Summer Shorts
A Short Story Anthology

Edited By
Madeline Smoot

Blooming Tree
PRESS

✳ ✳ ✳

Summer Shorts
Short Story Anthology

Blooming Tree Press

Illustrations copyright © 2006 by Blooming Tree Press
Copyright notices for individual contributors appear on the last pages of the book.
Cover art & Frontspiece by Elsbet Vance
www.bloomingtreepress.com

Blooming Tree Press
PO Box 140934
Austin, TX 78714

Printed in the United States.

Library of Congress Cataloging-in-Publication Data
Summer shorts : short story anthology / edited by Miriam Hees and Madeline Smoot.
p. cm.
Summary: A collection of stories and poems about the season of summer.
ISBN 0-9769417-5-9 (pbk.)
1. Summer--Literary collections.   [1. Summer--Literary collections.]   I. Hees, Miriam. II. Smoot, Madeline, 1978-   .
PZ5.S94 2006
810.8'033--dc22

                                        2006011316

Text set in Hoefler Text.

✳ ✳ ✳

Table of Contents

Illustrations

Wave Goodbye to Winter

By Kimberly Campbell

Pack up your coat,
And winter gear.
Jump in the pool —
Summer is here!

Mystery in the Mountains
By Dorothy Imm

"I can't believe you're leaving me out!" Even I knew I was wailing at Mom while we packed. But I didn't care. It was so totally unfair.

"It's *so* totally unfair!" I added.

"Miranda, for the bajillionth time, there are great activities just for kids in the evenings when the murder mystery game is played," Mom said. "Besides, you *think* you'd have fun, but you wouldn't. It's for grown-ups. You'd get bored."

"Oh yeah, sure," I answered, trying to make my voice as drippy with sarcasm as I could. I paused, laying a folded t-shirt on top of my swimsuit, then said, "Because dressing up, pretending to be someone else, maybe a princess or a spy, then pretending like someone's been murdered, and we're all suspects who have to solve the mystery — that sounds like such a boring, grown-ups-only thing."

We were getting ready for our family's summer vacation. When I first heard where we were going — a resort in the foothills of the Rocky Mountains where the guests get to act out a murder mystery every night for a week — I was SO excited. Then Mom and Dad explained to me and Rosey that only adults played the game. We would be sent off to do kids' stuff.

I sighed, a big puffy-sounding one, with a low moan thrown in. Mom reached over and laid her hand on top of mine in the

2

suitcase. Except for its size and gold wedding band, it could have been a kid's hand, with her chewed fingernails that were black underneath from gardening. Rosey sometimes joked at supper, "Oh, oh! Mommy! *SOMEone* didn't wash her hands!" Mom always laughed and told Rosey that even though it was hard to get gardening dirt out from under her nails, her skin was clean.

"I know it sounds fun," Mom said. "But it's for adults, like a book for grown-ups, and the murder mystery will be geared for adults, too. You would get frustrated."

"Great. So not only am I too young to play, I'm too stupid."

It was Mom's turn to sigh. "Miranda, stop that. Some things are just for adults, just like you're able to do some things that Rosey can't do yet. You'll understand better when you're older. Now run outside and get some fresh air. Thanks for helping, but I'll finish packing."

I nodded, but to let her know I wasn't buying this "some things are just for adults" stuff, I drooped out of the room with my head bent really low.

"Look, Randa! Cactuses!" For Rosey, the big thrill on the drive from the airport to the resort was the cacti growing everywhere. You'd think that seeing so many would make it less interesting after a while, but I guess not when you're five. She kept grabbing my arm with one hand and pointing out her window with the other.

I was going to say something like, yes Ro, they're *everywhere* out here, when Dad drove the rental car around a u-shaped bend on the crunchy gravel road. Instead I answered, "Forget cacti. Look, Ro! We're here."

Up above us, on the crest of a hill, was a long, one-story adobe building. Mom had shown me a picture, but I hadn't realized how soft it would look, like a building that's been dipped in white chocolate. About a foot down from the flat roof, a row of logs stuck out all along the wall in a straight line. There were lots of wide windows, each with a box of geraniums in front of it — their red blossoms so bright against the white walls, they almost looked like glowing lights.

"Welcome, welcome!" Even before we were all the way out of the car, a woman with a big puff of frizzy hair and a long, flowing sundress burst through the front door and swooped down on us. "You must be the Evans family!"

She turned and called up to the building, "Chester! Guests!" I guess Chester was used to being called like that because the door swung open again and a tall man came out.

"I'm Anna Holmeyer," the flowy-dress lady went on, "your hostess! Remember, if you need anything while you're here, 'Just ask Anna!' Oh Chester, they're in Suite 109. It's the north side." Chester squinted like he was trying to remember something. "Over there," she said with a wave. Chester nodded without saying anything and started hauling our bags toward the building.

Just Ask Anna turned back to Mom and Dad. "He's new. Our resort is so isolated. It intensifies the mood for mystery, but makes it hard to find help willing to make the drive! You know, you're the last players to check in. I think we've got an especially fun crowd for this week's game!"

She glanced at me and Rosey. I guess my face showed how mad I felt about being left out, because she added, "And kids, just wait until you see the water slides in our pool! And we've got some great movies lined up for tonight. Not to mention all the popcorn and cotton candy you can eat!"

Rosey squealed. "Mommy! Cotton candy! Can I have some now? Please? Please? Cotton candy!"

Mom shook her head at Dad. But it was a happy *oh boy, here we go* shake. Then she smiled at Rosey and said, "Not now, hon. That's for tonight. That's one of your special treats for when Mommy and Daddy are busy."

"Oooohh, Mrs. Evans, I do hope you remembered to bring some old-fashioned jewelry, whether costume or real," our hostess said in her isn't-everything-too-exciting-and-just-so-much-fun voice. We entered the lobby. "You've been assigned the role of Duchess Chaudin," she went on. "A down-on-her luck European wanderer. What else is in the character profile? Oh yes, you might be involved in smuggling! And Mr. Evans, you're going to be..."

But I didn't hear what cool fun role Dad would get to play. I ran across the lobby, away from the check-in desk, over to a huge picture window that looked out on a garden. Well, sort of a garden. There was a fountain with rust-orange rocks sprouting up around it, as tall as Rosey. They looked like they were growing out of the dusty gray soil — about the only thing that probably could grow here, besides cacti.

Then I saw the pool — not bad, not bad at all. It was really several pools, hooked together with waterways like creeks; there were kids floating between them on inner tubes. And whoa, the slides! There were six water slides. Some were wide and gently-sloping for little kids, and some were really high, with sharp turns and tunnels. Maybe I would have some fun, after all.

Mom put her hand on my shoulder. "Let's go look at our rooms, Miranda."

I turned and smiled up at her.

At the buffet breakfast the next morning, carefully balancing my plate loaded with stuffed French toast and maple-smoked bacon, I had almost completely forgiven my parents for leaving me out of the game.

Sitting down at our table, I caught sight of the Parker family and waved. They had one daughter, Emily, the same age as me, and I already felt like she was a new friend.

Mom took a sip of her coffee, then said, "So, what should we do..." But she was interrupted by a loud voice — a loud, shouting voice — from the lobby across the hallway.

"This is outrageous — OUTRAGEOUS," a man bellowed. The dining room went almost silent; you could still hear a few chinks of silverware on plates and little kids like Ro babbling.

"What kind of security deposit boxes are these?" the man went on. "I hope your insurance premiums are up-to-date. And where are the police? WHERE are they? WHEN did you call them?"

People bent toward the lobby now. A few grown-ups even got up and wandered that way. Mom sent some kind of silent message to Dad with her eyes because he nodded at her, stood up, and followed them.

We sat there, not eating anymore, all looking in the same direction, listening to the man shout about things being outrageous and shocking and demanding to know where the police were. You could hear a woman's voice too, but couldn't tell what it was saying. I guessed it was Just Ask Anna. But the angry man wasn't just *asking* Anna. He was definitely yelling all his questions at Anna.

Then Dad came back into the dining hall. His face looked tight. "Lisa," he said to Mom. "Where did you put your grandmother's tiara and bracelets last night? In our room or the hotel's security deposit box?"

"Security deposit box, of course," Mom answered. "Why? What's going on, David?"

Dad sighed and sat down. He took Mom's hand in his. "They've been robbed, Lisa. All the boxes were broken into. Everyone's valuables were stolen."

"Oh no! Nana's jewelry!" Mom said, with a little gasp that sounded like someone had hurt her. "It's been in our family so long." Dad patted her hand. Looking over at Rosey and me, she shook her head a little and blinked. She grabbed a napkin with her free hand and dabbed her eyes. "I was looking forward to giving those things to the girls one day," she said. She turned back to Dad. "Are the police here yet? Maybe they can recover some of it. Let's go see."

She wasn't the only one with that idea. By now almost everyone was filing out of the dining room, into the crowded lobby. The grown-ups all looked worried or angry, but the kids looked excited.

I said, "Hey, is it okay if I go say hi to Emily?" Mom nodded. Then she said to Rosey, "But I want you to stay here, with me."

Rosey didn't seem to care. She was jumping up and down and pointing out the windows. Spinning red-and-white lights flashed through the geraniums. The police were here.

I dashed over to Emily. I think one reason we'd formed such a quick friendship was because she was every bit as mad as me at being left out of the mystery game.

"Hi Emily," I said. "Hi, Mrs. Parker." Mrs. Parker nodded, but she wasn't paying real attention to us.

I pulled Emily away a few feet. "So listen. A robbery. A *real* mystery. Maybe we can find some clues. Help solve it."

Emily nodded in a matter-of-fact way, and I knew she'd been thinking the same thing. "I think it's Mrs. Holmeyer," she said in a low voice. "She has total access to those boxes, and she runs the game and tells the guests to bring fancy jewelry and stuff."

I nodded, watching Just Ask Anna's puffy hair bob as she talked with a lot of big gestures — pointing behind her, pointing at the doors — to a lady police officer.

"But she's so obvious," I said. "I mean, it would be stupid for her to steal the jewelry. She's the first person everyone will suspect."

I looked around the packed room. Word must have spread quickly through the resort; it seemed like every guest and a lot of the employees were in here. It could be anyone — there were so many — I didn't know where to start.

"Let's try to get closer," I said to Emily, tugging on her t-shirt sleeve.

We edged our way through the crowd, nearer to the check-in desk.

"I'm telling you, it must have *just* happened," Just Ask Anna was saying. "I always check the security deposit boxes every morning after going over the books. And everything was there an hour ago."

Emily shot me a significant look. Maybe she was right, maybe the thief was Anna Holmeyer.

But what if it wasn't? What if she was telling the truth, and it really had just happened? That would mean the jewelry couldn't have gone far.

The police officer seemed to be thinking the same thing because she asked if anyone had checked out yet. Just Ask Anna shook her head. The officer looked around at all of us.

"Have any of you seen anyone leaving the grounds of the resort this morning?"

There were a lot of murmured "no's" and heads shaking back and forth. The officer turned back to our hostess. "I'd like to ask you a few more questions in private. Can we use your office?" Just Ask Anna nodded and headed down the hallway behind the front desk.

Before following her, the police officer said to her partner who was standing like a guard at the front door, "Bill, call in and see if the judge received our request for a search warrant." Bill nodded and went outside to their car.

"Emily!" I leaned in and whispered to her. "If it's not Mrs. Holmeyer, the jewelry is still in the resort somewhere. Come on!"

I headed for the door leading to the rock garden, thinking we could take a look outside without attracting much attention. My heart thudded fast at the thought that the thief was still here. Probably in this room right now — looking harmless, but watching everyone very carefully.

As we went outside, Emily gave a little cry and tripped. She grabbed at me to catch herself, knocking us both down.

"Whoa, whoa, whoa! Are you girls all right?" It was Chester, the baggage carrier. He helped us up. I noticed his fingernails were black under the edges, just like Mom's. Maybe he was the gardener, too. Not that there was much to garden.

"Yeah, thanks," Emily said. "At least, I am. How about you, Miranda?"

"Yeah, I'm fine, thanks."

Chester smiled and strolled away, heading down the hill toward the pools.

Something scratched at my brain. Some idea, or something I needed to remember.

"Miranda! What is it?" Emily asked. I guess the something showed on my face, too.

"I don't know. Just now... I almost thought of something but I don't know what." I walked slowly over to the fountain and sat on the edge, staring away from the house, down the hillside, past the pools, at the dry, gray ground studded with bristly cacti. Then I swiveled and looked back up at the house, its smooth white walls so bright in the morning sunshine that it almost hurt to look at them.

Would the thief have risked hiding the jewels somewhere inside? Would he, she, or they have known how soon people would discover they were missing? Maybe not. Maybe the thief was as surprised as all of us by the shouting man. Where could you hide stuff in a hurry?

A bird zipped past, distracting me. It perched on the edge of one of the boxes of geraniums, warbling a piercing whistle of a song. Wow, what a postcard — bright blue sky, white walls, and a lemon-yellow bird surrounded by red blossoms and green leaves.

The thought that had been quietly scratching in the back of my head suddenly broke through.

"Emily!"

"What? What is it, Miranda?"

"Shhhh." I glanced back down the hill and lowered my voice. "I think I know who took the jewels."

"Better keep a close eye on that one," the police officer winked at Mom and Dad. "Smart as a whip." She gave me another broad smile, then headed out to the car to join her partner.

Two warm spots heated my cheeks as my parents both looked at me with big, proud, almost goofy-looking smiles.

"She's right, Miranda," Mom said. "I am still so impressed. Wow."

"I'll say, wow!" Emily bounced up and down a little on her feet, making her mom's arm, resting on her shoulders, rise and fall.

"Wow, wow, wowee kazowie, Randa!" Rosey's eyes were still round. I wondered if my own were wide and excited like that.

Guessing that the thief was Chester was one thing. Walking back inside, trying to look normal, not rushing an inch — in case he was watching us from the pool — had been a scarier, nerve-stretching thing. But then telling grown-ups, first Mom and Dad and the Parkers, then Officer Lowery (that was the woman police officer's name) was so intense I thought I might throw up, or melt.

But instead of getting annoyed with me, they'd all taken my idea seriously. I wondered why Chester had black dirt under his nails when all the soil outside was dusty and gray. I mean, when

I said it out loud to important, official adults, even I thought it sounded lame. There were probably lots of reasons his nails could look like Mom's after gardening.

But police officer Bill had immediately gone to ask Chester "a few questions." Then the search warrant came through, and Officer Lowery dug into the geranium flower boxes. And sure enough — oh, my skin still tingled when I thought of them pulling all that shiny, glittering jewelry out of the crumbly night-black soil.

Mom put her hands on my shoulders and squeezed gently. "And guess what?" she said. "I talked to Anna Holmeyer. And she said that she's going to change the rules this week. You and Emily, and any other children who want to, can play the mystery game with the rest of us."

I smiled so wide it felt like I always would be smiling from now on. Mom laughed her small laugh — not when she thinks something's funny, but when she's so happy it spills out in a bubble of laughter.

"You know, you'll need some jewelry for your costume," she said. "Would you like to wear Nana's bracelets? I think that would be fair, don't you?"

"So totally fair!"

Do Monsters Go to the Bathroom?

By Susan A. Meyers

Swoosh! Flip, flip, flip.

Swoosh! Flip, flip, flip.

Kenny knew he wasn't supposed to be playing in the bathhouse stall. He should have been standing in front of the sink washing his hands.

Instead he stood watching the toilet paper unroll and swirl and swish, down and round the flushing toilet.

Swoosh! Flip, flip, flip...

Swoosh! Flip, flip, flip...

Drip. Drip. Drip.

He heard them. Not the loud gushing sounds of water washing dirty hands, but fat, wet sounding drips dropping into an empty sink.

Kenny paused. He listened hard. He noticed how empty a bathhouse can sound when no one else is around. All his summer camp friends still sat around the campfire, roasting marshmallows and telling scary stories. He was alone.

A horrible thought crept into his mind. It sneaked right in and refused to leave. *Do monsters go to the bathroom?*

Kenny groaned. Why had he thought of that? It was a really bad thing for a person to be thinking when he was totally alone in a bathhouse. Yes, all alone with no noise but the drip, drip, drip of the faucet.

13

Whoosh... Whoosh...

Another noise joined the drip, growing louder and louder in his brain. It was his breath. And if monsters really did go to the bathroom, then their ears must be able to hear it too!

Rap. Rap. Rap.

Something knocked at the bathhouse door.

Do monsters go to the bathroom? Kenny really needed to know!

Creak...

He wished he could see through walls. Should he get down on his knees and peek under the stall? But what if something peeked back? Kenny bet a tasty boy would be just the thing for a monster snack.

Do monsters go to the bathroom? Something every kid should know!

Would a hairy monster, even one with yellow dots and a big purple nose, come out of the woods and into the bathhouse unless he really had to go?

Maybe if it really were a monster, it would be too busy doing its business to look for kids who played in bathhouse stalls.

Kenny froze right down to his feet. Except for his heart, which went thump, thump, thump.

"Kenny, are you in there?"

Saved! Yes, this was great! It was his camp counselor, Mike O'Day.

Kenny opened his mouth.

But then another thought crossed his mind. Was it Mike or an orange tongued, three-horned monster who sounded just like him? It made Kenny shiver and shake, and he wasn't even cold.

"Kenny?"

Slap flap. Slap flap. Slap flap.

Feet wearing flip flops walked across the floor. They stopped in front of Kenny's stall.

If it were a monster, shouldn't it smell? Maybe like a stink bomb, or an old skunk.

Kenny wrinkled his nose, sniff. Sniff. SNIFF.

He smelled sunscreen. The kind Mike kept in his fanny pack.

Tap. Tap. Tap.

Whatever it was knocked on the stall door.

"Hey, Kenny, you okay?"

He thought and then thought some more. Which was worse? Getting eaten by a monster? Or trying to explain to his counselor why he didn't answer when called?

He took a deep breath. "I'm here, Mike." He swallowed hard. With a shaking hand he opened the door.

Oh thank you, thank you, it was the real Mike O'Day!

"So this is where you've gone. What's wrong, Kenny? You're lookin' kinda pale. And you're all sweaty."

Kenny hung his head and confessed. "I've been playing."

Thump... thump... thump... the sound of his heartbeat was slowing down.

"Well, you're missing out on some great stories. Get your hands washed and get back to the campfire."

"Okay."

Mike turned to go.

And then Kenny's courage grew. "Hey, Mike, do monsters go to the bathroom?"

His counselor stopped and turned around. He shoved his hands in his pockets and looked him in the eye. "What do YOU think is true?"

Then Kenny knew.

Do you?

Misha and the Swamp Monster
By Caroline Young Ullmann

Misha was out of sorts, and she knew it. She shoved her damp hair out of her eyes and stalked around the lake.

"Misha, wait for me!" a whiny voice cried in the distance. "You're going too fast!"

She didn't answer, and she didn't slow down. She'd been looking forward all summer to visiting her aunt and uncle on their ranch in East Texas, and now everything had gone wrong.

"You're not even supposed to be here," she muttered. She was supposed to have flown to Texas all by herself. But, at the last minute, her parents said her 5-year-old brother had to come too because the babysitter had broken her leg.

It wasn't fair! Tad followed her everywhere — even once into the bathroom — and he never knocked before he burst into her bedroom.

It wasn't that she didn't love him. Tad was eager to share his muddy bugs and half-dead butterflies. His rich giggle sounded as though it started at his toes and bubbled up through his body. And now all the fifth-graders called her Misha because Tad couldn't say Michelle when he first started to talk.

Sighing, Misha swung around. The path was empty as far as she could see.

"Tad?" she called. "Hurry up! I'll wait for you." She adjusted her daypack. There was no sign of her brother.

Misha rolled her eyes. Tracing the paved path around the small lake her first morning at the ranch was something she always did. She hadn't even made it a quarter of the way around today.

The path circled the lake, but a thick belt of trees hid the water from view. She couldn't see the marshy zone between the trees and the water, which was good, because she didn't like to think about what lived there.

Toward the end of the walk, a rotted boardwalk maze led from the path out over the muck. Misha thought of it privately as The Swamp. Auntie Sal and Uncle Buck warned her every summer about the water moccasins and alligators.

"Misha, be especially careful this year," Auntie Sal told her last night. "It hasn't rained much lately, and the alligators haven't gotten enough to eat. They're hungry, and they're bold."

Remembering, Misha shivered.

"Tad, quit playing around," she yelled again. "It's getting hot. Let's go!"

She heard a high-pitched wail in the distance, but it sounded like an animal. She realized she'd been hearing the yowl ever since she started her walk.

Misha pushed away her unease. Tad had gone back to the ranch house, she reasoned. He was probably in the kitchen wheedling another hotcake out of Auntie Sal.

"Is it so awful to want to be alone?" she grumbled, walking on.

With a start, she realized she had nearly circled the lake. She was approaching the boardwalk that led into the Swamp. She increased her speed just as a long howl filled the air. The sound rose and dipped and rose and dipped and rose again.

It sounded like the same noise she'd heard before, but it was much closer. She broke into a run and sped past the board-walk.

Panting, she jogged into the kitchen just as Auntie Sal fin-ished the dishes.

"Where's Tad?" Auntie Sal asked. "Did he catch you up?"

Misha stared. She had convinced herself that Tad had wan-dered back to the ranch house. All of a sudden that seemed really stupid, but she couldn't tell her aunt that she hadn't looked for him.

"No, but I bet he's out in the barn," Misha said. She darted out the door.

Tad loved the barn. He had to stroke every animal — each chicken, horse and cow. This year Ranger, the big ranch dog, had given birth to ten fuzzy puppies. Tad had already named every one.

Misha pushed open the heavy barn door.

"Tad?" she called. She waited until her eyes adjusted to the dim light. Ranger and a pile of pups lolled in an empty stall.

Tad wasn't there.

She felt a surge of panic as she hurried toward the lake. Where did she last see him? Her throat felt so tight it was hard to shout his name.

She paused and heard the yowl again. Suddenly she knew where Tad was. He had gone into the Swamp to find whatever animal was making that awful noise. He was in the Swamp with the water moccasins and the alligators.

Misha raced back along the path toward the boardwalk and dove into the dark shadows of the Swamp.

"Tad! Tad, where are you?" she shrilled.

The boardwalk yawned before her. She could see black mud through gaping holes in the wood. Taking a deep breath, she slid out one foot, and then another. Her sneaker slipped on the green slime that coated the planks, and she almost fell. She let out a sob.

"Stop it!" she told herself fiercely. She didn't have time to be afraid. This was all her fault. She should have turned around when Tad fell behind.

The boardwalk tilted at a crazy angle. Tree roots grew right through the center. She'd have to climb over them to get to the other side. She swung across. A wedge-shaped head weaved toward her. She screamed. A black water moccasin slithered off a root. It plopped into the mud and swam away.

"Misha?" Tad's voice quavered. "Is that you?"

"I'm coming Taddy," she called. Misha forgot about the snake and kept going. She rounded a bend and stopped.

A white-faced Tad sat cross-legged on the boardwalk, eyes fixed on a swirl in the thick water. A filthy black puppy sprawled, asleep, on his lap.

She rushed forward and roughly hugged boy and dog.

"Tad, I was so worried!" she exclaimed.

"Blackie and I were scared," Tad said through his tears.

She pulled Tad to his feet. The puppy wriggled off his lap and yawned, exposing tiny teeth and a speckled tongue.

"Misha, wait. There's something bad out there," Tad said, turning to point at the soupy water. "It moved, and I got scared again."

Misha glanced at the mud and froze. Two blinking eyes emerged from the muck. A scaly head surfaced, followed by a horribly long body.

The water churned as a massive tail propelled the alligator's head onto the planks. In one move, it heaved itself onto the boardwalk and faced Misha and Tad.

The alligator was so big that its heavy haunches hung over the sides of the boardwalk.

"Misha, I want to go home *now*," Tad whimpered, pulling her hand.

"Hush!" she ordered. "We're going home, Taddy. But first I have to make the alligator go away."

Misha's mind raced. What could she do? She knew they couldn't outrun the alligator on the slippery boardwalk. She had to distract it so Tad could get to safety. In despair, she remembered her aunt's warning. The plump pup must look delicious.

She saw something move out of the corner of her eye and watched, horrified, as the sleepy puppy slipped between her legs and tottered toward the alligator.

"Blackie, no!" screamed Tad.

The alligator slashed its tail. It looked about ready to lunge. Misha grabbed the puppy and shoved her brother and the dog behind her.

"Tad, get back to the path," Misha gasped. She shrugged out of her pack. "And take Blackie."

"You have to come, too," Tad cried.

"I said go!" she hissed. She heard little footsteps move off, but she dared not turn to look.

She held the empty pack in front of her like a shield. For a long moment, she and the creature stared at each other. Misha was too afraid to cry. This was like a bad dream.

Suddenly, the beast scrabbled toward her, its long claws clicking against the wood. The alligator was so close she could hear its raspy breath. It opened its jaws wide. Misha was transfixed by its jagged teeth.

With a rush it was on her. She jammed the empty pack into its gaping mouth and leaped back. It snapped its jaws around the bag and shook its mighty head.

Misha whirled and ran.

Within moments she was back on the path. Auntie Sal ran toward her, carrying a shotgun. Tad and the puppy trotted behind her.

They all came together in a snarl of arms and legs and tears. The excited puppy jumped up against their legs.

"My stars, girl, I'm glad to see you!" Auntie Sal said. "Tad told me about the gator. Lord, you could have been killed! What on earth were you doing out there?"

The puppy sat down and let out a loud howl.

Misha broke free.

"You made that noise!" she exclaimed, dropping to her knees to examine the pup. She looked at Tad. "And you were looking for him, right?"

Tad nodded and flopped to the ground next to her.

"When you wouldn't stop, I went to the barn to see the puppies," he explained. "Blackie wasn't there. I told Ranger I'd find him. It was really scary."

Misha hugged Tad close. The puppy crawled into Tad's lap.

"Tomorrow morning, let's all walk around the lake together," Misha said.

The Camp Out
By Tricia Mathison

It was my first big camp out. I could hardly wait!
Dad said we'd go fishing if I could find some bait.
I'd dreamed of this so long and now I had my wish:
I dug for night crawlers to hook my first big fish.
I found some juicy worms and picked a perfect spot.
It was fantastic! You should see all that we caught!
Dad caught three catfish, and I got two rainbow trout.
I thought camping was the greatest. I had no doubt.
It was getting hot, so I looked around for shade.
That was one mistake I wish I had never made.
I saw some nice green leaves and sat down in a patch.
All at once I felt tingly and needed to scratch.
I felt very strange. I now itched from head to toe.
My skin got blotchy and a rash began to show.
My dad thought it was funny, but this was no joke.
Those cool, inviting leaves were really Poison Oak!
Covered in lotion, I climbed in my sleeping bag.
Camping out is great, but Poison Oak's a real drag!
Next time we go camping, I think I'll be just fine.
I hope Dad remembers to bring the calamine.

Why Do the Horses Stand in the Sea?
By Tovah S. Yavin

Kit let the warmth of the bonfire brush against her closed eyelids. She dug her heels into the soft sand and listened to the steady slap of the sea against the beach. She wanted to open her eyes, but she didn't want to see her cousin's scowling face, so she turned a little. That way, when she did look, she would see only the park ranger waving his pirate hat in the air and making silly "arrggh" sounds. As if that's how pirates really talked.

"The legend says," the ranger growled in the most pirate-sounding voice that he could manage on top of his Baltimore accent, "that a great Spanish galleon, filled with gold and treasure, was attacked by pirates. The crew and the horses on the ship were forced overboard. No one ever heard from the crew again. Arrggh! They probably became fish food, mateys! But the horses swam for their lives to reach this wonderful barrier island called Assateague. And here they have lived free ever since. Arrggh!"

Kit had heard the story many times. This ranger didn't do it as well as some of the others — but he was trying. Why did Tim have to sit there shaking his head and sighing loudly? He could at least act like he was having fun.

When the program ended, Tim jumped to his feet and stalked up the beach toward their campsite. Mom motioned for Kit to follow. Was she supposed to be his babysitter or something? He was a year older than her, for heaven's sake, and going into

8th grade. If he was determined to be miserable for this whole vacation, what was Kit supposed to do about it?

She followed him anyway, scurrying as fast as she could because he had a head start and was moving fast. By the time she reached their campsite, all she saw was Dad at the picnic table reading the newspaper under a flickering lantern. She slid into the bench across from him.

"How was the campfire?" he asked.

"Fine. They always tell the same story, but it's fun anyway."

Just then, Kit heard the clip-clop of horses walking along the asphalt road that wound around the campsites. They always came out at night, walking slowly, munching the scraggly grass that poked up in the clear areas that led to the dunes and down to the ocean. They were the wild horses of Assateague Island. Kit had snapped tons of pictures of them the first summer they had come here. Now she just liked to watch them.

The horses suddenly lifted their heads, whinnied to each other, and moved on. Kit didn't have to wonder why. Tim had just slammed the door of the bathhouse nearby and was stomping up the road as loudly as he could. When he reached the campsite, he leaned low to step into his small tent and pulled the flap closed behind him.

Kit looked across at Dad. "Give him time, honey, give him time," was all Dad said.

She woke early the next morning and, as always, loved being the first one up. She munched some cereal and waited for the sun to stretch itself higher in the sky. The air quickly grew warm, and Kit thought maybe she should try one more time to show Tim that this could be a perfectly fine vacation.

"Tim," she called quietly right outside his tent because she didn't want to wake her parents. "Tim," she repeated a little louder when she got no answer. She lifted the tent flap and peeked in. There was no Tim. His sleeping bag was neatly rolled and tied in the corner, and a few items of clothes were strewn about. But there was no Tim.

"Hey!" her cousin's voice startled her. She backed out of his tent and looked up, looked around, looked toward the ocean directly into the morning sun. A shadowy figure stood at the top of the dune with his hands on his hips.

"Tim?" she tried to shade her eyes.

"What are you looking for?"

"You."

"I just…

"Come here. I want you to see something." He turned and disappeared behind the dune.

Kit hurried after him.

The beach was littered with beautiful whole shells — usually there were only broken pieces by the time she got there. She followed her cousin, but couldn't keep her eyes off the sand and its treasure of stones and shells.

"Why do they do that?" Tim said as she drew close.

Kit looked up and saw four horses standing in the ocean, just deep enough to let the salt water lick around their hooves. They faced east across the water, standing still except for an occasional flick of their ears.

"Why do they do that?" Tim repeated.

"I don't know. I never — " Kit scowled, she had never seen the horses do this before. It wasn't fair that Tim would discover

something like this on his very first trip to Assateague. "Well, I've never seen them do that before, and I don't know why."

"They came down about a half hour ago," Tim went on. "From there." He pointed to another break in the dunes.

"A half hour ago?" Kit looked at her watch, and it was barely 6:30. "How long have you been here?"

"Since about 5."

"Wow." Kit focused on the horses again. "They're standing so still."

"And staring."

"Yeah."

"So why? Why do they do it?"

Kit just shrugged.

"I thought you knew everything about this place, the way you talk." Tim kicked at the sand then turned away from the horses. "So what is there to eat?"

Kit led him back to the campsite and showed him the two large freezer chests pushed under the picnic table.

"How come only one of them has ice?" Tim asked as he rummaged for cereal and milk.

"Because that one has the food that can spoil and needs to be kept cold."

"So why is the other stuff in a freezer chest, too?"

"Because," Kit sighed. "It's the best way we've found to keep the horses out of our food."

"Horses graze. They eat the grass and the shrubs. I've been watching them. They wouldn't eat this stuff."

"Well, they would if they could get to it. Trust me. I know."

"Yeah. Like you knew the horses stood in the ocean."

Later in the morning, when the whole family went down to the beach, the horses were gone. The beach quickly filled with people — some in the water, some stretched out sleeping on the sand, and kids with their plastic buckets building sand castles that would just disappear overnight. There were life guards, too, but no horses.

"Mom," Kit waited until Dad and Tim were in the water and much too far away to hear anything. "Do the horses swim?"

"Swim?"

"In the ocean?"

"Well, horses *can* swim. They'll do it if they are forced to. But I don't think they just swim for the fun of it or anything." Mom looked up from her book and smiled.

"But would they swim in the ocean?"

"Honey, I wouldn't think so."

"They stand in the ocean."

"They do?"

"I saw them. Early this morning. Standing in the ocean. Not too deep. They weren't really swimming. Just standing."

"Really? That's interesting." Mom waited a moment, then went back to reading her book as if it wasn't all *that* interesting.

Mom and Dad napped after lunch, and Kit spread her new shells across the picnic table to sort them. Tim sat across from her with his nose in a magazine. He was wiggling one foot back and forth as he read, and every minute or so he managed to kick Kit under the table. He didn't even bother to say excuse me. Finally, Kit pushed her shells down to the edge of the table and scooted out of Tim's line of fire.

"Sorry," Tim mumbled without looking up. But then he laid

the magazine down and watched Kit as she counted her shells. "Do you believe that stuff? About the horses?"

"You mean about the pirates and the ship?"

"Yeah, that."

"Oh, I don't know. But they came from somewhere."

"No one really knows?"

"That's what they say."

"And they don't belong to anyone?"

"Nope."

"Well, I like the horses."

Kit studied her cousin's face for a minute. That was the first time in a long time that she could remember him saying that he liked *anything*.

"We're kind of the same."

"The same?" Kit laughed. "You mean you and the horses?"

Tim nodded.

"How exactly are you like the horses?"

"That's simple. They got dragged away from their home and dumped somewhere that they didn't want to be. Now they just have to figure out how to survive on their own."

"But I still don't see..."

"And they're doing it, too. They don't need anybody."

Kit held her breath for a minute. When she and Tim were little, they had played together all the time. He'd been her favorite cousin. But, then his Dad died and he got so...something...gloomy, not mean, but not nice either, and he sure wasn't easy to be around any more. "You're not like the horses."

"Yes. I am."

"No one forced you..."

"Yes, they did. Mom wanted me out of her hair for a while. She never even asked me."

"But, anyway, you're hardly on your own."

"Yes. I am. I may not have to scrounge for food, but — you wouldn't understand." Tim grabbed his towel and started off towards the beach. "And I do know why they do it," he called over his shoulder.

Kit jumped up to follow him, but she didn't want to leave her shells lying around. It took her a few minutes to stow them safely away, and by the time she got to the beach, all she found of Tim was his towel. She sat down and tried to watch all parts of the beach at once — the sand stretching out on both sides of her and the dancing ocean in front. Still, Tim managed to surprise her when he suddenly appeared at her side, dripping salty drops of ocean all over her and the towel.

"Push over," he demanded, then plopped down, taking easily three-fourths of the towel for himself. That at least was something the old Tim would have done.

"So why, then?"

"Huh?" he turned to stare at her.

"At the picnic table, you said you knew why they do it?"

"Why — who does..."

Kit tried to jab Tim with her elbow, but he was too quick, suddenly thrusting himself out of the way and leaving Kit to flop flat on her back in the sand. Tim just laughed and held out his hand to help her up.

"Okay. I know why the horses stand in the sea."

"Why?"

"It's easy. Where are they looking?"

"At the ocean."

"What's on the other side of the ocean?"

"England. Europe." Kit shrugged.

"Okay. Too literal. Home. Home is on the other side of the ocean. It was a Spanish ship, remember?"

"So they're looking home?"

"Yup."

"These horses. After a couple hundred years. These horses..."

"Yup."

"You think they remember — Spain?"

"I'm sure the horses don't know anything about Spain." Tim shook his head and gave Kit an exasperated look. "But they know this isn't home. It's where they are — but..." Tim's voice faltered. He stared out like the horses had done — flicked his hair like the horses had flicked their ears, and sent strings of salt water down the sides of his face.

Kit wasn't sure what to say, but just then Mom and Dad came up behind them with beach chairs and extra towels. Dad dared Tim to race him to the water and off they went. Mom announced that it was Kit's turn to start dinner and pointed to her watch.

"Another hour and you need to head back," she said emphasizing the *you*.

When it was time for Kit to head back, she was glad enough to have a little time to herself. Most of the campsites were deserted, and she was going over in her head the steps for making tuna-noodle casserole. It was the dish she always made when they camped, because it was the only recipe she knew.

Then Kit spotted them and broke into a run. Three horses stood in the middle of their campsite — two had their heads stuck under the picnic table and the third was munching on a bag of apples — not just the apples, the bag too.

When Kit got closer, she saw that one of their freezer chests — the one with the dry foods — was turned over, its contents spilled across the ground. The lid that was supposed to be latched on to keep the horses out was lying on top of the picnic table — right next to Tim's magazine.

All the signs in the park told visitors to stay away from the horses because they could bite or kick. Kit didn't think about that. She ran up to one horse and pushed on his rump. He didn't even look up. She slapped the back of another one. He did look up — but only momentarily — then went back to the bag of potato chips that he was devouring.

Kit remembered the park rangers explaining that people foods, especially junk foods like a lot of this stuff, could be very bad for the horses. She had to try — for their sakes — to get them away from all this.

Kit looked around, grabbed the first thing she saw which was a pair of Tim's jeans left half in and half out of his tent, and started wildly swinging at the horses. She didn't want to hurt them, but they'd already eaten most of the food in the chest. She just had to do something.

Swish. Swat. Slap. She smacked them with the jeans as hard as she could. Each horse. One at a time.

They hardly looked up, and they definitely didn't feel the need to stop chewing. Not for a second.

Kit looked around desperately for help — hoping at the same time, that she would not see a ranger who would surely yell at her. And, thank goodness, she didn't see a ranger. The only person she did see was Tim, loping up over the dune, with his towel tossed over his shoulder.

"Hey, you," he said in a gentle voice as he approached the horses. "I know you're hungry, but this stuff will kill you. Move along. Go eat the grass you're supposed to eat."

One horse looked up from the last shreds of the bag of apples, whinnied happily, and moved toward the road. A second one licked the last salty specks of potato chip from his face and followed.

The third horse still had his head under the table. Tim flicked the horse's rump lightly with his towel. "You, too. Come on. Time to go." The horse pawed at a bit of lettuce and stepped backward, crushing the last tomato under his hoof, then followed his friends up the road. Kit watched the three of them walk off and could have sworn she heard one of them burp.

"See what I mean?" Tim said surveying the mess strewn about their camping area. "I told you I understood the horses. All you had to do was talk to them the right way."

"Tim!" Kit blurted, mouth open, hands on hips. "Look around! There's nothing left. They walked away because they just ate everything. It wasn't because of your magical voice."

"Well, believe what you like."

"And how did they get into the chest, anyway?" Kit demanded as she started cleaning up. "Could it be that you left the top off?" Kit pointed to the lid of the freezer next to his magazine.

Tim just shrugged. When Mom and Dad came back from the beach, Kit explained what had happened mentioning only that *someone* must have left the top off the freezer chest.

Dad said he'd been wanting to try the new restaurant in town, anyway, and Mom added that they could stop at the grocery store after they ate.

Kit wasn't sorry not to have to make dinner, and eating out was always fun. It was just the smug look on Tim's face that annoyed her.

When she woke the next morning, Kit headed straight for Tim's tent. He was gone, and she hurried to find him on the beach.

The horses were already there — standing in the sea — staring east across the ocean — just like the day before. She quietly sat next to Tim on the cool sand and watched. They looked like the same four from yesterday. One large one, two medium ones, and a smaller reddish brown one with a white tail. That was Kit's favorite.

They watched silently until the biggest one called to the others and led them back across the dunes.

"Wake me up tomorrow, so I can come with you," Kit said quietly. Tim agreed, and he seemed happier for the rest of the day. He helped Kit look for shells, chased her with the remains of a large horseshoe crab that he'd found, and poured a bucket of salty water over her when she tried to nap on the beach.

Still, it was good to be having fun with him again.

But the third morning that Tim woke her and led her silently to the beach, they found nothing. No horses. Just the wind and the water rushing in as if they were being chased.

"Something's wrong," Tim whispered.

"What?"

"I don't know. But there's something wrong."

They didn't have to wait long to find out. When they got

back to the campsite, there were rangers walking from tent to tent, waking people up.

"Hi," one ranger called as he approached their area. "Where are your parents?"

"Still asleep," Kit pointed to the tent.

"You need to wake them. We just got a warning of a hurricane coming. We're evacuating the park. You have until noon. I'll check back in about a half hour."

Kit woke her parents, and they all got busy taking down the tents and packing their gear in the car.

"What do the horses do when there's a hurricane?" Tim asked Kit.

"I'm not sure, but hurricanes happen here. The horses have come through before." She tried to sound confident, but she couldn't help wondering what *would* happen to the horses. Especially her little brown and white one.

When the ranger stopped back, he told Kit's parents where there were hotels inland and reminded them to stop at the ranger station to sign out before leaving.

When everything was packed, Dad thought they had time for a late breakfast before hitting the road. Mom started to prepare food, and Tim pulled Kit towards the bathhouse.

"I want you to see something."

Standing between the bathhouse and the road was the little brown and white horse.

"He's been standing there for awhile."

"Really?"

"He keeps looking across the road and then back this way. What's over there?"

"Just a kind of woody, marshy area. It leads to the Bay."

They both watched for a few minutes, then Tim said, "Come on," and moved toward the horse. The horse moved toward the road. Tim stopped, and the horse stopped. Tim took a few steps, and the horse took a few steps.

"He wants us to follow him."

"Tim, we can't..."

But the horse was waiting, so Kit followed, and the horse led them across the road and moved slowly into the woods.

Tim and Kit stepped gingerly over cacti and weeds and ducked to avoid low hanging branches until the horse brought them to a clearing and stopped. One of the other horses was lying down in the clearing, and two others stood at a distance watching. Tim walked slowly and steadily toward the horse in the clearing.

"I think its foot is stuck."

"Stuck?"

"There's a hole—and a lot of weeds and viney stuff. I don't think he can get up."

"What should we do?" Kit whispered. "There's a hurricane coming."

Tim pulled against the horse's leg, but it didn't move.

"Wait! Listen!" Kit called out. "I hear traffic on the road."

She made her way back, crushing prickly cactus under her sneakers and pushing branches away as they flicked at her face.

A truck passed, moving fast. A small car. Then she spotted one of the jeeps driven by the park rangers.

"Stop! Stop!" Kit yelled waving her arms. "There's a horse," she gasped when the ranger pulled over. "We think he's hurt or something."

The ranger followed her to the clearing, took out his radio, and called for help.

"They get tangled sometimes. We always check around here before a storm," he explained. "We'll take care of him, but you kids need to be out of the park."

Kit and Tim hurried back to the campsite where Mom and Dad were pacing and angry. Dad started to yell at them, but Mom handed out plates of warm pancakes, and soon everybody was too busy eating to do any yelling. On the way out of the park, Kit and Tim strained to catch a glimpse of the horses, but saw nothing.

When the park opened again two days later, most of the camp sites had puddles of standing water or scattered debris. They set up in one of the few dry ones and Kit and Tim hurried to the beach. There were no horses, but huge pieces of wood, shells, dead fish, and even bottles and plastic containers were scattered everywhere. They spent the day helping the rangers gather as much as they could into giant plastic bags.

Kit woke first the next morning, but she had barely stepped from her tent when she heard Tim stirring.

"Hurry," she urged, and Tim joined her in a few minutes. They hustled over the dunes to the beach, and there they were. The four horses. Standing. Staring. Just as before. They looked fine. All of them.

The little one, Kit's favorite, turned for a moment to look their way. And maybe he even nodded, before turning back to stare at the sea.

"So, you really think they're looking home?" Kit asked.

"Maybe. Who knows? But they seem to like it well enough here, anyway, don't you think? I mean, they seem to have made an okay life for themselves here."

"Sure," Kit answered.

"That doesn't mean they can't still remember their other life from before."

"Nope. Doesn't mean that." Kit agreed.

Tim's stomach growled loudly, and he laughed just as loudly. "Let's get something to eat."

Kit nodded and followed him back. There would be other mornings to watch the horses. Right now, Kit was thinking of a freezer chest full of her favorite muffins and donuts.

Adam's Quilt
By Valerie Hunter

"Adam! Time to get up!" Ma's voice cut into Adam's dreams, and he was instantly awake, scrambling out of bed and into his clothes. It was still dark outside, but Adam felt excited rather than sleepy.

In the main room, Ma was nursing baby Gideon and trying to get Fairby to eat her porridge, though the little girl still looked half asleep. There was a bowl for Adam, too, and Ma urged him to eat quickly. Adam checked his older brother Soren's pocket watch; it was four-thirty. Mr. Bloor, their nearest neighbor, would be arriving any minute to take them to the stagecoach.

Gideon was fussing, and Fairby was whining as Adam wolfed down his porridge. Ma looked harried, but she managed to flash him a smile. "Are you ready for our adventure?"

Adam smiled back. It was exciting to think that he and Ma and the little ones would finally be making the journey from Oregon to Kansas. Pa and his five brothers had left last fall, and it had been because of Adam that the whole family hadn't gone together. Adam had broken his leg a week before they were supposed to leave, and the doctor had said he needed to stay in bed for four months so that the bone could heal. Ma and Fairby stayed with him, and in January, when Adam was nearly better, Gideon had been born. That was why they had waited until July to go to Kansas —the trip by stagecoach, steamboat, and train was hard, and Ma wanted to wait until Gideon was bigger.

Adam heard Mr. Bloor's booming voice call to them from outside, and he jumped up. "I'll load the bags," he cried, grabbing the valises with their clothes, a basket with food for the journey, and Ma's sewing bag. Pa and the boys had taken the trunks with them last fall, and they were leaving the furniture behind because Pa could make new.

"Hullo, Adam," Mr. Bloor said as Adam came outside, loaded down with bags. "Let me help you with those."

Ma came hurrying out behind him with the box of bedding, then went back inside to fetch Fairby and baby Gideon wrapped in his quilt. Since it was so early, the summer morning was chilly, but Adam carefully kept his eyes off Gideon's quilt. He didn't want to think about it.

Ma and the baby sat in the front of the wagon next to Mr. Bloor, and Fairby and Adam curled up in the back amongst the baggage. Adam watched as their little cabin disappeared and realized he'd never see it again. It belonged to Mr. Bloor now, who was expecting his son and daughter-in-law to arrive from the east in a few months. Adam closed his eyes and tried to picture another family living there, but he fell asleep instead.

The next thing he knew, Ma was shaking him, and he opened his eyes to the summer sun. They were at the stagecoach station, and Mr. Bloor had already loaded their bags. Adam hopped down from the wagon, ashamed he had fallen asleep. He was ten years old, not a little baby! However, he soon forgot his disappointment as he bustled around with Ma, meeting the stage driver, an immense man named Mr. Henry, and his son Will, who looked about sixteen, the age of Adam's oldest brother Soren. Adam touched Soren's watch in his pocket, just to make sure it was there. Soren had trusted Adam with it when he left, and Adam would hate to lose it.

Adam held onto Fairby's hand and thought of his family in Kansas. It was a hard, long process to get mail from Oregon to Kansas or vice versa, and they'd only had one letter from Pa and the boys since they'd left. Each of his brothers had written part of it, and Adam felt envious as he read about them building the new house. Even Colton and Anson got to help, and they were just little boys, younger than Adam.

Adam felt a little better when he read Samuel's and Soren's parts of the letter. Samuel said he hoped Adam was feeling better, and that he was counting on him to help put up the pasture fences next summer. Soren wrote that he missed Adam's help holding the nails while he hammered. Anson and Colton weren't nearly as skilled.

Pa wrote only a few lines at the very end of the letter, warning Ma to keep a close eye on the money while she traveled. There had been many stagecoach hold-ups between Oregon and California.

"What money?" Adam had asked after he'd read the letter.

"The money your father left us for the steamboat fares," Ma said. Adam noticed that her forehead was wrinkled, the way it got when she was worried.

Now Adam whispered in Ma's ear, "You have the money, right?"

Ma frowned. "Shush! Yes, of course I do."

Adam wanted to ask where it was, so he could keep an extra close eye on it, but he didn't dare say anything else. There were so many people around who might overhear.

"Everybody best get aboard now!" Mr. Henry called in his loud, gruff voice. Ma shook Mr. Bloor's hand, thanking him for taking them to the station, and they got inside the coach.

There were six other passengers. Three were young men — two in rough looking clothes that were none too clean, and one in a dandified suit and a bowler hat. Then there were Mr. Tomkins, who was a merchant Pa knew; an older man; and a gray-haired woman with a pursed-up mouth.

Adam sat in a corner with Fairby in his lap. Ma was next to him, holding the baby, and the woman sat across from him. For awhile, they were all silent; it was still so early in the morning that Adam figured everyone must feel as sleepy as he did. Fairby drowsed in his lap, her yellow curls tickling his chin as he listened to the wheels rumble.

After awhile, though, the other passengers began to exchange pleasantries. The dandified young man, who was sitting on the other side of Ma, talked the most. His name was Thomas Crewe, and, like Adam, this was his first time on a stagecoach. "I have to admit I'm a bit nervous," he said. "You hear so many stories."

Mr. Tomkins shook his head. "Pshaw! Safer than traveling on your own, I'd say. And you saw Mr. Henry. A person would think twice before holding him up, wouldn't you say?"

"Well, I suppose so..." Mr. Crewe didn't sound very certain. "Still, he doesn't look like the most responsible man. Why, my bag could fall off the top of the stage, and I bet he wouldn't even notice! I wish he'd let me bring it in here."

"Use your head, Crewe," said the older man. "If we all brought our bags in here, there wouldn't be any room for us."

"Besides," said the woman in a voice loud enough to make

Adam jump, "if you have anything valuable in your bag, you should have had Mr. Henry put it in the safe box."

"What box?"

"The safe box on the back of the stage," the woman explained impatiently. "I gave Mr. Henry my money and jewelry to lock in there. Perfectly safe."

"I had no idea there was such a box," Mr. Crewe said. "Did the rest of you put your valuables there, too?"

The other two young men looked out the window and did not respond, but Mr. Tomkins and the older man said they had, and after a moment's hesitation, Ma agreed. Adam was surprised. She must have put the money there while he had still been asleep in Mr. Bloor's wagon.

"Well, don't I feel foolish," Mr. Crewe said. "I just didn't know. I'll have to talk to Mr. Henry the first time we stop and transfer my valuables."

Mr. Crewe began an animated discussion with Mr. Tomkins about the best banks in California, and the woman turned to Ma and Adam. "Foolish man," she snorted. "Imagine not knowing about the safe box!"

Adam hadn't known about it himself, so he kept quiet. Ma only smiled and inclined her head a bit.

The woman seemed bent on conversation. "I'm Miss Langenbrunner. I'm headed for a teaching job near one of the gold camps. They've just put up a schoolhouse, and they tell me the children there are as wild as dogs." Adam thought she sounded pleased by this fact, as though she was looking forward to putting them in their places. He was glad she wasn't his teacher.

"My, my," Ma clucked. "I was a schoolteacher myself, before

I married. Now I'm going to join my husband in Kansas."

"And these are your children? How old is the baby?"

"Six months."

Miss Langenbrunner frowned. "A hard journey for such a little thing. And you shouldn't keep him wrapped up so on such a hot day."

Adam was also wondering why Ma had kept Gideon wrapped in the quilt now that the day had grown warm. He wanted her to bury the quilt deep in one of their bags — or better yet, to leave it behind.

He was surprised when Ma said, "He's a delicate baby. I don't want him to catch a chill."

"Not likely, in this heat," Miss Langenbrunner said. "A fever's more like it."

Ma seemed to want to change the subject. "Do you like the quilt? Adam here made it himself."

Adam blushed, wishing Ma had kept quiet. She sounded so proud of him, but he felt ashamed. Everyone knew boys didn't sew. The only reason Adam had made the quilt was because he'd been so bored lying in bed while his leg healed. Ma had taught him how to sew, and he had made forty quilt squares during his time in bed. Then, even though he was up and about again, he found the time to sew them together into a rectangle. It wasn't nearly large enough to cover a bed, but Ma said it was big enough for Gideon, and she had quilted it herself just a few days before, sewing the front to several layers of old sheet for thickness and warmth.

Truth be told, Adam had enjoyed sewing — he liked the feeling of making something with his own hands, especially something so bright and colorful. Still, he was dreading what his brothers would say when they found out. His brother Eddie was especially good at teasing, and Adam knew he would never hear the end of it from him. Maybe he could convince Ma to throw the quilt away before they reached Kansas. Or better yet, he could take it upon himself to conveniently lose it.

Miss Langenbrunner leaned forward to examine the quilt, then turned her sharp gaze on Adam. "You made that, boy?"

"Yes, ma'm," he mumbled.

"Well, how about that." She fingered the edge of the quilt. "Not often you find a boy who does needlework. It's a pity that more don't learn, if you ask me." She gave Adam an approving nod, but he couldn't help noticing that the older man was looking at him as though he was a worm in the flour.

They rode on in the heat and the dust. Miss Langenbrunner talked about the last school she had taught at, and then quizzed Adam on his multiplication tables. Mr. Crewe continued to talk to the two older men, and the other two men talked quietly between themselves. Fairby hummed to herself, and Gideon fussed and then began to wail. Ma finally unwrapped him from the quilt, folded it carefully, and placed it on her lap, seating Gideon on top of it. He quieted down.

"Told you he was hot," Miss Langenbrunner said smugly, and Adam thought Ma's smile looked a little forced.

They rode on and on until Adam's throat felt like sand-paper — and his legs twitched with the urge to stand up. Gideon cried again, and this time nothing would silence him. Fairby joined in, and Adam's head began to hurt. He wished he was Will Henry, who got to ride on top of the stage with his father.

Finally, the stagecoach stopped. They hadn't reached their destination yet, but Mr. Henry said they could all get out for half an hour and stretch their legs. They were in a town that Adam didn't even know the name of, but all he cared about was getting out of the stage.

Adam held Fairby's hand and the food basket and followed Ma to the edge of town, where they could eat and walk around in peace. Ma nursed Gideon with the quilt spread across her shoulder, and Adam chased Fairby among the trees until she giggled and shrieked.

"I'll be glad when our adventure is over," Ma said. "I'm looking forward to seeing Kansas."

"And the new house," Adam added.

"And your father and the boys, of course!"

Adam nodded, but, as his eyes fell on the quilt on Ma's shoulder, he thought he could wait to see his brothers if all they were going to do was tease him. Maybe now was the time to do something about the quilt. "Can I hold Gideon?" he asked politely.

Ma handed the baby to him. She kept the quilt on her own shoulder. Adam sighed; he couldn't think of a way to ask for it that wouldn't be too obvious.

"What time is it?" Ma asked.

Adam pulled out Soren's pocket watch and sighed again. It was almost time to get back on the stage.

They stopped at the public privy to go to the bathroom first. As Ma took Fairby's hand and led her inside, she gave Adam the quilt to hold, though she looked anxious about doing it, as though she knew what he had planned. But once the door to the privy had closed, Adam found that he couldn't do anything with the quilt. There was nowhere to lose it, short of throwing it in a horse trough, and besides, Ma would notice it was gone as soon as she came out of the privy. He'd have to wait until they were on the steamer. Maybe he could throw it into the ocean; even if Ma noticed, there would be nothing she could do about it.

Adam used the privy next, and then they hurried back to the stage. They got there just in time; Mr. Henry started driving as soon as they were aboard. The stage was even more crowded, as a married couple had gotten on, and it took Adam a moment to realize that Mr. Crewe wasn't there.

The other passengers noticed, too. "Where's that young fool Crewe?" Miss Langenbrunner asked. "Do you suppose Mr. Henry forgot him?"

Mr. Tomkins leaned out the window so far that Adam thought he might tumble out. He called to Mr. Henry, "You forgot Crewe!"

Adam could hear Mr. Henry's voice rumble an answer, but he couldn't make out what he said. When Mr. Tomkins pulled his head back into the stage, his brow was furrowed. "He said that was Crewe's stop."

Miss Langenbrunner frowned. "Then why did Crewe say he was going to put his valuables in the safe box when we stopped?"

Nobody spoke for a moment. Then one of the young men said, "I'll wager he robbed the safe."

Mr. Tomkins stuck his head out the window again and had Mr. Henry stop the stage. They all got out and crowded around as he opened the safe box. There were several bags and valises inside — but they were all empty.

"How could this happen!" Miss Langenbrunner fumed. She shook a finger at Mr. Henry. "You promised me my valuables would be safe!"

Mr. Henry scratched his beard. "Lemme think. I unlocked the box so Mr. Crewe could have his bag— "

"He told us all his bags were up top!" Miss Langenbrunner sputtered.

" — and he took it and left," Mr. Henry continued. "Then I was about to lock the box when the horses spooked a little. I went to calm them down...wasn't gone for more'n a minute..."

"Crewe must have had a partner in town," one of the young men said. "Someone could have taken the money in less than a minute if he'd set up the scheme with Crewe ahead of time."

"But our money! What about our money?" Mr. Tomkins asked.

"Long gone now," said Mr. Henry.

"Well, aren't you going after it?" Miss Langenbrunner demanded.

"I'll send Will here back to town to report it, but I can't be turnin' around this stage. I'm duty bound to get to San Francisco in a reasonable amount of time. 'Sides, Crewe and his crony already have a half hour's head start—there's no way we'll catch them."

The older man grumbled and Miss Langenbrunner squawked and Mr. Tomkins decided to turn back with Will. Mr. Henry just climbed back on the stage and said he was starting the horses in one minute. The rest of them could get on or be left behind.

"Come, Adam," Ma said, and they got back on the stage. The summer air was hot, but Adam felt chilled inside, wondering how they would ever get to Kansas without money. Could Ma get word to Pa, so he could come get them? Even if she could, Adam knew it would take Pa a while to get to California, and they had no place to live in the meantime. Would he and Ma have to work to earn money for their passages? He thought panning for gold might be exciting, but Pa had told him that very few miners got rich, and the rest were just poor fools. Adam chewed on his lip, wondering what else they could possibly do.

He snuck a glance at Ma. Miss Langenbrunner and the older man were complaining loudly; the married couple clucked sympathetically; but Ma was as quiet as the two young men. She did not look as panicked as Adam felt, but her face was pale, and she clutched Gideon and the quilt tightly.

The rest of the journey seemed even longer than the first part. Adam wanted to ask Ma what they were going to do, but he knew that she would not like to discuss their problem in front of strangers, so he kept quiet. The stage stopped several more times, but the passengers all kept close together and close to the stage, so he couldn't ask then, either.

The farther the stage went, the more Adam worried, convinced that they would be stuck penniless in California forever. He looked at the quilt in Ma's hand and wished that his biggest worry was still what his brothers would say when they found out he'd sewn it. Now he wondered if his brothers would ever even see it.

Once during the long ride Ma squeezed his hand and whispered that everything would be all right. Adam tried to believe her, but he couldn't think of how it would be.

Finally, they arrived in San Francisco. Adam had been excited to see the big city, but now he felt only dread at the prospect of being stranded here forever.

Ma collected their things from the top of the coach while Miss Langenbrunner and the older man argued with Mr. Henry. Mr. Henry offered to take them back to Oregon for free, and Adam thought this idea didn't sound half bad. They could stay in their old cabin until Pa came to fetch them.

Ma, however, did not seem to even consider the idea. She said good-bye to their fellow passengers, asked directions to the harbor, and set off at a brisk pace. Adam was so focused on keeping up with her and not letting go of Fairby's hand that he couldn't ask what they were going to do.

Ma stopped at the wharf and found a quiet place for them to sit, out of the way of the crowds. "Ma, what are we going to do?" Adam finally asked.

"Why, buy steamer tickets and continue on our adventure, of course!" Ma said.

"But how — "

Ma smiled. "Our money wasn't in the safe box, Adam."

"It wasn't?" He felt a wave of relief, though he was still confused. "But you told Mr. Crewe..."

"I didn't want anyone to know where it really was. Now hand me my scissors, please. They're in my sewing bag."

Perplexed, Adam rummaged through the bag and gave the scissors to Ma. She handed Gideon to him, and then, much to his astonishment, began to snip away the stitches of the quilt's binding. When she had undone several inches of stitches, she carefully extracted their money from between two layers of fabric.

Ma laughed when she saw the surprised look on Adam's face. "It was the perfect hiding place, wasn't it? I have a little money in my purse, but I didn't want to carry much there in case of pickpockets, and I didn't feel safe having it out of sight in Mr. Henry's box. So I slipped it in the quilt while I was quilting it and figured no one would ever be the wiser!"

Ma left Adam on the bench with the little ones and the baggage while she bought the steamer tickets. Adam fingered the ragged edge of the quilt, still trying to realize that his quilt had saved the money. He blushed with horror when he realized he had almost tried to lose it.

When Ma returned with the tickets, she squeezed his shoulder. "I can restitch that seam in no time, and the quilt will be as good as new by the time we reach Kansas. Wait till your father and brothers hear about our adventure!"

Adam grinned, knowing his brothers would probably be envious. After all, they had never ridden on a stage with a real live robber before!

Ma took Gideon back and wrapped the quilt loosely around his shoulders; it was windy on the harbor. "He's getting so big, isn't he?" she said to Adam. "Before long the quilt will be too small for him."

Adam tickled the baby's foot. "I'll have to sew him a new one, once we get to Kansas," he said.

The High Dive
By Amy Fellner Dominy

My front door flew open, and Christie came busting in. "Janey!" she called out.

I sat at the kitchen counter painting my toenails Blueberry Blue. "Hey, Christie."

Christie lived next door, but she acted like my house was hers, too. She skidded into the kitchen waving a piece of paper in her hand. She looked like she'd just won the lottery or something.

"Hi, Mrs. Fields," Christie said breathlessly to my mom. Then she shook the paper at me. "You've got to read this, Janey."

I took the piece of paper and read: "Meadowlake Summer Swim Camp. For teens looking for more excitement, more challenge, more fun." I dropped the paper and turned back to my toes.

"We're not teens, " I said. "We're still eleven."

"Almost twelve. That makes us almost-teens. Besides, after summer's over, we'll be in middle school." Christie grabbed a licorice stick out of the tub on my counter and ripped off a hunk. "My mom called, and they said we could sign up. And, here's the best part," Christie exclaimed. "My sister's doing it, and she said so is Marlena Frost and all the cool kids that go to Dakota Middle School."

"So?"

"So?" Christie rolled her eyes at me. "We're about to be sixth graders, and what do eighth graders do to sixth graders? Make fun of them —*unless* the sixth graders are smart enough to become friends with the eighth graders *before* school starts by joining the same swim camp!" She took a gulp of air. "Get it?"

"Yeah, I get it." I dabbed Blueberry Blue onto my pinky toe. "It's another one of your plans."

"It's a great plan!"

"Your plans always end up with me in trouble!"

"They do not," she said, biting off another chunk of licorice.

"What about the camping trip with your dad? It was your idea to explore, and I ended up sprayed by a skunk. And remember your great idea to knock the wasp's nest off your house with a rock? You got away, and I got stung."

"Come on, Janey. You love to swim. You're the fastest kid in your age group every year. Remember last year — how you got to go to that special swim tournament? This way, you can swim against older kids."

I chewed my lip, thinking.

"You don't have to do this if you don't want to," my mom said.

But it wasn't that simple. Christie wanted to do it and we'd been best friends forever. I didn't want her to be mad at me. Besides, I did love to swim. I just wasn't sure about the rest of it. The flyer said "More Exciting" and "More Challenging." Christie was the brave one.

I guess Christie could tell I was nervous. She shook the half-eaten licorice rope at me. "Come on, Janey. You don't want to be a dork in middle school do you? Besides, it'll be fun. The flyer even says so."

The flyer said so. Christie said so. If only that little voice in my head said so. Instead it was saying, "Don't do it!" I took a deep breath. I told that voice in my head to be quiet. It was just for two weeks, after all, and I'd been going to Meadowlake Swim Camp every year. Besides, what if we got to be friends with Marlena Frost? How cool would that be? "Okay, let's do it," I said.

A week later, my mom dropped Christie and me at the Meadowlake Swimming Center for the first day of camp. Christie's sister had gotten a ride with one of her friends, so we were on our own. We carried matching yellow swim bags, each stuffed with swim caps, goggles, a towel, sunscreen, a lunch and money for a treat. The new bags were a present from my mom, and they were so cool. I hugged mine close as we passed the younger kids at the wave pool.

Our group met by the main lap pool in back. The pool stretched as long as our baseball field at school. One end had lap lanes, the middle had been roped off for diving, and the other end had a special section for parents with toddlers.

I swallowed hard when I saw our group. Was I short, or were they all tall? The nervous voice inside me started squawking again. I felt out of place. I even looked out of place. Christie and I wore new two-piece swimsuits. All the other girls wore one-piece suits with racer-backs.

Christie, on the other hand, was so excited she was bouncing on her glittery flip-flops. "There she is," Christie whispered. Marlena stood at the center of a group. You couldn't miss Marlena. She was tall and thin, like a model or something. My hair curled in weird directions but Marlena's looked like a surfer girl's — long and brown with blond streaks. "Let's try and get in her lane," Christie whispered.

Then a lady called out, "Good morning," and everyone turned to look at her. A bright yellow shirt over her swimsuit read, "Lifeguard." A red swim cap covered her hair, and goggles swung around her neck. I recognized her right away. She had been a judge at the swim tournament last year.

"Welcome to Swim Camp," she said. "My name is Linda. For the next two weeks, you can call me Coach." Then she saw me and smiled. "Hi, Janey. You still as fast as last year?" Kids turned to look at me, and I felt my cheeks get hot. Even Marlena stared.

As soon as Linda turned back to the group, Christie whispered to me, "You're famous!"

"Shhhh," I hissed and pointed to Coach Linda who was talking again.

"During this camp, we'll cover the swimming basics but we'll take it up a notch," Coach said. "We'll play underwater rescue games, climb our special rock wall, and for the grand finale — " she took a big pause, " — you'll all take turns off the high dive."

I gulped. I looked at the high diving board in the middle of the pool. I felt like a giraffe stretching my neck up, up, up to see. "No way!" I muttered.

The other kids murmured things, too. Most of them sounded like, "Cool," and "All right." Christie nudged me and whispered, "It'll be okay. Just like jumping on my trampoline."

I glared at Christie. I'd broken my arm on her trampoline

when I was six.

"For now," said Coach, "I'll break you up into lanes, and we'll do some swimming." Kids started pushing and shoving to get with their friends. The lanes all filled so fast that Christie and I stood on the Kool Deck, not sure where to go.

Suddenly, I heard Marlena's voice. "Hey you, fast girl. Janey?"

I nodded.

"You can swim in my lane."

Me? I mouthed. Christie jabbed an elbow in my back.

"Ouch!"

"Would you go?" she hissed, excitedly.

I clutched my new yellow bag and walked over to Marlena's lane. Christie lined up in the lane next to mine.

"I'm Marlena. This is Trisha and Becky," Marlena said. The other girls were eighth graders, too. They all smiled. That made me feel better, and I forgot about the high dive. Maybe Christie was right. This would be great.

We all jumped in the water and put on goggles and swim caps. Then Coach told us to swim up and back a few times to warm up. The idea was to swim on one half of the lane, then turn around and swim back on the other half. That way you didn't crash into anyone.

As soon as Coach announced a short break, I jumped out and found Christie. We huddled together and dried our hair with our towels.

"So, what is she like?" Christie asked.

"Nice. But guess what," I said excitedly. "I can swim faster than her, I just know it. I bet I pass her when we do our timed swim."

Instead of being excited, Christie looked horrified. "You can't!" she said. "She won't like you if you pass her."

"But I'm faster!"

"So?" said Christie. "There are more important things than being the fastest swimmer."

That afternoon, Coach Linda timed everyone for a fifty-yard lap. When my turn came, I got a really good push off. I zipped down the pool, flip-turned at the end and started back. Then, in my head, I heard Christie's words.

She won't like you if you pass her.

My heart pounded, but not because I was tired. A few yards from the finish, I slowed down. Coach Linda gave me a funny look when I climbed out of the pool, but Marlena beamed. Her time was 3 seconds faster than mine. "I'm glad you're in our lane," she said. "Come sit by me and the girls at lunch tomorrow."

I smiled back, sure I'd done the right thing. "Thanks!" Just wait until I told Christie. Marlena and I were already friends, and it was the first day!

The next day at lunch, Christie and I sat with the eighth graders. Christie's sister gave us strange looks from her table. "Jealous," Christie whispered to me. "Marlena's never been very nice to her. In sixth grade, she got teased for months before they left her alone."

I felt so lucky to be "in", that when Marlena asked if Christie and me could get ice cream bars for everyone, I said sure. We collected money, and then stood in line at the snack bar. When we got back, the girls were arguing about whether some singer's eyes were green or hazel. I got bored and stopped listening.

"Hello, Earth to Janey!"

Christie nudged me. Her cheeks had gone red and her eyes looked a little shiny, but I didn't know why.

"What?" I asked.

"Marlena's talking to us," she said, blinking funny.

"I said," Marlena drawled, "Did your moms make you carry those yellow bags? I mean, how embarrassing is that!"

My ice cream suddenly felt bad in my stomach.

"Twin bags — it's so elementary," Trisha added.

They all burst out laughing.

"Let me guess," Marlena added. "Your mom thought you'd look 'cute' in those bikinis."

That made everyone laugh again. Christie and I pretended to laugh, too.

But when we met the next morning for camp, neither of us had the bags. I'd told my mom there wasn't room for it. Instead, I shoved my things in a backpack like Marlena had done. We didn't say anything about it, but we both wore our one-piece suits from last year, too.

That afternoon I swam behind Marlena, and it seemed like every other minute I had to slow down or she'd kick me. I couldn't say anything, either. The fastest swimmer in the lane got to go first, and Marlena had the fastest time.

By lunch on Thursday, everyone expected us to get their treats. Only this time, Marlena didn't have enough money.

"I'll pay you back," she promised.

I stood by her seat for a minute. I wanted to say, "If I buy yours, I won't have enough money for mine," but I swallowed the words, and went to wait in line with Christie.

That afternoon, we lined up at the low diving board for practice. "This year, we're going to have a little contest," Coach said. "You'll dive as a team with the kids in your lane. I'll be the judge. The team that does the most dives with proper form and style will win an ice cream break, while the rest of the kids swim laps."

That got everyone's attention. Then Coach showed everyone the proper form and technique of a dive. "We'll practice on the low board for the next few days until everyone is ready. Now who wants to be first?"

The boys all fought to be first. An eighth grader named Andy won. He started to dive but then did a cannonball. Lots of kids laughed.

A tall kid named Frank went next. In mid-dive he stopped and did a half flip.

There was a class of moms and toddlers in the next section of the pool. The little kids started clapping at the splashes the boys made.

Coach blew her whistle. "All right, guys. This is serious. You need to learn this stuff for when it's time to go off the high dive. Goof off then, and you'll end up injured."

Injured! I closed my eyes and wished I could be somewhere else. Anywhere else.

"Hey, you okay?"

I opened my eyes. Marlena looked at me, her brown eyes worried.

"To tell you the truth," I said, "I'm not much of a diver."

"But you're a good swimmer," she said.

"I'm a little afraid of heights."

She blinked. "Well, get over it by next Friday. I want to win."

I looked around for Christie. She had gotten in a lane with sixth and seventh graders, and she liked them a lot. I caught her eye, and she waved. "You'll be okay," she mouthed.

The line for the diving board got shorter and shorter. The girls ahead of me dove with perfect form and made little splashes in the pool. Too soon, it was my turn. I stood on the end and tried to remember everything Coach had said. Arms overhead. Head tucked. Spring off the board. V at the waist. Break the water hands first. Smooth follow through. Toes pointed. I took a deep breath.

Here goes!

I jumped, twisted, and hit the water stomach first. *Smack.* I came up sputtering, my whole middle stinging with pain.

"You okay?" Coach asked. She bent down by the edge of the pool and helped me out.

A shadow fell over me. I glanced up. Marlena stood there.

"She's okay. Janey's tough. That's why we're so glad she's on our team."

I smiled weakly at Coach. "I'll be okay."

Wouldn't I?

I tried not to worry about it all weekend. I still had a whole week — I could learn to dive by then.

On Monday, Coach Linda worked extra with me.

On Tuesday, too.

And on Wednesday.

By Thursday, I was better but I still couldn't figure out how to get my arms in first. Everyone else made it look easy — even

Christie.

"You just get too stiff," Christie told me as we stood in line at the snack bar. "You gotta relax."

"How can I relax?" I said. "Tomorrow I'm supposed to go off the high dive."

We placed the order, and I pretended to be busy balancing snow cones. The truth is I'd decided to tell Marlena I couldn't do it. I didn't want to tell Christie though. I thought maybe she'd be mad or something. I'd tell Marlena as soon as I got back to the table and make it okay. I passed out the other snow cones, then stopped when I got to Marlena. "I want to talk to you about something," I said. I handed her the snow cone, took a deep breath and —

"Ick!"

I closed my mouth. "What?"

"It's strawberry not raspberry."

"I asked for raspberry."

"Well, it's not raspberry," she said. "I mean even you can tell it's not raspberry, right?"

I licked my lips. "Yeah, sure."

"Well, that guy just cheated me."

I didn't see how he'd cheated her, since I wasn't the one who'd paid for it. Marlena still hadn't remembered her money. Still, I felt like an idiot. I couldn't even bring back the right snow cone. How could I tell her I didn't want to dive? I'd do it, I thought. Somehow, I'd just do it. It would all be worth it when school started again. Besides, what else could I do?

I hardly slept Thursday night, but I got up early Friday morning anyway. This was the last day of camp, and I wanted it to be over. All I had to do was one little dive. My mom and dad told me I could do it. Christie told me I could do it. Marlena told me I could do it.

I couldn't concentrate all morning. I swam on the wrong side of the lane, and even Trisha complained about me being slow. Finally, Coach called everyone over. "Time for the dive competition."

I think I watched all the kids as they dived. I think I even cheered for Trisha and Becky, but I'm not sure. I was so scared. Then suddenly, Marlena was grabbing my arm. "You're next."

"Uh... why don't you go?" I said, my throat so dry I sounded like a chipmunk.

"We'll save the best for last," she said with a wink. "You're up."

Up. Why did she have to use that word? Slowly, I climbed the ladder. My head felt full of voices telling me, "You can do this, Janey!" Each step up, I took another deep breath.

"You can do this, Janey. You can do this."

I got to the top. I let go of the metal rails. My hands trembled.

"You can do this, Janey. You can do this."

I walked to the edge of the board. I put my hands in proper dive form, bent my knees and — froze.

Marlena called up from the bottom of the ladder. "You okay?"

I gulped. I wanted to yell back, but something was stuck in my throat. I think it was my heart. I inched a foot forward and looked over the edge at the pool below.

Oh no, oh no, oh no!

I had two choices. I could jump and die a painful death. Or I could not jump and completely humiliate myself in front of every kid I knew and start sixth grade as the biggest dork in school history.

I didn't know which was worse. Not that it was easy to think at the edge of a diving board, twenty feet up in the sky, surrounded by fifty kids screaming, "Dive already, Janey!"

Everyone at Meadowlake Swim Center stopped what they were doing and stared at me. Down below, the class of moms and toddlers bobbed in the water, watching. *I can do this*, I told myself frantically. *It's not falling, it's diving.* But who was I kidding? I was a lousy diver. A dive from this height wouldn't just sting, it would flatten me like a pancake.

My heart beat so hard, I felt it in my knees. Wobbly knees on a high dive are not a good thing. My feet gripped the diving board so hard, my toes turned white. I'd just painted my toes yesterday — Radiant Pink. I'd even used glitter to paint a flower on my right big toe. I gulped back a sob. My toes were too nice to end up dead.

From all around me voices were getting mixed up in my head. Christie, yelling, "You can do this." Hoots and catcalls from other kids. "Chicken!" "Baby!" My dad's calm voice, "You can do anything you want to do." Then, from right behind me I heard another voice.

"What's your problem?"

I turned around. Marlena stood at the top of the ladder. Even with wet braids, her hair looked perfect.

"I can't do it," I choked out.

Her eyes narrowed and suddenly she didn't look very pretty

anymore. "You have to. If you don't dive, we don't win. Even worse, I'm going to look like an idiot."

I blinked. "You?"

"I took you under my wing," she hissed. "If you don't jump, kids will laugh at me for being nice to a baby. I didn't need to be nice you know."

I could see in her eyes that if I didn't jump, she'd never be nice to me again. I'd ruin middle school for Christie and me.

Marlena lifted one foot onto the diving board and tapped it impatiently. Her toenails were painted red. Blood red. "Well?"

I licked my lips. My mouth had gone dry again.

"Maybe you just need a little push."

My stomach lurched in fear. "NO! Marlena, don't you dare!"

"Then dive, Janey."

"Haven't you ever been scared?" My voice squeaked with fear.

She cocked her head to one side, like maybe she was thinking about it, then looked back at me. "No."

Frustration bubbled inside of me. "You could make this okay. Kids would listen to you. You could tell them my eyesight went blurry or something."

"You want me to lie?"

"Then don't lie. Just tell them the truth. Tell them I got scared, and it's no big deal. So what if I'm not a good diver? I'm a fast swimmer."

"Not as fast as me."

My frustration turned to anger. Why had I ever let her beat me?

Marlena wagged a finger at me. "You listen to me, and I'll tell you what to do."

Then something inside me exploded. "No!"

She gasped like I'd slapped her. Maybe no one had ever told her no before.

I stomped a foot and my knee hardly wobbled at all. "I'm not going to listen to you." My legs straightened and my chin lifted. "I've listened for two weeks. Now, you can listen to me. I don't like waiting in line for your treats — and I want you to pay me back the money you owe. I haven't been swimming my fastest because I wanted you to like me, but now I think that's stupid. And," I sputtered, running out of breath, "I like my yellow bag even if it is goofy and matches Christie's."

Christie, I thought with a twinge of pain. I knew she wouldn't want me to say these things. She was my best friend, but I couldn't listen to her either. For once, I needed to listen to myself.

I took a deep breath. "I'm going to climb down that ladder, Marlena."

"You are so in trouble at middle school," she said as I grabbed the ladder railing. Her threat would worry me later, but right now that cool metal felt so good in my hand.

Marlena tossed me one more superior look, and then began a graceful run to the edge of the board and her dive.

Just then, a scream came from down below.

"Poop! Poop in the pool!"

A mom held up a flailing toddler, his diaper hanging by one side. Bobbing towards the open middle of the pool... like an innocent brown candy bar... was a piece of poop.

Marlena paused in mid-air, her arms in the perfect V, her

legs straight as a ballerina — her face frozen in wide-eyed terror — and down she went aiming right for the poop. No one even noticed me coming down the ladder. They were all doubled up and laughing their heads off at Marlena Frost.

That was two months ago.

As it turned out, people talk about that summer swim camp a lot at Dakota Middle School. And Marlena doesn't get to make the rules anymore. If she tries to get high and mighty, all you have to do is offer to buy her a brown candy bar — she gets a lot nicer after that.

Christie and I are still best friends. But now, when she tells me to try the bean burritos for school lunch or to take sky diving lessons with her, I just laugh. If she rolls her eyes at me, I roll mine back.

And next summer, I'm making all the plans.

High Dive
by Alison Dellenbaugh

Be calm, I tell myself. Be cool.
It's not that far above the pool.
Just ten more steps, now eight, now five,
'Til I'm the next in line to dive.
I wouldn't even try last year,
But now I'm older — what's to fear?
I can't believe I'm at the top!
Oh no, what if I belly flop?
And what if water fills my nose,
Or worse, I lose my swimming clothes?
The water looks so far away,
I wish I'd waited one more day.
There's still some time to change my mind...
"Go on!" shouts someone from behind.
I run and bounce and suddenly —
I'm in the air and feeling free!
Who cares if it's the perfect dive?
I took the plunge, and I'm alive.
And when I make my SPLASH! below,
I'm ready for another go!

The Water Fight Professional
By Angela Meuser

Some kids mow lawns to make extra money. Some kids sell lemonade. Not me. I spent the summer after my fourth grade year as Joey Michaels, Water Fight Professional.

The idea came to me at the age of five, on a church picnic of all places. Mom handed me a cup of water and told me to go dump it on my dad. Dad saw me coming, however, and offered me a dollar to dump the same cup on my mom. Mom got soaked and I got paid.

Apparently I fell asleep that night holding onto the dollar because the next morning I heard Mom say to Dad, "Look what you started. Watch him create a water fighting business."

The business was a great success. I advertised with a cardboard sign at the local park: Professional Water Fighter. A cup of water costs 50 cents. A water balloon costs 75 cents. The water gun costs one dollar.

You see, tossing a cup of water on someone was really quite simple. An unsuspecting stranger never saw it coming, because I could just act like I was drinking out of the cup as I walked toward them. A water balloon usually got a little more attention, so I would hide that behind my back. The water gun required a sneak attack. I had to climb a tree and wait for my target to approach. That's why it was the most expensive service to purchase.

The water gun was my favorite. It wasn't just any water gun. I started out with the Mega Drench 200, but decided to upgrade to the Galactic Turbo Drench 2000. It had much better accuracy. The Mega Drench always shot off to the left.

Being a water fight professional was a fun job. Once my service was requested, the victim who got wet immediately wanted revenge. I couldn't give the victim the name of my customer because I promised privacy, but I always recommended that the victim hire me to soak whoever had laughed the loudest when he or she had gotten soaked.

That kept me busy most of the time. When business was slow, I just volunteered my service to one random individual free of charge and that got things going again.

I pretty much had a monopoly on the market until my sister turned six. Christine showed up at the park the last summer before she started 1st grade. She hung up her sign that read: Super Water Fight Professional.

"That's a laugh!" I yelled because she had no experience whatsoever.

Christine stuck her tongue at me. A very mature business woman, I thought sarcastically.

Well, it was kind of cute. Even though her prices were lower than mine and came with free lemonade, I didn't worry. Who would hire a little girl to start a water fight when my booth was set up at the picnic table across from hers? Besides that, her balloons were all pink, and her cups had princesses on them. (They were left over from her birthday party.)

We quieted down when the first potential customer headed our way. "Good afternoon, ma'am. Is there anybody in particular that you would like to see get wet?" I asked the woman with a kindergartner in tow.

"What a great idea." The woman's head swiveled between my booth and my sister's. She turned her back toward me. "Aren't you adorable? Would you dump a cup of water on my husband?"

Christine did what she would consider a victory dance, but I just shook my head.

Christine picked up her paper cup and walked up to her victim with a smile. He smiled back and the whole picnic area turned to watch in anticipation. Christine dumped water on the man's shoe! I was appalled, but everyone else laughed.

Another member of the picnic headed our direction. Finally, I thought, they want to start some real action. But did the man walk to my table? No.

"Hey, sweetheart. Would you throw a water balloon at my daughter?"

Unbelievable!

Christine cradled the balloon in her hands as she walked back toward the group. She didn't even try to hide her weapon. Her target was a teenage girl, but it should have been a tree because that is what the balloon hit — not that it popped.

"That's an embarrassment to water fighters everywhere," I hollered, but for some reason the people at the picnic were applauding.

Christine bowed. Pathetic.

The teenage girl clapped the loudest. She leaned down to whisper in Christine's ear. My little sister returned to her table and pulled out my old Mega Drench 200.

"You snuck that out of my garbage can," I accused.

"Finder's keepers!" Christine yelled back before hoisting the gun that was almost as big as her entire body and pointing it directly at the teenager's boyfriend.

I could have called out to my sibling to angle the gun to the side if she wanted to hit her target, but I didn't. She had already made $1.50 more than me. There was no way I was going to help her steal my business.

The gun spit water out directly on the teenage girl who had hired Christine. That should do it, I thought.

To my surprise, the girl, now soaking wet, gave my little sister a big hug. "You're terrible," she laughed.

No kidding. I was so mad I picked up a green balloon that looked just like a grenade and prepared to hurl it at Christine's pigtails. "Go home, or get bombed," I threatened as she headed back my direction.

"I'll tell mom," she sang in her tattle tale voice.

At that point, I didn't care. "It'll be worth it," I said through gritted teeth.

Thus began the water fight to end all water fights.

To be honest, my little sis threw just as many balloons at me as I did at her, but I didn't even get wet. So of course, I was the one who got in trouble.

Mom restricted me from the park for the rest of the summer, which is actually fine with me. I wouldn't want to be blamed for "interfering" in Christine's lemonade stand. Besides, I started a new business. No, I'm not mowing lawns. That is a job for kids who don't own a Galactic Turbo Drench 2000 like I do. I am now Joey Michaels, Flower Watering Specialist.

The Mermaid's Scepter
By Sydney Salter Husseman

Emma walked along the sandy beach with her grandmother. Seagulls squawked as they flew to their nests on Haystack rock. Colorful puffins dotted the rock, waiting for their mates to bring food. Grandma loved to search for creatures in the tide pools around Haystack Rock.

"I see a purple sea star," Emma said.

"Where?" Grandma balanced on a half-submerged rock.

"Clinging to the rock — just under the water," Emma said. "Oooh, I see a little fish."

"Look at that bit of sea lettuce," Grandma said. "I saw a little crab hiding there."

The two peered into the pool of water until a wave washed over their toes.

"Oh, that's cold water," Grandma said.

"I see two orange sea stars," Emma said.

"I think the tide is coming in," Grandma said. "We'd better head back."

"Can we feed the gulls when we get back?"

"Of course." Grandma put her arm around Emma, but only for a minute. Emma raced toward the surf, then ran backwards like a sandpiper when a wave came close. Then she splashed in the small waves. She paused and took a deep breath of the salty smelling air. Emma walked along the edge of the water. Grandma walked on the drier sand.

"I found a shell." Emma held up a broken sand dollar to show Grandma. She gathered more shells.

"Come on, sweetie," Grandma called. "I feel raindrops falling."

Emma raced up to Grandma. "Hold these, please." She handed Grandma a handful of sandy shell fragments. "I just want to find one more."

"One more," Grandma said.

Emma ran to the water and stopped suddenly. A strange object bobbed in the surf. "Grandma!" Emma yelled. "Come look, hurry!"

Grandma walked quickly toward her. "What is it?"

"Look." Emma picked up the object. "What is it?"

"Well, it's a piece of seaweed, or kelp," Grandma said. "But how odd..." She took the object from Emma. It was a piece of kelp with the round air bladder at the top and a long stem. Except the stem was wound around and around in an intricate diamond pattern.

"Emma, sweetie. It looks like a scepter."

"A what?"

"A scepter — like a queen holds." Grandma's eyes twinkled.

"A mermaid queen." Emma lightly touched the scepter. "Are mermaids real?"

"Anything can be real in your imagination," Grandma said.

"I'm taking this back to the house." Emma held the scepter across both her arms all the way back to the beach house.

Grandma took a picture of Emma holding the scepter. Emma

spent hours staring at it and imagining the mermaid queen. She liked to think the queen had sparkling hair that shimmered like the ocean's surface on a sunny day. She imagined she had sea horse friends and swam deep with blue whales. The mermaid queen knew where all the ancient ships filled with gold and treasure rested on the bottom of the ocean.

On the last day, Emma returned her shells to the beach for other children to find. She saved one tiny whole sand dollar: mermaid money. She carefully placed it among the socks in her suitcase. After everything was packed, Emma picked up the scepter. It looked fragile and dry. She knew she couldn't take it home.

"Let's go," Grandma called.

"Wait. I've got to run down to the ocean one more time." Emma held out the scepter for Grandma to see.

"I understand," Grandma said.

The beach was empty, except for a flock of pelicans flying low. Emma ran to the surf and kicked off her shoes before they got wet.

"Mermaid," she called. "Here is your lost scepter." She threw the scepter into the waves and watched it bob until a big wave took it away. "Good-bye Mermaid Queen," Emma whispered.

Emma picked up her shoes and ran back to the car. Grandma wrapped her in a hug.

"Now, I'll always have a mermaid friend," Emma said.

Moon Smile

By Joanne Peterson

When I stay with Grandma,
We look for the moon.
We find Moon when it's slim and frail,
As thin as a fingernail.

We find Moon when it's big and round,
When she sits upon the ground,
Then slowly climbs up the sky,
A big balloon way up high.

"Look Grandma! There it is," I say,
"A beach-ball tossed too high at play."

Moon sails by the window,
Just out of our reach,
Sometimes shaped like a banana,
An orange, or a peach.

Tonight, moon shows up
Dressed in gold,
A bowl with more stars
Than she can hold.

Stars spill upon my floor.
Stars scatter out my door.

Moon becomes a big, bright smile.
Smiles while I sleep.
Smiles all the while.

The Nickname
By Bish Denham

Twelve year old Joshua scowled at his dad.

"I don't *want* to go to summer camp! It's some place out in the boondocks, miles away from my friends. It says here in the brochure that I can't even take my CD player!" He tossed it away from him as if it was poisonous. "They don't have video games, and no TV! And what if I'm the only African-American?"

"You won't be," his father assured him. "Trust me. You're going to have a great time at Camp Aqua Verde. You know I went there when I was your age."

Yeah, back in the Dark Ages, Joshua thought. *And there's nothing fun about being stuck way out in the country.*

"It's just for two weeks," his dad said.

Two weeks! He'd miss being with his friends and hanging out at the game-room. He'd miss TV.

There were four boys to a cabin.

George, Franklin and Bobby were all there when Joshua arrived.

At least we don't have to share bunk beds, Joshua thought. The councilor, a young man named Andrew, gave quick introductions then left the cabin.

"Ewe-a-newer?" asked George. He was stretched out on his bed chewing on a toothpick. Booted feet stuck out from the bottoms of washed-out jeans.

"A what?"

"Boys who have never been here before," he answered pushing a cowboy hat to the back of his head. "You know, a newbie."

"I guess so," said Josh. "I've never been here before." *And I don't intend to come back,* he added to himself.

"I'll be here for a month," Franklin said as he carefully organized his underwear drawer. He looked the opposite of George. He was all neatly ironed creases and carefully combed hair. "I've been coming for a month every summer since I was six."

Bobby sat cross-legged on his bed, with his back against the wall. Red hair curled out from under a baseball cap. "He thinks he owns the place," he said from behind a comic book he was reading.

"And you think you're smarter than God," said Franklin.

"It's starting already," George said to Josh.

"Kicker would be happy kicking cow paddies around a field all day," said Bobby.

"You'd think we'd be friends after being together every summer for the past five years," said George. "But we really hate each other."

Joshua's eyes went wide.

"Gotcha!" laughed George.

"Welcome to Antelope Lodge," said Bobby, "home of George, AKA the Kicker, Franklin known as the Snob and me. I'm called Nerd. Who are you?"

"I... I..." Joshua didn't know what to say.

"We'll figure that out later," said Kicker. "It's time to go to the Indoctrination Ceremony."

Toward the end of the first week, plans were made to go

camping. Up to that point, Joshua hadn't shared many activities with his bunkmates. All he'd done was sleep in the same cabin with them.

"Where are we going?" asked Joshua.

"Camp Wilderness," said Nerd. "It's about five miles from here. There's a lake. We get to fish."

"It's pretty cool," Kicker agreed. "Sleeping in a teepee, cooking up what we catch, telling ghost stories." Joshua was not excited about camping. Let alone fishing.

"And we have to hike there?" He didn't like the hiking part either. "And it's going to take how long?"

"The first mile is kind of hard," said Snob. "But the rest of the way follows the ridge and is easy. It can take three to four hours."

"Don't be a wuss," teased Nerd. "Maybe that's who you are, the Wuss."

"I am *not* a wuss," Josh said, hoisting a backpack to his shoulders.

"Ready boys?" Andrew popped his head in through the door. "Make sure you've got everything. You won't be able to come back for anything you forget. And remember, conserve your water. You don't want to drink it all before you get to the top of the ridge."

Snob was right. The first mile was hard. The trail was steep and rocky. Joshua was sure his pack was getting heavier with each step he took. His back felt like it was about to snap. He legs were aching, and he was having a hard time breathing.

"Half-way point boys!" said Andrew. He sounded too cheery for Josh's liking. "Anyone need a rest?"

The three musketeers looked at Joshua. "We're fine!" they said.

"What about you, Josh? Need a break?" asked Andrew.

"I'm... (pant, pant) no I'm... (pant, pant) just fine."

"It'll be easier coming out. Our packs will be lighter because we'll have eaten the food we're carrying. Sure you don't need a rest?"

"Well..."

"Wuss," whispered Nerd out of the side of his mouth.

Joshua glared at him. "No, really I'm *fine!*"

"Great!" said Andrew. "Another 15 or 20 minutes we'll be at the top."

Joshua groaned. Surely his legs would fall off before then. He concentrated on the ground in front of him.

If I just keep putting one foot in front of the other and don't look at how far I have to go... But he couldn't help looking up the trail every now and then. The top of the ridge didn't seem to be getting any closer. Sweat trickled into his eyes. When he tried to wipe it away, it made them burn. His shoulders felt raw from the straps of the backpack.

Maybe I'll die of thirst, he thought. *Maybe I'll trip and fall over the edge. They probably wouldn't miss me if I did.*

Just when he knew he couldn't take another step and his tongue felt like a wad of cotton, a cool breeze blew across his face. They had reached the top of the ridge. Far below they could see the valley they had hiked out of. The river, snaking through Camp Aqua Verde, looked like it was made of mercury.

"Break!" said Andrew.

They all collapsed to the ground and shrugged off their packs.

Canteens were opened and long, slow sips of water were taken. Kicker took out a bandana and drenched it with water. He wiped down his face and neck, sighing. Snob and Nerd did the same.

"Didn't you bring a bandana?" asked Kicker.

"No," said Josh through clenched teeth.

"Greenhorn, that's who you are," said Nerd.

Snob dug around in his pack and tossed Josh a bandana. "I always have extras. Don't leave home without them."

Josh would have been grateful if they hadn't been snickering at him. "Thanks a lot," he mumbled.

The rest of the hike went without incident. Most of the trail followed the ridge line. There were enough cedars and oaks to give occasional shade, and a steady breeze blew from the southwest.

They reached Camp Wilderness just before noon. It was nestled in a small ravine. A creek entered it from the north and had a dam on the south end. A large pond occupied the middle. Two teepees were pitched on the grassy banks. Several ancient oak trees grew near the pond. One of them had a rope attached to a branch.

Kicker, Snob and Nerd raced to a teepee, shedding their packs as they went.

"Before you guys go jumping in the pond, we need to make camp," ordered Andrew. "Go stow your packs. George and Bobby, I want you to look for firewood. Franklin, there's a bucket in my teepee. You get the water. Josh, you can help me rebuild the fire pit. We'll need some rocks. And be careful, Josh. Turn the rocks over slowly; keep an eye out for scorpions."

"Scorpions!" Josh turned pale and gulped.

"Yeah, you know," said Kicker, "those eight-legged critters with stinging tails?"

"They're everywhere; they're everywhere," Nerd chanted.

"You have to check your sleeping bag every night and your shoes every morning," added Snob.

"It's not as bad as they're making it sound, Josh," said Andrew. "Just be careful."

Josh expected a scorpion to jump out at him every time he turned over a rock. He didn't know what he'd do if he found one.

Probably yell like a fool, he thought. When none turned up, he felt like he'd been given a stay of execution.

Once camp was set up, Andrew let the boys go swimming while he made a quick lunch of peanut butter and jelly sandwiches.

As they walked to the pond, Kicker, Snob and Nerd started arguing over who would get to swing out over the pond first.

"You were first last year," Nerd said to Snob. "I was second and Kicker was third. So that means I'm first, Kicker is second and you're third."

"No, that's not how it was," said Kicker. "I was second, Snob was third and you were first. So I'm first, Snob's second and *you're* third."

"You're both wrong," said Snob. "*I* was second, you were first and Nerd was third. Therefore I'm first, Nerd's second and *you're* third."

"Why don't you just draw straws?" asked Joshua.

"That would make it too easy," said Snob. "Let's do paper, scissors, rock."

Kicker won first place, with Snob coming in second and Nerd third. Without being told, Joshua knew he would be last.

Kicker climbed up the boards that had been nailed into the trunk of the tree. He grabbed the rope and swung off the branch, hollering like Tarzan. When he was over the water, he let go. When he hit the water, he sent a shower of spray towards the boys on the bank. Snob was already out on the limb when Kicker started swimming back to shore.

"Look out below!" he yelled, cannonballing into the water.

"That's nothing!" said Nerd. "Watch this. Bombs away!"

Up to that moment, Joshua hadn't really thought about swimming in the pond. It was green and murky with slimy stuff growing along the edges. He was sure the bottom was muddy and that snakes lurked among the reeds. The three musketeers were splashing around and hollering.

"Come on Josh! The water's fine!" yelled Snob.

"Can't you swim?" asked Kicker.

"I can swim just fine," he said.

"What then? Are you chicken?" asked Nerd. "Maybe that's who you are, the Chicken, bawk, bawk, bawk."

Joshua gritted his teeth and climbed the tree. As he swung out he squealed like a pig. He managed to remember to let go and hit the water butt first. It was cold. For a moment he panicked as the green darkness closed over his head. Then everything went quiet. He swam to the surface and burst into the sunlight. In spite of himself, he was smiling and trying not to laugh.

"Lunch!" called Andrew. "Come and get it."

After lunch they went fishing. "Sometimes we catch a trout," said Nerd. "But mostly it's perch."

"I caught a catfish once," said Kicker.

"We found a great place to dig for worms by the dam," said Snob.

Joshua didn't say anything. He didn't want them to know how he felt about handling worms. He poked around with a stick, hoping he wouldn't find one. But he did. He picked the worm up between his thumb and first finger and quickly dropped it into a can they were using to collect them.

"Don't want to get your hands dirty?" asked Kicker. "Wow! Here's a big fat juicy one!" He dangled it in front of Joshua's face. Josh turned his face away, frowning.

"Don't tell me you're afraid of worms," Snob demanded.

"Maybe that's who he is," said Nerd. "The Worm."

Joshua was ready to slug somebody. He grabbed a worm and speared it with his hook. He felt sick to his stomach. He quickly tossed his line out into the water and hoped that would be the end of it.

The boys went to different spots along the bank of the creek. In just ten minutes Joshua had a strike.

"What do I do? What do I do?" he yelled.

"Haul in your line!" said Kicker.

"Get away from the reeds; it'll go for the reeds!" Nerd instructed.

"Watch out for that log!" warned Snob. The three boys raced to Joshua and continued to tell him what to do. As he hauled on the hand line, he thought his fingers were getting sliced open. He thought for sure he had caught a whale.

When he finally had it near the bank, Kicker said, "He got Old Fox!"

Nerd splashed into the water, grabbed the huge trout by the gills and threw it up onto the bank. It flopped about madly. "You got Old Fox! I don't believe it."

"We've been trying to catch him for years," said Snob.

Joshua watched the fish gasping, its gills were pumping, its mouth opening and closing, opening and closing. "What do we do with it now?" he asked.

"We eat him!" laughed Kicker, slapping Joshua on the back.

"Why don't we just let him go," said Josh.

"Are you kidding?" asked Nerd.

"No, I'm not kidding," said Josh. "Why not throw him back so you can try to catch him some other time? He's already lived a long time, why not let him keep on living? I mean, don't you call him 'Old Fox' for a reason?"

"Maybe he's right," said Snob. "What would we have to look forward to if Old Fox was gone?"

Kicker shook his head. "What's the point of fishing if you don't eat what you catch?"

Nerd picked up Old Fox and unhooked him. "Snob and Josh are right. He deserves to live." He handed the fish to Joshua. "You caught him; you throw him back."

Joshua didn't think about not wanting to touch the fish. He grabbed hold of Old Fox, waded out into the water, and gently let him go. He was sure the fish winked at him before swimming away. *Nah... couldn't be,* he thought. *Must have been a reflection of the light.*

Joshua turned out to be quite the fisherman. He learned how to remove the hook from the fish he caught. He learned how to clean them. Best of all he learned how to skewer them on a stick and roast them over the campfire.

"I know who you are," said Nerd as they ate dinner. "You're the Fish."

Joshua shook his head, smiling.

It had been a long day, and Josh was sore and tired. When he crawled into his sleeping bag he forgot to check for scorpions.

Luckily there weren't any. But Joshua couldn't sleep. He couldn't find a comfortable position. It felt like he was lying on a bed made of gravel.

He listened to all the unfamiliar noises: frogs down at the pond, an owl, things rustling and snorting. He pictured javelinas rooting around the fire pit. Then he heard a new sound—something crying, like it was hurt or lost. He tried to ignore it, but it didn't go away.

He peered through the darkness at the three musketeers. They were sound asleep. Joshua didn't want to wake them up. He knew they'd tease him about sounds that go bump in the night. He knew Nerd would make up a new name for him. *Bogeyman,* he thought.

He felt around for his flashlight and crept to the teepee flap, cautiously sticking his head out. A moon, nearly full, was dropping in the western skies. It was bright enough that he didn't need the flashlight, but he turned it on anyway, waving it towards the various sounds he heard. The rustling snuffles came from an armadillo. It wandered off when the light hit it.

The crying came from somewhere near the pond. He picked up his shoes, which were by the entrance, and steeled himself to leave the security of the teepee.

Joshua walked slowly. Every time he heard a noise he froze and aimed the light toward the sound. The crying got louder as he neared the pond. He was sure he knew what was making it. Then he saw it—a small dark lump, whimpering under one of the oak trees. A puppy!

Back at the teepee, the four boys woke up Andrew to show him Joshua's find.

"He can't be more than five or six weeks old," said Andrew. "He looks healthy."

"I wonder how he got there," said Josh.

"There's a ranch about half a mile from here," said Andrew. "He might have wandered off from there. We'll hike over tomorrow see if he belongs to them. Until then, you guys need to get back to sleep."

The boys made a cage for the puppy by encircling their backpacks. They gave him a little bread to chew on and a little dish of water. After he ate, he curled up and went to sleep.

Joshua slept too.

The people at the ranch weren't missing a puppy.

"I shot a feral dog a couple of days ago," the rancher said. "She was killing my sheep. Looked like she'd had pups. This one's probably hers. Same black and tan markings."

"Looks like you boys have yourselves a goshe," said the man's wife.

"A what?" asked Joshua.

"G-O-S-H-E, pronounced goo-sha. It's Apache for dog."

"Then that's his name," said Joshua looking down at the puppy cradled in his arms.

"Hey, Fish caught another one!" said Nerd.

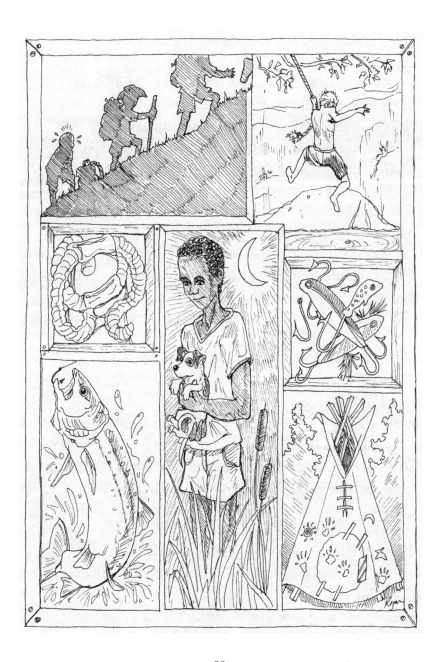

Joshua hauled in his line. Another perch. He'd already caught two, plus a catfish.

"We've got enough for lunch *and* dinner," said Kicker.

"What's our total?" asked Snob.

"Six perch, one trout and two catfish," said Josh.

"I say it's time for a celebration swim," said Kicker.

After they cleaned their fish and gave them to Andrew, the four boys went down to the pond. Goshe, the puppy, followed along, tumbling about their feet. They didn't know what was going to happen to him.

"Maybe the camp will keep him as their mascot," said Nerd. "I'd take him home, but we live in an apartment. They don't allow pets."

"I know I can't take him home," said Snob. "My little sister is allergic to dogs."

"We already have three," said Kicker. "So I can't take him."

"I'm going to ask my parents," said Josh. "Since I found him, I'd like to keep him."

Nerd climbed the tree and swung out over the pond. Josh was going second. He waited on the limb for Nerd to come to the surface before he jumped in. But Nerd didn't come up.

"Something's wrong!" he hollered to Kicker and Snob. "Get Andrew!"

Joshua swung out, hit the water and dove into the murky depths. He could barely see. He frantically felt around. His air ran out. He broke the surface, gulped in a lung-full and dove again. Then he saw Nerd's shadowy form. He hooked his arm under Nerd's and pushed off the muddy floor as hard as he could. He swam on his back, Nerd's limp body across his chest.

Andrew was in the water up to his waist and pulled Nerd to the bank. His head was bleeding from a large gash just above his forehead. Andrew checked his pulse, his breath.

"Is he dead?" asked Snob.

"He's got a pulse, but he's not breathing. Get my cell phone," said Andrew. "It's by my bedroll. Call the camp. Tell them to send for air-life rescue."

Kicker raced for the phone as Andrew began CPR. Snob ran and got Nerd's sleeping bag. Joshua went for the first aid kit. When the boys returned to the edge of the pond, Andrew had Nerd breathing, but he was still unconscious. They wrapped him in the sleeping bag. Andrew carefully lifted him and carried him up to the camp.

"They're coming!" Kicker said to Andrew. "Mr. Mallory said it would be 10 or 15 minutes before they got here. He said for you to call him as soon as you could."

Andrew pressed gauze pads to Nerd's head in an effort to stop the bleeding.

"He probably has a concussion," he told the boys. "We have to try to keep him from going into shock." They dried him off and wrapped him in another sleeping bag.

Andrew called Mr. Mallory, who owned the camp. "We've done everything we can, Mr. Mallory. Nerd's breathing, but he's still unconscious. We're just waiting now."

It was the longest ten minutes any of them had ever experienced. When they heard the sound of the helicopter, there was a release of tension. The three boys ran out into the field behind the teepees, waving Joshua's red t-shirt.

Nerd was awake by the time the 'copter landed. Kicker and

Snob explained who had pulled him out of the pond.

As the medical staff loaded him onto a stretcher one of the EMTs said, "He's going to be just fine, thanks to you guys."

"Josh, where's Joshua?" asked Nerd.

"I'm right here," said Joshua, resting his hand on Nerd's shoulder. He walked alongside the stretcher as they carried him to the 'copter. Everything was different in a new and wonderful way.

Nerd smiled up at him. "I know who you are, now," he said. "You're the Lifesaver."

Blame It on the Menehune
By Susan Zeller Smith

The first time Jake saw his dad's new pineapple farm on Kaua'i was also the first time he saw Tutu Akua. Well, really it was just a glimpse of a bent old man, stepping back into the lush growth of tree ferns.

Jake jumped out of his dad's Grand Cherokee, threw his duffle up onto the lanai, and ran around the house. The old man was gone. Jake looked around at the banana and mango trees, ti shrubs, and stone-edged ditch that gave shape to the cool, tiny backyard. Beyond the ditch stretched rows of pineapples, right up to the pali.

"Hey, Jake!" his dad called from the house. "Come on in and get your room squared away. Lots to do this summer!"

"Dad, who was that old man in the backyard?"

"Probably just an old-timer headed for that pile of rocks. It used to be some kind of shrine."

Over dinner, Jake's dad laid out the plans for the summer.

"I'm glad you're here, kiddo," he said. "I can use your help getting the fields in shape. Once you start high school in the fall, you'll probably want to be with your friends, not your old dad and his pineapples."

"Uh, can we do stuff besides the pineapples?" Jake asked.

"Sure," said his dad. "Did you know Kaua'i is the home of the Menehune? We can explore some of their ruins."

"What are Menehune?"

"They're the little people of the islands. They're about two or three feet tall, red-faced, and hairy. They work hard, but you'll never see them."

"Oh, yeah? Why not?"

"They do all their work between sunset and sunrise. If the project isn't done by dawn, it'll never get finished. The Menehune spend only one night on each project."

Jake made a face at his dad. "Right. And then I suppose the Tooth Fairy makes them breakfast."

Jake's dad laughed. "I'll let you decide that."

The next day Jake and his dad toured the fields. Jake discovered that the ditch in the backyard ran along the edge of the field, too. It came down from a spring in the hills, all three miles of it lined and edged with rocks.

"Did you dig this ditch, Dad?" Jake asked.

"No, it's been here as long as anyone can remember. They say the Menehune did it."

"Come on, Dad. You've got Menehune on the brain."

Jake and his dad squatted to look more closely at the stonework.

"These stones are so cleanly cut they fit together well enough without mortar to carry water without leaking. Ancient Hawaiians couldn't do this kind of work," said Jake's dad, pointing to the blocks on the bottom of the ditch. "Maybe it was aliens. Whoever put the rocks in, we need to pull them out, stack them, and fill in the ditch. So, let's get to it."

"Gee, I'd rather let the Menehune do it."

Jake's dad chuckled, tossed Jake some work gloves, and

reached for the first rock.

The next morning, Jake and his dad groaned their way through breakfast, their muscles aching after six hours of hauling rock and a fitful night's sleep. They walked slowly to the field, stretching to get the kinks out. They pushed through the line of tree ferns and stopped still as cold lava.

Every rock was back in place. Every rock Jake and his dad had pulled up and stacked was back in the ditch, looking like it had never been moved. Every single one.

An old man rose from his seat at the edge of the ditch.

"The Menehune don't like it when people mess with their work," he said.

"Do you know anything about this?" Jake's dad asked.

"I just told you—the Menehune."

Jake's dad blew out his exasperation. "Right. Jake, wait here. I'll find some guys to help us do this all over again." He stomped back toward the house, shaking his head.

"Hey, I saw you here the other day. I'm Jake." He eyed the old man skeptically.

"Aloha, Jake. You can call me Tutu Akua."

"Uh, how do you know about the Menehune?"

"Everyone on Kaua'i knows about them. Some believe they were the first ones to live here."

"Do they just build ditches?"

"Irrigation ditches, fish ponds, sacred places. You keep your mind open, Jake, and you will find lots of signs of the Menehune."

Jake made a show of looking around. "So, did they plant these pineapples? Think they'll do the dishes for me tonight?"

But there was no answer. The old man had disappeared again.

Jake, his dad, and two field hands pulled up and stacked stones and then filled in about a quarter of a mile of ditch that day.

"That should do it," Jake's dad said at the end of the day. "No vandal's going to undo all that work in one night. Jake, how about we camp out tonight and enjoy the stars?"

In the deep night, after the moon had set, Jake opened his eyes. Why had he woken up? Was it his father's snoring? The whining mosquitoes trapped in the tent with them? Then Jake heard it again. It was a sliding sort of scritching sound, and once in a while a short rumble like rocks laughing. Jake lay listening, barely breathing, until he could see shadows of branches on the outside of the tent. The sounds were gone.

"Dad, it's morning. Wake up." Jake jostled his dad awake, and they climbed out of the tent into the pink bird-song morning.

At least they thought they were awake. Maybe they were still dreaming.

The ditch was dug and lined. Again.

Jake's dad was speechless, his eyes as wide open as his mouth. Jake looked from the ditch to his dad to the ditch. Could it be possible? Jake, biting his lip, stepped closer to the ditch, bending to look for clues in the sandy soil.

"You won't find any footprints."

Jake jerked. Tutu Akua stepped out from the forest.

"I don't understand," said Jake's dad, running his hand through his hair. "No one was here last night. No one."

Tutu Akua stared steadily at Jake. "Did you see anyone,

Jake?"

"Ye — no, no, I didn't... see anyone," he said, unable to look away from Tutu Akua.

"I don't get it." Jake's dad looked along the ditch as though maybe he was mistaken about where they'd worked.

"The Menehune appreciate gifts of shrimp and poi," said Tutu Akua. He waved good-bye to Jake and walked away toward the pali.

"Dad, who is that old guy?"

"I don't know, kiddo. I'd never seen him before yesterday. What say we give this project a rest today?" Jake and his dad took down the camp and walked back to the house, Jake's dad stopping once to look back at the ditch. They spent the day at the beach, swimming and exploring ancient fish ponds. The rocks of the pond walls were as well cut as the rocks lining the ditch at home.

Back at the house that evening, Jake watched his dad stare at the ditch.

"Dad, Tutu Akua said the Menehune like shrimp and poi. Do you know anything about that?"

"Hmm? Oh. Legend has it that if you leave some, the Menehune will work for you."

"Want to try it?" Jake asked. "We've already staked out the section of ditch you want filled. We could just leave out some shrimp and poi, too. What could it hurt?"

Jake's dad snorted. "Jake, the Menehune are just a legend, a story to explain some very well-made rock structures. If you want to put perfectly good food out there, well, I'm sure the wild critters will love you for it. I'm going to bed. Tomorrow we'll tackle some rocks."

Jake waited until his dad was snoring to pack up the Menehune treats. He added some leftover grilled ahi and a couple of ripe mangoes, just to be on the safe side. He left the picnic at the side of the ditch, by one of the marking stakes.

He lay awake a long time that night, waiting to hear... something. He woke to a gray day of glistening green and delicate drops, not even knowing when he'd fallen asleep. He leaped out of bed and ran for the field, listening for the trickle of water flowing in the ditch.

Silence.

There was no ditch.

Tutu Akua nodded to Jake, raised a mango in salute, and was gone.

Thunder Guardian
By Sylvia M. DeSantis

When I was little, Rodney told me I could figure out how close a storm was by counting between the lightning strikes and the thunder. I didn't remember this until last summer, when I met someone who had weathered storms I couldn't even imagine. She helped me understand two things Rodney hadn't told me: Lightning comes in all forms and, sometimes, it strikes so close there's no time to count...

Everyone knows me as Tee even though my real name is Lateesha. But my little brother Paulie just calls me Ta. Right after school let out, when Momma and my stepdad, Rodney, said I should start looking for a job, I found out that you can call people all kinds of things and still not really know who they are.

It begins the morning I ask for some money so I can meet Madelyn down at the mall. Momma is in Boston at one of her conferences, and even though Paulie and I miss her during those trips, we love starting the summer with Rodney. He's still strict like Momma, but he always does special little things to celebrate the beginning of vacation when she's gone, like taking Paulie to miniature golf for no special reason or making eggs toblonero, my very favorite, just because. Even though Paulie is his son and I'm his stepdaughter, he treats us just the same. The one thing Rodney isn't so laid back about is handing over spending money.

"Now, Lateesha," Rodney says in that *you know we've discussed this* voice, "I'm thinking it's time you got yourself that little part-time job we talked about. Just something to get you started on saving for that phone." Rodney and Momma know how much I want a cell phone, and lately they've both been itching to see me in a part-time job *to learn responsibility*.

Rodney shakes his head and laughs when I run over to give him a big bear hug. I don't think the hug's going to work this time. "Janice said they still need someone at the Zip-N-Zap, and you like that place," he says, untangling my arms from his neck. Janice is Momma's friend who for some reason thinks I should spend my summer working. "That might be fun for you, and it's close. Start there, and see what they say." It's the third time this month he's suggested this, and he doesn't look like he's fooling this time. He waits a second and then gives me The Face. "We've talked about this, Tee. Do this for your momma and me?"

I close my eyes so I don't roll them, because that would definitely get me in trouble. If I stop by Zip-N-Zap and see what's up, at least I can tell him I tried. Plus, the job's probably already taken anyway, which means I can be home in an hour and still have time to read about Corey's secret affair with his wife's mother in my *Soap News Now!* before meeting Madelyn at the mall.

"Oh, Dad," I huff with a sigh so huge it blows my bangs straight off my forehead, "*alright*."

I walk through the sticky heat down Milton Avenue past Marion's Cleaners, the old deli, and a bunch of other stores tucked into the small shopping center on the other side of my neighborhood. I finally come to Zip-N-Zap, Cross River's idea of big-time fun, which isn't saying much. For thirty bucks an hour, parents rent one of the cinderblock rooms painted with stars and planets where Zappers, Zip-N-Zap hostesses, cut birthday cake and serve juice while kids scream bloody murder and climb on the huge, tangled jungle gym that winds through another room painted to look like the moon. Nobody I know would be caught dead on that jungle gym, and not just because it smells like pee. Everyone from school hangs out in Zappit Planet, the cool laser tag room in back. Last year Shelley Cabinski's parents rented the laser tag room for her birthday, which was less fun that it sounds since most of the boys in our class tried to fart every time they fired a shot. Shelley's dad finally made them stop, but by then it was time to leave. With any luck, I won't see anyone from school today.

I open the door to Zip-N-Zap and am blasted with a rush of freezing air that smells like cake, soda, and some other smell I can't figure out, but which reminds me of bleach. Standing behind the counter is the oldest Native American woman I've ever seen. Her face is so craggy she looks like she's carved in stone, but what really makes me stop is her eyes. They're black, small, and strong, like the espresso coffee Momma won't ever let me taste. She's got these crazy earrings made from some kind of stone, and they hang in her lobes like the night sky, they're so blue-black. I look away as a lady Momma's age comes out of the Staff Only door and stares at me. For some reason I feel squirmy under her gaze.

"Hi, uh, I'm wondering about the job," I turn and point at the Help Wanted sign, "for a new Zapper?" I think I'm starting to blush.

She makes a quick nod with her head, like a bird pecking a seed, as she pushes a pen and form at me from under the counter. "Fill out an application, and we'll talk." *Looks like the job hasn't been filled yet. Too bad.* Right then a girl wearing a headband bobbing with plastic planets swings out the same door, wheeling a huge birthday cake on a cart. Before anybody can even yell *watch out*, the old lady behind the counter loses her balance reaching for some party hats and trips right into the cart. There's a crash as the cart smacks the wall and the cake slides dangerously to the side, one huge corner hanging off.

"Therese! What are you *doing*? Are the bathrooms done yet?" The old woman stares at the floor and barely shakes her head as the manager screams at her. "Well, go on then. Marci!" she turns to yell at the stunned Zapper. "Why are you staring at the cake like it's going to serve itself? Get GOING!" Marci jumps to the cart, pushes the cake back to safety, and wheels it away into a room of shrieking ten-year-olds. As I lean on the counter to fill out the application, I see the old lady, Therese, shuffle toward the ladies' room with a roll of towels and cleaning supplies. I hadn't noticed, but her hair is long for an old lady's. It's really long, with some kind of funky ribbon with beads holding it together in a loose ponytail. Madelyn would love that ponytail holder. Then I notice something else. Therese moves in a way that seems almost violent, her bones jostling each other as she shuffles. Just as she turns to push the door, she looks back and catches me staring. This time I feel the blush color me right up to the roots of my hair.

When I was younger, Rodney and Momma used to call me Cocoa Cream. *Sweet cake dreams for my beautiful cocoa cream,*

Momma'd say when she kissed me goodnight, or *I know Miss Cocoa Cream will not be leaving those peas on her plate*, Rodney would say on the nights he'd cook. Rodney is white. In fact my biological father was black but so light momma says sometimes people thought he was white. I don't remember anything about him, since he died when I was a baby. Still, I never worried over his color, just like I don't care that Rodney is white. I love when Rodney and Momma stand next to each other with their bodies pressed together and their arms all wrapped around, and they look like the blackest night and the whitest sun, just soaking up each other's skin. Momma says there are a lot of people in the world who would love to judge us. I sometimes wonder if we should just be more worried about the folks in Cross River instead.

I push the application across the counter and wait to see what happens next. The manager scans it roughly with her eyes, and then looks at me, tilting her head to the side.

"You'll show up for your shifts?"

"Ma'am?"

"When you're scheduled," she says impatiently, "you'll show up for your shifts? Won't be calling off for this or that?"

"No, Ma'am." *Oh geez, I might actually get this job.*

"And you can work weekends? It's summer, so no excuses about homework, soccer practice, band meetings, none of that?"

"No, Ma'am. I mean, yes, I can work weekends."

"I'll expect you to always be your politest to parents. And to be nice to the children. Think you can manage that?"

"Yes, Ma'am. I'm fine with that. I have a little brother at

home and we do stuff together all the time. I'm always nice to him."

"Mmmm, yes, well...," she says, looking at me like I've said something wrong. Suddenly, I want this job more than anything.

"Alright then," she pauses, searching for name, "Lateesha. I'll see you Saturday morning at nine o'clock. We have two parties at ten thirty, and I'll go over things with you beforehand. Please don't be late."

"Ma'am?" I ask timidly, "what does the job pay?"

She sniffs as if I've told her something had gone sour in the kitchen. "It pays minimum wage," she says, already moving on to some other paperwork.

"Okay. Well, thank you. See you Saturday."

I step outside into the heat and realize I've been holding my breath the whole time. *Well, Rodney, now you've done it. I'm a Zapper!*

Saturday comes and goes in a blur of spilled juice, sticky ice cream and cake that's mysteriously gotten squashed in the tunnel that leads from Mars to Venus. Madelyn stops by and teases me about my headband with the bobbing planets, but I can tell by the way she looks at it that she secretly likes it. The manager, Mrs. Freedman, watches me closely all day. She spends a lot of time telling me what to do over the next two weeks, but when I basically get everything right, she starts to leave me alone. Things are going perfectly fine, until that awful Thursday.

I'm cleaning up the Saturn room, wiping up cake crumbs and wadding wrapping paper into the trash when I hear James and Barry, two kids from school. They're talking to Therese at the front counter. Well, not talking exactly. More like laughing at her. *Hey, Kimosabe, me wantum laser tokens! Come on, squaw, gimmee some tokens!*

I step out toward the front counter right as Therese starts to shake a little. She might have been cold, except a line of sweat has broken out on her forehead. James turns towards me. "Hey, Tee, we were just trying to get some Zappit tokens." He holds up a ten dollar bill. I take the money and give him the tokens. As James and Barry bolt for Zappit Planet's door, I turn to Therese. She's wiping the counter, trying to look busy. "I know them from school. They're okay guys," I shrug. Therese looks at me silently with her deep black eyes and turns away. *Okay, whatever.*

A few days later, as I'm leaning against the counter, watching the hot sun shimmer off the parking lot, some seniors came in. I recognize Dutchie Logan because I was on the field hockey team with his little sister last year.

"Hey, Tee, what's happening?"

"Nothing much. You guys want tokens?"

"Yeah." Dutchie lays down some money, and I start to count out tokens. Therese bumps up against something behind me, tripping and dropping her broom. When I look over, she's mumbling to herself in a weird way and nodding, like she's hearing some silent tune. Dutchie and his friends start to laugh and snicker. I roll my eyes and laugh a little until I see something funny in Therese's eyes, like storm clouds ready to break. I push the tokens towards Dutchie and his friends, and when I turn around to ask Therese if something's wrong, she's gone.

That night I tell Momma how Therese had acted kind of strange. Even though I feel kind of bad, I leave out the parts about how we laughed at her. Momma puts down the book she is reading. She had been so proud to come home from her conference and find me officially working for the summer, but for the first time since we've talked about my new job, she looks serious.

"Tee, do you wonder why a woman that old would be working someplace like Zip-N-Zap?"

"Well, I dunno. Same as me, I guess. For money?"

Momma looks straight at me. "Tee, a woman that age shouldn't have to work, not for minimum wage. She should be collecting Social Security or a pension. How old did you say she was?"

I know something's up when Janice stops by the next morning. Janice knows everything about everyone in Cross River, and Therese is no exception. *That's Therese Thunder, lives in the trailer park behind the old railroad station. Came to Cross River last year from Pale Bluffs after her daughter died, some kind of car accident. Hasn't got any family left. Talks to herself a lot. Strange old lady...*

When I see Therese a few days later at work, I steal a few sideways looks but can't face her somehow. Knowing about her daughter makes me feel weird. I'm not sure I should know something that private. When the door jingles, I look up and see Mrs. Freedman. She's stopped by to check the schedule and make some calls.

"I've had the absolute worst morning! First, I can't find the car keys, because who knows where Harold's put them, and then I end up in some huge backup on Highway 21 because some kids flipped a car last night and the police are still cleaning up the mess. Probably drunk Indian kids..." I stop listening when I see Therese stiffen.

Suddenly, I begin to understand, at least a little.

I think there's something I might want to say to Therese when, suddenly, she's out the door with that funny walk of hers, bones colliding with themselves fast enough to look like a jog. Without thinking about the look on Mrs. Freedman's face, I follow her.

"Therese! Wait! Wait up!" I catch her arm, and she slows just long enough to look at me before she speeds up again.

"Therese, I'm sorry. About your daughter. I'm sorry." I nearly whisper it, but I know she's heard me because suddenly she slows down and slumps a little, like a balloon losing air. She stops, looks at me, and crooks her finger. I should go back to work. I should apologize to Mrs. Freedman for running out like that. I should turn right around.

Instead I follow Therese without saying a word.

We walk for almost fifteen minutes until we come to a place I've never been to before. I can tell from the way I hear the river that we're somewhere near the old high school, but not in a spot I've ever visited. We're deep inside the rim of the forest that runs across the north side of town, the heavy trees lifting the heat and swelter of the sun off our shoulders. We walk for a few more minutes until we come to a small clearing. I know we're far in the woods because I can't hear traffic anymore, but I'm not really thinking of that. I'm wondering at what I'm seeing, my eyes big and round like Mrs. Freedman's when we bolted out the door.

In front of us is a rock ledge made of some kind of swirled pink rock that runs over and together in the most beautiful pattern I've ever seen, and beyond, a baby deer sips from the river with its mother by its side. I know as soon as I step hard on the dry branch that I've ruined the moment. The deer raise their heads and dart into the dappled forest behind them. Therese turns around and looks at me.

"Welcome, Lateesha, to my thinking place." It's the first time Therese has ever said my name, and the word sounds pretty in her mouth, like the softly running water next to us.

"Zip-N-Zap, it is a hard place to work, yes? My body does not like it there, and my mind, she wants to leave, but my soul tells me I have work to do." I look at Therese carefully. I have no idea what she's talking about.

"Lateesha, do you know me?" I shake my head. "Yes, yes you do. Because you are like me. We are of the earth, we have mothers and fathers, sisters and brothers. We are all connected. We look different, speak in other languages, but underneath, we are the same.

"People say things because they can — because to make fun of someone is easy. It's easy to be ugly." She takes a breath. "We fear and hate what we don't understand. Now, to understand, *that* takes courage. Do you have courage, Lateesha?" I try to look at Therese, to say something, but instead I'm mesmerized by the magical blue earrings, swinging like pendulums from her earlobes, reminding me of the first time I saw her at Zip-N-Zap. Then I surprise myself.

"No, I don't have courage. I'm a coward. I should have said something to James and Barry that day, but I didn't. And Dutchie. I should have told Dutchie and his friends to shut up but it's... it's so complicated." I don't know what to say.

Therese leads me to the edge of the beautiful swirled stone, sits down, and takes my clammy hand in hers. "You have more courage than any girl I know. I know what they say to you, Lateesha. About your color. About how you're not white enough for some and not black enough for others." I swallow. *How could she know? I never even told Momma or Rodney. About that day on the bus. Or the other times. The way people — other kids, even adults — would spit words at me in the cafeteria, on the bus, at the mall. They only know to please stop calling me Cocoa Cream. I'm too old for that I tell them, but it's really because coming from the wrong mouths the name had turned dirty and ugly.* I feel my eyes fill up. How does Therese know my hurt?

"I know you, Lateesha, and you are brave. You are like my Heather. My daughter Heather is with the Spirits now, but while she was here, she did beautiful and blessed work." Just when I think she might cry, she gathers herself up and stares straight at me with a look that reminds me of boiling storm clouds.

"Heather's Indian name means 'Guardian.' She is Guardian Thunder, watching over the lightning, sending her thunder message, helping the rain wash away the hurt so the Earth can start over again. You are a thunder guardian too, Lateesha. In your heart, you teach and protect."

I remember the times I've walked Paulie the long way home to avoid certain streets where I knew hate would be waiting, or the times I've heard the whispers but stood close to Rodney anyway, the best dad I could ever have, already knowing what kids were saying about my Oreo-colored family.

"Continue to teach your little brother by example, Lateesha, and love that stepfather of yours because he is a good man, no matter his or your color." Therese gently lets go of my hand, and, as soon as she stands, it begins to rain softly, thunder rumbling in the distance.

I look at her and know that it's going to be okay. For her. For me. For Paulie. For all of us who don't fit into a neat box. I realize right then how much I have to learn this summer, and not just how to run the register.

I watch Therese stand against that beautiful pink rock under the trees. She stands with her back straight, eyes clear, and torn old sneakers planted in a way that makes me wonder if she has solid roots far in the ground too. I finally understand how there's a place for us inside the thunder and rain if we can just find it.

Bummer It's Summer

By Gale Payne

Hall Bells Clang Cold And Gray
Last Day Of School's Today
Summer Day After Day
No Homework And All Play
Kids Shout, "Yippee Kiyay"
Teachers Sing, "Hip Hooray"

I Cover My Ears
I Swallow My Fears
No Yippee Kiyay
Not For Me, No Way

It Took All Year For Me
To Study, Learn, And See
How To Draw A Llama
Where To Put A Comma
Why We Do Language Arts
What To Call Body Parts
All This Will Be Forgot
Before It Turns Real Hot

Each Tock Of Summer's Clock
Finds Me In Greater Shock
So I Cover My Ears
Try To Swallow My Fears

And Blink Back Teabag Tears
Like All The Other Years
No Plans For This Summer
Bummer! Bummer! Bummer!

My Whole Block Left On Trips
I Stay Home, Bite My Lips
Don't Get To Take A Plane
A Bus, Tram, Nor A Train
It Takes Two For Word Games
The Twins Don't Know Their Names

Mom Won't Lend Me Her Broom
To Ride In My Own Room
Can't Talk To Lumps The Frog
Can't Play Chess With My Dog

Nothing Here, I'm Upset
No One To Dare Or Bet
No One To Speak French To
No One To Help Review
Can't Wait Till Labor Day
Still A Jillion Weeks Away
Summertime's Not For Me
Don't Need To Wait And See

Nothing Fun Comes My Way
Despite What Dad Might Say
So I Cover My Ears

Try To Swallow My Fears
No Yippee Kiyay For Me
No Way I Want This To Be
When Counting All The Ways
To Pass The Longest Days

An E-mail From Matt Greene
Fills My Computer Screen
"Want To Meet Up Some Time?
Find A Tree We Can Climb?"
"U the purple-haired guy?"
"Yep," he types in reply.

I Uncup My Ears
I Burp Up My Fears
"Yippee Hip Hooray
Summer's A-Okay!"

Spaceball
By Kay Pluta

It's going to be a long summer. My little brother, Roland, is going to drive me crazy. He always gets things wrong, and he won't listen.

Last week, he told Grandma he wanted to eat in the diving room. "It's a dining room," I've told him a hundred times. Roland wouldn't listen. Grandma told me "shhh." She let Roland wear his scuba mask at the table.

Yesterday, Roland asked for a soda from the bending machine at the grocery store. "It's a vending machine," I said. Roland said it had to be a bending machine because you bend over to get your soda. We yelled at each other so much that we lost our afternoon TV time.

Mom says if I can make it to suppertime today without fussing with Roland, she will take me to a baseball game on Saturday. Going to a baseball game is the one thing I want to do most of all this summer, but getting along with Roland won't be easy.

My second grade teacher, Mrs. Whirly, said the best way to stay out of trouble is to read. I get out my favorite book, *True Facts About Everything,* and turn to page twelve.

I am reading about "How Toothpaste Gets Into the Tube" when Roland bursts through the back door.

"You won't believe the new kids I met, David. They're teaching me to play SPACEBALL!" he yells.

"Calm down, Roland," I say. "It's called baseball."

"Noooo," says Roland. "It's Spaceball, and I need six mitts."

"Why six?" I ask. "How many kids are playing with you?"

"Two."

"Okay, so use your mitt and mine. Mine is in the basket in the garage."

"Two aren't enough. I need three for each guy."

I roll my eyes and take a deep breath. "You only have two hands, and you only wear a glove on one of them."

"Not these guys," says Roland. "They have six."

I shake my head and keep reading.

Roland stays put. "Does Mom have a mitt?" he asks.

"No, Mom doesn't play baseball," I answer.

"But yesterday I heard her say she couldn't find a mitt."

"She meant an oven mitt, silly."

Roland disappears. I keep reading.

I'm on the page about "Where Things Go When they Go Down the Drain," when Roland bounces back into my room.

"I only found three oven mitts. That's enough for one guy, but the other guy wants to bat. I need three bats."

I stick my finger in my book so I won't lose my place. "What kind of crazy baseball are you trying to play?"

"Not baseball, David," says Roland. "Spaceball!"

I speak very slowly. "There's no such game as spaceball. Why do you need three bats?"

"I already told you. My friends have six hands."

"I only have one bat. You'll have to look for something else."

I pull my book closer to my face and begin reading "Why

Cats Land on Their Feet."

Out of the corner of my eye, I see Roland grab a tennis racket, a ski, and a hockey stick out of my closet. I bite my bottom lip and keep reading while he crashes and thumps downstairs.

Just as I start "Why Roller Coaster Cars Don't Fall Off The Track," Roland darts into my room again.

"Now what?" I yell.

"The mitts aren't working, and all those things we were using for bats broke. We're all practicing pitching, now. I need six balls."

I slam my book shut and stand up. "Roland, what are you talking about? It's baseball, not spaceball! Nobody has six hands, and you don't use skis to bat balls!"

I hear a cough and look up. Mom glares at me from the

hallway. I think about homeruns and hot dogs.

"Okay, okay," I say, forcing a smile. "Show me what you're talking about."

I follow Roland into the backyard.

"You know this is nonsense, like everything else you come up with," I snarl under my breath.

Roland says nothing. He pulls on my arm and points.

I look. I see nothing but grass, the doghouse, our dog, some strange footprints, and a large shiny object floating over the trees.

I stand still, eyes wide, mouth open. One long skinny purple arm, then another, and another wave from the window of the space ship. Each hand is wearing one of my mother's oven mitts.

"Roland... Roland..." I whisper. Roland doesn't answer. He's poking around in the bushes.

"Uh oh, I think they took all the stuff with them," he says.

I try to speak but can't. Then I hear Mom call "David! Roland! Time to eat!"

It's suppertime, and I haven't fussed with Roland. That problem's solved, but I still can't believe Roland is right.

After we finish our spaghetti, Mom goes to get dessert out of the oven.

"Oh no, I've misplaced them again! Boys, do you have any idea where my oven mitts are?"

I turn and wink at my brother. This is going to be an interesting summer.

The Seal Of Marsh Cove
By Edith Morris Hemingway

Fog blew in wisps across the wide bay with snatches of bright sunlight above. It was the first glimpse of blue sky Bryn had seen in the five dreary days of her summer vacation in Maine.

"Ready to go, Bryn?" Dad called from the open door. "The sun is out. The tide is almost high, and, if we catch it right, we can paddle the canoe around the point and into Marsh Cove."

"Are you sure it's safe?" Mom said. "It looks a bit windy."

Before Dad could open his mouth to answer, Bryn jumped up from the couch and said, "We'll be fine, Mom. Don't worry." She shoved her feet into her sneakers and tied them. Then she grabbed her life jacket from the hook next to the door and ran outside.

Her younger brother was right behind her with his own life jacket in hand. "I want to go too."

Bryn groaned.

"Not this time, Michael," Dad said. "It's Bryn's turn."

They dragged the canoe down the rocky steps and far enough out in the water so it floated. After Dad fastened his knapsack around the thwart of the canoe, he held the boat steady while Bryn climbed in. Keeping low, she made her way up to the bow. Then Dad pushed it out a little farther and climbed in. Bryn's sneakers were wet and squishy and cold on her feet, but the sun felt warm on her shoulders.

"Is your life jacket fastened, Bryn?" Dad asked. When she nodded, he smiled, and she smiled back.

Bryn had practiced her strokes on a calm lake, but this was her first time out on coastal waters. Dad did most of the steering and the strong paddling. Bryn kept them on their course. They headed straight out from shore to get clear of the rocks and then turned up Gouldsboro Bay. Traveling with the tide, they didn't take long to round the point with its high rocky cliff.

Dad pointed up to the top of a tall fir tree. "A bald eagle," he said and reached out to hand her the binoculars. The eagle looked big even from this far away. She could see its white head twist around to look for food.

The family had walked up to this same point yesterday at low tide. Then the entire cove was a sea of mud with a few rocks poking up. Sea lavender and marshy grasses grew around the edge. It smelled like dead fish. Bryn had seen a man walking around in high boots, digging in the mud with a spade. Dad said he was clamming. Bryn wondered if all the fish, lobsters, and other creatures swam in and out with the tide.

Now, at high tide, Marsh Cove looked very different. Far out in the middle was one big rock jutting out of the water. Something long and dark moved up the side of the rock. Bryn looked through the binoculars. "I think it's a seal, Dad!" Maybe this was the one she had heard barking in the distance. Ever since she had done a report on seals in the sixth grade, she had hoped to see one in the wild. All week she had been watching for seals along the rocky ledges. Seeing one at the aquarium wasn't the same.

"Let's go investigate," Dad said.

They had been floating toward shore as they rested, but now they paddled a fast straight line toward the rock. The seal must have seen them coming because it slid off the rock into the water. Bryn groaned in disappointment.

"Take your paddle out of the water and be as quiet as you can," Dad said.

They sat there, watching, and drifted away from the rock. Bryn wanted to paddle back, but Dad shook his head and pointed down. Bryn saw a dark shadow, then one or two more. "Maybe they think our gray canoe is a big seal," she whispered.

Dad nodded and whispered back. "Could be."

Another shadow and another, closer this time, and then one whiskery nose poked out of the water. The nose disappeared just as quickly. They were getting braver — or more curious. Now two noses appeared on the left and one on the right. Pretty soon their whole heads were bobbing in and out of the water. One was sleek and black, another had circles around its eyes, and one had freckles on its face. The seals swam and dove all around the canoe, sort of like a game. When they stuck their noses out, Bryn could see their nostrils open and hear them breathe in the air. As they dove back down, they slapped their tails on the water and rocked the canoe.

The freckle-faced seal swam the closest, almost within reach — first on one side, then on the other. It seemed to look straight into Bryn's eyes, and she wondered if it would let her touch it. Very slowly she stretched out her hand a few inches above the water, and when the freckled nose came up again, Bryn felt a rough wet whisker brush across her palm. Maybe it wanted to touch her as much she wanted to touch it. Bryn thought she saw

fourteen seals in all, but they never stayed still long enough for her to be sure she counted right.

A shadow drifted over them as the sun disappeared behind a layer of clouds. The water became the same steel gray color of the seals.

"Time to head back, Bryn," Dad said. "The wind is picking up, and the tide is shifting." He looked at the choppy water beyond the point.

Bryn hated to leave the seals, but they, too, must have sensed a change. Now there were only one or two shadows flitting beneath the water. She saw one more glimpse of the freckled nose, and then they were gone.

"We need to paddle quickly, Bryn." Dad looked again at the white caps in the distance. He turned the canoe around with two strong sweeps of his paddle. "Do you remember the cross stroke I taught you?"

Bryn nodded and lifted her paddle out of the water on the right side of the canoe. Without changing her hand positions, she put it down into the water on the left side as far out as she could reach. Then she pulled it straight in toward the side of the canoe. Immediately they turned to the left.

"Good job," Dad said. "Out in the rougher water, the cross stroke will be harder to do, but we must keep the canoe from turning sideways in the waves. We could flip right over. And Bryn, get down on your knees in front of your seat while you're paddling. We need to stay low." While he talked, Dad moved up closer to the thwart and down on his own knees. "One more thing, Bryn. What do you do if the canoe tips over?"

Dad didn't sound scared, but Bryn could tell he was serious.

This was not a time to ask her own questions —just to answer and do exactly what he said. "I hang on to the side of the canoe because it won't sink." She remembered practicing it once when they first bought the canoe. But that was a warm sunny day on a smooth lake. Now just thinking about it made her shiver.

The bald eagle was gone from the top of the fir tree when they got back to the point. Along the way, for an instant, Bryn thought she saw one whiskery nose pop out of the water off to the left of the canoe.

Everything changed when they came around the tip of land and rock. The wind hit her right in the face, and a wave washed over the side of the canoe like a cold slap of water. Dad straightened them up before the next wave.

"Paddle with me as I talk, Bryn," Dad said. "Stroke, stroke, cross stroke, stroke, stroke, cross stroke." Bryn knew she couldn't take time to turn around and look at him, but it helped to hear him. And maybe it helped him keep his own rhythm. "Stroke, stroke, cross stroke."

Now she was sure she saw the seal out there just beyond the tip of her paddle. "Stroke, stroke, cross stroke," and she could look over and see that particular nose again. It was her special seal with freckles on its face.

Like riding a jerky roller coaster, one moment the bow of the canoe hovered up in the air, and then "bang" came down on the water before the next wave moved in. Sometimes Bryn couldn't even get her paddle in the water, and she stroked the air. But she kept on — stroke, stroke, and then she saw her seal every time she did the cross stroke.

Salt water stung her eyes and plastered her hair to her face.

Water covered her knees in the bottom of the canoe, but she wasn't cold anymore. She could hear Dad saying, "You're doing a good job, Bryn. Keep it up. Stroke, stroke, cross stroke."

Her arms were heavy. After each stroke, she felt as if she couldn't lift the paddle again.

"Stroke, stroke, cross stroke. I know you're tired, Bryn. We'll be home soon. Stroke, stroke, cross stroke."

She managed only one stroke for every two times Dad said it. But whenever he said cross stroke, she knew she could look over to her seal with its big round eyes. It seemed to be telling her, "Don't be scared. Reach out and touch me. Pull hard." Then her seal was lost in a wave again.

Finally Bryn could see the cottage. First a little dot she wasn't sure of, then the point and slope of the roof. Then she could see two dots standing outside. Then the two dots were Mom and Michael. She could tell Mom was standing still with her arms clasped tight in front of her. But Michael was running around, waving wildly to them. They should be turning in toward shore, but Dad kept paddling. Bryn wanted to turn around and ask him, but she knew she couldn't stop.

Dad's voice was hoarse and tired over the roar of the wind and waves. "Stroke, stroke, cross stroke." Now they were past the cottage and Mom and Michael! "Stroke, stroke, cross stroke. Keep on, Bryn. Just a little farther. Then we'll let the waves turn us back to shore. Stroke, stroke, cross stroke."

Bryn's arms ached. She could barely lift her paddle out of the water to reach out to her seal. But the freckled face was there, still encouraging her, making sure she was safe.

It happened quickly. They rode high on a wave, and as they

came down, Dad spun the canoe around. For a moment the canoe was broadside to the waves, and they started to roll to the right. Bryn didn't know what happened to her paddle, but she held tight to the side of the canoe. Dad slapped his paddle down flat on the water, and they rolled back up. Then they no longer fought the waves. The waves carried them now, too fast, toward Mom and Michael and the rocks on the shore.

Dad tried to slow them down by back paddling, but the rocks were suddenly on both sides of them. The canoe hit one on the right and bounced over to another on the left. Then a wave spun them around and wedged them in between two more rocks.

"It's shallow enough for me to get out, Bryn," Dad said. "Here, you use the grip end of my paddle to steady the canoe."

Bryn held the small end tight down in a crack between the rocks to keep them from tipping, and Dad stepped out up to his thighs in water. He worked his way around to the bow of the canoe, slipping once and pulling himself back up. Finally he dragged the canoe up on the dry gravelly beach.

Bryn's legs felt like spaghetti when she stood on the solid ground, and she couldn't keep her arms from shaking. Dad held her up and hugged Mom and Michael all at the same time. None of them could talk, and then they all talked at once.

When Dad let go, he took Bryn's hand, and they looked back out at the water. There was her seal with its whiskery, freckled face. Could it actually be smiling at her? It had followed them in closer to shore. Now it took one last look, as if assuring itself that Bryn was safe. Then, it disappeared under the water. Bryn watched for a long time. Finally, out beyond the rocks, amid the white caps of the waves, she saw its black head appear again and bob steadily back up Gouldsboro Bay toward Marsh Cove.

Sunlight broke through the clouds and sparkled across the water. The waves didn't look so scary now. Bryn raised her hand in farewell to her seal — her own special seal that had kept her safe and made this day so unforgettable.

At The Beach

By *Junette Kirkham Woller*

Summer sand hot on my feet.
Ocean waves don't miss a beat.
Tiny crabs nip at my toes.
Sun makes blisters on my nose.
Lacey foam on water floats.
In the distance I see boats.
As they sail, do they see me
While they float upon the sea?
I'd like to go way out there
Walk on the sea, float in air.
No one there to tell me "no."
I'd just go
    and go
        and go . . . .

Owen Nolan's Square-Wheeled Bike
By Alison Dellenbaugh

It was June 11th, and that meant two things: Owen Nolan was finally 11, and he could finally get another crack at his annual birthday wish.

"Time to blow out your candles!" said his mom. She led him to the dining table, where 11 burning candles perched precariously on top of a strawberry ice cream cake.

"Don't forget to make a wish," said his dad. Owen didn't need to be reminded. Every year since he was 7, he had made the same wish. He had wished for a bike.

He had gotten a tricycle. He had gotten a unicycle. He had gotten a musical skateboard and even a light-up motorized scooter. But never what he really wanted — a plain old two-wheeled bike like the other kids had.

So every year, his friends rode their bikes all summer without him.

Owen closed his eyes and made his wish. Maybe this would be the year he finally got a bike. He opened his eyes and blew out the candles.

Somehow, he doubted the wish would work this year either. His parents had those twinkles in their eyes that told him they were up to something weird.

"Come on outside," said his mom with a grin, after they ate some cake. "You're going to love your present this year."

"I'll love it if it's a bike," muttered Owen.

"It is," said his dad.

"A bike?" Owen asked. "A two-wheeler?"

"That's right," said his mom. "Come out and see!"

Owen ran outside and looked in the driveway. There it was — a yellow bicycle with tiger stripes. It wasn't a unicycle. It wasn't a tricycle. It didn't even have training wheels. It just had two wheels. But the wheels were square.

"See?" said Owen's dad. "A two-wheeled bicycle!"

His parents were so excited that Owen hated to mention the problem with the wheels. "Thanks," he said.

"Try it out!" said his mom.

Owen climbed on. He balanced himself on his feet, kicked up the kickstand, and tried to take off. The bike fell over, and he scraped his knee. He got up and tried again. This time his dad held the bike steady, but Owen still couldn't get the wheels to move. "I don't think it works," he said. "You probably just need practice," said his dad. "You haven't ridden many two-wheelers before."

"I guess so," said Owen, and his parents left him outside to practice.

Owen's friends Tony and Jared stopped by on their own bikes to see what Owen had gotten this year. "I like it!" said Tony.

"Really?" asked Owen. "Want to trade it for your bike?"

"Of course not," said Tony. "I only sort of like it."

"I've ridden a square-wheeled bike before!" said Jared.

"You have?" asked Owen.

"Yeah, one time in a science museum. They had it on a special track, one hump after another, so the ride was completely smooth."

"Let's build a road like that for it!" said Owen.

"It would be really tricky," said Jared. "All the humps have to be *exactly* the same size as the wheels. And you pretty much have to just go straight."

Owen frowned. "Never mind — that's too much trouble. And I was hoping to ride around the neighborhood with you guys."

"Better luck next year!" said Tony. He and Jared rode away quickly on their normal, round-wheeled bicycles.

Owen kicked the back wheel of his square-wheeled bike as he watched his friends ride away. Then he got an idea. He went into the garage and dug around until he found his old tricycle. He could replace the square wheels on the new bike with the back wheels of the trike! He carried the tricycle out to the driveway and set it down next to the square-wheeled bike. But he could tell, just by looking, that the tricycle wheels were way too small. Owen sat down on the driveway and rested his head in his arms.

The front door opened and his dad stepped outside. "Doesn't look like you're putting much mileage on those wheels yet."

"Not yet," said Owen.

"Is it the tiger stripes you don't like? Because we could have gotten leopard spots. They even had zebra stripes, but the bike was painted purple and we'd never seen a purple zebra, so..."

Owen sighed. He figured he should just tell the truth. "Dad," he said, "the bike has square wheels."

"I know!" said his dad. "Isn't it neat? I'd never seen one like that! Your mom and I figured it must be the new thing, and you could be the first kid on the block to have one. Maybe the first kid in town."

"Probably the only kid in town," Owen said. "The bike looks

cool, Dad. But square wheels don't roll very well. I doubt I can get it to go anywhere."

"I know squares don't normally roll," said his dad, "but I assumed they had thought of that if they were selling square-wheeled bikes."

"They hadn't." Owen stood up, grabbed the bike by the handlebars, and walked it around the driveway. Thump, bump, thumpity, bump. Thump, bump, thumpity, bump. "Even if it would go, it would always be a slow, bumpy ride."

His dad looked surprised. "I guess we should've tried it out first, but we didn't get it assembled until this morning."

"I can always ride my scooter," offered Owen. "It's a great scooter."

"It *is* a great scooter," his dad agreed. "But I'd hate to see you give up on the bike. I'll bet you can figure out something." He left Owen alone in the driveway again.

Before long, Jared and Tony rode back up. "Still can't get it to work?" asked Jared.

Owen shook his head. "Hey," he said, "do you think I could sell tickets to see it, and raise enough money to buy round wheels?"

"No one would pay for that," said Tony.

"Unless you have a whole science museum to go with it," said Jared.

"You're right," said Owen, jamming his hands in his pockets. "I guess I'll never have a real bike."

"You can ride mine for a while," said Jared.

"While we take turns riding your scooter," said Tony.

"Or your unicycle," said Jared. "I still want to figure that thing out!"

"A unicycle!" said Owen. "Why do my parents have to be so goofy? I ask for a bike, and what do they give me? A trike, a unicycle, a musical skateboard, and finally, a square-wheeled bike!"

"Are you kidding?" asked Jared. "Who else's parents would give such wild presents? I love your parents!"

"I think they're hilarious!" agreed Tony.

Owen looked at his friends. "That's because they're not yours," he said. "It's not so funny when you're the only one in town who can't ride around on your bike, because it has *square wheels*!" The thought of it suddenly did strike him as funny, and he started to laugh despite himself.

His friends started laughing, too, just as Owen's mom came out of the house with the rest of Owen's birthday cake. She was trying to balance it on three paper plates at once. "Boys, I saw you out here and thought you might want some... eek!" As she offered a plate to Owen, it slipped from her hand and flew across the driveway, landing cake side down near Owen's bike.

Owen started to groan, until he noticed his friends were still laughing. Soon, they were laughing even harder, and Owen and his mom couldn't help but join in.

"What a ridiculous day!" said Owen's mom. She turned to Owen. "Can you forgive me?"

"Sure," he said. "I already had my cake. Tony and Jared can have the surviving pieces."

"I mean for the bike," she said. "Your dad and I just thought it looked neat!"

"The bike?" Owen hesistated. "It's fine. I mean, I can't ride it, but it's cool to look at..."

Owen's mom started laughing again. "A bike you can only

look at but can't ride!" she said. "What a crazy present!"

Owen's dad joined them outside. "What's all this laughing out here?" he asked with a smile.

"Oh, nothing," said Owen's mom. "We're just admiring the world's most, um, *decorative* bike!"

"We'll save up to buy you another bike," said Owen's dad. "A regular one. You can set this one up as a conversation piece!"

"It'd make a cool sculpture for your room," suggested Jared.

"Or a really uncomfortable chair," said Tony, and everyone laughed again.

Owen studied the square-wheeled bike as his friends dug into their cake. "Hey," he said, "this bike might work after all."

"With wheels that don't roll?" Tony asked through a mouthful of cake.

"I'm not planning to ride it." Owen smiled at his family and friends. "You all gave me another idea."

The next day, Owen rode his scooter to the pool, the park, and his friends' houses, looking for all the kids he could find. "If I can borrow your bike for a few days this summer," he told each kid, "you can borrow my square-wheeled bike. If you can make it work, you can have my skateboard, my unicycle, and my light-up motorized scooter." By the end of the day, 23 kids had signed up to try it.

No one ever got the square-wheeled bike to roll well, but everyone had fun trying. Owen was almost a local celebrity. And best of all, he got to ride round-wheeled bikes all summer. He rode big bikes and little bikes, blue bikes and red bikes and black bikes, rusty old 10-speeds, shiny new mountain bikes, and BMX bikes covered with dirt.

Sometimes, he even joined in the efforts to make the square-wheeled bike work. Meanwhile, some of the other kids helped him figure out how to ride his unicycle, and Jared helped him program the musical skateboard to play their favorite songs.

"You know," he told Tony and Jared in August, "I don't think this summer would've been half so fun if I'd gotten a plain old bike."

"I can't wait to see what you get next year," Jared said.

When the next June rolled around, some kids were still trading Owen their bikes for his square-wheeled bike. Others asked for a turn with whatever he happened to get that year.

Owen's parents approached him before his birthday.

"So, do you want your own round-wheeled bike this year?" asked Owen's dad.

"No silly surprises, we promise," said his mom. "You can even help pick it out."

"Actually," said Owen, "I kind of like your surprises. But, instead of a strawberry ice cream cake, can I have pineapple upside-down cake?"

"Upside-down cake?" asked his mom. "Now *that* I can do!"

When Owen blew out the candles on the upside-down cake, he didn't wish for a bike. He wished that his new birthday present, whatever it might be, would bring him as much summer fun as the one before it. And from the twinkles in his parents' eyes, he knew that his wish would come true.

Lawnmowers
By Kelly R. Fineman

Sometimes there's a racket,
other times a hum.
Both sounds mean the same thing:
lawnmowers have come.

They skim across the yard,
cutting as they go.
Sometimes they move quickly,
other times they're slow.

The old man down the street
pushes his uphill.
That's how he must do it
or he'd take a spill.

His mower is quite old;
it has blades that twirl.
They make a click-clack noise
as they spin and whirl.

Our lawnmower at home
uses gasoline.
Once I get it started,
it sounds rather mean.

Dad says *I* must use it.
I don't get a vote.
But if I had my choice,
I would buy a goat.

Treasure at Cave Hollow Ranch
By Lisa Tiffin

Jack Richards and his twin brother, Nick, woke up with excitement. Today was the first day of the State Fair. Usually the twins didn't go to the Fair because they lived over four hours away in the city. But this year they had a chance since they were staying at their Uncle Joe and Aunt Audrey's horse ranch.

The twins had always dreamed of living on a ranch, and this summer their mother had surprised them for their birthday. It was hard work mucking out stalls, brushing the horses down, and hauling bales of hay, but the boys were happy to trade the morning work for the fun afternoons of horse riding, fishing, and hiking. And today, when Uncle Joe got back from his early morning trip into town, they were hoping he would let them go to the Fair.

"Nick, look at this!" Jack had just finished dressing and held out his hand to Nick.

"Where did you find this?" asked Nick. He took the envelope from Jack.

"It was on the floor. I think Aunt Audrey or Uncle Joe must have slipped it under the door while we were sleeping."

Nick carefully opened the large envelope. He felt the outline of an old fashioned skeleton key inside. He pulled out the key and noticed a small slip of paper. The paper had numbers on it: *N 42° 59.056 W 077° 43.957.*

"What do you think?" asked Nick.

Jack scratched his head and looked at the paper and then at the key.

"Well, I don't really know about those numbers, but maybe the key fits one of the barns."

The boys quickly put on their shoes and raced downstairs. Stopping only to grab the slices of toast and the juice Aunt Audrey had put on the counter for them, the twins ran toward the back door.

"What about the eggs and bacon?" Aunt Audrey hollered.

"No time," Jack managed through his last gulp of juice. He set his glass on the counter and followed Nick out the door.

Once outside, the boys looked around. In addition to the farmhouse, there were two barns, a fenced-in riding circle, a shed, and an old garage all on their Uncle's property. They quickly eliminated the riding circle and the open garage where Uncle Joe stored his old tractor and decided to concentrate on the shed and barns in their quest to discover what the key opened.

"Let's try the shed first," Jack said.

Nick agreed, and the boys ran to the shed. When they reached it, Nick pulled out the key and tried to match it with the lock on the shed.

"I don't think it's going to work," Nick said. "It seems like it's too big. What about the barns?"

"We've been in the new barn all summer," Jack said. "There's nothing in there but horses."

"Well, it must be the other barn, then." Nick turned and started towards the old barn, but Jack stopped him.

"I don't think we should go into the old barn." Jack shuddered at the thought of the old, dark barn. It had sat unused for at least twenty years, and he could only guess what they might find inside.

"Yeah, but what about the mystery key?" Nick asked.

"Well," Jack hesitated. "I guess we could just try the lock."

Nick grinned at his brother and took off toward the old barn. Nick reached the door first and stuck the key in the rusted lock. It fit perfectly. The boys exchanged nervous looks and began to push the door open.

"Hey, look." Nick pointed to a box in the middle of the floor. It was old and rusty, but it still looked out of place.

"Let's bring it outside," Jack said, glancing around at all the cobwebs.

Nick agreed, and, when they were out in the sunshine again, he lifted the lid. Inside was a gadget that looked like a bright, yellow cell phone.

"What is it?" Jack asked.

"It looks like a GPS receiver," Nick said. "My friend Ryan has one. He uses it when he goes hiking with his dad."

"Cool. Do you know how it works?"

"No, but I know how we can find out." Nick grabbed his brother's arm and raced toward the farmhouse.

Once inside, Jack and Nick sat at their computer and typed *GPS* in the search engine. Within a couple of minutes, they had found a website explaining how global positioning systems worked.

Jack's eyes lit up. "It uses satellites to show your position anywhere in the world."

"Cool." Nick could hardly contain his excitement as he

remembered the slip of paper he had found with the key. "Hey," he said to Jack, "These numbers must have something to do with this."

Jack looked at the paper. *N 42°59.056 W 077°43.957*. "Those must be latitude and longitude coordinates." They had studied latitude and longitude last year in social studies.

"Yeah!" Nick said. "The 'N' stands for 'north,' and the 'W' for 'west!'"

"Okay, now we're getting somewhere," Jack said. "The website says we have to be outside to turn on the GPS."

The boys went back outside, and Jack followed the directions he had read to turn the unit on. The receiver quickly blinked to life and gave them their exact location. Nick read off the numbers on the paper while Jack carefully entered them into the receiver. After Jack hit the enter key, the unit displayed a compass and route to the coordinates.

"Good job," Nick said as he looked at the screen. "It says we need to head about four miles north. We'll probably need the horses."

Jack hesitated. "What about the Fair?"

"Well," Nick looked at his watch. "We don't even know if we're going yet, and we have about an hour before Uncle Joe will be back, so what do you think?"

Jack bit his lip. "I guess we have time," he finally said, "but we'd better ask Aunt Audrey first."

"Fine with me," Nick said darting back into the house.

After getting permission, the brothers ran to the new barn and saddled up their horses. They rode close together, carefully following the compass on the receiver until they found themselves up on the outer ridge of the ranch.

The coordinates seemed to lead to a large fissure on the rock face at the edge of Uncle Joe's property. Suddenly, they noticed a path that led to a small cave.

"C'mon," Jack said, "The route points directly to the cave." He dismounted and tied his horse to a branch.

Nick jumped down from his horse and followed his brother into the dark opening. The boys waited for their eyes to adjust to the darkness of the cave.

"Hey," Nick whispered to his brother. "I can't hear the horses."

"Yeah," Jack replied waiting for the echo to pass. "This cave is soundproof or something."

The boys shivered in the darkness and began to look around.

"Are you sure we're in the right place?" Nick asked.

Jack looked down and pressed a button on the GPS receiver. The face lit up, letting off a blue glow. Jack shook his head. "We've lost the signal."

"Try going back to the entrance," Nick suggested.

Jack walked back to the opening of the cave and pointed the GPS towards the sky. "I've got it," he said, looking at the compass again. "It says we are within ten feet of the coordinates. It's got to be in here." Jack made his way back inside the cave.

"I wish we'd brought flashlights," Nick grumbled.

"Well, it's not much, but we could use the light on the receiver."

"All right. It'll have to do." Nick dropped down on his hands and knees and began to feel around on the floor of the cave.

Beside him, Jack flicked the GPS light on, and Nick suddenly noticed a large shape against the back wall.

"Look," Nick said. "Could that be another clue?"

Jack moved toward the back of the cave and found another envelope. "Let's take it outside and see what's in it."

The boys found their way out of the cave and immediately tore open the envelope. Inside was a letter.

> *Dear boys,*
>
> *Congratulations! You have found your first treasure using your new GPS unit. Aunt Audrey and I have really enjoyed your company and your hard work this summer. You are welcome at our ranch anytime.*
>
> *Love,*
> *Uncle Joe and Aunt Audrey*
> *P.S. We hope you enjoy the other present in this envelope. You have certainly earned it.*

Jack looked up from the letter. "What else is in the envelope?"

Nick grabbed the envelope and shook it upside down. Both boys let out loud whoops as they saw their present: two one-week passes to the State Fair.

June Bugs
By Tricia Mathison

I see the little June bugs
flying every day,
and I can't help but wonder:
is there a bug for May?

Picnic Point
By Lucy Ford

"I don't want to go," Jim said.

"It'll be fun," Dad said. He rubbed sunblock on Jim's back. "You just have to give it a try."

The dock heaved under Jim's feet. Uncle Brad's boat bobbed on the water. It didn't look safe. Jim glanced at the shady bank where their car was parked. This wasn't at all what Jim had planned for his summer vacation. He would rather toss rocks into the lake than ride a dippy-tippy boat.

"I'll be good," Jim offered.

"You can't stay by yourself," Dad answered. He snugged Jim's hat on. "Come on, you'll like Picnic Point. We can look for arrowheads, and there's a climbing tree."

"Is it that scary?" laughed Uncle Brad.

Jim mumbled. He liked Uncle Brad, who was big and tanned. He didn't want Dad to think he was a scaredy-brat either.

"Your Dad and I used to come here every summer with our Grandpa," Uncle Brad went on. "It's a special place."

Dad shrugged on a life jacket, while Uncle Brad swung an ice chest from the dock to the boat. Jim had his own life jacket. He slowly zipped it up.

"I'm hot," Jim complained, but nobody listened.

Uncle Brad offered his hand. Jim stepped warily onto the boat. It tipped under his feet. Jim stumbled to a bench.

"Sit tight until you get your legs," Uncle Brad said.

Jim clung to the edge of the bench. Strange noises gurgled and sloshed all around him. The boat lurched again as Dad stepped in, untied it, and pushed off from the dock.

"Next stop, Picnic Point." Dad settled on the bench beside Jim.

Uncle Brad sat down at the wheel. He turned the key. The boat chugged just like a car. Jim could feel the rumble through the seat of his pants. Jim watched their car get smaller as the boat floated away from the dock.

Suddenly the motor roared. The boat leapt forward. Jim gave a startled cry. He almost fell off the bench. The wind threw his hat on the floor.

The boat went faster and faster. Two lines of foam framed a curly V behind it. Wind clawed at Jim with icy fingers. The motor's howl was deafening.

Jim clapped his hands to his ears. His heart pounded. He hunched down beside Dad. The sun was in his eyes. He wanted his hat, but he was afraid to reach for it. More than anything, Jim wanted to be safe on shore. It would be warmer, and he wouldn't be bouncing around so much.

"Stop!" Jim yelled.

To his surprise, the boat did slow down. Dad leaned closer and put his arm around Jim's shoulders. "Look there, son!"

Squinting against the breeze, Jim turned to where Dad was pointing. The boat chugged closer to the rocky shore, where one pine tree grew apart from the others. A long branch reached over the water. On that branch was a big brown bird with a white head.

"It's an eagle," Jim said. He had never seen one before, but he knew what it must be.

"That's right," Dad said.

"Isn't he something," Uncle Brad said.

The bird's head turned with a snap, as if it had heard them talking about it. Jim saw the glint of its eye and the sharp curve of its beak.

Suddenly the eagle gathered itself. It leaned forward, wings opening wide, and kicked off the branch.

"I think he's spotted a fish," Dad said.

The eagle dove toward them, talons outstretched. It struck the water a short distance in front of the boat. Moments later it winged upward again. Something long and silver wriggled in its grasp.

"Whoo! He got it!" Uncle Brad cried.

The eagle flew in a wide curve, coming back toward its perch. Jim felt his heart soar with it.

As he turned to watch the eagle, Jim noticed there was another chair beside Uncle Brad's.

"Can I sit with you?" he asked.

"Good idea," said Dad.

Jim jumped up from the bench. He grabbed his hat and jammed it over his ears. Leaning on Dad's shoulder for balance, Jim made his way to the chair.

"All set?" Uncle Brad asked.

"Yeah," Jim said.

With a roar, the boat surged into motion again. This time Jim didn't mind. It was warmer with the windshield protecting him, and his hat stayed on.

Waves rushed past, sparkling in the sun. Spray burst up like fireworks. The motor was a steady buzz under his feet. Jim liked being able to see where they were going. He saw other boats passing by. Some of the people waved. Jim waved back.

Up ahead, a boat had stopped. A girl held up a red flag.

"They're water-skiing," Dad yelled over the motor noise. "Someone is in the water."

"Hold on!" called Uncle Brad.

He turned the steering wheel. The boat cut a wide arc, rolling in the water. Jim clutched his seat for a moment, afraid the boat would tip over. It didn't. It gave him a dizzy feeling, like being on a carnival ride. Jim couldn't help it — he laughed out loud.

Dad called, "Not so bad, eh?"

"Yeah!" Jim said.

Uncle Brad grinned. When they were past the water-skiers, he turned the boat back the other way. A sheet of spray flew up beside it. Jim reached out and let the water slap his hand.

They sped on across the lake. Blue water and blue sky were all around them. Jim felt like a mighty eagle, swooping and darting on Uncle Brad's boat. All too soon the motor's roar died back to a growl. Jim saw the shore ahead.

"There we are," Uncle Brad said. "Picnic Point."

"Ready to look for arrowheads?" Dad asked.

Jim couldn't believe it was already over. He did feel a little bit hungry, though.

"Dad?" he said. "After lunch, can I steer the boat?"

Ants
By Kay Pluta

Ants in the salad,
Ants in the dip,
Ants playing chase in the 'tater chips.
Ants in the pickles,
Ants in the slaw,
Ants diving high off my soda straw.
Ants in the cookies,
Ants in the cake,
Ants swimming laps in a root beer lake.
Ants in the burgers,
Ants in the cheese,
They don't say thanks, and they don't say please.
Ants disappearing.
Ants flee the park.
Look what I found — a hungry aardvark!

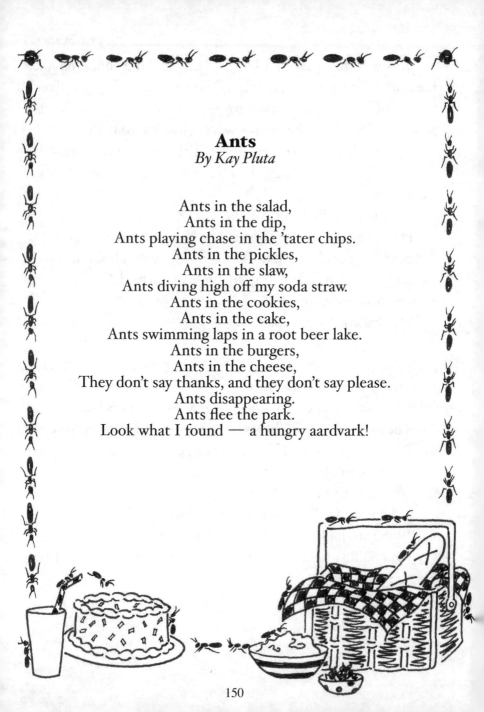

Margaret's Summer Treasure
By Alyssa Martin

To Margaret, visiting Grandma Viluna's house every summer was like entering a world of magic. Every knick-knack, teacup, and quilt had a story to go with it. Grandma Viluna herself was like a fairy godmother. She had curly white hair as soft and sweet smelling as cotton candy. She smiled all of the time, as if she was just about to say she had a surprise for you for being such a good girl. Margaret was always a good girl at Grandma's. At home she could be stubborn, sitting in front of a plate of sour-smelling squash until the sun went down. At Grandma Viluna's the food was always sweet. The carrots were covered in brown sugar, and the sweet potatoes had marshmallows on top. The ham had a glaze as delicious as dessert.

An afternoon spent at Grandma Viluna's was like discovering treasure. She always had something fun and exciting planned for them. When it was sunny, she and Grandma Viluna could spend hours picking berries and flowers in the field behind her house. On rainy afternoons Margaret would eagerly explore Grandma Viluna's large old house with its many rooms and deep closets. Sometimes Grandma Viluna would help Margaret make tiny pillows and blankets for her dolls out of colorful scraps of old fabric kept in a large cedar chest in the sewing room. Margaret loved to press the pedal on the sewing machine while Grandma Viluna carefully guided the fabric under the needle.

Today the summer rain danced on the awnings. Margaret

wondered how she and Grandma would spend the afternoon.

"Today we'll have a tea party," Grandma Viluna announced. "While I prepare our tea, you're going on a very important expedition! Take your doll, Molly, with you. I want you to find 13 diamonds that Grandpa Henry hid around the house. They're the size of your fist and as obvious as the nose on your face. If you find the diamonds, I'll have a special treat for you at teatime. Good luck, my love," she said, kissing Margaret on the forehead.

At first Margaret had no idea where to begin her search. She looked at her hand and made a fist. She scanned the parlor room and felt the excitement build in her chest. The idea of looking everywhere was a treat in itself, but to find 13 diamonds! Grandma Viluna told her that Grandpa Henry was a treasure hunter before he went to Heaven. They went on many adventures together in search of things they could make shine and sparkle.

"Too bad he wanted to get his hands on those pearly gates," Grandma Viluna often said when she reminisced. "Your grandfather could turn trash to gold," she told her.

Margaret thought of King Midas, whom she had learned about in school. She knew that was pretend, but what if it wasn't? She closed her eyes tightly and touched the closest thing, the piano, imagining the excitement of opening her eyes to a gold piano. No luck.

She decided to start her hunt upstairs. She ran up the long stairs, two at a time, and skipped down the narrow hall covered with gold-framed black and white photos of people she'd never met, some of them smiling and some of them looking very serious. She stopped at the end of the hall to look in her favorite secret spot. Grandma Viluna had a little chest of drawers where she kept fancy handkerchiefs and embroidered hand towels. Margaret sometimes hid Molly in the drawers when her cousin Robert came to play. Afraid of being teased for playing with dolls, she'd tuck her safely in amongst the pretty towels. Maybe the diamonds were hidden there. She closed her eyes and opened the first drawer. No luck. She quickly checked the rest to find only towels and handkerchiefs.

Next she went to the bedrooms. The door to her mother's childhood room was open. Margaret had slept in it just last night. Maybe she'd missed the diamonds. Grandma Viluna did say they were in an obvious place. She scanned the room with detective eyes. Pink canopy bed, small while nightstand, tall white dresser, just the way she'd always remembered. She looked at the collection of china dolls that sat on top of the dresser. They stared straight ahead, always patient and always pretty. Their painted lips wore their usual puckers. She looked at the basket of tattered books on the floor. No diamonds there. It was time to move on. She'd try Grandma Viluna's bedroom next.

She ran back down the hall and extended her hand to open the closed door. A diamond the size of her fist! The doorknob was a diamond! Her heart leapt. She giggled aloud. Now to count them all before Grandma Viluna rang the bell for tea. Margaret danced around the house tallying her windfall. She was rich! She was rich! The bell rang.

"Tea time, Sugar Pie!" Grandma Viluna chimed from the parlor.

Margaret raced toward the sound of her grandmother's voice, breathless with excitement.

"I found them, Grandma! I found all 13 diamonds!" she gasped.

"Aren't you a clever girl," Grandma Viluna said as she reached down to stroke Margaret's cheek. "You're still my most valuable gem, my dear," she said, bending down to kiss Margaret's forehead.

Margaret smiled at her grandmother, pleased to have solved the riddle. There was no beach, amusement park, or summer camp that could ever take the place of summers spent with Grandma Viluna.

"And now your promised treat, my sweet," Grandma Viluna said, reaching toward the tea tray. "To go with your newfound treasure, edible diamonds!" she announced holding out rock candy on a small white stick.

Margaret twirled the candy between her fingers and watched as it glittered in the sunlight that filtered through the lace curtains. She knew that the sugary candy wasn't made from diamonds, but with Grandma Viluna anything was possible.

The Magic Shell
By Marcia Strykowski

I'm not in the mood for this beach scene. School is finally done, and I want to enjoy every minute of my last summer before entering middle school. I'm dreading that big school full of a zillion new faces.

I like to make crafts and spend time in my room playing computer games and reading the latest fantasy books. Yeah, it can be lonely, but it sure beats having to watch my ex-best friend Kirsty hanging out with everyone but me. After six years, she told me I wasn't cool enough, and that I always had my head stuck in some fantasy world.

This morning, when we were getting ready to pile into the hot car, the last thing I wanted to do was climb in beside my sticky little sister and my even sweatier big brother. But I had no choice; I was outnumbered. Everyone but me was excited to go to the beach.

"Isabelle," my dad said cheerfully, "since you're the middle child, you get to sit in the middle." He always says it like it is some kind of prize, but I know better. I get to sit teetering on the bump of the backseat only to keep Jason from pinching Emily for two hours straight. I gave one last longing look at my cozy air-conditioned room, with my 3-D castle puzzle lying half finished on the floor, and then trudged back out to the car.

On the way, after Mom finally gave up nagging Dad to slow

down on the highway, we tried some guessing games — not that I wanted to play. I was too busy unsticking my cramping legs. The one time I played and tried to guess what Jason had seen, I said, "an alien on the side of the road?"

"There goes your imagination again, Isabelle!" Mom had said, smiling over the back of the seat.

Now, sitting here on the hot beach, I still feel grumpy. I keep finding myself thinking of last summer when Kirsty and I spent weeks setting up a two-member best friends club. Of course that was before she got in with the 'cool' kids. I hold my hand above my eyes to squint into the sun and wiggle my sand covered toes over the blanket — yuck.

Jason is getting all tangled up in kite string, and there isn't a breeze in sight. "Help me get this up, Izzie," he says to me. I shake my head no and flop down onto the blanket.

Then Emily starts whining, "Play in the water with me." I'm sure it's ice cold, so I ignore her.

I lather on some more sunblock and then get up to stretch. "I guess I'll start on my shell collection," I say with a sigh as I walk away from my family.

I stroll along, squishing my toes into the wet sand. My eye catches a sparkling glint from the center of a pile of rocks and seaweed. Reaching down, I pick up the most peculiar pink shell and flip it over several times. I peer inside.

"Hello," says a tiny voice. I spin my head around. I glance back at my family, all four of them accounted for. OK then, who spoke? Carrying the pretty shell, I race over to the dunes and search behind them — no one.

"Huh?" I peer into the shell again.

"Hi," says the same little voice. And then — I can't believe it — a tiny, tiny person uncurls out of the opening and lands right in the palm of my hand! My jaw drops a mile. She is light and wispy, like rose petals brushing my fingers. The little shell fairy bends to touch her miniature feet. "Ahhh, it's been so long since I've stood up." She smoothes out her lacy gown.

"But, what... who are you?"

"I'm Sophie. I can only visit for a few minutes because I'm needed at a council meeting."

"Is the meeting in here? Are there more of you?" I ask, examining the glistening shell.

"Oh, no," says Sophie. "There's a doorway at the back of the shell that leads to Trivelli."

"Trivelli?"

"A delightful place for my kind of folk."

Lavender spectacles sparkle above her tiny nose. "I like your glasses," I say.

"What glasses?"

"I see them on you."

"True, it *is* all in how you see things." The fairy, who now seems to be wearing green glasses, gives me a funny look. "OK, here goes," she says. "Because you have selected me on this special day, you are granted one wish."

Cool, I won a wish! How lucky! Things start looking brighter right before my eyes.

I consider all the different wishes I might have. My mind swims with possibilities — some generous and some not so nice (I snicker, picturing Jason with a monkey's tail). Hmmm. "Just one wish?" I ask.

"That's all. Of course any wish is already halfway to where you want to go."

I think some more. And then it hits me — I finally have the chance to wish myself back home hanging out with Kirsty! But do I really want to be with the new Kirsty? This is tough. I've got to blurt out something.

"My wish is to have fun with kids who like me," I say surprising myself.

"Done." The fairy claps her tiny hands. "Although of course you've had that all along."

"I have?"

"Sure, look again."

I glance around the beach. There's a cool breeze passing through, and the golden sun pours down like warm butterscotch syrup onto the mounds and mounds of vanilla sand that surround me. In the distance, I see silhouettes of fishermen lined up by the water's edge while seagulls swoop in and out among them. The sky looks bluer now, and a shiny red shape tells me that Jason finally got his kite up. Emily splashes around in the shallow, frothy waves, and Mom and Dad are actually holding hands side by side in beach chairs. It's peaceful here.

Sophie makes a dainty curtsy and then climbs back into her shell. I search inside for her, but it looks as hollow as when I found it. Is my crazy imagination getting carried away again? I wonder if this happens to other kids.

In middle school next year, there will be lots of new kids. All the small neighborhood groups will be mixed into one big class. Hey, who knows, maybe there'll be a bunch of us with crazy imaginations, and we can start a fantasy book readers club. A tingle of excitement for the future zips through me.

I stick my new shell into my pocket. It's really the only one I'll ever need. Racing back across the dunes towards my family, I shout, "Last one in is a rotten egg!" and then I leap into the shimmering water.

Slam Dunk Summer
By Lydia X. Allen

"Joe gets to go on an African safari, like an explorer, and see hippos, zebras, and probably crocodiles," Anthony announced at breakfast between bites of cereal. "And Cecile gets to go to Hawaii..."

"Anthony," his mom said, setting down a plate in front of his father, "please don't talk with your mouth full."

He swallowed "Hawaii! She gets to stay in a hotel right on the beach! She can just walk out her door and hang out on the sand, and go surfing all day..."

"Cecile surfs?" his dad asked, unfolding the sports page.

"I don't think so," Anthony admitted. "But she'll get to have room service, and watch fire dancers, and go to luaus. And even Kevin's getting to go to Camp Winnebago!"

"That's nice, dear," his mom said, sitting down on a kitchen chair. "Would you like some bacon?"

"So why can't I?" Anthony demanded, ignoring the platter his mom tried passing to him.

"You may."

"I can?" Anthony was amazed. He'd convinced his parents to let him go on a vacation, and it hadn't been hard at all! First, he decided, a trip to Disney World, then —

"Anthony? Earth to Anthony," his mom was saying. "I said you may have some *bacon*, not a vacation. But as I explained before,

160

because of Olivia's college tuition, this year we simply do not have the extra money to take a trip."

Anthony had heard it all before. His older sister, Olivia and her college tuition = no extra money = no trip. Olivia going off to college meant that he had to spend the first Saturday of summer vacation at home. It meant that he'd be spending *all* his sunny summer Saturdays and Sundays and every other day of the week stuck at home.

Anthony wiped his forehead with the edge of his t-shirt. He dribbled his basketball on the front drive, took a shot, then watched as it touched the bottom of the net and missed the basket. Again. The ball bounced down the drive with dull thuds, rolled into the street and headed straight for the next-door neighbor as she pulled letters from her mailbox.

"Nice try! That time it actually hit the hoop!" Mrs. Mitchell said as she stopped the ball with her foot, scooped it up, and tossed it back to Anthony "Don't worry; with practice and patience, you'll make a slam dunk one of these days!"

"Sure, thanks." He'd been practicing for two weeks, and he still missed the basket — every time.

Slamming the front door behind him, Anthony walked into the living room where his mom was folding clean clothes. He slumped on the couch and dropped the basketball on the floor. "I'm B.O.R.E.D."

"I know the cure for that," his mom said, rolling up a pair of socks.

"Yeah?" Maybe a movie, Anthony thought, already tasting the buttery popcorn. He could almost feel the cool air-conditioning of the theater.

"Yes." she stated. "The cure for being B.O.R.E.D. is W.O.R.K. And boy, do I have a job for you."

"What?" Anthony asked, not that he wanted to know.

"The garage is past due a spring-cleaning," she said. His mom sounded a little too happy, Anthony decided. "So it's officially time for a good summer-cleaning!" I want you to start by opening the door, reorganizing paint cans, hanging the garden tools..."

"OK, OK, I get the picture!" He had to escape before she recalled that his bedroom hadn't been spring-cleaned either. "I'm going, I'm going."

Sun streamed through the open door, highlighting the glorious mess of the garage. Anthony started lining up paint cans on a shelf. He set the cans in battle formation, with the light colors faced off to the dark. He placed trowels as cannons, screwdrivers as spears, and for a final touch, used garden gloves as flags.

He took a step back to admire his work and knocked into a large plywood board. The board crashed, which sent a two-by-four flying. The two-by-four landed on the carefully stacked firewood pile, which set off an avalanche of logs.

"Great, just great." Anthony muttered. He looked, then bent down for a closer inspection. Where the fire logs had been, there was now only what seemed to be a piece of pipe, or maybe a rolled up kite...

"Snake!"

"What's all the noise about?" Anthony's mom asked as she entered the garage. "I heard a huge commotion..." she stopped, her jaw dropped. "Oh my, what happened?"

"I found a snake!" Anthony said. "Do you think he's poisonous? Can I keep him? Please, please, please?"

"He's a harmless gopher snake, but he will bite," she said, closing her hand around its head and lifting it. "You may keep him, but only for a week. I'm not about to add mice to my grocery list, and I also want all of this picked up. Understand?"

Anthony nodded.

"Here's your new home, Snakey." The gopher snake flicked his tongue, almost as if he was saying he liked the old hamster cage Anthony had found for him.

Anthony rushed to finish his chore so he could get back to watching the snake. He loved the way its eyes seemed to glitter and how it wound itself up on the cage floor.

"Anthony!" It was his mom; he hoped she hadn't thought of more W.O.R.K. for him. "Anthony, there's a letter for you!"

Anthony never got mail, besides birthday cards from his grandma. "I wonder who it's from," he said, opening the Airmail envelope. He began reading:

Hey Tony,

Right now I'm on a broken cot in a stinky tent in Africa. The only thing hotter than the air is the boiled water we have to drink. I haven't seen one, zilch, nada, zero wild animals, except for the no-see-um bugs that have bitten me on parts of my body I didn't know I had. I did make a discovery; I get car sick, especially in four-wheel-drive Jeeps as they jump all over the dirt roads. That is why I am left behind at the campsite, where there is no T.V., no radio, not even a book to read, while everyone else gets to go off to see the wild life. Please write back A.S.A.P.

S.O.S. Your dying friend,

Joe

With a summer storm, and with all his friends out of town, Anthony gave upon having any kind of fun. He slouched, Snakey (in his cage) at his feet, in an easy chair in the den. His parents cuddled (yuck!) on the couch.

"Your sister Olivia called today." Anthony's dad said. He made it sound like she didn't call every Friday.

"Really, dear?" his mom asked. Anthony caught her giving a wink and an elbow nudge to his dad.

"Do you know what she said?" his dad asked, with a nudge back.

"What?" Anthony found himself asking.

"Well..." his dad winked. "She thought it'd be a great idea to have you come and stay in her dorm for the last weekend she's spending there."

A whole weekend in a college dorm? Anthony couldn't believe his ears.

"So, what do you say?" Anthony's mom asked.

"Yes!" Anthony yelled almost knocking over the cage. "Can I bring Snakey?"

"We'll have to ask Olivia about that." his dad said, then smiled "She wants me to drop you off this afternoon, then she'll drive back on Sunday night.

Anthony stuffed his backpack with a pair of jeans, a t-shirt, and two pairs of underwear. He threw the pack in the backseat of his Dad's car, and since Olivia okayed the addition of one gopher snake, he held the cage on his lap as they drove to the college.

"My roommate's gone." Olivia sounded so grownup, and looked it too, as she showed him her dorm room. "So you can bunk in her bed. Just throw your stuff down, and we'll grab a bite in the cafeteria. Then I was thinking we could go swimming, and then take the shuttle into town and catch a movie... everybody's going to be so jealous!"

"Jealous?" Anthony felt like he'd just gotten off a roller coaster.

"Of my absolutely adorable little brother!" Olivia pinched his cheek and shoved him out the dorm door.

Anthony discovered that being the little brother wasn't so bad on a college campus, and that being "absolutely adorable" only meant that everyone wanted to spoil him.

"Here are some chocolate-chip cookies," one girl said. "My mom just mailed them."

"Have these video games," said a boy. "I don't have time to play them anymore."

It also meant that all the students in the gym clapped and cheered when he dove off the high dive into the heated water of the pool.

"I've been waiting forever to see *Nordic Zombies*!" Anthony said later as they made their way into the theater. "But no one's wanted to go with me, besides you."

"Same here!" Olivia answered, paying for buckets of popcorn. They made themselves comfortable in the fold-down, velour-covered seats and watched the movie to the very end.

Anthony fell asleep that night in the borrowed bed of Olivia's roommate, awakening to the seven A.M. alarm of his sister's clock.

"I was thinking..." Olivia said, still dressed in her P.J.'s.

"You were?" Anthony asked. He sat up, rubbed his eyes and stretched out his arms.

"Hey, don't act so surprised!" Olivia threw her pillow at him then continued. "I was thinking we could spend the day at the race tracks, you know, watching the Formula One cars, eating hotdogs and maybe trying to get into the pits..."

"Really?" Anthony asked. He was wide-awake.

"Really," Olivia answered with a big yawn, "but you've got to promise me that tomorrow you'll help sort, pack, and load all my junk for the journey home. Deal?"

Anthony took her hand and shook it.

The weekend spent hanging out with Olivia passed more quickly than the fat, treaded tires of the racecars they'd watched rolling around the track.

"Tell us how the college visit went!" Anthony's mom said. She was waiting on the front porch when Olivia pulled into the drive. She planted a kiss on each of them. "We missed you!"

Hustling them in the house, she added, "Anthony, there's a postcard for you on the hall table."

The postcard had a picture of a palm tree with a hula dancer posed in front of it and fancy lettering that said, "Aloha From Hawaii." Anthony turned the card over to read the back:

> *Dear Anthony,*
> *Hawaii is nice and sunny, but I feel*

mean and sunburned. One day at the beach and I'm as red as a cooked lobster! And who'd've thunk, but I'm allergic to pineapples, mangoes, seafood, orchids, palm trees, grass skirts, and saltwater. Mom won't let me leave the hotel room; she's scared I'll have another allergy attack, and she'll have to spend another night of her "dream" vacation in the emergency room. What a nightmare!

Hope U R having fun!

Cecile

P.S. I got you a shark tooth necklace.

"I couldn't help noticing," Olivia said, her head in the fridge, "that for the couple of days I've been home, all I've seen you eat has been junk food."

"Junk food?" Anthony asked stuffing a chip in his mouth.

"So that is why," Olivia continued, "I am making lunch." She bustled at the kitchen counter for a minute then handed a paper plate to Anthony. "Ta da! Doesn't it look fabulous?"

"If you say so." Anthony answered staring at the strange green things spilling out of slices of lumpy brown bread. "What's that funny smell?"

"Just pinch your nose, and think of how healthy it is!" Olivia exclaimed, taking a generous bite of her own sandwich. "Go on, try it! It's one of my secret recipes, but being as you are my brother, I'll share..."

The phone rang before he could say he'd rather not know what the "secret" ingredients were. "I'll answer it," Olivia said, "so you can sit back and enjoy your meal!"

"Gee, thanks." As soon as she left the room, Anthony took his chance and dashed to the garbage can.

"Anthony!" Olivia yodeled as the sandwich slid to the bottom of the trash bag. "Kevin's on the phone!"

Anthony took the phone. "Hey Kev, how's Camp Winnebago? Having fun horseback riding, river rafting, eating grub?"

"You mean eating grubs," Kevin replied. "And roots, and berries half-pecked by birds. And the only thing I did with a river was fall in when I was trying to catch a fish for dinner — with my bare hands."

"No s'mores?" Anthony asked, dreaming of graham crackers, hot melted marshmallows and dark chocolate.

"No s'mores." Kevin sighed. "Camp Winnebago's a survival camp that I didn't survive. I somehow tangled with a bunch of poison oak trying to make my lean-to, caught the itchies, and got sent home."

"Sweet!" Anthony said. "You're finally back! Now you can come over and shoot some hoops!"

There was a moment of silence, then Kevin spoke, "Can't. At least not till my rash goes away. Sorry."

"Hey, don't act so down," Olivia said as Anthony hung up the phone. "I'm not saying I know how, and I'm not saying I'm any good, but I'll play basketball with you."

The summer sun flicked from the basketball backboard, and from the smiling face of the neighbor, Mrs. Mitchell. She had been plucking weeds in her front yard, but stood up when she spied Olivia and Anthony playing in the driveway.

"All right, Anthony," Olivia said, bouncing the ball to him. "Show me what you've got!"

Dribbling the ball, Anthony moved to the right, then left, then back again. He kept repeating, "Soft hands, eyes on the basket... Shoot!"

Sucking air in, he ran towards the basket and jumped, letting go of the ball. In slow motion, the ball arched, touched the rim, and swooped through. Anthony watched the net sway for a second before he started shouting, "Score!"

"Good one!" his sister yelled, chasing the basketball. "Think you can teach me?"

"Sure," he said. He liked the thought of being Coach Anthony. "It just takes practice and patience."

Anthony could've sworn Mrs. Mitchell winked as she asked, "Any more big plans for summer?"

"Who needs plans?" Anthony answered, then grinned. "But there is one thing I forgot to do."

Hey-Yo Safari Joe!

Sorry I didn't write back A.S.A.P., but I've been a little bit busy. While you've been lolling about in a faraway land, I've wrangled a wild snake, gone to college, dove from the high dive, and hung out at the racetracks.

Oh, and did I forget to say, I scored a slam dunk!

Anyways, get out of that tent and hurry home;

I want your help convincing the school principal to make summer vacation a few weeks longer. Cuz now I just need a break!

Hope 2 C U Soon!

Anthony

Summertime Feet

By Regina Kubelka

Sandy hair, muddy feet, grassy fields and swollen creeks,
the things that make childhood so neat.
Jolie and me with summertime feet,
Splashing through mud from a half-moistened creek,
Tying bacon to a string.
Here, you hold it Jolie, I don't wanna get pinched.
Plop them into a bucket... one... two... three...
Fishing for crawdads, Jolie and me.

"Let's jump into the creek!" suggested Jolie.
He inches into the water, now almost knee deep.
"How far should I go?" he dares.
Tip-tip-toe. A little more he goes.
Slip! Oh no! Jolie's fallen in. Now he's soaked to the core!
Oh Jolie, what now? Our moms will be really, really mad.
(Yours will be angry, but mine will be MAD!)

Gasp!
Here come our moms now!
Scramble, scramble. Where's my shoe?!
Oh Jolie, what can we do?!
Better be good, don't put up a fight.
They'll calm down by tomorrow night.

Then it's me and you again, my everyday friend,

For a game of hide-and-seek.
A wink and a snicker, given and received,
all is well on Willow Street.

Sulking, we march down the street and to our rooms.
Stickery stones under our feet, muddy shoes in hand.
Oh what a day of defeat.
Caught red-handed, just down the block from our homes
Smack-dab in the middle of Willow Street.
217 was mine, 219 was his, about as close as two friends
could be.
But now grounded to our rooms.
I can think of LOTS of places I'd rather be...

Like running barefoot through cool, damp grass in the dark
but moonlit night.
Pounce! The feel of warm, cement driveway beneath my feet.
Wet puddles of heels and toes follow me close as I sneak up to
Jolie's front door.
Knock, knock. I sure hope Jolie answers the door.
"Come in," I hear Jolie's mom say.
Oh boy, I'm gonna be in trouble again.
"Jolie's in bed, where you should be. It's late. Does your
mother know you're here?
You better get home, fast as you can. Do you want me to walk
with you dear?"
"No, I'm okay" I say.
"I'll be fast, like lightning in a storm. Please Mrs. Sealy, don't
tell Mom I was here."

Fast as lightning, like a quiet, sneaky snake across
Mrs. Sealy's lawn.
I tiptoe back across my warm driveway and to my
backyard's gate.
Open it slowly, don't make a sound,
Getting caught would be a big mistake!

Now under the covers, nestled in tight.
Yawn... Can't wait 'til tomorrow.
Good night.

Taking the Plunge
By Cassandra Reigel Whetstone

CLICK. CLICK-CLICK. CLICK-CLICK. CLICK.

"Ryan, what are you doing?" asked Grandma.

"I'm echolocating." I swam over to the side of the pool. "I'm pretending I'm a dolphin, and I'm looking for rings on the bottom of the pool."

"Well, Mr. Dolphin. It's time to take a break. I have something to show you."

I pulled myself onto the edge of the pool and wrapped my towel around my shoulders. "Grandma, I wish I could swim with real dolphins."

Grandma smiled. "Well, maybe you will. It's up to you to make your dreams come true."

Grandma held out a large gift bag. "I got you something special for your twelfth birthday next month, and I need to give it to you now." She handed me the bag. I pushed aside the tissue paper and pulled out two flippers, a mask, and a snorkel.

I was pretty sure that I was looking at snorkel gear, but there isn't a lot of snorkeling in Arizona. "What are these things for?"

"Happy Birthday, Ryan. It's time you finally get to swim in a real ocean. We'll practice snorkeling in the pool for now, and next month, we're flying to Hawaii."

"The ocean? Hawaii? Oh, Grandma, thank you!" I couldn't

believe I was finally going to see the sea!

She taught me how to put on the mask so that it fit snugly over my eyes and nose. I learned how to attach the snorkel to my mask, pull my fins onto my feet and jump into the pool.

At first the mask felt too tight and pinched my skin. But when I put my face in the water, the muscles in my face relaxed, and I could see the bottom of the pool clearly. I kicked my feet and swam the length of the pool. I couldn't believe how fast I could move with the fins. I must have gone from edge to edge in fifteen seconds.

For the rest of the month, I practiced gliding with my fins and breathing through my snorkel.

"This is great, Grandma. Will it be this easy in the ocean?"

"Almost. There will be waves rolling your body and fish swimming around, but you'll do just fine. We'll wear life jackets to be safe."

I knew I was a strong swimmer, but I had no idea what waves would be like, let alone fish nibbling at my toes. I smiled at my Grandma, but inside my stomach sank. What if I couldn't swim in the ocean?

A few days after my twelfth birthday, Grandma and I flew to Hawaii. During the flight I studied my ocean guide and memorized all the fish and other animals I might see. My head was swimming with images of colorful sea creatures.

We arrived at our hotel and got ready for our snorkel adventure. Early the next morning, we rode a boat out to a coral reef in the ocean. I couldn't stop jumping around because I was so excited.

"Ryan, you're going to make yourself sick if you don't settle

down," Grandma said. She couldn't stop smiling, though.

Finally, the boat reached the reef. Everyone got ready. We put on our wet suits, snorkel gear, and lifejackets. I climbed down the boat's ladder, eager to jump into the water. But when I reached the middle rung, I froze. My confidence evaporated, and I couldn't move. I just stared at the sea.

I wanted to turn around and climb back up. The boat seemed like the safest place to be. I started to think about sharks and barracudas. What if I sunk to the bottom? What if I forgot how to breathe through the snorkel? What if I got lost at sea?

Grandma was right behind me. "You're a great swimmer, honey. You just need to jump in."

Easy for her to say. I was stuck, clutching the ladder.

My heart was racing, and I blinked back tears.

I closed my eyes. I was just about to climb back into the boat when Grandma's words rang through my head, "It's up to you to make your dreams come true."

After a deep breath, I counted, "One, two, three!" and plunged into the water.

It felt like the waves were going to swallow me up. I immediately rose to the surface, but felt seasick as the water pushed me back and forth.

Grandma jumped in and swam to me. "Ryan, look down!" I put my head in the water. Hundreds of fish of all colors and sizes swam in the coral reef. There were blue-green parrotfish, lemon butterfly fish, trumpet fish, moray eels, and even a sea turtle! I could see the neon tentacles of the sea anemones. Black spiny urchins and brilliant sea stars clung to the rocks and coral.

It was as if I were looking through a spyglass and a magical wonderland.

Grandma watched a lobster crawling around the rocks while I swam after a unicorn fish. I was kind of far from the boat and turned to swim back when I heard a whistling sound. I looked around and saw a pod of spinner dolphins swimming straight towards me.

I would have been scared, but there wasn't time. Within seconds I was surrounded by dolphins. Some jumped into the air, spinning and turning somersaults. Others dove down into the water, and I could hear them clicking and whistling.

One dolphin swam next to me, and we stared into each other's eyes. My body relaxed and all of my ocean worries disappeared.

After a few moments, the dolphin slapped its tail, then joined the rest of its pod who were swimming circles around the group of snorkelers. I kicked my legs and followed the dolphins. I raced behind them while they leaped through the waves. Grandma clapped and cheered.

When the dolphins finally swam away, my legs were exhausted. I made my way over to Grandma, who helped me climb into the boat.

"Ryan, I'm so proud of you. You're a real fish!"

I gave her a wet hug and said, "Not a fish, Grandma. A dolphin!"

Summer in Pennsylvania

By Joan Hobernicht

One summer day in 1940, Bobby knocked on the door of his friend's house.

"Can Dickie come out and play?" he asked Mrs. Brown.

"*May* Dickie come out to play, not *can*. He has to let his lunch digest. Come back later." Mrs. Brown rudely closed the door in Bobby's face.

Bobby walked to the store on the corner. Tar oozed between his toes as his bare feet felt the hot road. Cicadas shrilled noisily in the big old magnolia trees. The Baker's shaggy old dog came to the end of his chain and barked at Bobby.

Across the river a long freight train moved noisily on the tracks. Bobby watched the smoke billow from the engine as it labored up the incline. It looked like a dragon belching fire as it stalked a victim.

The bell above the door rang as Bobby entered the dark store. Scents of kerosene and cheese blended with the smell of linseed oil on the floor.

Miss Minnie stood behind the counter. "What can I do for you, Master Bobby?" she inquired. She was a skinny old lady who did not like noisy boys.

"I'll take a bottle of Coca Cola and a Clark bar. Just put it on my old man's tab," Bobby said.

"No, your dad gave me orders. You and your brother are not

179

to charge anything to him."

"I don't have no money," Bobby said.

"I see. Well then, I must ask you to leave, Bobby Knight" Miss Minnie looked suspiciously at Bobby until he was out the door. "Don't hang around asking customers for money, either," she called after him.

Bobby walked along the cracked sidewalk. "Step on a crack, break your mother's back," he recited. He deliberately walked on every crack. "I don't have a mother, so who cares?" he said. Bobby's mother had died so long ago that he couldn't remember her at all. He shoved his hands deep into the pockets of his blue-bibbed overalls. He felt a marble in the right-hand pocket. Without taking it out of his pocket, he rolled it around with his forefinger and thumb.

"Hey, Bobby, want to go to the swimming hole with us?" Pot Lid Jones and Froggie Vasovitch ran up from the river's bridge to where Bobby stood. Pot Lid was thirteen, tall and thin. His hair was dark and curly. Froggie was plump. He wore thick glasses.

"No, not today," Bobby answered. "I want to make some money to spend at the carnival when it comes to town."

The last time Bobby had gone with the older boys, he had gotten into trouble. They had taken Edie Comstock's clothes and hidden them while she was swimming in her underwear in the swimming hole. Bobby had been grounded for a week.

Bobby searched through the trash pile behind the grocery store and found several empty aluminum cans. He filled a discarded cardboard box with the cans and a tin platter that someone had thrown away.

"Bobby! Bobby! The junk man is here," Bobby's younger

brother, Jimmy, called excitedly.

The two boys ran home as fast as they could. There on the porch was the junk man. His dark face crinkled as he smiled. "Do you have any scrap iron for me today, boys?" he asked. The rotten floor boards of the porch squeaked as Mr. Pete walked towards them.

Jimmy ran ahead to the pile of iron, copper, and aluminum stacked beside the house. The boys had worked hard all summer digging for scrap iron in the dump near the old cemetery. Jimmy and Bobby had separated the metal objects from the foul smelling rubbish. Bobby added his newfound treasures.

"How much do we have there?" Bobby asked. He was hoping they had enough for money to go to the carnival that would soon come to town.

Mr. Pete pursed his lips as he bent down to the pile of metal on the ground. He was tall and thin. "Well, now, the iron is pretty good but those cans aren't tin. Aluminum doesn't bring me as much," he said.

"How much? How much?" Jimmy jumped up and down with excitement.

Mr. Pete pulled out a five-dollar bill. "There it is, take it or leave it," he said.

Jimmy took it before Bobby could say anything. "I thought aluminum cans were worth more than tin ones," he protested.

Mr. Pete grinned, but his eyes looked hard and cold. "If you don't take what I give you, I might not stop next time," he said. He scooped up the metal and got in his beat-up old Model T truck. It chugged on down the road.

"Gimme that money," Bobby said.

"Huh uh! He gave it to me," Jimmy said, and he ran toward the store.

Bobby ran fast and tackled Jimmy at the knees. Jimmy fell onto the hard pavement and bumped his nose. Blood poured from his nose, and he cried.

"Oh, boy, now I'm going to get it," Bobby thought.

He found some rags in the kitchen drawer and dipped them in the water barrel. "I'm sorry I hurt you. Give me the five dollar bill, and I'll go get it changed," he said.

Jimmy sat on the porch steps and held the wet rags to his nose while Bobby ran to the store.

The bell over the door clanged loudly as Bobby ran to the counter. "Miss Minnie give me four one dollar bills and two fifty cent pieces," he shouted.

"Slow down Master Bobby, I won't change your money unless you buy something first," Miss Minnie said firmly. She looked at him over her glasses.

"O.K. give me two bottles of coke, then," Bobby said.

Miss Minnie took two bottles of Coca-Cola from the ice-box behind her. "That will be ten cents," she said primly. She took the five-dollar bill from Bobby and gave him four one-dollar bills, one fifty-cent piece and four dimes.

"I need to share this with Jimmy. I want two quarters," Bobby said.

"You have your change, now leave," Miss Minnie said.

Bobby ran out of the store and down the street.

Jimmy's nose had stopped bleeding when Bobby got back to the house.

"Here is your money, Jimmy, you get two dollars and four

dimes," Bobby said. "I get two dollars and just one fifty-cent piece."

"Are you sure, Bobby? It doesn't seem right that I get four pieces of coin and you only get one."

"It's all right, mine is bigger." Bobby handed Jimmy the glass bottled Coca-Colas and the boys popped the metal caps off with the bottle opener. They drank the soda while they watched cars going by on the highway in front of their house. It was the main road between Route Forty and Somerset. A lot of cars and trucks went by.

The boys counted their money again. "The rides at the carnival are ten cents. I can buy twenty rides and still have enough money for cotton candy and a soda," Jimmy said happily.

"I want to try the shooting gallery. Maybe I can win something," Bobby said. The boys hid their money under the mattress of the old iron bed they shared.

"Let's go up and swing on the grape vines," Bobby said.

"Dad said we shouldn't," Jimmy protested.

"Dad's at work. He'll never know," Bobby said.

The boys watched for a chance to dart across the highway. They ran up the side of the mountain until they got to the big oak trees. Grape vines and cherry bushes grew close to the trunks of the trees. The floor of the forest was filled with broad-leafed plants. Squirrels ran along the branches, chattering as they scolded the intruders. Snakes slithered in the tall green grass. Frogs croaked from a nearby pond. Jimmy and Bobby rested in the shade of the bushes for a while.

"That oak tree there has a lot of grape vines on it," Jimmy observed.

Bobby took his folding knife from his pocket. He cut a vine close to the trunk of the tree. Bobby unwound it from the trunk until he had about ten feet of vine. He tugged to make sure the top of the vine was attached firmly to the tree.

"Let me! Let me!" Jimmy said.

"No, I have to test it first," Bobby said. He grabbed the grape vine with both hands and ran toward the edge of the creek bank. His legs wound around the bottom of the vine. He sailed out over the creek and hollered, "Whee! Whee!"

Jimmy grabbed the vine when it came back. He ran fast and swung across the creek. As the vine returned back across the creek, it came loose from the top of the tree with a loud snap. Jimmy fell in to the creek.

"Jimmy, Jimmy," Bobby shouted. He ran to the edge of the creek bank, but at first he couldn't see Jimmy. Then he saw him lying face down in the water.

"Help! Help!" He shouted at the top of his lungs.

"What's wrong?" Pot Lid came crashing through the bushes followed by Froggie.

Bobby pointed to the edge of the bank and cried, "Jimmy fell into the creek."

Both big boys scrambled down the side of the creek. "Go to the store and tell Minnie to send help," Pot Lid told Bobby.

A car's brakes squealed as Bobby ran across the highway in front of it. "Quick, Miss Minnie, get help, Jimmy fell in the creek," Bobby said as he ran in to the store.

"Land sakes, that creek isn't deep enough to drown in," Miss Minnie said.

"But he fell from a vine and he isn't moving," Bobby said. He pushed his blond hair from his blue eyes and looked imploringly at Miss Minnie.

Miss Minnie took the telephone receiver and turned the handle on the telephone box. "Operator, sound the siren," she said.

When two men working nearby heard the siren, they came running to the store. Mr. Johnson still had his barber's apron on. Mr. Kett had been working in his garden. He wore a large-brimmed hat and gardening gloves.

"Follow Bobby," Miss Minnie shouted to them.

They ran across the highway and up the mountain path to the big oak tree.

"He's over here, " Pot Lid shouted as the men approached the creek bank.

The big boys had pulled Jimmy from the creek, and he lay on the mossy bank.

"I heard him moan. He's alive," Pot Lid said.

But Jimmy did not open his eyes.

"Don't move him. He may have neck or spinal injuries," Mr. Johnson said.

"Bobby, run and tell Miss Minnie to call the fire department. Tell them to drive the ambulance as close to us as they can and to bring a gurney," Mr. Kett said.

Bobby did as he was told.

The firemen parked on the highway and folded up the gurney. They carried it up the mountain.

"Jimmy's face isn't as white, and he is breathing, but I wish he would wake up," Mr. Johnson said.

"He has a large purple bruise on the front of his head. He

may have a concussion," Mr. Kett said.

"Did you move him?" the older fireman asked the boys

"We had to move him out of the creek, or he would have drowned. But we didn't move him more than we had to," Pot Lid said.

"Let's get him to the hospital and see what the Doc can do," the younger fireman said.

The two firemen placed the gurney close to Jimmy's side. Then one of the firemen took hold of Jimmy's shoulders, and the other fireman grabbed his legs. They gently moved him to the gurney. They lifted the gurney, and its legs unfolded. They wheeled the gurney down the mountain path to the ambulance.

"Can I go, too?" Bobby asked.

"No, you better go find your dad," the older fireman said.

"Come, Bobby, we'll go get your dad," Mr. Kett said.

"I have to go back to my barber shop. Mr. Santo has half a haircut, and he'll be hopping mad if I don't finish it," Mr. Johnson said.

Mr. Kett and Bobby rode in Mr. Kett's truck to the sawmill west of town where Mr. Knight worked.

"Dad, Jimmy's hurt bad," Bobby said. He ran to his father who was stacking a pile of lumber.

"Whoa, now, son, take it easy," Mr. Knight said. He knelt down and looked at Bobby. "What happened, Mr. Kett?" he asked.

"The boys were swinging on the grape vines. One broke, and Jimmy fell in the creek. He is unconscious. He is in the hospital at Zion," Mr. Kett said.

"I told you not to swing on them vines." Bobby's dad looked

angry.

The hospital in Zion had only four rooms. Jimmy was in the one next to the nurse's station. Bobby and his dad rushed to Jimmy's side. He looked dazed and bewildered. "I know I'm in the hospital. Am I going to die?" he asked the nurse.

The nurse was Doc's wife. She was old and fat. Her gray hair was wound around her head in a braid. She wore glasses. Her clean white uniform smelled like soap. "No, you just got banged up a bit. Your arm is broken. Doc put it in a cast. Does your head ache?"

"Yes, it does ache something fierce," Jimmy said.

"Just lie still. I'll get an ice pack for you," Mrs. Doc said kindly.

Jimmy's head was bandaged. One arm was in a plaster cast.

"Are you going to be all right?" Bobby asked.

"I broke my arm but I'll be O. K.," Jimmy said.

"I'm glad to see you are alive, son. I will go to talk to the doctor, now," Mr. Knight said. He was a big man. He wore coveralls that had sawdust on them from working in the sawmill.

"Your son has a mild brain concussion and a broken arm, but he will be all right soon," the doctor said. He was an old man who had no hair. He wore thick glasses.

"When can we take him home?" Bobby's dad asked.

"I want to keep him here overnight just to make sure that his concussion is better. You can come about ten tomorrow morning and take him home," the doctor said.

Bobby's grandpa came to take Jimmy home the next day. Grandpa King had a beard and his hair was gray. His face was lined with laugh lines. He was always telling jokes. He took Bobby and Jimmy to his house. "Your grandma and I are going to keep an eye on you two until school starts next week," he said.

"May I go to the carnival?" asked Bobby.

"You'll have to ask your dad that one," replied his grandfather.

Jimmy lay on the couch in the living room. Miss Minnie and Mrs. McGuire came to see him. Most of the grown-ups in town visited Jimmy. Pot Lid and Froggie came to see him. Jimmy was the center of attention. No one said anything to Bobby. He sat on the steps at the back porch and put his head in his hands.

"I want to thank you boys for helping our Jimmy," their grandma said. Her eyes crinkled when she smiled at Pot-Lid and Froggie. Bobby's grandma used a cane when she walked. Her back was bent over. Her gray hair was short. She gave everyone a big piece of freshly baked chocolate cake and a glass of milk

Jimmy slept at their grandparents' house that night.

Bobby slowly walked home.

"I want to talk to you, Bobby," his dad said.

Bobby stood in front of the table where his dad was sitting.

"Sit down, son." His dad said.

Bobby sat on the edge of the chair.

"I trusted you to watch out for Jimmy, but you disobeyed me. Jimmy could have been killed. Jimmy said you sold scrap metal to Mr. Pete. I'll need that money. The doctor bill has to be paid. Go get me that money now," Bobby's dad said.

Bobby fought to keep back his tears. "Yes, sir, do you need Jimmy's money, too?"

"Yes, I will, bring it all to me," Bobby's dad said.

Bobby gave his Dad all of the money they had received from Mr. Pete.

"I guess I can't go to the carnival, now," Bobby said

"No, you can't. You must go to your grandpa's house as soon as I leave for work tomorrow morning. Mind your grandpa and grandma and stay out of trouble," Bobby's dad said.

Bobby went to his grandparents' house every morning. He helped his grandpa tear down an old shed. They saved the boards and piled them neatly by the garage. He pulled and straightened the nails and put them in an old coffee can. He read to Jimmy and helped his grandma with the dishes.

One morning as Bobby walked to his grandparents' house he heard the music from the carnival that had just come into town.

"I hear the carnival," Jimmy said. "I wish we could go to it."

"We don't have no money," Bobby said.

Their grandpa came into the kitchen where the boys were eating breakfast.

"Bobby, what do you have behind your ear?" he asked. He reached up and pulled a shiny new quarter from behind Bobby's ear. He gave it to Bobby. "Oh, my, here's another one behind your other ear." He gave it to Bobby, too.

"Well, Jimmy, you are growing quarters, too," their grandpa said, and he removed a quarter from each of Jimmy's ears. The boys were amazed.

"How do you do that?" Bobby asked.

Their grandpa's eyes twinkled. "Someday, when you are grown, I'll show you," he said.

"Thank you, Grandpa. Do you think we can go to the carnival now?" Bobby asked

"Oh, yes, can we, please?" Jimmy said.

"If you help Grandma this morning, I'll go with you this afternoon to the carnival for a while," their grandpa promised.

The boys picked vegetables from the garden and helped their grandma clean them.

"Will Dad be mad at us for going to the carnival?" Bobby asked.

"You are my daughter's sons, and I am sure your mama would want you to have fun. I am in charge of you today, and I say you can go to the carnival," Grandpa said firmly.

Bobby rode on the Ferris wheel and the Looper. Jimmy rode on the Carousel. His arm was in a sling, but he held on to the horse's reins with his good hand.

They saw the bright lights and heard the loud music. They met with their friends and ate cotton candy. Their grandpa sat on the bench and watched them.

Lifeguard Lexie
By Shelby May

My first year at Camp Abalone, the summer of 2036, on the island of Quinn 9, meant being away from my parents. They were once again in Timberland, studying the habitat of the pinbill. I knew a lot about the pinbill, a newly developed species that adapted easily to its environment. But my first year at Camp Abalone also meant I'd be studying something too—something I knew nothing of, something that was far more peculiar than the dinky pinbill. My study would focus on what seemed a nearly extinct species. Its name, *his* name to be exact, was one Cody Cartwright.

Cody Cartwright, the sole lifeguard at Camp Abalone for the past three summers would now be having an assistant for the first time: me, Alexis Fernbury. Yet when we met, beyond his brilliant suntan and glossy blonde hair, I knew he must be the last of his kind—the kind that was ready to tell me what I'd done wrong before even introducing himself.

"Don't step onto the dock without absorbers! You must wear absorbers at all times!" Cody hollered at me.

My feet were actually quite happy to be bare; the smooth plastic planks were warm to the touch. But from my backpack I dug out my absorbers, something my grandmother called flip flops. I thought about Grandmother Ky. She was so excited about me coming to Camp Abalone. She had her own memories as a camper here. She could remember when abalone actually grew on the offshore reefs — back when the idea of *farming* aquatic delicacies would have made her laugh.

Yet after slipping my feet into the absorbers and facing Cody, the tall, blonde, waterman, all I could think was that I must have marked the application wrong. Instead of 'lifeguard,' I should have checked 'counselor.' It might have made things easier.

"So you're fourteen. You're tall for fourteen, which, I guess is good. But are you strong?" Cody asked next. He lowered his Rebels, sunglasses with triple lenses for a mega UV screen. And that's when I knew my father had gotten it all wrong. He'd said I'd be perfect as a lifeguard because I swam like a mermaid. And I had believed him. But then again, I've always been a sucker for fairy tales and for what my father believed I could do. But now I could see I wasn't going to be a lifeguard, not even an assistant lifeguard. I was going to be a slave, if Cody had anything to do with it.

"You do know SDD, right?" Cody pressed. I nearly fell off the dock. Didn't this Mr. Lifeguard know that sonar detection devices were lousy human lifesaving systems? Cody really was proving to be a rare species.

I cleared my throat. "Sonar?" It wasn't much of an answer, but it just shot out of me. Cody glared. I went on. "I just think sonar tech can never be as good as... just paying attention with our senses."

"So then, what you're saying," Cody stopped to yank on a rope that was making a kayak leap from the water, "is that you're *sensitive*. Correct?" He let go of the rope, and the kayak landed in perfect position against the dock.

Suddenly, after only minutes of standing in this beautiful preserved habitat, I wanted to hook myself to the nearest hovercraft and go home. I had just been accused of being sensitive — like it was a *weakness*. Who cared about swimming in aquamarine coves or hiking inland where untamed boars supposedly lived. I wanted to head straight back to Trawntown. Trawntown, where my best friend Lan and I would do exactly what we did last summer: Stuff ourselves with dehydrated cherries, view those idiotic game show reruns, and lounge by the pool after dark. (Allergic to sun and fresh fruits, Lan had this strange idea that those old game shows weren't actually rigged.) But the truth of it was that I couldn't do the same things I did last summer. I couldn't let my father down. And I definitely couldn't let Cody Cartwright — whose name I now figured sounded like a cowboy's, rustic and old fashioned — know he'd gotten to me.

I cleared my throat. "Well, I just think our senses are like instruments — natural born devices."

"I see. Yet you lack the sense to wear sunscreen?"

My throat tightened again. I could feel myself entering anger mode. My mother somehow disabled her anger mode after years of viewing my father's rise beyond the Richter. But I wasn't that experienced. My voice tracked high then low, "Well, I infuse with Invisalight each morning, SPF 100." Anyone under sunlight as much as lifeguards would know this product. It saved people from graffings and elims, expensive body part renewals. I finally took a breath allowing pride to take the place of anger.

"So why is your face so red?" He said without looking up.

"I'm just hot."

And while my anger took a dive inside of me, embarrassment took its place. Cody laughed so hard, reminding me of steam, the kind that melts plastic, the kind that spits from espresso machines, the kind that fogs mirrors so there's absolutely nothing to see.

Cody was my worst nightmare. And to think I'd dreamed for a whole lunar cycle about him, wondering what he'd be like. I'd worked out hard to get in shape for this job too. I even started a swim club to help train kids younger than me. But as I turned away from Cody I heard myself say, exactly like Grandmother Ky would say backing her scooter out of the driveway, God help me get out of here alive.

Later, at the dining hall, I pushed open the fingerprinted metal door. A nice woman named Jude introduced herself. She told me where to sit, and I inched by the faces of campers smothered in first-day-at-camp-jitters. They sat staring at the full cows, or milk pitchers, on the tables in front of them. It made me remember the stories grandmother Ky told me. She had said milk would be from powder, and the eggs from powder too, but everything would still taste good because I'd be so hungry. I doubted it when she told me. I doubted it now as I took my seat next to Cody who ignored me. I asked what was for dinner.

"Did you confuse me with the cook?" he asked back.

Maybe he was trying to be funny. But even Jude, who had been a Camp Abalone counselor for thirteen years, didn't think it was funny. She just shook her head. "Ignore him. He's a grump and a half." And I did, happily. But I was still curious about dinner — and hungry. When they rolled out the trays with bowls of steaming something, I decided Grandma Ky went to camp in the "old days" of bad food. Now the food had to be good.

Never underestimate the wise words of your grandmother.

The dirt-brown water with uncooked carrots was supposedly stew. Yet it soon became rain when some kid named M.K.

started splashing his stew with a spoon. Powdered or not, I had to agree with the kid. The stew wasn't worth eating, so why not make rain? In fact I laughed, which endeared me to the campers immediately. However, Cody Cartwright, the cowboy, was about to tan my hide with his sour look.

Later when things calmed down, Jude leaned over and whispered something to me. She said that in all her thirteen years here, first-night stew usually just sat cold in bowls. "Maybe after tonight the cooks will finally change their menu."

I asked her about the powdered eggs and milk then. Jude yawned, a giant basketball of a yawn. "Yeah I guess so, but you get used to that. Especially if you're hungry. Still, I think the stew should be served to the pogs."

A man walked by as Jude was saying this. He stopped and added his fifty cents worth. "Even the pogs won't touch it. What does that tell you?" But he smiled and introduced himself as Mr. Okeehoomerummer, or Mr. O., the camp director. His smile turned up in the corners of his mouth and his bald head was shiny. Right away he reminded me of an Id, a character from Lan's favorite game. His shape was sort of egg-like, and he seemed friendly, but with a big brain. But I didn't tell him that. Instead I stuck with Camp Abalone lore, keeping things safe.

"My Grandma went to this camp fifty years ago," I blurted. Both Jude and Mr. O. looked surprised. "She told me I should ask about the wild boars in the hills."

"Wild boars?" Mr. O. exclaimed. "There are just pogs here now, Alexis, only pogs."

I shrugged my shoulders then followed some counselors outside.

Of course Camp Abalone would have pogs — part pig,

part dog — they'd become invaluable to households, not just their ability to eat human garbage, but they were pretty cute and lovable too. And now that they'd been G'd, they no longer smelled, and their waste was recyclable. Grandmother Ky had said humans would be G'd, or genetically altered, just like pogs some day, to which my father said what he always said — "tell me something new."

But I had something new to tell him. Cody was a pure living monster disguised as a lifeguard. He was a lifeguard that somehow got every single camper (especially girl campers) to sign up for Water Works.

Water Works to me was just another title — a title that meant I had to yank all seventeen kayaks off the rack and drag them to the shore while Cody stood there squinting, smiling and talking to the campers. There were girls who hung on his every word, boys who interrupted with questions like how deep is the ocean or what happens if there's a tsunami. Honestly, by noon that second day of camp, not only was I parched from the heat and hard work, I was also ready to clobber some of the campers. They were just acting so stupid.

That's not to say I didn't like them. Some were okay. The cautious ones reminded me of seals inching into the water. The confident ones jumped from the dock. Some were really entertaining to watch. But still, paying so much attention to every camper was exhausting. By the end of the day, Cody's sonar detection did seem an easier way to keep track of the swimmers — especially when he looked fresh as a cucumber, while I felt as wilted as a leaf of lettuce left out in the sun all day.

To make a long day longer, when the campers returned to their cabins, Cody and I had to clean up the Water Works area.

We put away the kayaks, and together we lifted the heavy buddy-tag board to bring it inside the equipment shed. But after Cody locked up the shed and we were ready to leave, he turned to me and said one word. "Telemetry."

I smiled like a dope. It's just that I know a lot about telemeters. Lan's parents happened to be telemetric engineers. Maybe it was the first time Cody had seen a smile on my face, but all of sudden he was so excited. "Just think, Alexis, no need for buddy tags, no need for buddies. It's better than SDD," he added, "because it's not just underwater, but everywhere!" His voice raised a note, "If a camper slips underwater or swims across the cove and climbs the cliff, we'll know. Wherever anyone is, we'll know. Even if someone's in the bathroom..."

"Wait, wait." I had to interrupt. I had to tell him what I knew. "Telemetry doesn't always work..."

"Yeah, if a kid takes the device off. But we're going to make this permanent."

"How?" I knew that telemeters, like campers themselves, came in all shapes and sizes.

Cody took out a pocket-sized metal box from his backpack. Inside the box were cells the size of fingernails. "Tomorrow I'll just attach these little tippers to everyone's swimsuits. I mean, what kid will take his swimsuit off?"

I was stunned by the idea. I was also stunned by how Cody was talking to me. For the first time I really felt like his assistant.

First thing the next morning, the sun beat hot. The wind stood still. From the dock I stood watching as the campers geared up for a kayak trip. I was keeping a close eye on this one kid M.K. again. He was sneaky. He'd be in the equipment shed one minute and at the fish lagoon the next. I'd noticed from the two days before that he didn't buddy up easily. He was alone or in motion almost all the time.

I looked at the fluffy gray clouds on the horizon. I began to imagine a full day of kayaking with the rest of the splashy, giggling campers. At least they'd be having fun. I heard Cody as he began to attach the telemetric tippers onto their swimsuits. He told them it was like a micro-machine that would report to another machine so he'd know where everyone was. No big deal. Except for M.K. As Cody clicked the tipper onto his shorts, M.K. hollered, "Hey, don't trap me!"

Cody told M.K. it wasn't a trap, just a way to keep track. M.K. answered back, "Yeah and what if you drown, can we keep track of that?"

"No one's going to drown," Cody said, "It just makes it easier, alright?"

Meanwhile I began helping the others strap into their neon PFD vests. Everyone talked in circles. The boys predicted what they'd find in Orange Cove: knuckle fish, lava rocks, and fossils. The girls predicted what the boys would really do: lose their paddles while trying to splash them. I started to laugh along with them. That is until Cody glared at me and shook his head as if I wasn't really his assistant but just another camper.

It bugged me, but I didn't say anything. And once we'd paddled outside Abalone Cove, the navy blue of the deep sea calmed me. I relaxed and followed behind the last of the fifteen kayakers. Yet I sensed that even on this beautiful day, even with Cody's fancy telemetry, I needed to pay attention.

Besides that, I needed Cody to trust me. I felt proud that after three days of camp I knew the names of all the kids. I knew who liked the ocean. I also knew who'd rather play on the shore than swim— like M.K. He didn't even get his feet wet if he could help it.

So, even though everyone had passed Cody's water safety test, I felt like I should especially watch out for kids like M.K. In fact, he was in the kayak in front of me. I was glad he seemed so confident. But suddenly he was doing something that Cody believed no camper would ever do. M.K. was taking off his swim trunks.

"Hey!" I yelled.

It was strange how the wind changed directions at the exact moment M.K. tossed his trunks up and out of the kayak. But he didn't even turn around to look at me. He just kept paddling in his underwear. No big deal.

I kept paddling closer to M.K. But I had to wonder. Hadn't Cody been alerted? Did he even know M.K.'s trunks had slipped away like jellyfish? I was about to beep him. Yet at the same time I could see something happening to another kayaker, Lucas, who was just beyond M.K.

In a flash of peaky waves, Lucas was heaved to a tilt in his kayak. I knew he was a strong swimmer, even if he was small for his age. But the wind began pushing from all directions, tossing him one way, then another. The gray clouds were darkening too. And the ocean shone black as lava. And then I smelled rain. Maybe M.K. did too. He finally looked at me. But we were too far from Abalone Cove to turn back.

Cody beeped me at last, but there was static, his voice rough. He wanted to know if I was alright. He said he couldn't see me. The telemeter and the GPS tracking had failed somehow. I should have been afraid. But for half a second I had to think maybe I'd become a real human being to him.

I answered that I was fine. "M.K. though..." I started to say. But nothing had really happened. M.K. continued to paddle in his underwear, and was now almost to Lucas. I told Cody I was headed towards Orange Cove and heard through the crackle that he'd made contact with the Coast Guard. Instantly I looked in the direction I hoped the Coast Guard would be coming from.

But then M.K.'s kayak was out of sight! My heart jumped into my throat. My eyes darted everywhere until I spotted him in the water beside Lucas. One kayak had capsized; the other one was already drifting away. "M.K.! Lucas!" I heard myself yell to them.

M.K.'s arm shot up into the air as if to signal — a human signal.

I gripped the paddle and stroked the water forcefully. When I got near, M.K. was splashing and karate chopping at the ocean. He managed to explain that he'd jumped in when he saw Lucas go over. But now I understood why M.K. never even inched into the water at camp. He could swim, but the ocean was no friend.

M.K. and Lucas would stay afloat with their bright PFD vests attached. I knew that. But I had to guess that Cody wouldn't know both boys were without kayaks. It began to rain heavy, seeded drops. While Cody surely would guide the others to safety, it was up to me to bring M.K. and Lucas in. It was up to me despite the sting of rain and the fear that whipped at me in the wind.

It proved too difficult for either of the boys to climb into my kayak. They began to panic. I had to make a decision. "M.K.," I instructed, "You and Lucas hold tight onto this rope." I threw out the docking rope. It felt like a braid in my hands.

Cody beeped, reporting he and the other campers were safe in Orange Cove. "We'll be there soon," I told him. I started to panic then. How many campers were with him? Did he know I had two? My voice sharp and strong I yelled, "Did you get a head count?"

His answer, after too many seconds, dropped low as an anchor, "You have two?"

"Yes, we're okay."

Lightening then thunder cracked and boomed nearby. "M.K., Lucas, you guys hold on," I yelled to them. "Watch out for each other. We gotta get to shore fast." I dug my paddle into the raging water. They gripped the rope behind me.

Once we could see the group on the shore it seemed we traveled that much faster. Still the boys gulped mouthfuls of seawater. And they shivered cold. Finally, when we pulled that

waterlogged kayak onto the sand, we all took the deepest breath of our lives. I'm sure of it.

Some kids pointed at M.K. in his underwear then. But really everyone was too tired, too wet and too numb to really laugh.

Cody's voice sounded strained and tired as well, "The telemeter gave a reading... indicating someone was almost to Quinn 10. What happened to you guys out there?"

"What didn't happen is more like it." M.K. said, shivering. "We didn't drown, thanks to her. Thanks to Lifeguard Lexie. So you can save your devices... for other devices."

M.K. put his arm across Lucas's shoulder. They made their way to where the other campers had gathered.

"Where're his shorts?" Cody asked out loud.

"Quinn 10 it sounds like." I answered.

Minutes later we were helped onboard a rescue boat by the Coast Guard. The rain had let up, and the wind had calmed. Though the ocean swells were still rough, I balanced against the boat's smooth railing. The horizon looked empty. I was amazed at the way the weather could change so fast.

"So, Lifeguard Lexie?"

I turned around to see Cody. His tone had changed. Like the weather, it'd gone from stormy to calm. And though I felt strong, after everything that'd happened, all I could do was shrug my shoulders. Besides, nothing we could have said right then would have been good enough.

Arriving in the small harbor of Camp Abalone was like coming home. I helped unhitch the kayaks that'd been towed by the Coast Guard. I helped pull them to shore, then lifted them onto the racks with Cody. Never had I felt so tired and so alive at the same time.

Later that night in the dining hall, my face felt hot and my shoulders ached. You could hear the buzz of campers talking about the kayak trip. Full cows slowly became empty cows, powdered milk or not. We were served hamburgers and French fries. You'd think they'd taste like they'd been made way back in 2006, but everything was pretty fresh. I studied Cody for a second. Yeah, I understood why the girls at camp could fall for a face like that. I guess you could say he was one of a kind. But then I got a reading no telemeter could detect. Cody was telling Mr. O. how "the campers got so worried about Alexis out there. I didn't even think they'd noticed her these past few days."

Like how you didn't notice me? I wanted to say. But I didn't. Cody was watching me now. Not because my face grew redder or because I'd slipped my feet out of my absorbers. I could sense his appreciation. I could also sense something else. Butterflies had started climbing into my throat. I swallowed, but couldn't help but smile.

And M.K.? He was watching French fries fly across the dining hall, one at a time. Tomorrow he and I would go exploring for untamed boars.

Camp Charivari

By Christine Gerber Rutt

Creeping
'round the forest,
watching for wild bears.
All we see are scratched trees and striped skunk
hairs.
—

Slimy
on the bottom,
shiny on the top. Diving
off the wooden raft — doing belly
flops.
—

Crunchy
on the outside,
mucky goop inside.
Hot dogs and S'mores, flaming-hot,
char-fried.
—

Zizzing
in my ears
and whizzing round my bed.
Swip. Swaap. Mosquito splats on my
head.
—

Scratches
down my arms. Bites
up my legs. Soggy socks.
Collected rocks. Now home to ham and eggs.

Backyard UFO
By Elizabeth Tevlin

Libby and Angie examined the strange circle, maybe 8 feet across, of flattened, discolored grass in Libby's backyard. Angie was baffled but didn't say so.

"A crop circle," breathed Libby.

"A what?"

"A crop circle. You know, when a field of grain gets mysteriously leveled in a big pattern. They're usually circles. Farmers all over the world wake up and BAM! a humungous crop circle in the hayfield. People think aliens make them," Libby explained.

"Wow," said Angie, "a UFO in your backyard. We only have a cat. Should we tell your parents?"

Libby shook her head, "We need more proof first. Let's put up the tent and sleep out here tonight. We'll catch those little green men red-handed!"

The girls pitched the tent under the apple tree, then flopped inside. Their faces shone with the heat.

Libby opened the flap to let in some air. By the back door, they could see a crumpled wading pool. Libby's brother Zak had punctured it yesterday with his action figures. Wet Zak-sized footprints on the patio headed toward their neighbor's pool today.

That evening Angie and Libby went through their list again.

"Flashlight?" Libby asked.

"Check."

"Camera?"

"Check," Angie said, "and we also have snacks and comics to read 'til... well, until the aliens arrive." Angie peered out the tent door. "Do you think they're out there right now?" she whispered.

"You don't have to whisper," Libby said. "Even if they're out there, they're miles away. They won't hear you — unless they're reading our thoughts. And then whispering won't help anyway."

Angie shuddered. She tried not to think of anything.

Libby was still thinking though. "Why put a crop circle here?" she asked.

"Maybe it's a sign on a space highway. Like, 'Yield to Oncoming Starships'?" Angie giggled nervously.

"So, the whole universe is looking at my backyard? Even into my window?" Libby said, lunging for the door to see how her bedroom window looked from outside, at night.

"You'd better keep your room clean if you want to make a good impression!" laughed Angie.

That was the last laugh of the evening. The familiar daytime sounds faded into unfamiliar nighttime sounds. Prowling raccoons sounded like alien footsteps (if they even *had* feet). Rustling leaves sounded like a spacecraft shimmering into view.

Every few minutes, they unzipped the flap and poked their heads out.

"What are we waiting for?" asked Angie. "Lights? Noises? A knock at the door?"

Suddenly, they heard and felt it — an ominous rumble, like the planet was growling. They froze. Three blinding flashes in quick succession illuminated the girls' pale, frightened faces. Then three thumps sounded right above their heads.

"Run!" Libby screamed. They frantically unzipped the tent. Stumbling for the house, they fell inside the kitchen door.

Snap. Libby's drowsy mum switched on the light.

"Mom, I... aliens... a spaceship... save us!" The girls' voices tangled into one.

"Spaceship? Sounds more like a thunderstorm. I was just going to check on you." She peered out. "The wind may be blowing some apples off the tree."

No way were they going back out. Aliens could come and make apple pies if they wanted.

The girls slept in Libby's bed.

In the morning, Angie and Libby rolled up their sleeping bags. Angie picked an apple up off the ground. "Looks like our UFO was an 'Unthreatening Fruit Object,'" she said. "Libby?"

Libby was staring into her neighbor's yard. Another crop circle! Well, not a circle exactly, more like a rectangle.

"A landing strip!" figured Libby.

Angie dropped the apple and ran to Libby's side. "There's probably a whole fleet of UFOs here!"

Four kids in swimsuits poured out the neighbor's door, followed by their dad. He waved at Libby and Angie. "Gonna be another scorcher." He fiddled with the garden hose. "I'm setting up the sprinkler today. Feel free to come and cool off."

"Thanks," they replied and bolted behind the house to discuss their new clue. But Libby's mom was there, testing her repair on the wading pool.

"Good as new," she smiled. "Libby, can you blow this up, please?"

Libby and Angie took turns puffing, and the pillowy sides rose. Zak ran out.

"Put it over there," he said. "It's the best spot for jumping in." He was pointing right at their crop circle.

"No way. That's where the aliens landed!" argued Libby.

But Zak was already dragging the pool over the crop circle where it fit... perfectly.

"Um, Libby," Angie pulled her friend aside. "The crop circle is the same size as the pool, which has been sitting on that grass for, like, a week. Maybe our UFO was an 'Uninflated Funtime Object.' Zak's pool!"

The girls burst out laughing, then ran to put on their bathing suits. They splashed and swam till sundown.

"That looks fun," said one small green creature.

"I told you. We have to wait till they're done."

When night fell, two green forms dipped their toes in the wading pool.

"Aaaahhh." It was hot in their spacecraft too.

Hurricanes

By Mindy Hardwick

"Hurricane coming," Dad said. The morning summer sun cast rectangular boxes across the coffee table.

"Something smells." My brother crinkled his nose. White powdered sugar crumbs coated his lips.

"Maybe it's you," I said. "*My* deodorant is working."

Greg held his nose and rolled his eyes at me.

"Wipe your mouth," I said. "Don't you know anything?" I smirked at Greg.

The TV announcer pointed toward a swirling white mass that was moving up the Southern coast.

"Are we still going to the beach?" I already had on my new blue swimsuit under my long matching blue T-shirt. Aunt Celia's green two-door Pinto pulled into the driveway.

Dad squinted at the screen. "Hurricane won't be here before tomorrow."

"Did you see?" Aunt Celia pushed open the screen door. "Hurricane coming."

Dad lit a match. He stuck it into his pipe and took three puffs before answering. "Yeah." He rolled his eyes.

My brother and I grinned at each other. Dad and Aunt Celia were siblings, just like us.

"Going to be a wild ride at the beach," Aunt Celia said.

I picked up my plastic pink bag and slid my novel from the

209

coffee table into the bag.

Greg pushed open the screen door. "There's no wind out here."

"Not yet," Dad said. "But there will be."

"Are you going to sit outside?" I asked. Back home before Mom and Dad were divorced, Dad had always sat outside in the thunderstorms. As the lightening flashed and the thunder rolled, Dad would take his pipe to the front porch and watch the storm roll across the sky. Mom would hustle Greg and me into the basement with a small radio so we could track the storm as it moved across the town. Dad had only ever come to the basement once. The sky had turned green, and the air had gotten very still. "Tornado," Dad had said. "Get into the basement." The sirens had wailed. I had covered my ears. The tornado hadn't lasted long. When we had come out, the neighbor's above ground swimming pool was at the high school across the street and an uprooted tree lay across the backyard.

In the living room, Dad turned off the TV. "Probably," he said.

"Ready?" Aunt Celia opened the screen door. I crawled into the front seat of the Pinto.

"Jen, you were in the front last time." Greg hit my shoulder.

"Too bad," I said and gave him my evil older sister smirk.

Greg pushed the backseat forward into my back. I screamed.

"Enough," Aunt Celia slid the keys into the ignition. "Get in and buckle up."

The beach was ten minutes from Dad's house. We rolled

down the windows, and the hot breeze blew through my hair.

"How come you don't have palm trees here?" I asked. Every summer Mom took us to San Diego to visit her side of the family. There were always palm trees lining the roads.

"Not the right climate," Aunt Celia said. Her voice rose in pitch. I prepared myself for one of her teacher talks. Aunt Celia was a seventh grade science teacher. Since I had just finished my seventh grade year, I figured she assumed I was one of her students who had returned for a summer session.

In the backseat, Greg played drums with his hands on the seats. Ka bum. Ka bum. Ka bum. The hand-drum moved and played on the back of my seat. Ka boom. Ka boom. Ka boom. Every time Greg's hands hit my seat, I felt their imprint in my back. I clamped my lips shut and didn't say anything. I wasn't going to give him the satisfaction of knowing he was bothering me.

"Have you talked to your mom?" Aunt Celia asked. Greg's drum stopped.

"Not for a few days," I answered. My voice raised in pitch to polite girl tone.

"Probably should give her a call," Aunt Celia took her eyes off the road and looked at me. "She'll be worried."

"Okay," I mumbled.

"We can stop by my house. You can use my phone," Aunt Celia said. "If you don't want to call with your dad around."

"Okay," I said. Greg's drum started against the seat.

It was our first summer of joint custody. Dad had us for a two-week vacation. We were on the East Coast visiting his family. Then, Mom had us for another two-week vacation. We were going to the West Coast to visit her family.

"Aren't you lucky?" Mom had said. "You'll get to see both coasts this summer."

"Yea," I muttered. I didn't want to see both coasts. I wanted to stay at the pool in our own state that didn't have a coast and swim with my friends.

Aunt Celia slowed and pulled into a black asphalt parking lot.

"Where's the beach?" I asked. Hills with grass surrounded us.

Aunt Celia popped the trunk. "Behind the dunes." She waved toward the hills.

Greg pushed against my seat. My knees buckled into the front dashboard.

"Stop," I pushed back hard. Greg crashed back to the backseat.

"Get out," Greg yelled.

I picked up my plastic bag and pulled out sunglasses. I moved the sunglasses around on my face, and flipped down the front visor so I could see them.

Greg hit the seat behind me. "Get out."

"Something the matter?" I asked and smiled my evil big sister grin at him. "Do you want something?"

Greg hit the top of my head. "Get out."

I unfolded my legs from the seat. I still wasn't used to how long my legs had gotten. It seemed like one minute I was able to squeeze in small places, and the next I couldn't squeeze anywhere.

Greg pushed out from the backseat and glared at me.

"Race you," I said, and took off running toward the dunes. Greg's small legs thumped behind me. I knew I'd win. I always won. Greg's legs were too small.

I came up on top of the dunes, and could see for miles into the horizon. The waves crashed in large white caps on the beach.

"Aunt Celia," I called. "Look at the waves!"

Aunt Celia puffed as she came up out of breath beside me on the dunes. "Hurricane is coming," she said.

"Is that what happens?" I asked and pointed toward the crashing waves.

"Yep, the hurricane is still miles out. But the waves tell us there is a storm out there." Aunt Celia waved her hand toward the horizon.

"But there's no wind." I pointed toward the still sky. "And it's still sunny."

"Storm hasn't hit land yet," Aunt Celia said.

Greg whooped. "The body surfing is going to be great." He rolled down the sand dune. His small body tumbled over and over. Sand was in his hair when he stood up. "Come on," he called.

Aunt Celia took my hand. "Ready?" she said and squeezed my hand.

The momentum of the run down the sand dune carried our legs forward as our plastic towel bags knocked against each other on the run downhill.

Greg stripped off his t-shirt and dropped it in a pile on top of his orange beach towel.

"Stay together," Aunt Celia called. "The force behind the waves will carry us down the beach."

I tossed my t-shirt and shorts into my plastic bag and followed Greg to the water. The Atlantic water was warm. In the Pacific Ocean, we always inched into the water one toe at a time. The water never seemed to warm up, and there was always a cool breeze blowing over us. Today, the breeze was hot, and the warm water felt like a lukewarm bath.

Greg moved toward the crest of the wave. The wave broke over his head. He disappeared and resurfaced, like the wet seals that lay on the rocks in San Diego. Aunt Celia and I placed ourselves on either side of him. The water pulled us backward.

"Here we go," Aunt Celia cried. The water lifted us onto the white crest of the wave. I held out my arms and lay flat on my stomach. I made sure my mouth was closed tight. I knew the water of the ocean was not like the chlorine water of the pool. The ocean water crept in anyway and made me gag.

The wave carried me into shore. A flat body surfer. My legs scraped sand. Aunt Celia and Greg lay next to me with large grins on their faces.

"Hurricanes are fun," I cried, and hopped into the crest of the waves.

Aunt Celia pointed toward the orange and blue color splotches of our towels. "Don't loose sight of those," she said. We had already moved an inch past them on the first wave. "The force under the waves is strong."

The afternoon sun moved in the sky as we moved further down the beach with each body surf.

"I can't see our towels." I looked down the beach.

Aunt Celia pointed in the direction we had come. "Way down there," she said. "Are you ready to go?"

My legs shook as we walked down the beach. It seemed a lot farther on land than in the water. Greg ran and splashed in the small waves on the shore.

"They don't have hurricanes on the West Coast," I said.

"They have other things," Aunt Celia said, "like earthquakes."

"Mom wouldn't take us outside in an earthquake," I said.

"Your dad always liked adventure," Aunt Celia said. She stopped. "I'm out of breath. Need a break."

"Mom doesn't," I said. I kicked the sand. It flew around me like a small dust storm. "Don't do this, don't do that," I mimicked Mom's voice.

"She's just watching out for you," Aunt Celia said.

"No she's not," I said. "She's scared of everything!"

"You miss your dad," Aunt Celia said.

The tears gathered behind my throat. I didn't cry that spring when Mom came home and said the judge awarded her custody with visitation rights to Dad. I didn't cry when Dad told us goodbye, and I didn't cry the first time we went to see Dad in his tiny new basement apartment. He served us spaghetti, and we tried to pretend everything was just like it had been at home.

Now all the tears came pouring out. I nodded.

Aunt Celia held out her arms. I stepped into them.

"He's still with you," Aunt Celia said. "Even though he's not living with you."

I looked at her. "No he's not. He's gone."

"Aren't you down here when a hurricane is coming?" she asked.

I nodded my head.

"You could have stayed home. You could have sat on the beach and not surfed the waves."

"But I didn't," I said. "I loved surfing the waves. I liked being carried half way down the beach."

Aunt Celia nodded.

"I like adventure," I said. "Like Dad."

Aunt Celia pulled me close. "Afraid so," she said.

On the way home, I let Greg have the front seat. I didn't kick him once. When we got home, Dad was cooking dinner.

"Have a good time at the beach?" He sprinkled oregano into the red spaghetti sauce.

"Yep," I said. "And we want to go tomorrow too."

Dad glanced at the TV. "I don't know. They're starting to clear the hotels and storefronts."

"Just for a little while," I said. "Not to swim. Just to watch."

"Maybe," Dad said.

The hurricane hit the next morning. The trees swayed. The water crashed on the beach. The shops closed. Dad took us to the beach, just to watch.

"I'm not getting out," Greg said from the back seat of the car.

"I am." I grinned at Dad. "Just for a minute."

Dad and I stood on the boardwalk. The wind whipped our hair. The spray from the water crashed against our cheeks.

I took his hand. He held on and squeezed hard.

Gone Missing!
By Susan Sundwall

The car tires crunched on the gravel road that led to the strawberry field. Corinne and her mother had come in the cool dusk to pick strawberries at Aunt Jenna's farm. Her cousin Kayla waved as Corinne got out of the car. They always spent the first week of summer vacation together.

"There's a big surprise in the barn," Kayla squealed.

"Did Tully have her kittens?" Corrine loved Kayla's large tabby cat.

"Sure did," said Kayla. "They've had their eyes open for a week!"

"Oh Mom," cried Corinne, "may I go see, pleeeease?"

"Go on," said her mother, "but remember, you promised to help pick berries for your dad."

Kayla and Corinne bounded into the barn. A great bundle of fur lay on an old gray blanket. Corinne gasped as she looked down at Tully and her six sleeping kittens. She knelt beside the blanket and ran a finger gently over the little bodies. Tully arched her back and gave a soft *meow*.

"Do the kittens have names?" she asked.

"Not yet," said Kayla. "I convinced Mom to wait until you got here."

"Cool!" exclaimed Corinne.

"Corinne!" That unmistakable Mom voice.

"Ugh," said Corinne, "I better go out and help pick. Meet you back here in half an hour? I pick fast!"

"Deal!" said Kayla.

Two buckets of strawberries later, Corinne was back in the barn and examining the kittens. Two of them had white foreheads, and three had black tipped tails. But wait! Weren't there six? As Kayla came through the barn door Corinne called out, "How many kittens were there?"

"Uh... six," she answered. "Why, has one gone missing?"

They looked everywhere. Then Corinne noticed a loose board in the barn wall. There were bits of fur caught in the wood and dig marks in the ground outside.

They followed the path leading from the barn to the creek and saw more bits of fur all tangled in the scrawny tufts of crab grass. "Weird," said Corinne. Soon they were in tall wet weeds and Corinne's sneakers slid in the mud. She fought to keep her balance but — kersplat! Yuck... her shorts were all wet! A quick movement caught her eye, and a dark tail swished through the reeds.

"It's only a muskrat," said Kayla. It scurried away when Corinne stood up. Where was that kitten? It was getting dark, and Corinne imagined the poor thing alone and frightened in the woods.

What would steal a kitten, Corinne wondered? Another cat or maybe a hawk? She looked up and shivered, imagining the shadow of dark wings. Just then she heard a soft noise, a meow? She ran quickly toward it and spotted a rotting log near a big willow tree. Peering inside she saw two bulging eyes.

"Kitty," she said softly. She waved Kayla over, but as she got near, a fat green frog leaped from the log and headed for the gurgling creek. They began to giggle, and then heard the crying sound again. Corinne crept to the edge of a hollowed out space in the bank. She spotted a small burrow and saw two tiny ears sticking out... kitten ears!

"Kitty!" she cried, but as she bent to reach for the kitten she heard another sound — a hiss. "Uh oh," she said, "I hope that's not a snake!" She peered along the edge of the bank and saw a small brown weasel glaring at her from a few feet away. She gulped. There was no time to waste; she had to act. Corinne lifted the kitten whip-fast from the burrow and ran. "Come on!" she screamed at Kayla. "I sure hope it doesn't chase us," she said, bolting away.

They raced through the grass in squishy sneakers as Corinne clutched the little ball of fur against her t-shirt. People in the strawberry field looked up as they made for the barn.

"Corinne!" her mother yelled. "What on earth is wrong?"

Corinne and Kayla flopped down on a hay bale near the barn door and began to laugh.

Aunt Jenna poked her head out of the barn. "Is that the one gone missing?" she asked.

"There was a weasel," Corinne said breathlessly.

"It must have stolen the kitten through that loose board in the barn," Kayla gasped. "Corinne grabbed her away just in time!"

"Well, we've had quite a rescue!" Her mother came up beside Aunt Jenna.

"That must have been Pesky," said Aunt Jenna. "That weasel's not right in the head, always poking around looking for trouble!"

"I saw the kitten in its burrow," said Corinne. "Why would Pesky take a kitten?"

"She may have lost one of her babies to a fox or some other animal," said Aunt Jenna.

"And wanted to adopt a kitten!" Corrine added. She looked out at the strawberry fields and thought about poor Pesky, and then she held the frightened kitten against her cheek.

"I think this is the first kitten we should name," said Kayla.

"I know her name," Corinne whispered as the kitten snuggled close. "I found her by the willow tree near the strawberry fields," she said. "I'll call her Willowberry." She stroked the kitten under the chin, and the kitten agreed with a soft meow.

Vacation Instructions
By Cindy Breedlove

I'm going on vacation
And leaving Bert behind.
My aunt's suppose to feed him.
She said she didn't mind.

I wrote some notes to help her,
And taped them round about.
I wrote how she should pet him
And watch— he might jump out!

I think he'll prob'ly miss me,
So one note I wrote big:

Please play
with Bert so
he's not
A lonesome
guinea pig.

Ogopogo
By Gloria Singendonk

"Canada? We're going to *Canada* for summer vacation? Isn't it, like, cold and snowy all the time? Why would we want to go there?" Josh asked, looking at his parents like they were from another planet — which they must have been to have thought of this idea.

"Because your Uncle Oliver rented a cabin up there on a lake, and he's invited us to share it for a week," his mother answered.

Josh's dad scanned through a brochure with a sparkling lake surrounded by mountains on the cover. "On Okanogan Lake. Its somewhere in British Columbia... above Montana, I think. And according to this brochure, it can actually get very hot there in the summer."

Josh rubbed his forehead, carefully avoiding touching his dark hair, which was gelled into spikes and dyed yellow on the tips. "But you said we'd go scuba diving again this year." He looked from one parent to the other. "I thought we'd go back to, like, the Caribbean or Mexico or somewhere exotic, not some scrubby lake in the middle of nowhere land." He'd been taking scuba diving lessons since he was nine, and every year since, they had gone on a scuba diving vacation. He'd thought for his fourth year, since he had earned his cave diving certification with his dad last year, they'd go some place even more exotic than before.

His mother touched his arm. "Oh Josh, settle down. Your cousin Kyla says she's scuba dived there in the past. Besides, maybe the two of you can do something different for a change."

"Oliver is bringing his boat," his father said, looking over the rim of his reading glasses. "There's stuff to do on top of the water too, you know."

Josh frowned. "Yeah, but I'd rather explore a sunken ship or a coral reef."

"Oh, you never know what you might find up there," said his father.

Later that month, they landed in the lakeside city of Kelowna. After gathering their luggage, they met Uncle Oliver in the airport, and he took them to the cabin.

"Hey!" Josh's older cousin Kyla called, running down the drive toward the car, her long, blonde hair flopping in a ponytail down her back. "Great to see you!"

"Hi," said Josh, helping to empty the trunk of luggage. "I brought my wet suit. Did you rent us some diving equipment?"

"Yeah, but you won't need that wet suit. A full-body dry suit is better for the cold water in the lake, so I reserved some with our equipment. We'll go first thing tomorrow to pick everything up. As soon as we get back, we can head out."

"Tomorrow? That's, like, a whole day away. What are we going to do until then?"

Kyla grinned. "The cabin is stocked with all sorts of board games."

Josh rolled his eyes. "Great." This vacation was going to be worse than he had thought.

Uncle Oliver held the door open for them. "And we brought a tube for some water fun. If we're lucky maybe we'll see Ogopogo."

"What's Ogopogo?" Josh asked.

Kyla glanced over her shoulder toward the lake at the front of the cabin and shielded her eyes from the setting sun. "A sea monster."

"Yeah, right," said Josh, looking doubtful. "You mean like that one in Scotland... the Loch Ness monster?"

"Precisely," said Uncle Oliver.

"It was in one of the pamphlets I was reading," chimed in Josh's dad. "The native people believe there's been a creature in Okanogan Lake for thousands of years. The pamphlet said that there are still about six sightings every year, but nobody's been able to prove it actually exists."

Josh shook his head. "I'll believe it when I see it."

The next day, Uncle Oliver took them into town to pick up the scuba gear. By the time they arrived back at the cabin, the weather had turned from warm sunshine to heavy clouds with strong winds.

On the dock in front of the cabin, Uncle Oliver unsnapped the canopy of the boat. "Not the best day for being out in the water."

"But a great day to be under it!" said Kyla, pulling in the line that secured the boat to the dock.

Josh nodded as he jumped into the boat. Uncle Oliver motored across the choppy lake while Josh and Kyla put on their scuba gear.

"Is here good?" Uncle Oliver asked over the noise of the

engine. They were near an outcropping of land some distance from any houses.

"It's great, Dad. I haven't been over to this side before." Kyla turned to Josh. "My friend Andrew and I dived nearer the cabin last year."

Uncle Oliver cut the motor and threw the anchor over the side.

"Let's go!" said Josh. He clamped his mask down over his face and rolled backwards off the side of the boat.

The deeper they dived, the murkier the water became. Josh turned on his handheld underwater light and followed Kyla toward the landmass. She stopped, beamed her light at him to get his attention and then pointed at a black spot on what must have been the bottom of the outcropping they had seen above. A cave! Josh signaled that he understood and shot back up to the boat.

"We found a cave! Can we have the diving rope?" Josh asked Uncle Oliver when he reached the surface. "Please?"

"A cave? Are you sure you two should be going in alone?"

"We're both cave certified," said Kyla. "We'll be fine."

Uncle Oliver threw the rope to Josh. "Okay, but be careful."

They descended back to the cave entrance and secured the rope just outside. Josh took the other end and headed into the cave with Kyla close behind. The interior was as black as octopus ink. Their lights barely penetrated its depths. Josh's heart beat faster — finally an adventure. He swam ahead, the beam of Kyla's light adding to his own as they moved further into the cave. A little ways in, Kyla's light waved back and forth. Josh blinked, trying to see what she was shining her light on. He looked over his shoulder. She seemed to be signalling him. Shining his light on her, he interpreted her hand signals. She was saying she was afraid and wanted to get out.

He considered going on without her, but knew that was foolish. One never went diving alone, never mind in a dark mysterious cave. He turned back for one last attempt to penetrate the darkness with his light. He swung it back and forth across the cave. The beam caught a movement just ahead of him. He quickly shone back on the area. Nothing. And then he felt something swim under him. Something big.

Kyla grabbed him and swam to the entrance. Josh let her pull him as he beamed his light around and around, but he saw nothing else.

"That was cool!" he said, breaking the surface.

"That was not cool!" cried Kyla. "That was one of the scariest things I've ever experienced in my life!"

Uncle Oliver leaned over the boat, his eyes full of concern. "What happened? What's the matter?"

"There was something in the cave," said Kyla. "Something very big."

"Ogopogo?" asked Uncle Oliver, his eyes twinkling.

Josh grimaced and shook his head. "No way!" But then he remembered the feeling of that thing swimming under him. Could there really be a sea monster in the lake?

"So you think you saw Ogopogo, do you?" laughed Josh's mom when they got back to the beach.

Josh shook his head and pointed at Uncle Oliver. "I didn't say that, he did."

"It could have been!" Kyla said, pouting. She unzipped her dry suit and climbed out of the boat. "It was large and lumpy and swam very fast — right under me!"

"Did you know there's a reward for proof of Ogopogo's existence?" asked Josh's dad. "It was in one of those pamphlets Oliver sent down."

Josh stroked his chin. "Like how big of a reward?"

"I think it was two hundred and fifty thousand dollars."

"Wow, that would pay for a lot of scuba trips," Josh said, rubbing his hands together. "Uncle Oliver, do you have an underwater camera?"

Grinning, Uncle Oliver winked at Josh's dad. "Why, yes I do."

"Do you think I could borrow it? And can we go back out there?"

"I thought you said there was no such thing as a sea monster!" Kyla said, her hands on her hips.

"For that much money, I'll take a chance," Josh said.

Kyla shook her head. "Not me, cousin. You're on your own. I won't be scuba diving in that lake again."

Josh sent his dad a pleading look. "You'll come with me, won't you?"

"All right, but if we see a real sea monster, we're out of there."

Back in the water, Josh and his dad entered the murky cave armed with flashlights and a disposable underwater camera. Kyla had come for the trip, but stayed on the boat. This time Josh's dad took the lead, pulling the tethered rope with him. He swept his light over the right hand side of the cave, while Josh took the left. The beam of Josh's light caught movement. He pulled the camera up to his eye, gripping it tightly in his right hand. Could there really be a sea monster? He swam closer, trying to see whatever was moving in the viewfinder. Suddenly, his feet were pulled down as something wrapped around his ankles. Struggling to hold onto the flashlight and camera, Josh kicked and wiggled, trying to get free of the grip of whatever had captured him. "Dad! Dad!" his mind screamed, but there was no way to call out through the scuba equipment. In his struggles, the camera went off. The light flashed brightly in the dark cave. As quickly as he'd been grabbed, he was let go. Feeling the last of the constraints drop from his legs, Josh kicked away, swimming toward his father's beam of light.

He grabbed his father's shoulder and signalled *let's get out of here. NOW*. His father's eyes looked puzzled, and he shrugged. *GO NOW,* Josh signalled again.

Okay, his father signalled back. Their lights flashed the sides of the cave as they raced to the entrance. Another movement along the left wall caught in Josh's beam. He kicked faster, but his father stopped and shone his light in the area. Hesitating, Josh slowed and added his beam to his father's. A red and yellow blob bounced in the current. A limp inner tube, its towrope still attached, was caught on rocks along the side of the cave.

He'd been caught by an old water toy, not by the tail of some sea monster! Josh and his dad unhooked the towrope from the rocks and rose to the surface.

"What did you find?" Kyla asked, helping Josh into the boat.

"Nothing worth two hundred and fifty thousand dollars," he

said, deflated. He told her of his fight with the old inner tube as he helped his dad haul it into the boat.

Kyla frowned. "Well, it might not have been a sea monster, but getting caught in a rope down there is dangerous enough. I think that's all the cave diving for this trip."

"Yeah, maybe we should take up water skiing."

A week later, the plane for home roared through take off. When it levelled out and the seat belt sign pinged off, Josh's mom handed him a package of pictures. "Here's the film from the underwater camera. I had them make duplicates for Kyla, so these are yours. Amazingly, only one didn't turn out."

Josh flipped through the pictures. He smiled at the ones of him and Kyla fooling around in the lake. When he came to the one that hadn't turned out, he peeled off the 'Could Not Process' sticker the photo shop had placed on it. It was pretty black, but Josh realized it must be the one from inside the cave. He could just make out his flippered foot, but what was that around his ankle? It was too thick to be the towrope for the inner tube... and were those green scales along its length?

"Mom, can we come back here next year?" he asked, pocketing the picture.

Peanut And The Bone Chomper

By Pamela Kessler

Fireflies blinked their secret codes against the darkening summer sky as Matt and his friend, Jake, lumbered over to the tent for their Friday night camp-out. The branches of the maple tree hung heavy in the humid air while the crickets began their nightly serenade. Peanut, Matt's dog, followed along, running circles around the boys' legs.

Jake tripped over the rambunctious, brown dachshund. "Does Peanut have to come along?"

"He's our guard dog," Matt said. "I told you my dad and I found a pile of gross, left-over bones when we were setting up the tent. Something is out there eating creatures alive," Matt said in a spooky voice.

"Oooh, I'm scared," Jake razzed. "I'm sure a seven-pound dog will be a great help."

Matt laughed as he unzipped the flap to the tent and tossed in the sleeping bags. "I think we have everything— a flashlight, games, pillows, soda, and chips."

"Sounds like it to me," Jake said.

The boys climbed into the tent. Matt zipped the flap so Peanut couldn't escape, and unrolled his sleeping bag. His back was leaning on the tent wall when he felt something brush past. "Did you feel that?"

"What?" Jake asked.

"Something's out there."

"I'm not scared, Matt." Jake said as he unrolled his sleeping bag.

Peanut jerked his head up and looked toward the screened flap on the tent. Matt looked too. He thought he heard a sniffing sound. "Jake, did you *hear* that?"

They listened, motionless. Soft sniffing could be heard, and the thin fabric of the tent moved in and out with each sniff.

"Look!" Matt cried. "Something's out there!"

"I see it, too. What is it?" Jake's eyes were as big as saucers.

Peanut darted for the flap; he barked and scratched at the flimsy tent material. His nails were getting caught in it.

"Peanut, come here!" Matt called out to his ferocious mini-beast.

Suddenly, a loud yelp came from outside the tent. Peanut barked back. The hair on his neck stood up like a punk rock star.

"Get the flashlight, Jake," Matt called. "Maybe I can see what's out there." He grabbed the light from Jake and shined it through the screen. A pair of eyes glowed back at him. "Ah!" Matt fell back, and the flashlight rolled away.

"What is it?" Jake asked.

"It looks like a big dog or something." Matt felt around for the flashlight. "All I know is we've got to get out of here!"

"How?"

"I don't know, but I don't want to end up as a pile of bones!"

The creature outside growled and scratched at the base of the tent. Matt darted to the screened flap and shouted, "Get

outta here!" He stomped his feet. Jake jumped up and joined in until finally the animal ran off.

"Come on, let's make a run for it!" yelled Matt.

Matt unzipped the flap, and they bolted for the house. Peanut was close behind; his stubby legs had to work twice as hard to keep up with the speedy boys. Just as they neared the back door, the animal jumped out from behind the bushes. The boys froze in their tracks.

Peanut charged over to the animal and sprang up like he had bounced off a trampoline. He tried to bite at its face. The animal edged back while Peanut continued his guard. His teeth snapped like a tiny crocodile's as his jaws opened and shut.

"Jake, let's go!"

Matt's parents heard the racket and ran into the kitchen as the boys scrambled in.

"What's going on?" Matt's mom asked in a panic.

"Peanut, where's Peanut?" Matt grabbed an apple from the counter and raced back outside.

Peanut was still holding his ground. The large tan creature crouched down; he growled, ready to pounce.

"Peanut, come on boy!" Matt called.

Peanut dashed toward Matt, and the angry beast hustled after him.

"Look what I've got!" Matt shook the apple to get the animal's attention, and then threw it toward the tent, and it rolled inside.

Distracted, the animal bounded after the apple into the tent. In a sudden brave dash, Matt followed behind the animal and pulled the tent zipper closed, locking him inside. He growled and scratched and tried to get out.

"Matt, get away from there!" Mom called from the door-way.

"It's a— a coyote!" He tried to speak between breaths.

"What, a coyote?" Dad looked shocked.

"Remember the bones, Dad? I bet it was the coyote that left those bones under our tree. He probably wanted Peanut for his next meal!"

"We'd better call Animal Control before he gets out of that flimsy tent," Dad said.

From the kitchen window Matt and Jake watched the tent walls puff in and out like an inflatable moon walk from the trapped coyote inside. "I hope he doesn't tear our tent," Matt said. "We won't be able to have any more camp-outs this summer."

Soon the men from Animal Control arrived. They placed a large cage at the flap of the tent. One man held the cage door up while the other carefully unzipped the flap.

The coyote lunged into the cage, thinking he was free, but the man holding the door quickly let it drop. The coyote growled and paced in the cage. After he settled down a bit, the men put on heavy gloves and lifted the cage onto the truck.

"I guess you boys had an uninvited guest at your camp-out tonight, huh?" one of the men said. "We've had several reports of this rascal nosing around the area."

"That coyote was scared and hungry. You were lucky to get away from him without getting hurt," the other man added.

"My dog, Peanut, saved us." Peanut ran up to Matt, his tail wagging with excitement when he heard his name.

"You mean that little dachshund stood up against this big coyote?"

Matt picked up Peanut and rubbed his cheek along the dog's soft, dangling ear. "This little dog can be pretty tough. If Peanut hadn't come between us and that coyote, I don't know what would have happened." Peanut licked Matt's cheek, not realizing he was a hero.

"Well, I guess he deserves an extra bone tonight." The first man rubbed Peanut's head and got into the truck. "Good-night, boys," he said.

Matt and Jake waved as they watched the truck back out of the driveway.

When the truck disappeared into the distance, Matt turned to Jake and said, "Let's go check out the tent. If it isn't too messed up, you still want to have our camp-out tonight?"

"Well... only if Peanut comes with us," Jake said.

"I thought you said a seven-pound dog wouldn't be any help," Matt joked. "Come on, let's go!"

Peanut agreed with a hearty *YIP* and raced ahead to the tent.

Porch Swing
By Elsbet Vance

On the porch swing
      Painted boards squeak
Chains from rafters
Rattle and creak

Nothing to do
Lay in the shade
Turn on the fan
Drink lemonade

Watching the clouds
Drift away and
Cover the sun
Wishing they'd stay

Even the dog's
Too hot to move
Lazing around
Summer's slow groove

Grandma and the Water Park

By Marilyn E. Freeman

Grandma poked her head into the room just as Allen and I were getting out of bed.

"Amy, Allen! Wake up, sleepy heads. The sun is out nice and bright. Today is going to be a beautiful day."

"Good morning, Grandma. You seem so cheerful today," I said.

"What do you think about a trip to the new water park?" she asked.

"Water park? We would love it! Do they have slides and stuff like that?"

"Yes, I think so. I heard it's really nice. We can spend the whole day there. I know they have a snack bar where we can get our lunch," added Grandma.

"Snack bar? Yum, let's go!" said Allen.

"Can we go right after breakfast?" I pleaded.

"Yes," said Grandma cheerfully. "I think I can still fit into my bathing suit."

The chatter at the breakfast table was all about the water park. I couldn't believe how much fun we were having with Grandma. We didn't miss our friends at all. We missed Mom and Dad, but we talked to them often on the phone.

The ride to the water park was fun. We talked about what we would do that day. I wanted to go down the big slide. Allen wanted to ride the canoe down the waterfall. Grandma wanted to relax under a nice shady tree, and then maybe float in the pool on a raft.

"Grandma have you heard of those long tubes of styrofoam they call noodles? You can sit on them, or you can wrap them around you and float. They're a lot of fun."

"Noodles? Amy, you eat noodles—you don't float on them," answered Grandma. "How in the world can you hang on to a noodle?"

"You'll see. They have them in all colors, and they're fun to play with in the pool," added Allen.

We couldn't believe how crowded the parking lot was when we got to the park. The park swarmed with people. The lines to the slides and other attractions were long. Allen and I didn't mind the long waits. We loved being there. Grandma found a lounge chair in a nice shady spot under a tree.

"I'll sit here and you can get in line for the slide," she suggested. "I can see the slide and the pool right from here."

It seemed like everyone was in line for something. There were lines for the many slides, lines for the snack bar, lines for the rest rooms, and lines to rent floats. Grandma went in and out of the pool while Allen and I enjoyed the attractions. Grandma was thirsty and decided she should get cold drinks. She told us she would be right back

I lost sight of Grandma for a moment, but then I saw her searching to get into one of the lines. I quickly noticed she was in the wrong line. By the time I reached her, she was already half way up the stairs.

"Grandma! What are you doing?" I yelled.

"I'm in line to get us some cold drinks," replied Grandma.

"No, you're not!" I shouted. "You're in line for the Super Colossal Slide."

"I'm what?" yelled Grandma.

I started laughing. "Grandma, you're in line for the slide."

"No! I can't be in line for the slide! I'm getting cold drinks. I don't want to slide! I have to get out of this line," shouted Grandma. Just at that moment the line started moving faster. The kids behind her started shoving. I could see Grandma near the top arguing with the little boy behind her.

"Lady, please move up some. We want to slide," said a little boy.

"You don't understand, I don't want to be in this line," said Grandma with a sigh. "I have to get out of this line."

"Sorry, Lady, you can't get out now. You are already on the steps. You have to keep climbing," said the little boy.

Allen saw me standing near the slide and hurried over, "Amy, what's all the excitement about?"

"It's Grandma. She is on the steps for the slide, and she wants to get back down. The kids behind her won't let her get off the steps. They keep shoving her forward," I answered. "Grandma thought she was in the line for cold drinks."

Allen laughed so much his stomach hurt. "Poor Grandma, it looks like she is going to take a super colossal slide into the pool."

"Allen, we have to do something! What can we do?" I asked.

"Nothing, she is almost to the top. We can't help her now," replied Allen still laughing. "Just stand here and watch the show."

Grandma was almost to the top of the slide. I could see her talking to the little boy in back of her. "I can't go down this slide," Grandma told the little boy. "I just can't."

"Lady, don't be afraid. I'll help you. It's fun, you'll see." he replied.

"You don't understand. I want to get down from here," said Grandma. "Now!"

"Lady, there is only one way down. You'll have to slide down," said the little boy.

The other kids in line started yelling at Grandma to move a little faster. They all wanted their turn at going down the slide, and she was holding up the line.

I was horrified at what Grandma was going to have to do. Allen was still roaring with laughter. "Don't you care about Grandma?" I asked.

"Yes, of course I do," answered Allen. "She'll be fine. She won't get hurt. It's only a slide."

"Are you crazy?" I yelled. "It's the Super Colossal Slide — the fastest, highest slide in the water park!" This only made Allen laugh more. Tears ran down his face.

Grandma was at the top; it was her turn to slide down. The little boy stood close behind her. "Okay, Lady, it's your turn. Just sit down and slide." he said.

"NO! I can't!" shrieked Grandma. The kids in line kept yelling for her to hurry up and slide.

"Lady, why did you get in line to slide?" asked one girl.

"I didn't! This is a big mistake!" cried Grandma.

"Come on I'll help you," said the little boy. "Sit down"

Grandma sat down but refused to let go and slide down into the water. "I can't do it!"

"Wait!" I yelled as I raced up the steps of the slide. "That's my Grandma! I'm going to slide with her!" I hurried up the steps and sat behind Grandma, grabbing onto her shoulders.

"Okay, Grandma," I whispered. "Let's show 'em how to really slide. Ready?"

Grandma let go of the slide and covered her eyes. The whole park could hear Grandma yelling, "EEEEEEEEEEEEEEE!"

Allen rolled on the ground with laughter. All the kids in line were clapping for Grandma.

Grandma hit the water like a cannonball. When she came to the top, she looked like she'd seen a ghost. Her face was white, and her eyes were wide open with a wild stare.

"Grandma, are you okay?" I asked. "Did you get hurt?"

"I'm okay. I just don't want to talk right now," she said as she climbed out of the pool.

"Grandma, I think you broke the speed record coming down the slide," laughed Allen.

I gave him a poke in his side with my elbow. "Allen!"

"I just want to go back to my chair and rest for a few minutes," said Grandma. "Then we can get some lunch. First, I'll make sure we get in the right line."

Allen and I both laughed. We went in the pool near Grandma while she rested.

"Allen, I was just thinking," I said sadly. "I wish we had more time to stay with Grandma. This has been our best vacation ever. I can't wait to see what we'll be doing tomorrow."

Billy-Bunter
By Goldie Alexander

Molly held out the meat. "Come on," she called to the bird. "Take it."

A beady eye watched her.

"Molly, you'll scare that thrush," Grandma called through the open window. "Move to where he can't see you."

"Okay." Molly placed the sliver on a ledge. Trying to avoid leaning on her sprained ankle, she limped away so that the bird couldn't see her, but she could see him.

The thrush's head was grey and smooth. His eyes were like berries. His wings were brown and speckled. His beak and legs were black as ebony.

Molly watched him glance around. "Come on," she whispered. "Take it."

The bird cocked his head. He called, "Coo... weee." Then he used his beak to pick up the meat and flew with it to the back of the garden.

Molly leaned on the windowsill and peered out at the garden. "Lucky thing," she said enviously. "Wish I could fly."

Grandma laughed. "That'll teach you to watch out for unexpected waves."

"Wasn't my fault," Molly said, nearly in tears. "That wave was just too big."

Grandma hugged her. "A sprained ankle could happen to

anyone. It's just bad luck."

Though Molly hugged Grandma back, nothing could make her feel better. She lived in the city where life sometimes felt terribly cramped. She loved getting together with her cousins, Tony and Jacob. All winter the three youngsters had been looking forward to spending their summer holidays at the beach. They all owned surf-boards. All three enjoyed staying in a seaside village where they were allowed to freely roam. As Grandpa said, "You have to be sensible. If you don't talk to strangers and avoid anything dangerous, I see no reason to restrict you."

The cousins had explored the sand-hills that led to the beach. They had roamed through grass and shrubs that hid small animals and insects, and they had searched rock pools for unusual shells and sea creatures. But most of all, they loved to surf. So it was bad luck that, on Molly's second day, an extra large wave had picked her up. The wave had thrown her into a sand-bank on her ankle, and she'd twisted it very badly.

When Molly tried to get back up, her leg hurt too much to stand on.

While Tony stayed with Molly, Jacob ran home to fetch Grandpa. Behind his sunglasses, Grandpa peered at Molly's ankle. "Poor thing," he said and gave her a piggy-back ride all the way home. By the time they got to the house, Molly's ankle was swollen to twice its normal size.

Grandma inspected it and shook her head. "No more swimming till that gets better." She put an icepack on Molly's leg. "That'll help get the swelling down," she told Molly. Then she tied an elastic bandage around the ankle so Molly could stand on it.

But the ankle still hurt. Molly couldn't stop crying.

She had thought the only thing that could mess with this holiday was rain. How wrong she was. The weather was perfect: warm days, cloudless skies, golden sands, and heart stopping white waves. But instead of swimming and surfing, she could hardly move out of the house.

Meanwhile, Jacob and Tony were up first thing to go to the beach. They only came home for lunch. Then all they could talk about was how much fun they were having. The boys were learning to ride large boards. When the surf was down, they explored the sand hills at the back of the beach. They waited for the tide to go out, so they could wander over the rocks looking for crabs and sea-shells. They brought back some of their finds. Once Tony found a large conch-shell that was almost intact. Then Jacob brought home pieces of driftwood that the sea had battered into interesting shapes. But right now all Molly wanted was to ride the waves. A sprained ankle stopped her from doing too many things. Most of the time she was so angry she could hardly open her mouth except to say "yes", "no," and sometimes "maybe."

The day after Molly sprained her ankle, Grandma asked her to help bake gingerbread-dolls. Molly rolled out the dough. Then she rolled the dough into balls. Finally, she shaped the balls into heads, bodies, arms and legs. She gave the dolls sultana mouths, cherry noses and jellybean eyes. Then she piped pink and white icing sugar onto the bodies. Now the gingerbread dolls looked like they were wearing pants and vests. She was so busy that when a bird cried "Wotch-soo-wee," she hardly bothered looking up.

"Look!" Grandma cried. "That bird's here. Billy Bunter is back."

Molly peered at the grey thrush with the black beak. "What did you call him?"

"Billy Bunter." Grandma sprinkled flour into the bowl. "When your great-grandmother was your age, there were books about a boy called Billy Bunter who had lots of adventures."

"Adventures?" Molly was interested enough to momentarily forget how angry she was. "Tell me some."

"Billy Bunter went to boarding school where he solved lots of mysteries. Pass me the sugar, will you?"

Molly did. She said "What kind of mysteries?"

"Oh, he found lost treasure. And once on a dare, he stole the headmaster's silver cup. But he stood up for weaker, smaller boys. He was always stopping bigger boys from bullying littler kids."

Molly said, "What about the girls?"

"No girls. It was a boys-only school."

Something odd struck Molly. "What's Billy Bunter got to do with grey thrushes?"

"Billy Bunter was fat and greedy like some of our birds. What Billy Bunter liked best were midnight feasts. Back then, boys brought some of their own food to boarding schools. They called them Tuck-Boxes."

That sounded like fun. "You mean they had fridges in their rooms?"

"Those boys slept in dormitories. Lots of kids in one very large room. Back then there were no fridges. Boys were expected to bring food that would stay fresh."

"Oh. Like what?"

Grandma wiped down the bench. "Fruit cakes. Biscuits. Sweets. Mince pies. But the interesting thing about Billy Bunter was that he always shared his feast with any boy who had an empty Tuck-Box."

Midnight feasts! Great idea, Molly thought. Why can't we have one here?

"Anyway," Grandma was saying, "The name stuck to anyone who ate too much."

Molly smiled to herself. Didn't both her cousins boast that they could eat a large carton of ice-cream all by themselves? What if we have a feast tonight? Molly thought. Maybe my gingerbread dolls will be ready to eat.

Just then a grey bird appeared at the window. His beak tapped on the glass as if to command some attention.

"Look Grandma, Billy Bunter's back for more food. What can I give him?"

"Those thrushes eat worms and snails," Grandma replied, "so they love fatty food. Give him a little grated cheese. And talking about food," Grandma held up floury hands. "Let's get these dolls into the oven."

Baking took up the rest of the morning. Molly's ankle was far too sore to do much else. Though Grandma offered, "What about I show you how to knit?" Molly shook her head. All she wanted was to get back into the surf, and now she couldn't. It was so unfair.

Later that day, Molly hid three gingerbread-dolls in her room. That night she tried shaking her cousins awake. "Surprise," she cried. "Midnight feast. Look at what I made."

But Jacob and Tony weren't interested.

Jacob didn't open his eyes. Half asleep he mumbled, "Go way."

"Go away Molly," Tony murmured. He also went straight back to sleep.

Days drifted by. A steep track led down to the beach. But Molly's ankle hurt too much for her to even think of tackling it. "Anyway," she said morosely when Grandma suggested it, "Why go to the beach if I can't swim?"

"You can always watch the boys," Grandma suggested. "Grandpa will help you get onto the sand."

"But I'll only get sunburnt."

"Not if I smother you in sun-cream," Grandma said quickly.

Molly shook her head, and her lower lip stuck out in a sulk. Just sitting on a beach could only make her feel worse. Why ask Grandpa to help her make the difficult trip up and down the sand hills just to feel miserable?

For her, this holiday was a terrible flop. What made things worse was watching Jacob and Tony coming home every afternoon over-the-top happy.

All Jacob could talk about was tackling giant waves and riding crests.

All Tony could talk about was surf-boarding. The only thing that could cheer Molly up was Billy Bunter. "All I ever do is feed you," she mock-grumbled, watching the thrush swallow scraps of cheese. "You've gone through a packet in just a few days. But you're even thinner than ever."

Right then a couple of long tailed birds flew overhead. "Kwock-kwock," they cried and darted across the verandah.

"Shoo, shoo." Grandma raced out of the kitchen to chase them away.

Molly giggled. Grandma looked so funny when she got cross. White hair flew everywhere. Her spectacles nearly fell off her nose.

"Those wattlebirds!" Grandma cried on her return. "They really hate having Billy Bunter around."

Molly shook her head. She felt sorry for Billy Bunter. "Why are those birds so mean?"

"Each bird has to look after his own patch," Grandma replied. "Wattle birds won't have other birds hanging around." Then she added, "If you keep giving Billy Bunter cheese, and don't make any sudden movements, soon you might even have him eating out of your hand."

Molly spent a lot of time feeding Billy Bunter. Soon the bird was brave enough to sit next to her hand, though never on it. Wouldn't it be wonderful, she thought, if she could convince Billy Bunter to sit on her shoulder? That would show he wasn't frightened of her. Hadn't she once seen a nature film where certain birds like rosellas were brave enough to do just that?

Grandpa let Molly borrow his digital camera. He showed her how to use it. Molly took lots of photos of birds. Most were of Billy Bunter. Using the camera was fun.

Even so, surfing was still better.

One afternoon Molly noticed a black cat in the garden. The cat had a missing eye and only one and a half ears. He was the largest cat Molly had ever seen. She went to shoo him away.

The cat took absolutely no notice.

Then suddenly he sprang onto the ledge where Billy Bunter

was perched. Just in time, Billy Bunter chirruped a warning "wotch-soo-wee" and headed for his favorite tree.

Molly watched anxiously. That cat was quick and strong. He looked hungry—hungry enough to catch and eat a tasty-looking bird.

Would Billy Bunter be okay?

Grandma didn't seem worried. "Billy Bunter's used to cats."

"Who owns him?"

"That cat's wild. Feral."

"How come he's here?"

"People bring pets to their holiday houses. Sometimes the cats get lost. Or their owners forget to take them home. Don't blame the cats. Hunting birds comes naturally to hungry cats. It's just that birds can't defend themselves."

The next day, there was no sign of Billy Bunter. Molly wandered through the garden. She looked behind bushes and up trees, but no Billy Bunter. Molly worried all day. What if that cat had caught him?

But Grandma said, "Stop worrying, will you? That bird's a survivor if ever I've seen one."

All the next day, Molly kept popping outside to look for Billy Bunter. Once she thought she heard his whistle from a tree in the next door garden. She slowly limped towards it. But when she peered over the fence, all she could see were more wattlebirds and some tiny yellow wrens with very loud voices.

Suddenly that same black cat she had seen before slunk out from a bush. Molly usually loved cats. But wasn't there something mean about this animal? Maybe it was the way his one eye glared at her. Molly had the feeling that this cat didn't much like children. Maybe it was because he'd been in many fights. As well as that missing eye and torn right ear, he'd lost some of the fur on his left back leg.

Molly shivered. It was easy to picture that cat hunting rabbits and birds. It was easy picturing that cat catching them. She knew cats often liked to play with their catch. Grandpa said this was the way they survived in the wild. But all Molly could think was, "Poor Billy Bunter." Now she was sure that she knew what had happened to him.

"Psst..." she hissed at the cat. "Go away."

But all the cat did was yawn and continue strolling away from the house.

By the end of the week, Molly's ankle felt strong enough for her to stand on both feet. Grandpa helped her carry a boogie board to the beach. Molly surfed. She dog-paddled and floated. She swam over-arm and back-stroke.

It was wonderful to be back on this beach playing in the surf.

That very day a family moved in next door.

The first Molly knew about it was seeing a car pull into the drive. She watched a girl climb out and then lift a little boy out of his car seat onto the ground. The girl had long brown hair, and she was small and thin. All the same, something about the way she held herself told Molly that the girl was also twelve. Not that Molly didn't enjoy being with Jacob and Tony, but having someone new can always add more interest.

That afternoon she went to the beach with the boys. Molly was careful to watch out for any extra large waves. They had a wonderful time. Towards dusk, they returned to house. After they'd eaten and helped Grandpa put the clean dishes away, Molly went into the garden to see if Billy Bunter was around.

There was still no sign of him.

She was about to go back inside, when she glimpsed that girl from next door.

They stared at each other. Molly wasn't sure if the girl's stare was friendly. But as Grandpa kept saying, "If you don't smile and say hi, you can't expect the other person to smile back."

So, scooping up a basketball Tony had left in the garden, she peered over the fence and cried, "Hi. I'm Molly. Want to play?"

The girl smiled and nodded.

"I'm Jenna," she said, walking towards her

Molly helped Jenna over the fence. As they threw the basketball to each other, Jenna said, "I'm real keen on surfing."

"Me too," said Molly. Then she added, "I'm here with my cousins. We go surfing every day."

Jenna's face lit up. "Dad's just bought me a new boogie board. Can I come with you?"

Molly nodded. She remembered the little boy she'd seen Jenna help out of the car. "Is that your brother?"

"Sure is. He's Max, and he's two."

"Lucky you." Molly tried to keep the envy out of her voice. "I don't have any sisters or brothers."

"But you have big cousins," Jenna pointed out. "I have to babysit Max. I adore Max, but he can't do much. I think cousins would be much more fun."

Just then Jacob and Tony came out of the house. "Meet

Jenna," said Molly. "She wants to come surfing with us."

Everyone smiled at each other.

"Let's play basketball," said Jacob. "Boys against girls."

"Okay," said Molly. The boys won the first game. Then they all swapped sides. Jacob played with Jenna, and Molly played with Tony. This time Jacob and Molly won.

They played and played until it was too dark to see each other or the ball.

It was all so much fun, Billy Bunter completely slipped Molly's mind.

The rest of that week, the youngsters were so busy surfing, playing ball, and helping Jenna look after little Max, the time just flew.

Molly wished she could stay for another two weeks. Every so often she remembered Billy Bunter. What might have happened to him? Then she would go outside and search right through the garden. Twice she glimpsed that black cat with the missing eye, but there was no sign of the bird.

Surely poor Billy Bunter had been caught and eaten. Surely he was no longer alive.

But on the last night of their holiday, Grandma called the youngsters to the window. "Look who's visiting us."

And there was Billy Bunter, flanked on both sides by two baby birds. The babies' mouths were wide open. They fluffed themselves up to twice their size in an effort to be noticed.

"Seems that *he* is a *she*," Grandma chuckled. "All those babies. No wonder Billy Bunter was getting thin — she was keeping those hungry youngsters happy. Told you that bird was a survivor."

Molly reached for her camera. She took shots of the birds until her battery ran out.

Then she took a fresh packet of cheese out of the fridge. She said, "Billy Bunter? No way. How about we call her Billy-Mae?"

Troll In My Tree House
By Kathryn Lay

On the first day of summer vacation, I tripped over a troll watching cartoons on my portable battery-operated television in my tree house.

"Aaargh!" I screamed.

"Aaargh!" The troll screamed back.

I scooted back against the treehouse wall and stared at a boy-troll with a round face, a long crooked nose, and a tail sticking out of his brown shorts. He blinked wide eyes at me and scratched the orange tuft of hair on his head.

"Who... who are you and what are you doing in my tree house?" I asked.

The troll stood up and folded his thick arms. "You live in a tree? And what a marvelous tree home you have, human boy."

I frowned. "I don't live here. This is my own private place. No one's allowed." I pointed at the sign I'd painted that hung near the ladder. "See, 'Andrew's Place. No Trespassing! No girls, parents, or bullies."

With a smile, the troll patted himself on the chest. "I am not a girl or a parent. And I only bully those who bully me." He stood tall and put both hands on his hips. "I am Thomas. I am a troll."

I snorted. "Yeah? You look more like a gnome. Aren't trolls supposed to be scary and mean?"

Thomas's lip trembled. My jaw dropped when he then fell down and beat his fists against the floor, kicking like my three-year-old sister when Mom says no to ice cream for dinner.

"Boo hoo, you are a mean boy. I am a troll. Everyone in Trollsville calls me little one and pushes me down. My sisters tell me what to do all the time and call me names and say I could not even scare a human. So I ran away. I like boy's house in tree. I stay here or I will cause big trouble for human boy."

With that said, Thomas wiped his eyes and walked over to plop onto my bean bag and stare at Bugs Bunny.

Trollsville? Where was that, somewhere between Unicorn City and Wizard Town?

I walked over to the ice chest to grab a root beer and cold candy bar.

"Hey, you pig. Where are all my sodas and snacks?"

Thomas waved a chubby hand at me. "Not much food here, but you can bring more later."

I was really mad then. This troll outcast was telling me what to do in my own tree house. I was about to tell him to take a hike, when my oldest sister poked her head over the ladder.

"Andrew, Mom said it's bedtime. You can't hide up here all night," Jeannine said.

"No girls allowed," I yelled.

Jeannine stuck her tongue at me. "Hmmph, who wants to come inside anyway? You'd better hurry down, or Mom's coming up after you."

She disappeared down the ladder.

Thomas waddled over to me. "Human boy doesn't like his sister?"

I shrugged. "I have five sisters. Why do you think I hide up here?"

Thomas plopped down beside me. "I don't like my troll sisters. They push me down and sit on me. Hey, I could eat Andrew's human sisters."

I backed away. This guy was weird. Even for a troll.

"Listen, I've got to get to bed before Mom grounds me again. You can't hang around here. Go on back to Trollsville," I suggested.

But Thomas just shook his head. "I won't go back until my sisters beg me and call me a fearsome troll. I will go with you."

"You can't," I shouted. "My family will see you."

Thomas tapped his chin. "Which room is yours?"

I pointed to the upstairs window in the corner. "That one. Why?"

Thomas walked to the only window in the treehouse and climbed onto the branch beside it. "Thomas will sneak inside and see Andrew's real home. But I must go only in the dark or the sun will turn me to stone."

And then he was gone. I climbed down the ladder as quick as I could. This was getting too strange. I had enough trouble finding somewhere to be alone without being bugged by my sisters. I didn't need a troll following me everywhere too.

I ran inside the backdoor, closing it quietly. But Mom can hear a mouse sneeze. "Andrew, is that you? If you don't brush your teeth and get into bed, you're grounded for the weekend."

"I'm going now, Mom," I said. Inside my room, I stuffed my desk chair under the doorknob and ran to my window.

"Yaaa!" I yelled when I opened the curtain and saw Thomas stuck to the window like a giant spider.

"Yaaa!" He yelled back.

I unlatched and raised the window carefully as Thomas held on. When the window was open, he slid inside.

He ran and jumped on my bed, curling into a ball on my pillow. "This bed is too soft, but I am tired and will sleep here."

"Hey," I said. "You can sleep in the chair. That's *my* bed."

Thomas was already snoring. No way was I sleeping with this guy — his breath was worse than the trash can in the school cafeteria. I threw a blanket over him, covering that orange hair and grabbed another blanket. With a grunt I curled up in my only chair and tucked the blanket all around me.

I dreamed of voices and movement. I dreamed of being wrapped in the blanket and carried away while people argued.

"Hurry quick, the day will come soon," a gruff voice said.

"Shut your mouth, I almost dropped him. King Rufus will be angry if we hurt his runaway son," a gruffer voice said.

Suddenly I fell out of the chair. At least, I thought I fell out of the chair. I struggled in the blanket and pushed it away, catching a long breath.

Two creatures stared down at me, their eyes wide as saucers and mouths open. Those mouths had a lot of teeth.

"Uh oh, this is not Thomas," one said.

The other shook his head and tugged at his green beard. "No it is not! The King will be mad. We captured the human and left Thomas behind."

I scooted away. These were trolls. Big, scary ones. Not like Thomas at all.

"Take me home," I gasped.

Both trolls shook their heads. "That would be a bigger mistake. We will take human boy to the King. Maybe he will keep this boy instead of son."

They each grabbed me by the arm and dragged me inside a dark, smelly cave. I stared at the throne in front of me. On it sat the biggest, ugliest two-headed Troll. He stared at me and snarled. Both heads snarled in unison.

"What have you brought your King?" the face with the crown asked.

"Dumb King," the other head said. "It is a human boy sitting on your floor."

A hand reached up and slapped the non-crowned head. "Shut your mouth. You are not King this year," the other head said. He pointed to me. "Who are you, human boy?"

I swallowed and tried to stand and bow. "Excuse me, your Trollness, I'm just a kid who found a troll in his treehouse. I think these trolls grabbed me by mistake. Thomas was sleeping in my bed."

The King gasped. His other head laughed.

I glanced at my kidnappers, but they had already run away.

"Hmm, will your family eat my Thomas?"

I shook my head. "Oh no, my parents are vegetarians. My sisters will probably drive him crazy but..."

The King waved a hand at me. "Your talk is boring. Go down to the room behind throne and tell my Troll Queen that I say to cook boy..."

I gasped.

The King cleared his throat. "I don't mean to eat boy, I mean to cook food for boy."

"But I want to go home," I said.

The Troll King nodded. "Soon. It will be good for Thomas to practice scaring human boy's sisters."

I started to tell him that they'd probably scare Thomas more, but both heads closed their eyes and began to snore. I tiptoed toward the cave's entrance, but two troll guards stood with their backs to me. Instead, I ran to where the Troll King said I could get some food. Maybe the Queen would send me home.

I walked down a long, dark, smelly corridor until I saw light coming from a side cavern. When I walked into the room, three girl trolls and one Troll Queen screamed.

I decided to be polite and not scream back.

"Oooh, Mother, it's so ugly!" a young troll screamed. Her one eye blinked at me.

I was just glad they each had only one head.

"I want to squash that ugly boy-thing," a warty-headed troll said.

The last sister grinned at me with pointed teeth and patted her purple hair. "Do not squash him, I think he is cute."

I backed away. The Troll Queen stared at me like any mom would, or maybe she was sizing me up to see if I'd fit in the roasting pan.

"Did the King tell you to come here?" she asked.

Quickly, I explained what happened and how I was brought here by mistake instead of Thomas.

The Troll sisters laughed. "Thomas is a dumb troll. He is not scary, he is not strong, and he is not a good Troll Prince."

"Maybe if you were nice to him…" I suggested.

They laughed louder, even the Troll Queen. "A troll son does not need to be nice, he needs to be tough."

I shrugged. I guess they were right. Maybe Thomas just didn't understand his sisters.

They offered me something to eat, but the bowl of food was green and brown, smelled like a day at the dump, and I was sure

I saw something moving around in it.

The Troll Queen left to teach Troll Terrorizing. I was left alone with Thomas' sisters.

It wasn't long before I knew why Thomas had run away.

"This boy will do Thomas's chores," the warty sister said. The other two agreed and put me to work.

I spent all morning breaking the breakfast dishes, feeding the bats, stirring a huge pot of grey lumpy stuff for lunch, and listening to the sisters laugh at me. Even my sisters weren't this bad. Well, almost, but at least they didn't stick their warty faces in mine and demand I count how many warts they had or grin at me with yellow, pointed teeth.

By the time I was promising to never complain about my

sisters again, the Troll King came into the room and grabbed me by the shirt. "It's time for this human boy to go home. Thomas is ready to come back."

I couldn't imagine why.

The same troll guards who brought me here put a blindfold on me and led me home through an underground tunnel. I remembered they couldn't go out in the sun or they would be turned to stone. They popped open a patch of grass that led into my backyard.

"You will go home now. The King's son has returned to Trollsville."

With a shove, I was pushed out of the tunnel and the trap door closed behind me. I ran across the yard, hugged the tree with my tree house in the branches, then ran inside my house. I wondered what Thomas had done all morning.

My room was clean, cleaner that it had been in a long time. On my desk was a note from Thomas.

"This is an awful place. Human sisters made me clean Andrew's room. And they try to hug me and tell me that I am a cute little troll. They even made me take a bath! There is no home like a Troll home. You can come and visit me someday. But leave human sisters at home."

I smiled. Sisters were sisters everywhere. I pulled a cave lizard from my pocket and went to find them.

Ice Cream
By Sally Clark

Licking
ice cream,
summer passes
in long, slow
licks, then
drips
down
the cone.

Hurry —
eat it fast.
Summer is gone
before you know!

The Diver

By Suzanne Kamata

Frances lay in her feather bed, listening to thunder roll through the summer night.

Wind lashed the eaves. The white pines danced, shaking their boughs to the rhythm of the rain. Even though she couldn't see Lake Erie from her bedroom window, Frances could picture the roiling waves lit by flashes of lightning.

It came as no surprise to see her father in his captain's uniform the next morning. "A load of copper went down last night," he explained to her while she rubbed the sleep from her eyes. "My divers are going to try and salvage it."

Frances nodded gravely. Her father was known to be the best wreck diver on the Great Lakes. He'd received a letter from President Theodore Roosevelt himself commending his efforts.

She hoped that the crew of the ship was able to escape, though she knew many men had died in such storms. She watched her father adjust his navy cap and ran over to give him a hug.

"Be careful, Father."

"Oh, don't you worry about me. Be a good girl and help your mother and I'll be back before you can say 'Jumpin' Jehosephat.'"

Her mother watched this familiar scene from the stove. "Why don't you stir up these griddle cakes?" she called out to her eldest daughter. "Your brothers and sisters will be awake soon."

But Frances was already dashing out the door, through the yard and into a copse of trees, down to the riverbank where she could watch her father's boat glide down the river.

Oh, and how she wanted to go with him. She wanted to watch the divers bring up treasures from the sunken ships. She imagined chests of jewels, underwater kingdoms, and strange speckled fish. And then she imagined herself down there, too, diving.

When her father returned two weeks later, his curly black hair a wild halo, his face burned red by wind, he was smiling. He burst into the dining room where his children and wife were having their supper and broke into a jig. "We found the ship and we pulled up all the ore. Made a pretty penny for ourselves, we did!"

Frances's mother smiled. "I'm just glad you're safe."

After the captain had eaten, clearing his plate three times, he settled into the rocker at the hearth and lit his pipe. Frances sat down on the rug at his feet. She knew that it was time for one of her father's stories. He puffed for awhile, rocking slightly, a faraway look in his eyes.

Frances waited patiently, quiet as a river rock.

Finally, he began. "Did I ever tell you about that time I saw a mermaid?"

Frances shook her head. "No, Father. Please tell it."

"Well, I was just a lad back then, a cabin boy. We were sailing off the coast of Florida in search of sunken treasure. We'd been on open water for over two weeks with nothing but gulls and pelicans for company. I was leaning over the rail, trying to spot a flash of gold down in the depths, when a ripple of water caught my eye.

"I saw the tail end first, thick and muscular and covered with green scales. When they caught the light, they shimmered like emeralds. 'Here's our treasure boys,' I called out. I was bedazzled, you see. All I could make out was brilliance. But when the other sailors came forward, they blanched with horror. They had seen a woman's head and shoulders attached to that tail. She had masses of snarly green hair with bits of shells sticking to it. And her face, well, it was the face of death — lips the color of blood, skin a pale blue."

Frances bit her thumb. "What did you do, Father? What did you do?"

He rocked and puffed a little more before continuing the story. "Well, all of us knew that if she started singing to us, we'd be doomed, so we plugged our ears with rags. As fast as we could, we set sail for home."

"And you were all right?" Frances asked breathlessly.

He pounded his chest. "Every one of us, safe and sound."

"Oh, Father. Do you think there are mermaids in Lake Erie?"

The captain reached up and twirled his moustache. "I wouldn't doubt it, Frances."

Just then, Frances noticed her mother standing in the doorway. Her lips were pressed tightly together. "There you go again," she said. "You'll be giving the child nightmares."

"Oh, I'm not scared," Frances protested. "Please, just one more story."

But the captain glanced at the woman in the doorway and

shook his head. "Not tonight, my sprite. It's time for bed."

Frances stood up, but something kept her in place. She felt she would never be able to sleep unless she told the captain what was in her heart. "Father, I want to learn how to dive."

Suddenly, he turned serious. "It's dangerous work, you know. Ninety-nine out of a hundred men can't do it. Go under too deep and your nose might start bleeding, your head might start hurting. You could even suffocate."

Frances kept her eyes on his. "I'm not afraid, Father. And you know I'm a good swimmer. I can hold my breath just as long as any other boy or girl."

He was silent for what seemed like an eternity. Finally, he smiled and said, "Well, I was about your age when I started diving. I guess now is as good a time as any."

After that, the captain started taking her out on his boat with him. She watched the crew constantly and asked questions about their equipment. If her father thought that she would get tired of her diving fantasy, he was wrong. The more she learned, the more she wanted to dive.

One day, as she was leaning over the railing, gazing at the bubbles from the divers below, her father came up beside her and lit his pipe. He squinted into the sun and chewed on his pipe stem for a moment. "A barge went down on Lake Huron. It's stuck in sand fifty feet under. We're going to have to go out there tomorrow. Do you want to come?"

Frances nodded, trying to contain her excitement. Maybe she would finally get a chance to dive.

They sailed to the site of the sunken ship. That first day, the owner of the ship was onboard. Frances couldn't help but feel sorry for him as she stood beside the man. His mouth drooped with sadness. His shoulders slouched.

"You know, there is one article in that boat that I'd like to secure," he said. "There is a diamond ring in my cabin that I prize very highly. I wonder if your father would get it for me?"

"I'll get it for you myself!" Frances cried.

The man smiled sadly, but Frances was already thinking about plunging into the water the next morning.

Frances stood on deck and watched the divers prepare. The lake was almost as smooth as glass. It was a little chilly, but Frances knew the divers would be warm in their full-body suits.

Her father was about to hoist the diving helmet over the first young man's head when the diver suddenly clutched his stomach. He bent over, as if in pain. His diving partner and the captain came quickly to his aid and helped him sit down. Soon, they were peeling him out of the diving suit.

"Must be the curse," a voice growled behind her.

Frances felt a shiver down her spine. She turned her head to see a man with a bristly chin talking to another, clean-faced boy.

"Curse?" the boy asked.

"Aye. Some say the spirits of drowned pirates are down there, roiling up the water, trying to protect their booty."

Frances saw the boy gulp with fear, but she tossed her head. That man was just telling stories, and they weren't half as good as the captain's tales. Besides, Father was always talking about what a superstitious lot his men were. Spirits indeed. The diver probably just ate a rotten egg for breakfast.

"Well, I guess there won't be any diving today," the captain said, taking off his cap and wiping his forehead.

Frances stepped forward. "I'll go, Father. Please. I'm ready. I've been practicing for weeks now and the lake is so calm."

He studied her for a long moment. Frances saw a glimmer in his eye. His mouth turned up at the corner. "Alright then. Let's get you into this suit."

Frances squealed with delight. She wanted to throw her arms around the captain's neck, but she would have been embarrassed with all those men watching.

With her father's help, she wriggled into the diving suit. She stood still while he fitted the helmet over her head. The copper globe was heavy and she had to stand with her feet apart to brace herself. She could hear the grinding of bolts being screwed into place. Through the latticed window at the front of the helmet, she watched her father connect the oxygen tube to the helmet. Everyone was speaking, but the words were muted. Even though she was surrounded, she felt curiously alone. The added weight made her feel clumsy. She had to hold her father's arm as she walked.

The Captain had decided that Frances would go down with one of the most experienced divers on his ship to inspect the damage. He would be manning the compressed-air apparatus that would send oxygen to his daughter.

Through the window of her helmet, Frances saw a flicker of fear in her father's eyes. "Don't worry, Father. I'll be back safe and sound faster than you can say 'Jumpin' Jehosephat.'"

He nodded. "That's my girl."

She watched the elder diver begin climbing down the ladder hooked to the side of the boat. Then she followed him into the cold depths of the lake. She concentrated on each step, each breath, doing her best to stay calm.

The water felt tight around her legs. Then it was girdling her hips, hugging her chest. She hesitated just a moment before immersing her head. The water pressed on her from all sides. Looking up, she could see the murky figure of her father leaning over the side of the boat. Sunlight speared the water, illuminating particles. It was like peering into a soft, green cloud. A fish — a perch, maybe — swam past her mask. She wanted to stand there for a moment, just watching, but she remembered that there was work to be done.

She took another step down the ladder. Her breath came out in tiny puffs. She suddenly felt weak and tiny in comparison to the mighty lake. Still, she slowly continued her descent. At last, she reached the bottom rung and stepped onto the sand. She paused for a moment. There, just twenty feet away, was the sunken barge. The sight of it filled her with excitement and renewed her energy. Her companion moved toward it. She followed close behind.

He climbed over the wall of the ship and stretched out his hand to help her. She let him pull her overboard. When she saw the cabin, she stepped out ahead of him and pointed to her chest. She wanted to go in first.

The other diver nodded and waited at the entrance while she entered the cabin. She unlatched a light from her belt and beamed it into the room. She saw a chair and a fish and then, through the blur of water, the nightstand where the man had left his ring.

Just then, her head began to throb. She realized air was no

longer coming through the tube and into the helmet. She jerked on the rope around her waist, to alert those on deck that there was a problem. And she waited.

She remembered her father's words about the dangers of the deep. It felt as if her nose had started to bleed. She took a step forward and stumbled, dropping the light. Suddenly she was on her hands and knees. She turned her head, trying to spot the diver behind her, but the bulky helmet made this impossible. All she could see was a cloud of sediment swirling in her wake. She became very still, thinking to preserve her energy, and held her breath. Her lungs began to ache. Although it was dark and the lamp was out of reach, she began to see flashes of brilliance at the edge of her vision.

"It's true then," she thought, remembering the words of the grizzled sailor. "This ship is cursed."

Everything was going black. Her eyes closed. But then something large churned the water around her. With her last ounce of energy, she opened her eyes to see a huge tail covered with opalescent scales. The water fizzed and sparkled. She felt strong arms lifting her back onto her feet. She could see fingers fastening the light to her belt again. Air whooshed into her helmet and she took a deep breath. Just then, she saw a swirl of green hair, lips the color of coral. The mermaid fluttered her fingers and swam away.

Frances just stood there for a moment. When her lungs had stopped aching, she carefully approached the nightstand, pulled open the drawer, and snatched the box containing the diamond ring.

She turned slowly and found her companion diver there,

right behind her. He held out his hand and guided her back to the ladder.

A few minutes later, with the aid of the other diver, she crawled onto the deck of the ship, still clutching the box. A round of applause greeted her. Her father gathered her into a hug.

"We were so worried about you. Young Sam tripped over the air compressor, and the tube was knocked loose. What a terrible experience on your first dive!"

"I'm all right, Father," Frances said. Although she had never been so scared or exhausted, she felt that this was the happiest moment in her life.

The owner of the sunken ship bowed to her. "You are an incredible girl," he said. "For your courage, I would like to reward you with the diamond ring that you have retrieved."

Frances shook her head, remembering that the ring was the man's family treasure. "No, you keep it," she said. She had something better. She had her own story to tell that night in the rocker in front of the fire.

Lost in the Cow Pasture
By Marion Tickner

I love going to Grandma's during summer vacation. Grandpa lets me ride with him on the tractor. Grandma lets me help pick wild berries. But this year I hadn't counted on being here for a giggly girl's birthday party. I hope her brother Ben is there.

"Did you wash your hands, Henry?" Grandma asks.

That's the way it is with grandmas, always asking if I'd washed my hands or behind my ears. I expect next she'll be checking between my toes.

"Grandma, I'm only going to Ben's house," I tell her.

"You're going to Amanda's birthday party."

I want to go to a girl's party as much as I want to go to the dentist. No way of getting out of it either. I could pretend to be sick, but that would be no fun.

"Amanda is your cousin, and I expect you to be on your best behavior." Grandma hands me the present she'd wrapped. She gives me a swat on my rear and says, "Get along with you now."

I shuffle on down the road, hoping Amanda won't think I'd picked out that plastic jewelry. How long does a girl's birthday party last, anyway?

"I'll be just in time for cake if I walk slow enough," I tell myself. "Hope it's chocolate."

I've been to Ben's house before, so I know that his place is just around the corner from the cow pasture. I could cut cross-lots, but I might get lost. That sounds like a good idea, though. If I get lost, I won't have to show up at all. Amanda will never miss me, and Grandma will understand.

I come to the cow pasture and stop to look over the situation. What would be the best way to cross the fence? If I climb over, I might get caught on those little wire thingies. I'm not quite brave enough for that. Can I slide under? I can almost hear Grandpa say, "Make up your mind, boy."

"Okay, Grandpa," I tell myself, "I'm going for it."

I kneel down and push the present to the other side. Then I lie flat on my belly, close my eyes and wiggle my way underneath like a snake. Ouch! Something like a buzzy tingle attacks my back. An electric fence! Did I get electrocuted? Serves them right for making me go to that dumb old birthday party.

When will Grandpa find me? Grandma will cry. Mom and Dad too. I open my eyes. If this is heaven, it doesn't look any different than the cow pasture. Guess I didn't get electrocuted after all.

I grab the present, stand up and rub my back. What if there's a bull in here? Too late to think about that now. No way am I going under that fence again.

"Keep going," I say out loud to encourage myself.

Rats! Something feels soft and squishy under my foot. I take a peek. Yuck!

"Moo!" I look up into the brown eyes of an animal. I lose no time getting to the nearest tree and hauling myself up. Do bulls climb trees?

The animal looks up at me, moos again, and then wanders

off. I watch him go and make sure he's far away before I even think about getting down.

"Hey, Henry, what're you doing up there?" Ben's standing at the bottom of the tree, holding a brown paper lunch bag.

"Getting away from the bull."

"There's no bull in this pasture, nerd." He sits down and laughs.

"Did they send you to look for me?" I ask. "What've you got there?"

Ben opens the bag and looks inside. "No. I ran away from the party. They're playing some stupid game with blindfolds on."

"How in the world do I get down?" I want to see what's in that bag.

I reach my leg for a branch and drop down. The seat of my shorts catches on something and I hear the most awful ripping sound. The package reaches the ground before I do. And I land smack on top of the fancy pink bow, putting it out of commission forever. No way can I go to a party now. My shoes are a mess and my pants torn.

Ben dips his hand into the bag and brings out a big hunk of chocolate cake with gooey chocolate frosting. "I'll share with you."

My favorite. I sit down beside him and watch him break it into two pieces.

"Amanda's birthday cake," he explains. "I didn't stay for the party, so I brought some of it with me."

We sit here under the tree, the two of us, eating chocolate cake with nothing but our hands.

"At least I left all the candles," Ben says, as if that makes it all right.

"You're going to get it when you get home," I tell him, wiping my sticky, chocolaty hands down the sides of my shorts.

"So are you," he reminds me.

"At least we don't have to go to any dumb old party."

We both fall over, laughing.

Sea Rescue
By Patti Zelch

Patrick sat on the edge of the dock waiting for his grandfather. He dipped his toe into the warm water. Ripples circled away from his foot. Patrick leaned forward. He could see the turtle grass waving with the current on the bottom of the bay. It would be a good day for snorkeling, he thought. The clear water would make it easy to spot the bright-colored fish that darted around the reef.

Screech, Screech! Patrick looked up and saw an osprey. The large brown and white bird flew to the nest it had built over the summer. Patrick had watched the hawk fly away every morning. Later, it returned with twigs clamped tightly in its beak. Back and forth, back and forth it went, day after day. Now, the finished nest rested on top of the old telephone pole near the gravel driveway that led to Patrick's grandparent's house.

"Ready for a guy's day of fishing?" called Grandpa. He walked down the ramp carrying a trolling rod with a golden reel in one hand and his battered tackle box in the other. "We'll make the last day of your summer vacation a special one. Just the two of us out on the water."

Patrick laughed when he saw Grandpa. He was wearing a t-shirt with the words, "Fish to live, Live to fish!" embroidered across the front. His favorite fishing hat shaded his face. Hooks and lures, some with red and orange feathers, covered the wide

278

brim.

Patrick jumped into the boat. "All set. The bait bucket and cooler are right here."

Grandpa handed him the sleek black rod. Patrick placed it into the holder with the other rods. They stood like proud soldiers lined up for inspection — lines strung, hooks sharpened, waiting for their orders.

Grandpa climbed aboard. "Untie her," he called as he started the engine.

A whiff of gasoline filled Patrick's nostrils. He heard a gurgle and a sputter, and then the steady whine of the motor as the propeller began to whirl.

Nana stepped out on the back deck and waved. "Be sure to bring back dinner," she called, as the boat pulled away from the dock.

Patrick plopped into the seat next to Grandpa. They entered a channel that weaved through an area of trees and scrubs. The twisted roots of the mangroves whizzed by as the boat made its way toward the open water of the ocean.

"Want to take the wheel?" Grandpa asked when they cleared the cut. He slid over and made room for Patrick. "Keep the compass on 150 degrees. That'll get us to the deep water."

Out of the corner of his eye, Patrick spied a flash of silver-gray. He turned his head and saw two bottle-nosed dolphins racing beside the boat. Minutes later, they leaped over the white splash of waves in the wake that followed behind the boat's engine. The sun glistened off their shiny backs.

Grandpa busied himself getting the rods ready for fishing. "Slow her down," he said after baiting the last one.

Patrick nudged the throttle downward until the boat slowed to trolling speed.

Grandpa let each line out then stepped back to survey his work. "Looks good. Now we wait."

Morning gave way to afternoon. The scorching rays of the sun beat down on Patrick and Grandpa.

"We haven't even had a nibble," Patrick said. "And I'm hot!"

"Maybe that's why they call it fishing and not catching," Grandpa remarked. "Keep an eye out. We don't want to disappoint Nana."

Patrick sat in the bow of the boat. A soft mist sprayed his face. He ran his tongue over his lips and tasted salt. He wished he were back with Nana drinking a nice cold glass of homemade lemonade. Patrick glanced up and saw a frigate bird. It circled high above, looking for baitfish. Suddenly it dropped out of the sky and swooped across the top of the water. A few seconds later, it soared into the air. A fish dangled from its talons.

Patrick sighed. He's doing better than we are. Our fish box is empty. He lowered his eyes and stared into the endless water. Patrick liked the way the ocean changed colors. In some places it looked turquoise; in others, it was a mixture of deep blues and greens. In the distance two white balls caught his attention. He watched the balls dip under the water and then pop up again.

"Grandpa, look over there!"

Grandpa slowed the boat and looked in the direction Patrick pointed.

"They're trap markers, nothing special," he said.

"I know what they are. But look, they're moving. They go

under, then come up further away."

Grandpa watched the balls disappear. In a few minutes, they bobbed to the surface.

"That is strange," he said. "Let's take a look."

As they got closer, Patrick noticed a large shadow hovering in the water below the markers.

"There!" he cried. A sea turtle's head broke through the surface. A yellow cord was coiled around its neck.

Patrick watched the turtle gulp in air and then disappear below the surface dragging the balls with it. Minutes passed. Patrick heard splashing. He turned and saw the sea turtle.

Its flippers slapped at the water as it struggled to keep its head above the water line. The turtle's nostrils opened wide. It sucked in air. Then, its flippers stopped moving, and the turtle slipped into the blue darkness of the water.

Patrick peered into the ocean. "I think he's choking!"

"Not much we can do about it," said Grandpa. "That line needs to be cut from around his neck."

"We can't just leave him like that," Patrick said. "I can grab the end of the line if you get the boat close enough."

"It won't be easy," said Grandpa, edging the boat forward. "He'll dive when we get close."

Patrick nodded and then wrapped one hand around the side rail. He leaned out of the boat and reached with the other. His hand closed around the trailing end of the weathered cord. He lifted the line from the water. All of a sudden there was a tremendous tug. The slippery rope was wrenched from his hand.

Patrick leaned his head against the railing. Tears stung his eyes.

"Well, we gave it a try," Grandpa said. "Best head home. Nana's waiting."

Patrick sprung to his feet. "No! We've got to try again. I can do it. I'll hang on tight this time."

Grandpa smiled. "That's what I wanted to hear! Let's do it!"

Patrick leaned out of the boat again. "Hold tight, hold tight," he repeated to himself.

There it was! Patrick closed his hand around the rope, pulled it from the water and wrapped it around a cleat.

Bang, thump! The turtle's shell beat against the side of the boat. It thrashed and jerked, straining to get back into the water.

The turtle's head rocked from side to side. Its strong jaws snapped open and closed. With each move, the rope tightened around its neck.

Patrick looked down at the turtle. Two frightened eyes, as big as tennis balls, stared back at him.

"Don't be scared," he whispered. "We're here to help."

The turtle's eyes rolled closed, and it became still.

Grandpa slipped his fillet knife under the rope. The line was so snug against the turtle's neck that the sharp point nicked its skin. Patrick watched the trickle of blood drip into the water. The turtle didn't move. Grandpa yanked the knife upward and sliced through the rope. Free from the line, the turtle fell into the sea.

Patrick stared into the water. Where was it?

He stood up and scanned the surface. Nothing!

He ran to the other side of the boat. Lifting his hand to block the sunlight, he searched in every direction.

There it was! Patrick spied the turtle riding a wave off in the distance. It stretched its neck and looked right at Patrick before diving into the deep purple water.

"Do you think it knew we were here to help?"

"I'm sure it did," answered Grandpa. He untied the rope and began pulling it up. "Give me a hand, Patrick. There's something heavy on this line."

Together they hauled up the rope. Tied to the end was a cement block.

"Well, I'll be!" said Grandpa. "That's what was pulling him under." He turned toward Patrick. "That turtle would have drowned if you hadn't seen those markers." He reached out and hugged Patrick to his chest. "Good job, my boy."

Grandpa put the boat in gear and headed toward home. Patrick settled into his seat. He ran his fingers along the slick yellow rope lying in his lap. He looked back at the deep water one last time, then turned and watched the shoreline come into view. He was anxious to tell Nana all about his special day. He knew she wouldn't care about the empty fish box either.

Catch Of The Day!
By Doris Fisher

I grabbed my bait, my hook and pole
And skipped down to the fishing hole.

I bet I'll catch a fish to eat
As I sit here and cool my feet.

Perhaps a bass, perch, or trout —
I'll jerk my line and pull it out!

How proud and happy I will be
To boast and brag to family.

What's that? A nibble on my hook?
I stand and splash to take a look.

I lift my pole and see the line.
Yippee! A minnow suits me fine!

Our Mom, The Crazy Genius
By Tracey Miller

Outside my bedroom window, waves of heat squiggled up from the sidewalk. My brother Mack and I were perched right under the air conditioner vent, and we *still* couldn't get cooled off! Even when the ice cream truck came around the corner playing "Pop Goes the Weasel," we weren't interested. It was too hot to move!

"I'm gonna melt." Mack gasped as he slithered down on the bed.

"I know. I can't even think anymore." I groaned.

Mack kind of growled and slid further down the bed. Soon he'd be sprawled out in a puddle on the floor.

We heard Mom coming down the hallway. She was probably bringing us clean clothes to put away. I had tried to tell her that "summer vacation" meant just hanging out and enjoying the good life. She wasn't a big fan of my complaining, so, that day, I got to put up Mack's laundry, too. If she was bringing us more clean clothes, I could not handle it! It was too hot to do anything but lay here!

Sure enough, Mom had her hands full of laundry. "Hey! What are you guys doing?"

She was smiling. That was positive!

"It's too hot to do anything," Mack moaned and slid a little further down the bed.

Mom laughed. "Why don't you jump on the trampoline? It isn't *that* hot."

Was she batty? Had the heat gotten to her brain?

"Mom, the trampoline is outside." I reminded her.

"Right." She said.

"And, outside is HOT!" I said.

"And, we'd be JUMPING! *That* would make us hotter!" Mack

added.

Mom paused, thinking for a minute. She reached into the laundry basket and threw us our swim suits. "Put these on."

Mack and I stared at each other. She HAD lost her marbles. The public pool was closed all week because of some hole that had to be patched — right in the middle of summer! Talk about horrible timing!

"Where are we going to swim?" Mack and I asked at the same time.

Mom grinned wickedly. "Just get on your suits and meet me downstairs."

It was sad that Mom had lost her mind at such a young age. It must have been all that laundry folding. But when Mom said something, you did it. So Mack and I showed up downstairs wearing our swimming best. Mack even had our dinosaur floaty.

Mom snatched the floaty from Mack and tossed it on the couch. "Follow me, sad, hot children!"

We glumly followed our nutty mother. Did she think a pool had appeared in our backyard? Did she forget we lived thousands of miles from any ocean and at least a hundred from the nearest lake? The heat had zapped our Mom!

Outside, she patted the trampoline. "Hop on."

Mack and I looked at each other in surprise. That black trampoline was H-O-T! The sun beat down like a huge bonfire in the sky! Obediently, though, we tiptoed onto the mat.

Mom jogged over to the edge of the house. She bent over and began working on something we couldn't see. Mack gave me a sad look and made a "crazy" twirling motion next to his head.

Then we saw it. Mom's great, crazy plan. The water hose! She grinned like a mad scientist and stuck the sprinkler under the trampoline. She turned the water on full blast! It shot up and through the thick black trampoline mat. Everything got slick and wet. Mack and I realized the genius of Mom's plan! We were too old for skipping and jumping in the sprinkler, but this was something new! And it was great!

After a few hours of this chilly play, the neighbor kids began to peek over the fence. Mom said we could have our friends play, too, as long as we took turns jumping.

As the sky got dark and the crickets began their noisy summer song, Mom made us come inside. We both complained loudly. We were exhausted, but neither of us was ready to quit our new game.

"I promise you can do it all again tomorrow. Just wait for the sun to come up, okay?" Mom said, toweling off Mack's wet head.

"You know, Mom, we thought you were crazy from the heat. But you could be the biggest genius I know!" Mack told her.

Mom laughed and popped him with the towel. "It's a crazy kind of genius — kinda like Dr. Frankenstein. Just wait until you see what I've come up with for dinner!" She let out an evil laugh and, hesitantly, Mack and I followed our crazy genius Mom into the kitchen.

All the King's Horses
By Bevin Rolfs Spencer

Never before had Jo seen so much space. Sky and land went on forever without the interruption of even one single tree. Occasionally they'd pass a black and white metal sign announcing a town with a population of twelve. This just confirmed for her that no one wanted to live in such a wasteland of dust and wind.

"How could a whole town have fewer people in it than my entire fifth grade class?" Jo asked, picking out a post office and a few scattered trailers as their minivan zoomed through the postage stamp of a town.

"Welcome to Wyoming," said Jo's dad, grinning.

"Isn't it great?" Mom chimed in.

"Fishing!" yelled her little brother, Matt. He couldn't wait to get there.

Jo sighed. Why couldn't they go on a normal vacation? All the kids from her Pennsylvania town were headed to the beach. She pictured the popular kids lounging in the sun strategizing how they'd rule Woodburn Middle School next year. Not that she was popular. Jo closed her eyes. She dreaded middle school even more than Wyoming.

Dad left the highway for a bumpy, dusty dirt road that led to their final destination: Hawk Rider Ranch. After unpacking, Jo stood on the front porch of their cabin. She gazed out across the sagebrush, listening to her parents gush about the scenery.

"But what's there to do here?" she said, crossing her arms over her chest. The cabin had no television, no phone, no stereo, no nothing — nothing but beds and chairs.

"Plenty," said Dad. "There's riding, hiking, fishing and canoeing."

"Fishing!" whooped Matt again, racing around the cabin with his pole.

Jo rolled her eyes. She said, "I'm not interested in any of that."

But after the first full day of not being interested, Jo was lonely and bored.

The second day she sat on the back porch of the dining hall and watched a white camper van with Canadian license plates pull in. The doors flew open, and a family she hadn't met spilled out, shouting and running in all directions.

"Emily, help your brother!" yelled a short woman in Bermuda shorts, a tank top, and round, red sunglasses.

"I'm trying!" called a girl with straight blonde hair down to her waist. She grabbed a little boy under his arms and hoisted him off the ground while he kicked and squirmed.

Jo smiled to herself. She'd done that maneuver with Matt. At the same time, the girl struggled to drag a suitcase down the narrow, rocky path to the cabins.

"Hey, can I help?" Jo called, springing to her feet. Emily nodded and Jo took the suitcase and followed them down the hill to the cabin right next to theirs.

Emily dumped her brother in the doorway. He raced inside, and Emily held the door for Jo. "Thanks," she said. "I'm Emily. We went to Yellowstone for the weekend."

Jo liked her friendly blue eyes. "Jo."

"Boy, I'm glad you're here, eh? We got in a week ago, and there's been nobody to do anything with."

Jo perked up. "I know. It's so boring here."

"Hey, let's go exploring tomorrow!" Emily announced as if they'd been friends forever.

Jo hesitated. Exploring sounded like hiking, which sounded like she'd be participating in Hawk Rider Ranch activities.

Emily now held the cabin door closed against the raging tide of her brother who was threatening to make a run for it. He acted just like Matt.

Jo laughed. She'd never met Emily before, but somehow she knew right away they'd be friends.

After breakfast, Jo and Emily sat together on the sunny back porch of the dining hall. The smells of fried bacon and pancakes wafted out the kitchen door and mixed with horse flesh and leather as a group of riders walked by on a morning ride.

"So where should we go?" Jo asked as the riders disappeared down the hill.

Emily grinned. "Don't know. That'll be the adventure part." She stood up and squinted against the sun. "We better get some supplies first."

Together, they rounded up backpacks, water bottles and sunscreen, and the ranch cook, Anita, gave them some snacks to bring.

"Let's just head up that way," Emily offered, pointing in the opposite direction of the riders. And they set off to explore Hawk Rider Ranch.

The morning grew hotter, and Jo was glad to have brought water with them. The girls followed a horse trail up and away from the ranch, talking non-stop.

"I'll be going into grade 5, eh?" Emily said. Jo liked the funny way she had of saying things.

"I'll be in sixth," said Jo, as the familiar dread of starting middle school gripped her. She didn't feel ready or confident about tackling a whole new school.

When they stopped talking, the absolute stillness of the trail engulfed Jo. Sometimes the only sound was the wind as it spoke through the trees, bending the branches and making them moan. The quieter it became, the more Jo felt she was being watched.

Jo huffed and puffed as they chugged up the trail, and Emily's face was red.

"Woo Hoo!" Emily yelled. "Look at that view. Maybe we'll find some secret caves or old Indian teepee rings up here."

Emily's enthusiasm was catching. But after another hour of staring down at the ground looking for rings of rock or caves, they'd come up empty.

Jo was about to say that maybe they should head back, when she smacked into the back of Emily who had stopped dead.

"Shhh," Emily said and pointed. "Look."

"I don't..." Jo started. Then stopped. She did see something. And it was moving. She felt a rush of adrenaline. What was it?

"Let's go," whispered Emily. She veered off the trail, creeping slowly down the hill into thick trees and brush, following the dark shadow.

Stumbling, Jo tried to keep up. Her entire body was on alert, ready to turn and run if whatever they were following decided to turn on them. The tree limbs bent together, forming a canopy above the girls, spreading out bits of light like a patchwork quilt on the ground.

Out of breath and sweating, they caught the movement again. This time the shadow climbed up and around some rocks. Reaching the crest of the hill, they stepped out of the trees into an open meadow that spread wide before them, an oasis of green grass and flowers. And they weren't alone.

Jo and Emily looked at each other. They were amazed to discover that they had been following a horse. Six horses in all stared back at them, their dark eyes curious.

"Horses?" Jo was shocked.

"Do you think anyone knows they're here?" Emily couldn't keep the excitement out of her voice.

Jo didn't know anything about horses, but it seemed strange to find them in this remote meadow. The girls moved closer to them, then sat themselves and their packs down next to a fallen log.

They threw out some ideas about what they'd discovered. Were these wild horses? Wild, spirited, magical horses? Living in this secret valley, away from everyone? Emily pointed to a black horse that emerged from behind a tree. "He's got a bridle on, but the reins have snapped off."

Jo saw what Emily was pointing to. Whatever had happened to that horse, he'd escaped from somewhere. "Maybe they all escaped together."

"And ended up here," said Emily, "to form a kingdom all their own." Emily's eyes got big as she stared off into the distance. "I think we were meant to find this place, Jo. I think they need us."

Jo felt the magic seep into her skin. It DID feel like they were meant to be there.

Emily suddenly jumped up off the log, hands on hips. "They need us to protect their secret valley from invaders. Like knights!"

"Except without the armor," said Jo. "Protectors of a secret kingdom of horses."

Jo had never had a secret place before — a place away from her family and far, far away from home. She looked at Emily, an idea forming as she spoke. "Here, the horses rule." Emily nodded, her eyes bright. Jo said, "But we are all-powerful and say who can enter and who can't."

Emily said the kingdom needed a name. She came up with two French words: *Monde Cheval*. The world of horse.

The next day Emily and Jo knighted each other in a special ceremony. They picked wild flowers from the meadow and tied the stems together, making a wreath for their heads. Jo found a long branch they called the knighting stick, which they used to tap each other's shoulders, signifying them as knights.

"We swear allegiance to Monde Cheval, from this day forward," they recited.

Afterwards, they celebrated their knighthood with molasses cookies they'd brought from the ranch and a thermos of lemonade.

Every morning the girls shrugged off ranch activities in order to get an early start to Monde Cheval. No one seemed to notice that they had developed an avid interest in hiking. Emily marked the turn-off to Monde Cheval with a purple hair ribbon, making it easier to find.

Soon the horses got used to their presence, especially since they brought them snacks like apples and carrots. Emily showed Jo how to feed them with an open palm. They watched and studied the rulers of the kingdom and soon gave out names.

The large, black horse with the remains of a bridle was King Brutus. He kept a lot to himself, but was often seen in the company of a female horse with an extraordinarily long, red mane.

"That's Queen Lady Bird," Emily announced one day. "She's so delicate looking, like a bird."

The horses paired off or worked their way around the meadow as a group, eating grass, nosing each other, or standing in the shade of a tree. Emily and Jo worked up names for a royal family, including Princess Pegasus for a small, white horse, and Prince Blaze for the brown horse that was always near her. Jo had never been around horses before and was amazed at how easily she could now approach them and stroke their noses and necks.

Once, in the early morning, they watched Princess Pegasus, Prince Blaze and a young horse they'd named Cap, because of the small fringe of hair between his ears that looked like a hat, buck and kick at the air as if they were playing a game.

Emily and Jo would survey their antics from atop a nearby hill, making up stories about the history of the kingdom. They decided that it was a refuge for all horses, especially those with broken souls, and that all who were lost could belong there. But the kingdom was to remain a secret from the human world. Only Jo and Emily were allowed in.

To Jo, in the dazzling light of the kingdom, anything felt possible. She was a knight, and nothing else — like gossip or sixth grade — mattered in Monde Cheval. It seemed like nothing could disrupt the serenity of their secret world.

But they were wrong.

As the second week began, Emily and Jo arrived at Monde Cheval to find Princess Pegasus had come up lame. She put no weight on her left back foot. Emily let out a little cry of alarm.

"Maybe she hurt herself while she was playing with Blaze the other day," Jo suggested, remembering how the horses had run and kicked at one another.

Emily winced, gingerly touching Pegasus' swollen ankle. "Do you think she's broken it?"

Jo shrugged. She had no idea. "Maybe it's just a sprain. Should we wrap it up like you would for a person?"

That sounded like the best idea they had. Carefully, with Jo talking quietly into Pegasus' ear, Emily used an extra shirt she had to bind up the horse's ankle as best she could. But by the next day, it was obvious Pegasus was in pain. She wasn't moving or eating.

The brave knights of Monde Cheval felt helpless. Their magical world began to fade as they realized what they had to do. Emily's eyes filled with tears. "We have to help her."

But help meant telling. Help meant revealing Monde Cheval and the end of their kingdom of horses. Jo didn't want their magical world to end, even if it was pretend. King Brutus seemed to sense their decision as he pranced around the perimeter of the meadow. His great head shook, and they could hear his whinnying as the girls headed down the trail, back to Hawk Rider Ranch.

At first Mr. Sawyer, the ranch manager, didn't believe them. But as they began to describe the horses, his face changed. "That's my lost herd you're describin'," he said.

Jo and Emily were shocked.

Then Emily said, "It makes perfect sense. King Brutus broke his reins when he tore the hitching rail and escaped. We just didn't know he'd escaped from here!"

That's when Mr. Sawyer called Wayne. "He's a famous wrangler from Dimwitty, Wyoming," he told the girls.

The girls took in Wayne's pressed wrangler jeans and well-worn boots and shirt. He didn't look all that famous or impressive to Jo.

"Never met a horse he couldn't track," said Mr. Sawyer, smiling. "And I need them horses back. Got a big crowd comin' in next week."

Wayne stared down at Jo and Emily, unsmiling.

"One of the horses is hurt," Emily explained. "It looks like it's her ankle. She won't eat or drink."

The girls tried to explain to Wayne where to find them.

Mr. Sawyer frowned. "No place like that up there. You girls makin' this up?"

"No," they said.

But Wayne couldn't find it. The girls waited anxiously for his return with the horses of the kingdom, but he came back alone for two straight days. And Mr. Sawyer grew anxious.

"You'll just have to take the girls with ya," he told Wayne, who frowned deeply at this.

"Emily's ridden before. You can put a lead rope on Jo's horse." Mr. Saywer scratched his head. "I need them horses back, Wayne."

And this was how Jo and Emily found themselves perched atop two horses, getting set to wrangle with Wayne. Jo rode a sure-footed mare named Buttermilk, and Emily was on an opinionated pony named Trojan. Jo's stomach felt tight as they set off up the trail, but after being around the horses at Monde Cheval, she didn't feel as afraid as she might have. Wayne still attached a harness and lead rope to Buttermilk as an extra precaution.

The trail to Monde Cheval looked different to Jo on horseback. She felt the closeness of the pine trees all around her, the cool scent of their needles rolling over her like sea spray.

When they finally reached the meadow, Jo felt like a traitor. The horses of Monde Cheval whinnied at them, and the horses they rode called back, in recognition. They dismounted and led their horses over to where Pegasus still stood, under a tree.

Wayne examined her leg. He scratched under his hat. "I'll have to bring a vet up to her," he said, looking around. "We'll take as many back as we can."

"Blaze will stay with her," said Jo. "I don't think he'll leave her."

Wayne looked at her with surprise, but said nothing.

When they got back on their horses, Wayne explained what was going to happen. "Should be slow and easy going," said Wayne. "We'll just encourage 'em on down the trail." Emily and Jo both gripped their horses a little tighter.

Wayne expertly trotted his mount around to where Lady Bird and Brutus stood under a tree. He twirled a rope in the air and called "Yip! Yip!" Lady Bird moved forward, and Jo recognized Cap as he darted out, his back legs kicking. Soon the horses formed a single line and headed up and out of the meadow to the trail that would take them back to Hawk Rider Ranch.

Buttermilk navigated the trail with her head down as Jo watched the horses scurry down the switchbacks, their shoes clanking against the rocks. Soon, the narrow trail of the woods opened up onto a flat area filled with sage brush. Out of nowhere, King Brutus erupted from the trees, his body crashing through the brush. He ran to the front of the line and began to lead the horses in the wrong direction — away from the ranch.

"Blast it!" Wayne yelled. "Hold on!" he called to Jo, and suddenly they were running too. Jo was almost blasted out of her saddle as Buttermilk struggled to keep up with Wayne's horse. She caught hold of the saddle horn and Buttermilk's mane, bending her knees and holding on tight! Emily bounced along behind them.

Wayne pulled up alongside Brutus and tried to turn him. Brutus picked up speed. Then a shot rang out. Wayne reached down and grabbed his bull whip, swirling it over his head and snapping it with a loud CRACK! Alarmed, Jo let out a shriek. With the snap of his wrist, he cracked the whip again, and the group of horses turned as one.

All of them were at a dead run gallop now. Dust and dirt flew in the air as the horses ran for home. Jo was full of electric energy, like someone had plugged her finger into a socket. Feeling the horse run free beneath her, with the scenery whizzing past, was exhilarating and scary at the same time. She wondered if this was how it felt to fly.

Emily whooped and hollered behind her, letting out a "Yee Haw!" as the horses climbed the last hill before plunging down the trail back to the corral.

With another crack of the whip, Wayne forced Brutus to make the last turn into the corral. He ordered Emily to stand just outside the gate as Jo and Buttermilk skidded to a halt in front of the tack shed.

Breathing hard, Jo might as well have been on a roller coaster ride. Looking at the horses now, she saw them for the animals they were. King Brutus and Queen Lady Bird blew hard through their noses, the sides of their bellies heaving from the run.

Wayne secured the horses in the corral. His face was red and sweaty, with a line of dirt just below his hat.

"You girls okay?" he asked.

Jo and Emily looked at each other.

"That was so cool, eh?" Emily said. Despite having had to give up Monde Cheval, they had to admit that wrangling had been the time of their lives.

The two weeks at Hawk Rider Ranch had flown by, and now Emily and Jo faced each other in the parking lot to say their good-byes.

The horses of Monde Cheval were back at the ranch, but Jo and Emily had decided that was the reason they had found it to begin with. "You had to be worthy of heart and mind to enter there," said Emily, "and we were. They never would have found Pegasus without us."

Jo hugged Emily. She had shared more with Emily in that short time than with friends she had known for years.

"We'll write," said Emily. "And come back next year."

Yes, thought Jo, that was certain. Jo couldn't imagine not coming back now. She had to check on Princess Pegasus and King Brutus, along with the rest of the royal family. And she was determined to become an expert rider, maybe even wrangle herself one day.

Wayne had taken a vet up to treat Pegasus. It would take awhile for her to recover from her sprain, but she would be all right. Prince Blaze had stayed with her, just as Jo had predicted.

"We'll never forget Monde Cheval," Emily yelled from the window of their camper as they pulled away.

Jo waved until her arm hurt. No, they would never forget their secret kingdom of horses, she thought as she climbed into the mini van next to her brother Matt. Jo felt ready to face home, and sixth grade. She was a knight, after all. A knight not without armor, she decided. It was just invisible.

Fish Rescue!

By Amy Oriani

"Hey," my cousin Alex shouted. "There are fish down here!"

He was at the bottom of a dry waterfall trail, and I could barely see him through all the branches and rocks.

"Fish?" I called back from the top of the earthen dam. "How could fish get down there? That's crazy!"

But I went to see anyway. I followed the dry creek bed and found Alex standing by a small pool of water. And he was right — there *were* fish in there! There must have been about twenty, including a giant catfish.

"They must have washed over the dam after the storm yesterday," I said. "And now they're trapped."

"Come on," said Alex. "We have to save them!"

"And quick," I said. "The water's already warm — we have to get them out before they cook!"

We didn't have any fishing nets, so we grabbed some buckets and plastic bags from the cabin and raced back to the little fish pond.

We poked some holes in the bags and dragged them through the water, hoping to scoop up some fish. No luck.

The bucket worked better. When we laid it on its side, sometimes a fish would swim right in! The tricky part was tipping the bucket right-side-up without letting the fish escape. We lost a couple, and then — "Got one!" Alex yelled.

A little sunfish was swimming in circles at the bottom of the bucket. "Quick, get him back into the lake," I cried. We scrambled back up the rocks, water sloshing everywhere. At the lake, we tipped the bucket over and dumped the fish out. He swam away with a flick of his tail.

"Come on, let's get some more!" Alex said.

"You keep trying with the bucket," I said. "I can catch them with my bare hands."

"Oh, right," my cousin scoffed.

I waded into the center of the pool and stood very still until all the mud had settled. I pretended I was just another rock, and after a while the fish forgot I was there and began to swim around my feet.

A fish came closer. I leaned down, my hands close to the water... and grabbed. "Rats, missed it!" I grumbled.

"See — told you," Alex said.

I waited some more. The big catfish swam by. "Oh, please," I breathed. I put my hands in the water and held them very still. The catfish nosed around the dirt by my hands, and I grabbed it! "Got him!" I yelled. "Bring the bucket!"

My cousin raced over. "Hey, you did it!" he said, impressed.

The catfish was so big it couldn't even straighten out in the bucket. His skin was covered with scars, probably from his bumpy trip down the waterfall. "Come on, big guy," I said to the fish. "Let's get you back where you belong."

It was a hard climb back up the rocks with the heavy fish flopping around in the bucket. When we tipped him in, he seemed glad to be back in the cool lake instead of that hot little puddle.

He swam close to us for a while, then headed out into deeper water. "Bye," we called.

"OK, let's get the rest," I said.

Down we went, to finish the job. Between the bucket and my hands, we caught all the fish. We got pretty good at planting the bucket at one end, then walking slowly toward it, chasing the fish right into its mouth. We could catch two or three at a time that way.

By the time the last fish was caught, it was getting dark. We dumped the last bucketful into the lake just as the sun was going down.

"Whew!" said Alex. "Who knew summer vacations could be so much work?"

"No kidding," I said. "But come over here." I was walking through the long grass on top of the dam, out where it was dark. "Looks like we get a reward for all that work."

"Reward?" asked Alex, catching up with me. "What kind?"

"Look down there," I said.

Millions of twinkling dots were appearing in the grass. It looked like someone had turned on Christmas lights in the field. "Lightning bugs!" Alex yelled.

They were everywhere. It was beautiful. Then I ducked as a dark shape flew low over my head.

"And bats!" I called.

Hundreds of bats were flying out of the pine forest, darting right over our heads as they headed to the lake to skim the surface for bugs.

The two of us stood there, watching the show. The lightning bugs were making constellations in the grass; bats were squeaking overhead; and below the calm lake surface, our fish were enjoying their newfound freedom.

It was the best reward we could have asked for.

Hummingbird Song
By Kristy Dempsey

Humming, drumming, whirring, zip
Flitter-flutter, flower-sip
Trilling whisper, trembling wings
Spritely, whizzing buzz that rings
Music written on the air
Floating here, then darting there
Of all the songs this small bird sings
Its sweetest song is sung by wings.

Low Tide

By Katharine Folkes

"Hot! Hot! Hot!" Meg yelped. She was in such a hurry to get to the beach, she'd forgotten her shoes.

She and her younger sister, Patsy climbed up the path through the high sand dunes at the end of the street. The hot white sand with waving sea oats, burned Meg's winter-tender feet.

"I can't wait 'til supper!" Patsy, said, trudging through the loose sand, beside her. She'd remembered her shoes.

"Well, we've got to catch them first!" Meg answered, leaping down the dune.

It was the summer of 1950, their first day at the beach, and they were going crabbing.

The two sisters carried string, chicken necks, wire traps and a big plastic bucket.

They could hear the gentle lapping of the waves as the tide slowly inched out to sea. It was the perfect time to catch blue crabs.

"Hello, beach! We're back!" Meg yelled.

Patsy danced around in circles, traps and string whirling through the air.

"This looks like a good spot," Meg said.

Dumping their load, the girls pushed sturdy sticks with string attached, into the wet sand a few feet apart. They tied a chicken neck to the other end of each string and fastened

them to the inside of the traps. Walking down to the water, they placed the traps about a foot deep, so they could see when they caught something. Then they washed the chicken smell off their hands.

While they waited, they wandered down the beach and watched the hermit crabs move about in the small tide pools. Patsy squatted down to play with them and let them crawl into her hand. Meg sat beside her, staring out at the Atlantic, day-dreaming and enjoying the smell of Gabby's lotion she'd slathered all over herself. It was one of her favorite smells.

After awhile they went back to check the traps.

"Look! There's three in this one!" Patsy cried. They ran to look in the others. There were two more in another one. They pulled the traps up out of the water. Getting the crabs into the bucket was never easy. The blue crustaceans grabbed hold of the wire trap with their claws, and the girls had to shake and shake and bang the trap on the side of the bucket to make them turn loose.

Patsy and Meg were trying to make the last crab let go when it fell out right on Meg's foot. Before it could bite her toe, Meg reached a practiced hand down, grabbed the crab behind his claws, and quickly dropped it into the bucket.

"Almost got me!" she said, laughing.

After a couple of hours the bucket was full. The crabs' claws made a clicking sound as they tried to climb out. Carrying it together, the girls decided to take a short detour home, around the end of the island through the shallows. As Meg and Patsy sloshed along, they saw something large and round on the bottom in front of them.

"It's a horseshoe crab!" Patsy cried, excitedly. They put their bucket down, and Patsy handed her traps to Meg. Patsy picked up the huge thing — she never seemed to be afraid of sea creatures — being very careful to keep its long stinger angled away from them. Turning it over, she saw the female's eggs, so she gently put it back in the water.

Horseshoe crabs probably hadn't changed the way they looked in a million years, Meg thought, walking up the road toward home.

"Oh, how wonderful!" their mom exclaimed, as the sisters came into the back yard, and she saw how many they'd caught. "Let's get them in the pot!"

After the crabs had been cooked, Mom, Meg and Patsy stood at the kitchen sink.

"Cleaning these crabs is my least favorite part!" Patsy said, making a face, "but I sure do like eating them."

"Wish we hadn't caught so many!" Meg said. "We did too good a job."

Mom laughed. "Bet we don't have any left over!"

Later, after homemade peach ice cream, the girls collapsed together in the big Pauley's Island hammock hung between two oaks. Music from their parents' Victrola brought the voice of Bing Crosby singing "Dear Hearts and Gentle People."

"Boy, I'm about to pop!" Patsy said, sighing contentedly.

Meg had one foot dangling, pushing them back and forth. "Me too," she echoed, looking up at the stars. She was thinking of a poem she could write about today. Maybe she'd tell about a hermit crab that had outgrown its shell, or a blue crab that was determined not to get caught.

"Let's tell ghost stories!" Patsy said. "I bet I can scare you!"

"Bet you can't," answered Meg.

After a while they just lay there listening to the cicadas compete with the sound of the waves. Finally, they poured themselves out of the hammock and went to put their shovels and buckets by the back door, ready for tomorrow.

They were going clam digging at low tide.

Rocky Road
By Darlina Chambers

"I watched the vid of your bedroom," I said. "You painted every wall a different color?"

"Oh, Alyah, not every wall," Chandra said, "two are red. The green and orange walls are supposed to brighten things up." Chandra settled into a transmitter chair in her colorful room. She'd made the changes since I had moved to Oklahoma Skybase a week earlier.

"They do," I said. "Especially with the golden dragonflies and flowers. It's way out cool!" Running my fingers through my hair, I flipped a curl over my shoulder and waited. Chandra moved her face closer to the camera, a habit she had when transmitting messages. I looked into her nostrils as they grew bigger on the screen.

"I saw your vid." The nostrils backed away, showing Chandra's face. "The round walls in your bedroom are pretty. Are they steel?"

"Aluminum. It's lighter."

"And your backyard is awesome." Chandra leaned back in her chair.

"Yeah, since we built our house above Oklahoma City, we have to choose plants the sun won't fry. Mom said that at six thousand feet above the Earth's surface we're at about the same elevation as you are in Colorado Springs, but we're closer to the equator." I reached for the candy dish and pulled out a strawberry Zonka Bar, my favorite.

"Your mom always plants nice gardens." Chandra lifted a cup from her chair arm. No telling what she drank — probably one of her famous concoctions. "Even with robotic landscaping, my mom has a brown thumb. It's embarrassing. All those people flying over our backyard only see brown spots and tangled vines. They probably check their GPS units to make sure they're not flying over the Sahara Desert."

"Maybe we can put a pond in it," I said.

Nostrils again.

"Back away, would you?" I asked.

"Oops, sorry." She sat back and adjusted the camera, making her whole body visible. "I don't know about you, but none of my fifth grade teachers taught me anything about building ponds."

"Next week during summer break, I could fly to Colorado Springs. I'll e-mail my mom's landscaping program to you. It has plans for cool ponds, and the instructions are super simple. We'd have one done in a snap."

"Are you sure we can do it?" she asked.

I set my Q82 helicopter down on Chandra's concrete heliport. Ponytail swinging, she ran from the house and threw her arms around me. We'd dressed the same — tank tops, shorts and sandals. No surprise there.

"Took you long enough, Alyah girl," she said. "I thought you left an hour ago."

"You know my mom. She programmed my helicopter for the slowest and safest route. I'm lucky I didn't get here sometime next year." I grabbed my suitcase. Arm in arm we walked into the house.

After quick hellos to Chandra's parents, she and I walked out to the plastic deck in her backyard. Everywhere else, bushes and grass had started turning green weeks earlier. Here, the brown grass and dead shrubs clued me in to how bad Chandra's yard would look this summer. What'd I gotten myself into?

"Let's get this job started," I said, acting like I knew what I was doing.

Chandra pushed a button on the picnic table. A twelve-inch flat screen popped up. Chairs swiveled out from the center, looking too decrepit to hold anyone.

Ydan, Chandra's younger brother, banged his arms on the kitchen door, dragging out two chairs. "Here Alyah. Make yourself comfortable."

Hmm, I thought. He's not turning out too badly. It would help if he stood straight and his clothes didn't hang so loose, though. "Thanks."

"Get lost, scab face!" Chandra grabbed at a chair.

"Here maggot." He shoved it toward her then stomped off.

"My brother, the creep. You wanna take him home?"

"No way! My little sister's more than enough." I pulled up the computer file I'd e-mailed and navigated through the landscaping program's initial screens.

"Stop there." Chandra pointed. "Click the budget icon."

I did. A screen opened with a chart that listed yard things — rocks, trees, bushes, flowers. The dollar amounts sat empty.

"Mom said we can spend eight thousand dollars on our 'little pond.'"

I gasped. "She can't be serious. I'll bet even little ponds cost more than that. And we have to cover a big area."

Chandra planted her elbows on the table and rested her chin on clasped hands. "She's serious. Eight thousand tops. I knew we couldn't do this."

"It'll be enough. We'll put some prices in here and make it be enough. Program, input costs, one thousand for rocks." I turned to Chandra. "Rocks are probably cheap."

"Why would anyone pay for rocks when they're lying all over the place?"

"You know, you're right." I stood and walked to the side of the deck. I leaned over the rail and looked around the corner at rock-covered hills. "Palmer Park is across the street. There're more than enough rocks there for thousands of ponds. I wonder why no one has ever thought about using them." I looked back at Chandra.

"Well, they're kind of white looking. Maybe people don't like white rocks."

"I don't have a problem with them. Do you?" I walked back to the chair and sat, crossing my legs.

She shook her head.

"Good. Zero dollars for rocks. That leaves us with eight thousand dollars to spend on a pond liner, pump, trees, bushes, flowers, and two goldfish — one for you and one for me. Let's finish the budget after we select the best pond." I opened the *Ponds* screen.

"Oh, look," Chandra said. "There's one that's shaped like Florida where my grandparents live. I'd like that one, so I can think about them when I see it."

"I don't know," I said, "it looks astronomically big."

We walked to the edge of the deck. Chandra held her dad's laser over the side and measured the space below for the pond. Fifteen feet by four feet. It would fit perfectly.

Back at the computer, Chandra picked out the plants, and I dragged them around the virtual pond. I typed dollar amounts into each cell in the budget spreadsheet, saved and then exited the page. We filled out an order form, using her mother's credit information, and sent it to Another World Nursery.

With our supplies coming the next day, we had no time to waste getting started. Early June weather in Colorado Springs might be cold enough to snow or hot enough to roast hotdogs over a heliport's concrete. This afternoon was hotdog hot.

I should've kept my big mouth shut about building a pond during summer break. Who knew a fifteen by four foot Florida hole would take us so long to dig? I mean, Chandra's robodiggers had spent an hour already and still had half the pond to go. We sat there watching, bored beyond book facts.

"How many rocks do you think we'll need?" I asked, watered-down Jupiter Juice in hand.

"Pull up that diagram on the computer again, the one with the plants already in place." Chandra scooted her chair out of the sun, where she'd been tanning her short legs. "Yeah, that's the one. Drag the rocks over, using different shapes and sizes."

Using the curser, I moved rocks to get a good balance around the pond. The same minute we finished, the robodiggers flew toward the shed. The doors unsealed, and the robots darted inside.

"Looks like we're done digging," I said. "Let's get the rocks first thing in the morning."

"Yeah. I've had enough hard work for one day."

The sun rose over a cloudless sky, warming the calm morning air. We climbed into Q82's front cabin. Airlocks tight, I touched the ignite button. The engine started. Propellers whirled, lifting the chopper into the air.

In less than a minute, we flew over Palmer Park, scanning for an outcrop of rocks big enough so that we'd only have to make one stop.

"There," Chandra said. "In front... under our feet now."

I landed on the heap. We hopped out and looked around.

"These are perfect," Chandra said.

"Excellent. Let's load them up." I looked at my wrist computer. "Open Chandra's pond program. Final screen. Quantify rocks by size."

"Fifty-six small, thirty-two medium, ten large and three giant," the computer said.

"Q82," I said. "Release robobirds."

A panel on the chopper's side unsealed. Chandra and I pointed at good rocks, and robobirds swooped down, picked them up and loaded them into their compartment. After fifteen minutes, we had our rocks onboard.

Whir, whir, whir. Circling propellers drew my attention. A pea green chopper hovered above us. A Park Ranger, probably flying his morning rounds. Wind from the landing helicopter whipped my hair, and I felt the splatter of gravel eat at my bare legs.

The ranger jumped out and walked toward us. "Morning ladies. I see you've gathered a good collection of rocks."

"Yes sir." I pointed. "Chandra lives across the street, and we're building a pond in her back yard." Whirring robobirds seemed to grow louder, hovering around us as we waited for the ranger to move on.

"Sounds like an ambitious project."

The ranger wiped his nose on the back of his shirtsleeve. I hadn't noticed any snot on his sour face.

"I'm sorry to have to tell you this," he wiped his nose again, "but you're going to have to get your rocks somewhere else. Regulations state that no one can remove anything from the park. That includes animals, vegetation and ore."

"We're not taking that many," I explained. "One hundred and one to be exact. And most of those are very small."

"What if everyone who came to the park took one rock?" the man asked. "We get millions of visitors in here each year. It wouldn't take long before there'd be nothing left."

I looked at Chandra. She shied away, her cheeks pink with embarrassment.

"But we already spent our budget," I said. "Can't you make an exception, just this once?"

"No exceptions. You have to put them back."

I slumped my shoulders, trying to look desperate. "But we really, really need them."

He looked at me with a tight face, like Dad when he starts to get mad. "If you don't, I'll have to take you to jail." He pointed at Q82. "Now, tell the chopper to reverse the robobird's sequence and return the rocks."

No one had to say *jail* to me twice. Or to Chandra. She looked like she might wet herself.

I climbed into Q82. "I'm sorry."

Chandra climbed in bedside me. "What're we going to do?"

I wished I knew.

"I've got it!" I snapped my fingers as Q82 landed on Chandra's helipad. "All we have to do is change our order. We'll buy a smaller pond liner, maybe Oklahoma. It's shaped like a pan and you'll always think of me when you see it." I smiled.

Chandra shook her head.

Hmm, what else? "Cutting the number of plants and other stuff in half will give us enough money to *buy* the rocks. Okay?"

"But we already have that big hole dug." Chandra whined. "That was a ton of work."

"The robodiggers will refill it. We'll lose some time. But that's all." I jumped out of Q82.

"Do you think the pond will still be big enough to see when flying over the yard?" Chandra's voice still carried a small whine.

"Everyone will see it. I swear!"

Chandra paused on the front porch. "I don't know, Alyah. I've never even been to Oklahoma."

While Chandra filled two glasses with Lilac Lemonade, I went to the back deck. Suddenly, a message hologram appeared in front of my face:

Ms. Chandra Martin,
　　　　Thank you for your order. Everything is in perfect

condition. This morning's delivery completes our no return/no refund transaction.

Sincerely,

Mr. Sloan Davies

Another World Nursery

I looked over the deck railing. Below sat piles of plants, mulch and a Florida pond liner. "No return? No refund? No way!" I closed my eyes, then opened them. The message still floated in front of me. "Go away!" It disappeared seconds before Chandra stepped onto the deck.

"Here, let me help you with that." I grabbed my glass and the plate of chocolate chip cookies Chandra carried on a tray. "You know I was thinking. I looked at the size of your yard again and Oklahoma is going to be much too small." Almost a lie, but not.

I bit off a chunk of cookie and took a sip of lemonade. Ugh! Sweet and sour mix. My tongue didn't like it, but I kept from making a sour face like the Park Ranger.

"You're good at making creative drinks and snacks with your food processor. Great lemonade! Cookies too." I watched for her response to my sell job. She listened as she set the tray on the table. "Just right for a hot day." Now for the zinger. "How about we set up a lemonade stand like we did last summer? We can *earn* the money for our rocks."

"Let's just put more plants around the pond. That would be easier. Besides, Oklahoma is okay. Isn't that what you said before you moved?" she asked a little meanly.

This wasn't the time to argue about why I'd moved. Dad's helicopter company had transferred him. Did she actually think

I liked being away from her? Why did she think I was really here? It certainly wasn't to build a stupid pond. "I'd prefer that you come to Oklahoma when you miss me, not stare at some old pond. Besides, how hard can selling cookies and lemonade be?"

"We were little kids last year," Chandra said. She stuffed a cookie in her mouth. Crumbs tumbled down her chin. "Besides, our moms bought most of them."

"No way! The neighbors loved them. And with Academy Boulevard's air traffic merging onto Maizeland Road now, I think lots of people will stop. We'll make up exotic names for the treats and paint crazy signs to make everyone curious. Come on, it'll be fun."

Chandra's eyes grew wider. I almost had her.

"Can't you just see Florida over the rail?" I asked. "I mean, come here. I want to show you something." I grabbed Chandra's arm and pulled. "Look, it's already waiting!"

Robolifters and diggers put the pond liner and plants into place. The fish swam in a container under the deck's shade. I kept them out the work program, leaving Chandra with the honor of emptying them into the finished pond later. She sat now with her legs propped up on the table, tapping into her wrist computer.

"Okay," I said. "What are the snack's names?"

"I think we should sell three drinks. I'll make Martian Melonade with watermelon and lemons, Orion Orange Slush with oranges, ice and cream and Plasma Punch with lemon lime soda and cherry juice."

"Sounds great!" I said. "And cookies? How about Chocolate

Stinkbugs?"

Chandra wrinkled her nose. "You can never go wrong with good old fashioned Chocolate Chip."

"Alright," I said, disappointed that Chandra got to have all the fun naming things. "Hey, do you have any of that paint from your bedroom left over? We can use it to make signs."

"What are you making signs for?" Ydan asked as he stepped onto the deck.

"Why are you always hunching over us?" Chandra asked. "Can't you tell Alyah's not interested in a slouch like you?"

I glanced at Ydan's face, which was as red as a laser beam.

Ydan hit Chandra's shoulder. "You're a jerk. I don't care about your stupid pond anyway." He stomped off. The deck rattled under his size ten sneakers.

"You know, we could probably use his help," I said.

Chandra glanced at me. "I'd rather do without rocks than have to babysit him."

"Okay, then. Where's the paint?"

It was another hot day, with an afternoon forecasted to be in the nineties. Good! Heat, sweat and mild sunstroke meant more customers. Chandra carried an armful of boxes to the front yard and dropped them at my feet. I pushed a button on the side panel of a large box. The sides opened, four legs extended, and a table flipped upright on the grass. Small boxes jackknifed into chairs, and, in no time, we'd set up our stand. I taped a white paper tablecloth, stamped with dragonflies and flowers, onto the table.

On the grass I nailed flat banners for overhead traffic while Chandra pounded in vertical signs for people who drove cars, bikes and motor scooters. We listed drinks at nine dollars a glass and cookies at seven dollars each. Our profit would be slim, so I raced back into the house and grabbed cups and napkins, but skipped the paper plates.

Chandra followed me out and set two pitchers on the table. One held an orange liquid, the other red. Then she carried out a plate of cookies and the pitcher with melonade. We sat together and waited for customers.

By 2:00, we'd sold two pitchers of punch, four of orange slushes, one and a half of melonade, and had used enough ice to cover the North Pole. The chocolate chips melted in our cookies and reflected the sun like pools of dark mud. They still tasted delicious. But try telling that to would be customers. The temperature had climbed so high, that even Chandra's mom had stopped coming out to buy another cookie or to try another drink.

"How cheap did you say rocks are?" Chandra asked.

"With our profit so far," I said, "we can buy half of what we need."

"We haven't had a customer in over twenty minutes, and it's getting hotter," Chandra complained. "Let's call it good at half the rocks. No one will ever know but us, and I'm willing to let it slide."

The front door banged shut. I looked back. Ydan, dressed in a red and white uniform and jetpack, jumped down the steps.

"Hey," I yelled. "Where you going?"

"Air-soccer tournament." He stood straighter than before. I walked over to him. Yep, he was at least two inches taller, and a little cuter in that uniform.

"Where's the game?"

"Freedom Elementary, your old school."

"Well, good luck." I turned. "Chandra, I have a great idea!"

"Oh, wonderful. Another idea."

"No, this one is good."

I throttled forward, and Q82 headed west toward Freedom. I spied the crowd long before we arrived. It looked like most Colorado Springs residents stood under the game, watching the players fly above them, kicking the ball over their heads. A big banner across the playground read, "City Championship Tournament."

"Chandra," I said. "We can place that rock order now. Any color you want."

We set up our stand next to the Parent Teacher Organization booth where adults sold eagle t-shirts.

Customers flocked to our stand.

"Give me a Plasma Punch. And a cookie."

Orders came so fast, Chandra couldn't direct the food processor quickly enough. Then, around 5:00, the last game ended, and people started leaving. My hands felt gross from sticky juice and melting cookies. Tired from standing most of the afternoon, I sat. A woman from the PTO table walked over.

"Looks like you had a good afternoon," she said.

"We did." I smiled. "We need the money to buy rocks for a pond we're building in Chandra's backyard."

"What great entrepreneurs," she said. "And I'm glad you picked our school to host your sale. We can really use the donation."

"Donation?" I looked at Chandra.

"Why, yes," the woman said. "Didn't the principal explain it to you? For every sale you make, you donate fifty percent to the PTO. It's common practice."

"But that's four hundred and fifty dollars," I whined.

"Lovely," the woman said, extending her hand.

Day four. Hot. A pond with water pumping through a ceramic frog's mouth, surrounded by plants and bushes. Gaps showed between green where robolifters had no rocks to place. I wanted to cry. After counting and recounting our money, we still came in fifty dollars short. I looked at each gap, deciding which one would go unnoticed if we didn't fill it with a rock.

"We could return the fish," Chandra said. "They're not used."

"I need to tell you something. You received a message after the plants came that said our order was nonrefundable. I thought I could get all of this to work out anyway. I'm sorry I didn't tell you. And I'm sorry I let you down."

"You didn't let me down, Alyah." Chandra put her arm around my shoulder. "This has been a lot of fun. I've missed you. The pond isn't what's important to me. You are."

"I've missed you, too." I blinked back a tear, turned and gave Chandra a squeeze. I took a deep breath. "If you can stand me for another five minutes, I have one more idea that might work."

"You go girl, even if it takes ten."

"Computer, begin new search... landscape materials... rocks... sale." We waited five seconds before a screen opened. "Hey, these are man-made."

"They look like the rocks in Palmer Park," Chandra said. "And they're selling at twenty percent off. After tax and delivery, we'll have enough money left to pay back my mom for the drink and cookie supplies. Let's place the order."

The delivery arrived the next morning in the rain. Robolifters put the rocks in place while we got drenched. Draped in slickers, Chandra's parents and Ydan came down the stairs to see our project. I walked under the deck and picked up the goldfish container. My shoes squished in the mud as I ambled alongside the pond's beautiful garden. I handed the fish to Chandra.

She flipped the lid open and then looked at me. "Thanks for your idea about putting this pond in our yard, and making sure we got it right. It's so pretty. But it's not perfect until it holds two friends." Chandra lowered the container to the water and poured the goldfish into the pond. They darted from edge to edge, exploring new territories but always checking back to make sure the other swam nearby.

I Wonder What the Clouds Taste Like

By Diane Gonzales Bertrand

Would a cloud taste of sugar
like spun candy from the zoo?
Would a cloud's taste be smoky
like Daddy's barbecue?

Would clouds taste like marshmallows
and leave a sticky paste?
Would clouds taste like candy sticks
and leave a minty taste?

Would clouds taste so lemon sour
I'd pucker up my lips?
Would clouds taste so cola sweet
I'd want another sip?

Would clouds taste spicy hot
like chilies and tomatoes?
Would clouds taste soft and mushy
like scooped mashed potatoes?

Would a cloud taste pink like gum
as I blew bubbles out?
Would clouds taste white like soap suds
so I must spit them out?

Would clouds taste sharp like onions
and even make me cry?
Would clouds taste cool like ice cream
and make me wish for pie?

Would clouds taste so peppery
that one bite makes me sneeze?
Would clouds taste slick and lumpy
like spoons of cottage cheese?

Would a cloud taste creamy smooth
like frosting on a cake?
Would clouds taste buttery crisp
like waffles Mom bakes?

Would a cloud's taste tickle me
like sodas fizz my nose?
Would clouds taste cozy and warm
like soup warms up my toes?

Would clouds taste coconutty
and get stuck on my teeth?
Would clouds taste like caramels
and get stuck where I can't reach?

Could I grab a little taste
before clouds disappear?
Will clouds melt or spin away
before the taste was clear?

I wonder what a bird tastes
as it flies through the sky.
As I gaze at summer clouds,
I only guess and sigh.

I wonder what the clouds taste like.

Bottle It Up
By Heath Gibson

Paw Paw is a dirty old man. No, really he is. I can't remember him ever being clean. Not in the morning when I climb out of bed on the back porch he and Granny made into a room for me, not in the evening before I fall asleep after they make me watch reruns of *I Love Lucy*, and definitely no time in between. The knees of his pants are permanently stained with dirt, little traces of soil fill the wrinkles and cracks of his stubby hands, and I am not even going to talk about his fingernails.

But it is more than the way he looks. It's also the way he smells. Standing next him, my nose fills up with this smell that's like wet earth — you know the way dirt is right when you push a shovel in the ground, or the way a flower bed smells when you're on your knees pulling weeds. That smell seems to fill his skin, and I think maybe seep out of his pores. But it's not the bad kind of dirty. It is the good kind. And it is a nice smell that reminds me it is summer.

Since I was five, Momma has been sending me here to South Mississippi to spend most of the summer. Kids in my class at school get to go to fancy summer camps every year, but Momma can't afford that. So I guess she figured this was the next best thing. And that's OK with me. I've always liked it. I like it because Paw Paw is kind of crazy-wacky. *Different* is what Momma has always said. And different is exactly what the summer should be.

"Rise and shine, Indiana. Time to hit the floor," Paw Paw calls from the kitchen. My name is really Jason, but he calls me Indiana because I love *Raiders of the Lost Ark*. Every summer we watch it together, and I remind him at the end that I'm going to be like Indiana Jones one day. And every time we watch it, he says the same thing. "Heck son, forget 'one day.' Why not now?"

I don't like mornings nearly as much as Paw Paw does, so it takes me a while to get myself out of bed. He walks to the back porch, coffee cup in hand.

"Come on now, son, it's time to hit the floor and get this day started. You can't sleep your life away." To Paw Paw, sleeping past 7:00 A.M. is wasting the day.

I roll over and pull my arm out from the covers. I slap my hand against the floor. "Is that hitting the floor good enough?"

Paw Paw laughs a little and takes a sip of coffee. "You must have got that from your mother. She did the same thing when she was your age. So I guess I've got to do the same thing I did to her."

He grabs the covers with one hand and snatches them right off the bed. "Time to get going, Indiana. There's treasure out there waiting for us." He turns and walks back to the kitchen. He knows that will get me up.

I stand out of bed and pull on the jeans and t-shirt I left lying on the floor by the bed. I don't worry about putting on shoes because I never have to wear them when I'm here.

Paw Paw is sitting at the table when I walk into the kitchen, rubbing my eyes awake. A plate of bacon and eggs sits in the spot across from him. Granny fusses at him all the time about eating that kind of stuff at his age, but it hasn't stopped him yet. I'm glad because it means I get to eat it too, not cereal every day like back at home.

"Get you some food in your stomach so we can get going. The river and marshes are waiting."

I sit down and start shoveling eggs into my mouth. I eat fast. I might take a few minutes to get going, but once I do, I don't slow down much. Paw Paw likes that about me.

I put the plate in the sink when I finish. Paw Paw is already waiting for me on the back steps. I step out the back door, and the humidity wraps around me like a wet blanket. Most people hate it, but not me. It's the exact opposite of the dry town in west Texas where I live. I mean, the dirt out there is hard and dusty, the trees are short, and what grass that does grow is not the kind you want to lay down on.

Here with Paw Paw and Granny, the air is kind of heavy and wet like a bathroom after a hot shower. The grass grows thick and soft, and the whole world seems to be green. Everything is green except the brown river that spreads out through the whole town on its way to the Gulf of Mexico.

The river is my favorite. Me and Paw Paw don't go fishing in it; I don't really get to go swimming in it either. We do something better. We search for *treasure*.

We don't dig for gold or look for some chest that some long-ago pirate buried somewhere. We look for *bottles* — bottles made before there were twist-tops and bottle caps. We also look for buttons made before there was plastic. But most importantly, we search for traces of a town that disappeared a long time ago — the town that was here when Paw Paw was a little boy.

Before the big shipyard, the paper mill, and three chemical plants, Oak Point was a town where boats of all kinds came in from the Gulf of Mexico. They also came down the Pascagoula River delivering all kinds of stuff to be sold in the shops that lined Main Street right down to the city docks. Everybody that lived here had something to do with a shop or the river.

For a long time it was the only town in the county with a big supermarket, the only place you could get parts for a broken down truck, and the place to go to get a pile of flounder for fish fries on Sunday afternoon.

I know all this because Paw Paw has told me so many stories about it that I dream I lived back then. Paw Paw, in his crazy way of doing things, stands up on the coffee table in his dirty cover-alls like it's a stage.

He tells me long stories about fishing boats, about the trolley that ran through town, and about how when he was a kid he and his brother would collect bottles people threw off the trolley. They would get a bunch of bottles and turn them in at Mr. Toups' store for candy and maybe a couple of nickels.

When he finishes up on the coffee table, he tells me the same story again, but in a different way — with a big photo album filled with old black-and-white pictures of Main Street, the trolley, and old black men sitting on buckets fishing with cane poles down on the river.

But the town is different now, and the river is different, but there's still good things for us to find there. Most of it might be junk to most folks, but they're artifacts to me and Paw Paw.

"Indiana, no time to waste. Here, take your tool." He hands me the metal rod we use to shove into the mud on the banks of the river to see if there is anything hard underneath. Paw Paw carries the small shovel and the machete. We walk around to the front of the house.

"So where are we hunting today?" I ask.

"Well, Indiana, last night after you fell asleep I took a look at my old maps. There's a place down behind the Dantlers' property where I think we might have some luck."

Paw Paw has these old maps from before every road was paved and when the trolley still winded around town, crossing the river here and there. The maps also show where the local dump sites used to be before there were garbage trucks. Those are the best places to look. But most of those places are by the river, and a lot of the land has washed away or is now under water.

We walk down the sidewalk side by side. We don't ever drive to where we dig. It just wouldn't be the same if we did. We pass house after house, and Paw Paw waves to people sitting on front porches and ladies digging weeds out of flower beds. I wave too, even though I don't know them and they don't know me. It's just the friendly thing to do.

The only person we don't ever wave at is Ms. Mabel. She lives down by the river, and she has all these signs posted up everywhere that say, "Keep Out," "No Trespassing," and "Trespassers will be prosecuted." I guess Paw Paw figures if she's not going to be friendly to anybody, then we shouldn't be friendly to her. I don't know, but I do know it makes me nervous to walk by her house. It's painted grey. The curtains are always closed. And her flower beds have nothing but dirt in them — they're not lively and colorful like everybody else's in town.

We finally make it to the Dantzlers' property. We walk along the edge of the property, along the side of the house, and down to the river. This is another wacky thing about Paw Paw. He doesn't ever ask if we can be on people's property. Of course, that is half the fun.

"Alright son, start getting that rod down in the ground. Them bottles ain't going to jump out of the ground and land in your hand."

I walk along the bank and shove the metal rod in and out of the ground as fast I can. I have to be careful not to do it too hard because I could break whatever is down there. I shove and pull, shove and pull until my arms and shoulders are burning.

We get to a part of the bank where a tree is in our way. Paw Paw and me get on our hands and knees and crawl under the limbs. I like getting dirty.

"Now be careful, Indiana. You know this mud gets soft as your Granny's mash potatoes."

As soon as the words come out of his mouth, my right leg sinks down into the mud all the way up to my hip. My face is just about in the water.

Paw Paw laughs. "Now watch out, you get too much of that pooh pooh mud on you, and Granny's not going to let you back in the house." He calls it pooh pooh mud because that's about what it smells like. But I don't care. We're looking for treasure.

He pulls me out, and my leg makes this nasty sucking sound when it pops out. Good thing I don't have to wear shoes because I would have lost one there. We keep walking on the bank, but Paw Paw stops real quick.

"Well, look at that." He points to the bank about eight feet in front of us. Blue glass shines in the sun. "Indiana, get that rod, and check that spot right there."

I slosh through the water to the spot where the glass is scattered. I shove and pull, shove and pull, and on the third one, the end of the rod, touches something solid.

"Here Paw Paw. Dig here."

He eases down on one knee and starts digging. In a few minutes, we have three bottles. Paw Paw puts them in a bag and stands up. "Well, I'd say we've been lucky today. We better get back before it gets too hot out here, and your Paw Paw falls over dead."

We sneak back through the Dantzlers' yard and head down the sidewalk. My heart is still beating pretty fast, but it nearly stops when we get to Ms. Mabel's place. She's outside sweeping her sidewalk. We don't ever see her much, so it's weird when we do.

"Paw Paw?"

"What you need, son?"

"How come Ms. Mabel has all them signs up around her house? And why doesn't she ever wave like everybody else in town?"

"Well, let's just say she got tired of people bothering her and trying to get on her property."

"Why would people want to get on her property?"

"Indiana, there's treasure on that property that lots of people want to get their hands on. And if anybody ever does, they'll be famous for sure."

"What? Come on Paw Paw. Are you serious?"

"There are bottles and bowls and pots in this place that are so old they're not even made of glass. They are made of *clay* — from when the Pascagoula Indians used to live on the banks of the river."

My eyes get all wide and strain like they're trying to jump out of my head. "Indians? Here?"

"Yep. There was a group of Indians that was going to be

attacked by the tribe in Biloxi. But the Pascagoula Indians weren't fighters. They didn't want to fight, and they didn't want to die in battle. They knew that's what would happen if they tried to fight the Biloxi tribe. So what they did was they had a ceremony, and the whole tribe held hands. Then they started singing this song together. And while they sang, they walked down in the river and drowned, leaving all kinds of artifacts behind. That's why people still call it the Singing River. Sometimes at night, right when the sun is going down, if the wind is blowing in a certain direction, you can still hear the tribe singing their song."

"So, how much is out there?"

"Don't really know. Ms. Mabel nor anybody in her family has ever let people out there to see. People have tried to get out there, but none of them have had much luck.

She even turned away a bunch of people from the university who wanted to pay her a lot of money to let them study the property. She said all she could do was show them some of the items people in her family had found out there."

"Have you ever tried to sneak out there and look, Paw Paw?"

I have to say that I did one time. But only once. Ms. Mabel called the cops on me, and they were there before I got through the backyard."

"You went to jail?

"No, but I wish they would have taken me. Your Granny looked like she was going to explode right out of her skin when they dropped me off. She said unless I felt like cooking my own meals from then on, I better stay away from Ms. Mabel's property. So, that's what I do."

"But I bet you'd still like to see what's out there."

"Indiana, you have no idea. I dream about getting out there at least once a week. But it's going to have to stay a dream. I'm sure somebody will get out there one day. And if they find what I think is out there, they will be famous for sure. Famous I tell you."

We don't even make it home before my brain is already churning with how I'm going to be the one to find out what's on Ms. Mabel's property. I'm going to be the famous one. I'm going to be just like Indiana.

Bullfrogs warn me one last time that I shouldn't go. Their deep belches and croaks remind me that Paw Paw will probably be mad at me for doing this. But he ought to know Indiana wouldn't let somebody being mad at him stop him. So I'm slipping down the back steps at four o'clock in the morning. I know I said I didn't like mornings, but it's still dark, so I'm not sure it counts as morning.

I ignore the warning of the bullfrogs. I tuck Paw Paw's straw hat down on my head, grab the metal rod and shovel, and head toward Ms. Mabel's to find what nobody has found, to find my little piece of fame.

Being out at four o'clock in the morning in a town like Oak Point is like being in a place that only lives during the daylight — no cars on the road, no lights on in any houses. I could walk down the middle of the street, and nobody would see me. But I don't. I stay on the edge of the sidewalk, close to the edges of yards. And I even walk part of the way through patches of woods and empty lots just to be safe. I walk fast, almost jogging because I want to make sure it's still dark when I get to her house. It is dark — dark like I have never seen.

The only hard part about getting on her property is keeping from running into trees that cover the side and back of her property — all of them with "Trespassers Will Be Prosecuted" signs nailed to them to tell me I'm doing something wrong. But it doesn't feel wrong. It feels good — exciting, like something right out of a movie. I'm not Jason. I *am* Indiana.

I make it to the part of the property where the trees stop and the marsh begins. I can smell the river close by. The river has this smell about it that's like a mixture of metal and fish. But it's good smell, the smell of summer. I don't have the machete so I just walk straight into it.

I try to be careful, moving slow to keep the tall grass from cutting me. Marsh grass is like razors if you brush it just right. That's why I'm wearing long sleeves. Sleeves can't protect my face though. I try to brush the grass to the side and tuck Paw Paw's hat in front of me, but some of the grass catches me on the cheeks anyway. After about forty yards, the wind blowing across my face tells me I have liquid on my cheeks, and I know I'm cut. I don't care. I can only hear the singing of the Pascagoula Indians in that wind, telling me to come find them.

After a while of fighting the marsh and mud, I make it to the bank of the river. I squat down to catch my breath and wait for the sun to come up. The one thing I know about the river is alligators — I did two science projects on them for school. And I know that nighttime is feeding time for alligators, and the bayous are filled with them.

When the sun comes up, they go back to the banks and soak in the sun. I'm not about to go stomping off in the edges of the water, knowing a hungry gator might want me for a snack.

It seems like I only wait seconds for the sun to start turning the sky from black to light gray. I guess it's because I have the song of the Pascagoula to keep me company. The light comes fast, and as soon as I can see down the bank and make out the line of the water, I step out of the marsh into the water and start slugging through the mud.

It's hard going. I keep sinking up to my knees, and I have to use the shovel to pull myself out and forward. The smell is so awful I swear the sewer is emptying somewhere close by.

I'm not really sure where I'm headed. Ms. Mabel owns 100 acres of riverfront property. The spot could be anywhere on this 100 acres. And I'm not really sure I'll know the spot when I come to it.

It's daylight, and the song of the Pascagoula is gone, so I don't have it to tell me when I'm in the right place. I just hope I find another clue.

After what feels like forever of stomping and struggling along the river bank, I stop because the land does. Water bends around a small point, going inland and making it impossible for me to keep walking. I could follow it inland until it gets shallow enough for me to walk across, but I don't have time for that. I need to move fast.

So I just jump in — up to my neck. My feet barely graze the soft bottom, and every time I try to put a foot down to stand up, my shoe sinks, bringing the water up to my mouth and stinging the cuts on my jaw. I quit trying to stand up, and I swim, which isn't easy when you're holding a metal rod and a metal shovel. It's like I've got rocks in my pockets.

I finally make it to the other side and have to crawl on my hands and knees to keep from sinking into the ground. I have never seen quicksand, but this stuff has to be pretty close to it.

I stand up, leaving the rod and shovel on the ground. I lean over, wipe my hands on my knees, and breathe hard and fast. When I catch my breath, I pick up the rod and shovel and keep moving. I make it about twenty more yards before I feel something break in the mud under my right foot.

My heart immediately starts pounding harder, like it's trying to jump out of my chest. I drop the rod and plunge the shovel under the spot where my foot was and pull up hard. I dump the mud over on the bank. In the mud are pieces of clay — pieces that look like they used to be the sides of a bowl.

I start digging around me faster and faster. And all the work gives me is more mud. I know I'm close. I pick up the pieces of clay and put them in my pocket. I'm thrilled I found pieces at least. But Indiana wouldn't be satisfied with that.

I get a sudden burst of energy. My feet forget they're walking in mud. It's almost like walking through a parking lot, my feet move so fast. I come around another point, and there it is — the spot. I know it because the marsh that lines the river becomes hard ground, a mixture of white sand and brown dirt.

I turn to walk up on land, and I notice claw marks in the mud on either side of what looks like a slide going into the river. I know from my science projects that it's where an alligator slid from the bank down into the water. I stop moving and look up on a wooded area. My eyes scan back and forth, waiting to see an alligator lying in the sun. But it is clear — only sand, leaves, and pine straw.

I walk slow, watching the ground for signs of hard clay so I'll know where to dig. I brush away pine straw with my feet. I sweep to the left and then to the right, staring hard at the ground. I step a few more times and make a big sweep with my left foot. I feel something like a rock run across the bottom of my shoe. I drop to my knees and brush away the sand and dirt with my hand. I cut my hand across the palm.

I yank my hand back to see blood mixed with the dirt covering my palm. I don't even care. I really don't even feel any pain. I look down to see what cut my hand and see two arrowheads hiding in the ground. I grab the tip of one with my fingers and pull it out of the ground.

Right in my hand is a piece of a world no one knows except for in books. And I'm holding it. I raise my hands in the air and take a breath to yell up into the sky I'm so happy. But I don't let that yell out. Can't, unless I want to get caught.

I put the arrowhead in my pocket and pick up the other one and do the same. I scan the area again, trying to decide where to look. My head can't make sense of anything. The excitement seems to be taking over my brain, keeping me from making any kind of decision. I just turn around and around, waiting to see something that will lead me to another treasure.

When I'm nearly dizzy from all the turning, I notice a small mound about four feet high. It doesn't look natural. It looks like somebody made it.

On the edges of the mound there are tons of pieces of clay everywhere. But I don't want pieces. I want something whole — a real treasure. Something that will make me famous.

I use the metal rod to probe down into the ground, working my way around the mound and then outward away from it. I plunge the rod slow, not wanting to break anything below. Sweat is running down my face. The sun is up good, and the heat of Mississippi in the summer beats down on me hard. But I can't stop searching.

I plunge and pull, plunge and pull, feeling a little bit of panic twisting around my stomach. What if I don't find anything? I don't want to do all of this for a couple of arrowheads. I want something big.

When the panic is just about to the point where I almost feel sick, the metal rod glances something hard in the ground. I yank the rod out of the ground and start digging. The ground and my arms feel like they weigh as much as the pine trees that are doing nothing to keep the sun off me. But I force my arms to keep going.

About a foot and a half down, I find it — my treasure, my piece of time and history that nobody else could get. I'm the only one. I'm just like Indiana.

I scoop the clay bowl with both my hands like I'm holding a newborn puppy. There are no designs on it, just a few lines. It's still the greatest thing I've ever seen.

I stand up and run to the top of the mound and force my mouth to yell, "I DID IT! I AM INDIANA!"

And then I hear it — what sounds like a giant cat hissing at me. I turn and see a huge alligator standing about twenty yards away. I look down at the ground and immediately know the mound I'm standing on has been made — by her. It's her nest.

I freeze, feeling my chest heave up and down, up and down. My mouth is held open, letting air rush in and out. I can't move, don't know where to move. Alligators are super fast, and I'm standing on her nest.

She hisses again, long and loud. She starts to inch toward me, but I still can't move. My legs just won't do it. She keeps moving. And I keep doing nothing. I grip the bowl in my hand and think maybe I can throw it to distract her enough to run. But I can't let go of my treasure.

The alligator makes another quick move toward me, and all of a sudden my legs decide to work. I bolt off the mound heading for the water. I don't know what makes me think that is a good idea. My legs are heavy, but they're moving, moving like the hard ground has suddenly turned into marsh mud.

I hear the alligator scurrying behind me. I push harder, sweat pouring down my face and my arms, and my treasure still in my hand. I hit the edge of the river, and the sound of scurrying feet gets closer. My head starts thinking about people sneaking in but never getting to show their treasure to anyone.

My arms pump as hard as my feet. The noise of scurrying feet attacks my ears. The sound of leaves, grass, and water mixed together shove me forward.

I make it across the small canal I swam through earlier. The sounds are gone, but I don't turn to see if the alligator is still behind me. I keep running, the marsh grass slashing and cutting my hands, begging me let go of my treasure. But I won't let go. I will be famous, just like Indiana. Paw Paw will be proud of me. I will be like him.

I can see glimpses of the trees in Ms. Mabel's yard, the orange letters of the signs that told me to stay away. Run, run, run, my brain screams at my legs. I jump over a limb, a hole, and one more log. My legs push hard and stretch long. My body shoots out of the woods.

And my face slams into the ground.

Mud is in my eyes and up my nose. My right hand is still clenched around my treasure, so I wipe away the mud with my left. I roll over and look back to see what made me fall. The handle of Ms. Mabel's cane is around my ankle. And Ms. Mabel is standing over me.

I was a trespasser, but I wasn't prosecuted. I didn't get to keep my treasure, and I didn't get famous. What I got was Granny's fly swatter across my butt and a whole day sitting on the couch staring at a TV that wasn't on. I thought Granny was going to shake my bones right out of my skin when Ms. Mabel took me back to the house. And I thought Paw Paw's face was going to split; he was smiling so big.

I wanted more than anything to take that bowl and the arrowheads home with me at the end of the summer to show everybody that I really am a treasure hunter. Instead, all I have is a story that nobody is going to believe. That's the only bad thing about stories, memories, laughs, and fun. I can't bottle it up and take it with me. Then again, if I could, I guess summer wouldn't be the same, wouldn't be as good, wouldn't seem like a treasure all by itself.

The Land Of Summer
By Madeline Smoot

The dog disappeared.

Sam shook his head and blinked his eyes. "Pookiepoo?" he called for his little sister's dog.

No answer. No yelp. No wagging tail.

Sam sucked in a huge breath of air. "Pookiepoo," he screamed louder than a tornado siren.

Still nothing. The dog always came when called. Sam bit the bottom of his lip. The dog had definitely disappeared.

He dropped his book on top of the pile of books from his summer reading list. His mom would kill him if he didn't finish it, but his little sister would kill him if he didn't find her dog.

Sam tiptoed over to the spot where the dog had disappeared. He searched the bushes for Pookiepoo fur. He searched the sky for UFOs that might have beamed the dog up. He didn't find either. He didn't see anything unusual until he reached the spot where Pookiepoo had disappeared. There in the grass sat a small circle of metal. Sam bent down and saw a disc about the size of a half dollar. It blinked every few seconds like the LED on his computer. Sam stared at it for a moment, then reached out to pick it up. As soon as his skin touched the surface, waves of dizziness slammed into him, nearly knocking him over. He just managed to grab the little disc before he blacked out.

He woke up standing in the sun. Sam shut his eyes and shook his head to get the fuzziness out. This couldn't be right. He shouldn't have woken up standing in the sun. Didn't you normally fall down when you passed out?

After a few deep breaths to get rid of the jitters he still felt, Sam opened his eyes.

"Oh," he muttered to himself. It felt like an understatement. He stood alone on the top of a hill with a world laid out before him. In front of him, a path led down to what looked like a huge beach resort. He could see little tiny dots out in the ocean that he assumed were people. Bigger dots looked like sailboats. He turned to his right, expecting to see jungle or something. After all, everyone knew tropical islands had jungles. He had no doubts he'd ended up on a tropical island.

Sam was wrong. Instead of jungle, he saw sports fields just like at the park across the street from his house. He counted eight baseball diamonds and twelve soccer fields. There were even tennis courts and basketball courts, something the park at home didn't have. Before Sam could turn to see what was down the next side of the hill, he heard a whistle. Spinning around quickly, he saw a girl his age coming toward him.

"A rooker," she called out. "I found a rooker."

"Huh?" said Sam. He looked around, but he didn't see anything. "What's a rooker?"

The girl laughed. Sam smiled too. There was something about her laugh that made him relax. He hadn't realized how nervous he'd been on this strange hill by himself.

"You're a rooker." She stopped only a few feet from him. She stuck her hands in the pockets of her board shorts. "You're new.

We call new folks rookers. It's like some word someone brought in." The girl shrugged and grinned. "I don't know."

"How'd you know I was new?" asked Sam.

She laughed again. "You looked lost, even from behind."

Sam looked down at the ground and wiggled his toes in his sandals. "Where are we?"

"Summerland."

"Summerland?" Sam looked around at the beach. "Like fairy heaven?"

The girl shook her head. "Do I look like a dead fairy?" Without waiting for an answer, she grabbed Sam's hand and dragged him around the hill, pointing as she went. "It's the land of summer. Look: there's the lake and the camp and the amusement park."

Sam stopped moving, which jerked the girl to a stop. His eyes got bigger than the disc he still held in his hand. In front of him was the biggest theme park he'd ever seen. The roller coasters and Ferris wheels seemed to stretch all the way to the horizon. He could even see a midway and rides for smaller kids.

"It's even bigger than Funfun Land, and that's the biggest

park in the world." Sam turned to the girl. "I've wanted to go all summer."

"See?" She smiled and tried to pull him along some more. "It's summer here all the time. It's like a vacation that never ends."

"How long have you been here?"

"I was six when I got here, and well," she stared at the sky for a moment, "I'm not six now."

"Oh." Sam held the disc up. "Did one of these bring you too?"

She nodded but stuck her hands behind her back and stepped away. "If it touches skin, it'll send you Away."

"Home?" asked Sam.

"This is home." The girl frowned. "That sends you Away. Be careful with it. After a little while most of us throw ours in the sea so we won't accidentally touch it."

Sam nodded, but he wasn't sure yet he wanted to stay. He stuck the disc in the pocket of his shorts that didn't have a hole. The disc faintly glowed through it.

"So, where do you want to go first? I was headed to camp." She stuck out her hand. "I'm Winnie by the way."

"I'm Sam." He shook Winnie's hand, and the two smiled at each other. "Uh," said Sam, "I'd love to go to the roller coasters, but I think my dog's here somewhere. I guess I should find her." Sam didn't feel to enthusiastic. After all, it was just his little sister's dog. The theme park seemed to be calling him to come play.

Winnie's smile vanished from her face. "You brought a dog here? Are you crazy?" Her voice lowered to a whispered hiss.

"What's wrong?" he whispered back. "I didn't bring the dog

on purpose. She found my disc first."

"This is bad." Winnie paced around the hill staring at the ground. "Very bad. We have to find that dog fast." She paused to look at a footprint in a spot of mud, but it was clearly human not dog. "If Queen Petra or one of her followers finds your dog first, she'll eat it or worse."

Sam felt like a thousand little spiders had just started to lightly run across his skin. He bit his lip and resisted the urge to shiver. He couldn't imagine what could be worse than being eaten. His sister would kill him if anything happened to her precious Pookiepoo.

"Do you know where it went?" Winnie kept pacing.

Sam looked wildly around. "She could be anywhere," he said. "Pookiepoo! Here girl. Pookiepoo."

"You're dog's name is Pookiepoo?" Winnie looked like Sam had just grown four or five extra heads.

"It's my sister's dog."

Winnie looked doubtful.

"She's four. She was two when she got the dog, and pookiepoo was her word for puppy."

"Uh huh," said Winnie with a ghost of her formerly radiant smile. "Well, is there something Poopie Poo really likes to do?"

"Pookie — like KEY — poo loves to swim. Didn't you say something about a lake?"

"Yes!" Winnie grabbed his hand and spun him around to the left. "Come on!" She started pulling him along a trail that meandered down the hill. As he ran, Sam could see a beautiful blue lake with sailboats and motorboats pulling water skiers. In an area roped off with buoys, people splashed and swam with inner tubes.

"Who's this Queen Petra?" asked Sam between gasps. "Why does she eat dogs?"

"I don't know," Winnie gasped back. "I don't think so." The two reached a flat part and nearly fell they were running so fast. After a few stumbles, they regained their balance and started running again.

"Queen Petra was the first person to find this place hundreds or thousands of years ago. It's hard to say since we don't really keep track of time here. I've never actually seen her. Anyway, after a while she got bored and decided she wanted other people to enjoy this fantastic place she'd discovered. She figured out how to make the discs and sent them out to the Away place to bring unhappy people back here."

"She must be some kind of brilliant scientist." Sam glanced at the flashing light glowing through his pocket. "I don't think I could make a transporter, especially one this tiny."

"You might, if you had nothing else to do." She made a movement that might have been a shrug, but since she was running, it was hard to say.

Sam just gasped. His lungs felt like they'd fallen into the kiln in the art room at school. Winnie must be in really good shape if she could run like this and talk at the same time. Sam thought there was a chance he'd spontaneously combust if he had to do this much longer. Maybe hours of video games really weren't the best thing for him after all. Who'd have thunk Mom could be right?

"Since she got here first, she got to be Queen. Normally,

she's really nice, but she got bit by a dog one day and got really mad. She told everyone the next time she saw a dog she'd chop off its tail, fry it alive, and have a huge feast. And Petra always keeps her word."

Sam felt sick, and not just from all the fast running.

"So you can see why we've got to find your dog first." Winnie slowed them down to a walk.

Sam just nodded. Even if he wanted to, he could never go home if Pookiepoo got eaten.

He could never face his little sister. Ever.

In front of them, the lake flowed to the horizon. People of all ages tanned on the shore or swam in the water. Kids played ball, and two pairs of teenagers were playing chicken in the deeper water. Everywhere people were having fun, splashing and shouting. But there was no Pookiepoo. No happily yelping dog running up and down chasing balls or swimming in the lake.

"Juliet," called Winnie. "Juliet!"

A tall, extremely pretty girl in her early teens turned and waved. Winnie and Sam went over to her.

"Who's this?" asked Juliet. She eyed him critically for a second before her eyebrows shot up. "Winnie, did you get your very own rooker? Your very first — and so cute." Juliet gave Winnie a knowing glance. Winnie rolled her eyes, and Sam couldn't help thinking that older kids were so weird with their obsession with the opposite sex.

"Juliet, this is important," said Winnie. "Did you see a dog? Sam here accidentally brought his, and we think it might have run down here."

Juliet bit her lip and turned to Sam. "Was that sweetheart

yours? She just loved the water. Romi and Remi were playing with her before Alex caught her."

Winnie cursed.

Juliet nodded. "That dog was a smart one. She didn't want to go with Alex and growled at him and everything. He caught her though. Who knew Alex could work a lasso?"

"Rat's brains, horse hooves, and crow's feet," swore Winnie.

"Who's Alex?" Sam had to ask even though he knew the answer wouldn't be good.

"A worm's butt," said Winnie.

"Alex is a suck-up to Queen Petra," said Juliet. "He's always trying to insinuate himself into her inner circle. He wants power and for Petra to give him special privileges. He'll bring your dog right to her."

"Little humbug. Petra should send him Away if you ask me." Winnie kicked a rock at a garbage can.

Juliet rolled over onto her stomach. "No one asked you, or me, or pretty much anyone else. You know the rules. Anyone who wants to stay can. No exceptions, no exclusions. As long as Alex likes it here, there's nothing we can do."

Winnie sighed, and then turned to Sam. "Well, at least we can try to save your dog. Let's see if we can get to the palace before Alex." She grabbed his hand and pulled him into another run. He had just enough time to look back at Juliet and wave before she was gone, lost in a sea of full time vacationers.

"How're we going to beat Alex to the palace? He must have a pretty good head start." Sam couldn't believe it. That last run must have really gotten him in shape. He wasn't winded at all, and they were running even faster this time. That, or the island was starting to get to him. Sam wasn't sure he really liked that last idea.

"He may have left before us, but he's trying to walk a resistant puppy. I've never done that, but I can't imagine it's easy."

"It's not."

"So, Pookiepoo has to be slowing him down. If we can get to the palace first, we can stop him before he shows your dog to Petra. Then you can send your dog Away. All you have to do is touch some part of it with your disc. Just be sure not to touch it yourself or you'll go too."

"But where will Pookiepoo go? Will she be back home, or will she be standing in the middle of a street?"

"I don't know. I've never known anyone to go back. Does it really matter? Anything's better than being eaten."

Sam pictured his sister's dog being hit by a car. That definitely didn't seem any better than being eaten.

Even though they ran at top speed, they never passed Alex and Pookiepoo. They saw a go-kart track and a miniature golf course and ran over a bridge with people floating in inner tubes in the river underneath, but there was nobody leading a dog. All too soon they stood in front of a huge skyscraper.

"This is the palace?" Sam asked. "It looks like a huge New York City hotel." There was even a revolving door in the center to walk through. He could just catch a glimpse of a huge pool complete with water slides at the back.

"Petra calls it the palace, so we call it the palace." She led him through the glass revolving door into a long, brightly lit hallway.

On either side were rooms filled with video games or ping-pong tables. There was even a movie theater.

"Wait a minute," said Sam slowing down a tiny bit. "*The Sacred Sword of Himeji* doesn't come out for another couple of months. How do you have it here?"

Winnie looked back. "Time works different here, I think. It's slower or something. It's probably out now back in the Away."

"What?" Sam came to a complete stop. How long had he been gone? What had his family been thinking? He now knew he'd have to go back so they would know he was okay and not worry.

"Winnie?" Sam walked a little faster to catch up with her. She'd started weaving in and out of corridors with more and more people.

"Yeah?"

"What year did you come here?"

Winnie slowed down while she was thinking. "The Southern states had just voted to secede, and Papa wanted to enlist to fight them. Mama was crying, so I went outside to hide in the barn. I found a disc in the hay. I guess that was what, 1861?"

Sam didn't say anything. He wasn't really sure when the Civil War started, but that seemed about right. Winnie had to be over 150 years old! Sam felt numb. Winnie only looked like she'd been here maybe four years. If he didn't hurry, his whole family might be dead by the time he came back. He began to walk faster. The little bits of conversation he heard gave his feet additional speed.

"Did you see him strut through here carrying that sweet little..."

"Taking right to her to..."

Sam grabbed Winnie's hand, and this time he dragged *her*.

At last, the crush of people eased up when they entered a huge ballroom. Sam's throat closed up as he heard a dog bark. Without a single "excuse me" or "pardon me," he pushed and shoved his way to the front.

"Don't you dare eat my dog!" he screamed as he pushed through the last group of people.

A hush went over the room, and everyone froze except Pookiepoo and the teenage girl she was playing with. They were wrestling in front of a large chair. Pookiepoo kept nipping at the girl's heels, and the girl would laugh and roll Pookiepoo over.

"Pookiepoo," he said with relief. The evil Queen must not have seen her yet.

When Pookiepoo heard her name, she barked and ran over to Sam. She jumped up to kiss his face. Sam wiped off the dog drool, for once not caring about the slobber. He leaned over and hugged his sister's puppy. "You're okay."

"So this must be your dog," said the teenage girl.

Sam looked up and noticed for the first time that she was blindfolded. She stood up and with her hands feeling in front of her walked over towards Sam. Before she could get very far, Pookiepoo ran and tried to barrel her over. The girl laughed and petted the dog.

"I'm Petra," said the girl. "What's your sweetie pie's name?"

"Um, I'm Sam, and that's Pookiepoo," said Sam.

Petra smiled. "What a perfect name." She bent over to rub Pookiepoo's belly and cooed, "That just is the perfect name for you, sweetie pie, isn't it? You are just such a pookie poo aren't you?"

Sam rolled his eyes. He would never understand girls. Then he wrinkled his forehead. "Wait a minute," he said. "You can't be Queen Petra. Queen Petra found this place and must be really old, like thirty, and she hates dogs, but you seem to really like Pookiepoo. I have to get her out of here before the mean Queen gets in here."

Petra frowned and sat down on the floor next to Pookiepoo. She kept rubbing the dog's belly. "Well," she said, "I did find this place when I was eight. I think I'm probably about seventeen now, so I've been here maybe nine years, much longer than anybody else."

"I told you time is different here," said Winnie.

"And I don't hate dogs." said Petra. "I just got mad one day and said something really stupid. But the things I say I want or wish for seem to happen here. I'd said I'd eat the next dog I saw. So when I heard that Alex had found a dog he was bringing me, I just made sure I didn't see it."

"That's why you're blindfolded," said Sam.

Petra nodded. "But it's starting to itch, so you might want to take her home now. I'm assuming you came from Away? It's the only place a dog could have come from."

Sam nodded then realized Petra couldn't see him. "Yes. I want to go back. I probably should leave right now before more time passes."

Petra looked surprised. "Why? The disc will take you to the moment you left. No one will even have noticed you were gone."

"Really?" The gnawing feeling in his stomach eased up. His sister would still be able to sleep with Pookiepoo tonight. "I wish I could stay longer." Sam turned to Winnie. "I would really have liked to ride those roller coasters, but I should probably get Pookiepoo home before Petra accidentally sees her. I don't suppose the disc will bring me back?" he asked Petra.

"Did you eat anything?"

"No."

"Then you should be fine. For some reason, all the people who leave here without touching the food are able to come back. My friend Ariana does it all the time. Don't ask me how the discs work. I didn't make them."

Sam's eyebrows came together. "I thought you did."

"Me too," said Winnie.

"No. I got lonely and wished that I could have more people. The next day, eight people showed up on the hill holding discs. People have been coming ever since."

Sam and Winnie looked at each other and shrugged. That mystery was something he could figure out next time he was here — after he'd ridden the roller coasters.

Sam went over to Pookiepoo and put his arm around her neck. "See you soon," he said to Winnie and Petra. They both smiled, and Winnie waved. Sam stuck his hand in his pocket and touched the disc.

Again the dizziness hit him, and Pookiepoo whimpered. His vision went black again for a second. When he could see, he realized they were in the backyard. His mom was calling him from the back door.

"Sam? Samuel!" she screamed. "What on earth are you doing?

I bet you haven't finished your summer reading have you? How will you be done by the time school starts if you don't read?"

Sam didn't answer any of the questions. All he really wanted to do was grab the disc in his pocket.

About the Authors

Goldie Alexander lives in Melbourne, Australia. She writes novels, short stories, articles, and scripts for adults and various child audiences. She likes to delve into various forms of writing and is passionate about fine-tuning her own work. She lectures in Creative Writing and frequently speaks at schools, clubs, and festivals. Visit Goldie on the web at www.goldiealexander.com.

Diane Gonzales Bertrand's poem was inspired by her daughter Suzanne, who first said, "Mom, I wonder what the clouds taste like." Diane is the author of many bilingual books for children including *The Empanadas that Abuela Made* and *My Pal, Victor*, winner of the 2005 Schneider Family Book Award.

Cindy Breedlove lives with her husband, son, and two guinea pigs in Indiana. She spends her summers growing vegetables and flowers in her gardens. She likes to watch the hummingbirds come to the flowers. She doesn't like the raccoons visiting her corn patch.

Kimberly Campbell's stories have been accepted by *Pockets*, *On the Line*, *Shine Brightly*, and *Kid Zone* magazines. Her first children's book is a biography of Richard Peck (Enslow, Fall 2007). Kimberly lives in Newnan, Georgia, with her sweet husband Jim and their lively daughter, Anna Marie. Visit her online at: www.KimCampbell.smartwriters.com.

Darlina Chambers enjoyed her educational career working for schools, theSpace Foundation (under NASA grants), and technology-based learning corporations. Today she takes pleasure in writing fiction about characters that have futuristic adventures. Darlina shares her life with her husband Gregg, grandchildren Alec and Alyah, and bouncy Bichon Bailey.

Sally Clark lives in Fredericksburg, Texas, where her favorite summer pastime is to write poetry sitting on her balcony, enjoying the shade. She has published numerous poems for adults, but this is her first children's poem, published with Blooming Tree Press. You may contact her at auslande@ktc.com.

Alison Dellenbaugh lives in Sarasota, Florida, with her husband, two young sons, and a lop-eared house rabbit. She already has a round-wheeled bike, so for her birthday, she wants a book contract. Feel free to drop by her web site at: www.alisondellenbaugh.com.

Kristy Dempsey lives in Belo Horizonte, Brazil, with her husband and three young children. Her home is a whirr of constant activity, just like the hummingbirds winging outside the window by her desk. Kristy drinks far too much Diet Coke in an effort to keep pace.

A fourth generation Virgin Islander, **Bish Denham** says living there "was like being inside a pirate's treasure chest, lots of history, lots of inspiration for writing." Her mother was the first one to recognize she might have a talent after she wrote a three page essay when she was eight. Bish currently lives in Texas with her husband and two dogs.

Sylvia M. DeSantis is an instructional designer, English/Women's Studies instructor, and landlocked mermaid who lives in Pennsylvania. When she's not dipping her fins in the ocean, she enjoys writing Young Adult fiction, poetry, and essays. Her work has recently appeared in the *Chicken Soup for the Soul* series. She'd love to hear from you at: wordsong@sylviamdesantis.com.

Amy Fellner Dominy is an MFA graduate of Arizona State University. Amy writes children's fiction as well as adult and children's theatre — her plays have been produced across the country. She's a member of SCBWI and The Dramatists Guild. Amy lives in Phoenix, Arizona, with her husband and two children.

Kelly Fineman lives in Cherry Hill, New Jersey, with her husband and two daughters. She enjoys writing, watching her daughters' soccer games, and spending time with her family. She hires a guy to mow her lawn.

Doris Fisher has three picture books scheduled for release in 2006 and 2007 — *Happy Birthday to Whooo?, One Odd Day,* and

My Even Day. She is a former kindergarten teacher whose poetry, variety word puzzles, and articles have appeared in more than ten different children's magazines. Visit her website at: www. abcdoris.com.

Katharine Weeks Folkes, aka Kay, was born in Georgia, and enjoyed many summers at St. Simons Island. San Antonio, Texas, however, is home. She and her six-year-old granddaughter, Kayta, enjoy writing short stories together.

Lucy Ford is the pen name of fantasy writer Deby Fredericks, whose children's stories have appeared in magazines such as *Boys' Life*, *Ladybug* and *Babybug*. Her novel, *The Magister's Mask*, was a finalist for the 2005 Independent Publisher Book Award (IPPIE). Fredericks lives, writes, and wrangles children in Spokane, Washington.

Marilyn E. Freeman lives in Florida with her husband, Bruce. She has two daughters and ten wonderful grandchildren. She has been published in several magazines. She is the author of two children's books, *Summer Adventures With Grandma* and *Pasquale's Journey*. She is a graduate of the Institute of Children's Literature.

A native Mississippian, **Heath Gibson** did not find the joy of children's literature until he was an adult. But since falling in love with the genre, he has used the unique landscape, people, and voice of the Gulf Coast region to fuel his writing. He currently lives in Atlanta, and he is working toward an MFA in writing for children at Hollins University.

Mindy Hardwick holds an MFA in Writing for Children and Young Adults from Vermont College. She has published articles on the craft of writing for children. This is her first published short story. In the summer, Mindy loves to swim in large ocean waves. Visit her website at: www.mindyhardwick.com

Edith Morris Hemingway, a graduate of Spalding University's MFA program, is co-author of two Civil War novels for children. She lives with her family in Misty Hill Lodge, a secluded 1930s log cabin in Maryland. Her favorite summer vacation activity is kayaking on the coast and lakes of Maine. Visit her at www.ediehemingway.com.

Joan Hobernicht is a retired country schoolteacher. Her stories were published in *Highways and Buyways*. A Christmas story was published in *The Havasu Connection*. Two children's stories were published in *The Magic Lark Journal*. A story was published by *Long Story Short*. She has three unpublished novels on the shelf.

Valerie Hunter is a Language Arts teacher for grades six through ten in Wood-Ridge, New Jersey. Her stories for children and young adults have appeared in magazines including *Cricket*, *Cicada*, *Boys' Quest*, *On the Line*, *What If?*, and *The Moo-Cow Fan Club*.

Sydney Salter Husseman lives in Utah with her husband, two daughters, two cats, and two super-sized puppies. She enjoys writing novels and stories, reading all kinds of books, decorating birthday cakes, and traveling anywhere. Last summer she took her family (and puppies!) to Cannon Beach, Oregon, for a family reunion.

Dorothy Imm moved so often when she was growing up that she doesn't know where she's from. She lives in Ohio now, in a house that's usually full of children and always full of books. You can read another of her short stories at: www.viatouch.com/learn/storystation/stories/mikeandgreenwood.jsp.

Suzanne Kamata grew up in a small town on the shores of Lake Michigan. She now lives in Japan, near the Pacific Ocean. She has never been diving, but she loves to take her twins to the beach whenever possible. Her other stories for children have appeared in *Cicada* and *Ladybug*.

Pamela Kessler resides in Illinois with her husband, son, and three dogs. Some of her published credits include, *Bible Pathways for Kids*, *Writer's Digest Writer's Forum*, *Institute of Children's Literature*, *Simple Joy*, and *Write from Home*. Members of her large, extended family are the inspiration for many of her stories.

Kathryn Lay is the author of 1200 published stories and articles for children and adults, including a short story in the anthology *A Glory Of Unicorns*. Her children's novel, *Crown Me!* (Holiday House, 2004), won the 2005 Texas State Reading

Association's Golden Spur Award, Check her website at: www.kathrynlay.com.

As an English teacher, **Alyssa Martin** has always admired the way children write stories straight from the heart, letting characters take them to the moon and back. Her goal is to tap into that courage as often as possible by writing for an audience that loves dreams and magic.

Tricia Mathison lives in Lake Mary, Florida, with her husband and two children. She absolutely loves summer, especially going for a swim or eating a popsicle on her back porch. Tricia contributed a story to *Mistletoe Madness* and has written for *Highlights*, *Guideposts for Kids*, *Hopscotch*, and *Wee Ones* magazines.

Shelby May finds future fantasy stories sublime. Her lifelong love for the fun, exciting, and dangerous ocean inspires much of her work. And when characters must shape up and believe in themselves, she's rooting for them, even if they make a mistake. Visit Shelby at: www.shelbymay.com.

Angela Meuser studied journalism at the University of Oregon. She now lives in Boise, Idaho with her husband and three children. Besides being a full time mom, she teaches aerobics, coordinates a support group for teenage moms, and writes freelance. Her dream career is that of picture book author.

Susan A. Meyers is the author of several short stories and the children's book, *Callie and the Stepmother*. She lives in Oklahoma with her husband, Joel and son, Tre. You can visit Susan's website at www.susanameyers.com.

Tracey Miller is the mom of four kids who give her all of the crazy story ideas she can handle! She is also a freelance educational writer and claims that working from home in your pajamas is the only way to go. However, she is thrilled to think her writing may go further — reading a library book is always more fun than taking a test in school! Her favorite children's authors are Roald Dahl, Madeline L'Engle, and C.S. Lewis. Tracey's hobbies include making (and eating) chocolates, reading, and watching movies.

Amy Oriani lives in Minnesota with her husband, two sons and a cat with half a tail. Her stories and poems have appeared in *Highlights for Children*, *Wee Ones*, and *KidTime* magazines. Amy grew up in Pennsylvania, where she spent many summer nights on the dam featured in "Fish Rescue." Although she still greatly enjoys bats and lightning bugs, these days she is happy to let her sons be the ones to grab the fish with their bare hands.

Gale Payne practices law and writes poetry and novels for children. All four of her grandparents immigrated to the United States from Europe. Because none could read or write, Ms. Payne vowed to be a writer. She lives in Fort Lauderdale, Florida, with her husband and two daughters.

Joanne Peterson, a member of SCBWI, writes for children and adults. Her writing has appeared in books, magazines, and poetry collections. She lives on the Olympic Peninsula in Washington State and can be reached at jopete71@msn.com. The imagination of her grandson, Roman, inspired "Moon Smile."

Many years ago, **Kay Pluta** found writing stories a pleasant escape from the boring chore of second grade penmanship exercises. Fueled by a wonky imagination and the sounds of laughing boys and purring cats, the grown-up Kay Pluta continues to write. Visit Kay on the web at www.kpluta.com.

Christine Gerber Rutt is co-editor of *Parenting Pages*; a freelance writer and translator; and a baby sling instructor (www. babyslings.ch). She lives in Switzerland with her Swiss husband and their two daughters. She's discovered that the perfect S'more combines crisp American graham crackers with dripping Swiss chocolate and gooey marshmallows.

Gloria Singendonk is a freelance writer with a passion for history and Canadiana in general. Her family of three adventurous boys has vacationed on Okanogan Lake many times and although they've never seen Ogopogo, they still watch for it every trip.

Susan Zeller Smith writes picture books as well as fiction and nonfiction for older kids. She loves to research her stories, especially when they take her to Hawaii. She lives in Utah with her husband, two kids, a border collie, and two hermit crabs.

Madeline Smoot loves to read but hates shelving books. Since a career as a librarian seemed out, she decided to become an author and an editor instead. This is her first anthology with Blooming Tree Press. Visit her at her website: www.madelines moot.com.

Susan Sundwall writes short stories, children's plays and non-fiction articles. Her picture book, *Bandy Bandana*, featuring the lovable pup Bandy and his many colorful bandanas, is available on Amazon. She lives with her husband and Springer Spaniel, Libby, in upstate New York. She has three sons and four grand-children.

Bevin Rolfs Spencer is a writer and educator of young children and their families. She lives with her husband, two children and a dog. Bevin writes novels and short stories, and when she's not chasing after her kids, loves to read, write and go play outside.

Marcia Strykowski works at a public library and enjoys music, theater, crafts, and family get-togethers. Publishing sales include *Blooming Tree Press* (anthologies), *Boys' Quest, Celebrate, Confetti, Dragonfly Spirit, Flicker, Fun for Kidz, Highlights for Children, Hopscotch for Girls, On the Line, Short Stuff, Story Friends, Wee Ones,* and *Whimsy.*

Elizabeth Tevlin has written lots of funny stories and articles for children. She is also an artist using very unusual materials: paint swatches and fortunes from inside cookies. Elizabeth lives with her husband and daughter in Ottawa, Canada, where winters can be very cold, so she likes her summers hot!

Marion Tickner delves into her childhood as she writes for children. Like Henry, she once found herself caught by the seat of her pants in a tree and had to be rescued by a visiting friend. She doesn't climb trees anymore, but she enjoys vacationing in the Adirondack Mountains. Marion has been published in several children's magazines as well as the *Mistletoe Madness* anthology. She lives in Syracuse, New York, with her husband and can be contacted at mmt4@juno.com.

Lisa Tiffin is a writer from upstate New York, where she lives with her husband and twin sons. In addition to articles and literature study guides, she writes fiction for young people and has recently completed her first adventure novel. She can be reached at acbooks@rochester.rr.com.

Caroline Young Ullmann was in second grade when she wrote her first book. It didn't get published, but she still has it. When she grew up, she worked as a reporter and editor at several newspapers. Now, she works at The Seattle Public Library and writes for young people.

Elsbet Vance is a writer of fantasy novels, poems, and an illustrator of children's books. She enjoys curling up absolutely ANYWHERE with a good book. She lives in South Carolina with her husband and two children, whom she homeschools.

Cassandra Reigel Whetstone writes poetry and stories for children. Her work can be found in children's magazines, including *Highlights* and *Ladybug*, And In Blooming Tree Press's *Mistletoe Madness*. She lives Northern California with her husband, two children, and two dogs — all of whom love to swim in the ocean.

Junette Kirkham Woller, a member of SCBWI, is a freelance writer with a background in the Fine and Performing Arts. Her writing has appeared in newspapers, magazines, newsletters, books, and poetry collections. Experience as a music teacher, professional model, handspinner, weaver, calligrapher, bookbinder, and toastmaster are resources for her work.

Tovah Yavin lives in a Maryland suburb of Washington, DC, where history, geography, and government have inspired many stories, poems, and novels. But few of the sights in the area have intrigued her more than the horses of Assateague Island who do, indeed, come down to stand in the sea.

Patti Zelch taught in elementary and middle school before giving up teaching to devote herself to writing for children. The idea for her story, "Sea Rescue," came after she and her husband saved a sea turtle from drowning while they were fishing in the Florida Keys.

About the Illustrators

Regan Johnson is an author and illustrator living in Austin, Texas. She is a member and chairperson of the Society of Children's Book Writers and Illustrators. Her artwork has appeared in juried art shows, picture books, young adult novels, and soon a manga novel. Her first picture book with Blooming Tree Press, *Little Bunny Kung Fu*, debuted in 2005. Her love of animals started her interest in drawing. Her continued love of animals is why she has so many pets today.

Matt Jones is an artist and illustrator in Austin, Texas, and a member of the Society of Children's Book Writers and Illustrators. He creates original artwork for children's books, murals, theater design, graphic design, web graphics, and comics. Throughout his artistic career, Matt has taught middle and high school students.

Regina Kubelka is a published illustrator working in various mediums such as watercolor, pencil and digital mixed media. She has a Bachelor of Fine Art in Illustration from Rocky Mountain College of Art & Design. You can check out more of Regina's work by going to her website at www.illustrationcentral.com.

Nancy Miller was raised in Boise, Idaho. She grew up sketching and drawing to her hearts content. It wasn't until high school that she learned about the world of illustration. Her illustration work has received an honorable mention in the Society of Writers and Illustrators Illustration Contest, and was accepted in the Society of L.A. Illustrators West Competition.

Robin Patterson lives in Brossard, Quebec with her husband, two sons, two hamsters, a few turtles and three zillion tropical fish. She is an illustrator, portrait artist, designer and children's art teacher. She also writes stories, articles and poetry for both children and adults. She wears many hats.

Wendy Wolf is an artist and writer who lives near Seattle with her wonderful husband and 10 cats who make her smile every day. She's 44, has freckles, and is a vegetarian. She loves reading (preferably with a cat on her lap) and food (especially when someone else cooks).

About Blooming Tree Press
Creating Hope, Encouraging Dreams

Blooming Tree Press is located in the beautiful city of Austin, Texas and is dedicated to publishing quality books for young readers and adults.

The company is named after an inspiring woman, Mildred Bloom, who in her ninth decade continues to encourage and create hope in all who are fortunate enough to know her. Blooming Tree Press will continue to offer adventure, mysterious excitement, hope and wholesome reading for the young and the young at heart.